With devastating insight and shocking candor, Barney Leason reaches deep inside America's corporate kingdoms and reveals the white-hot ambitions, sexual obsessions and shameless pleasures of Wall Street's giants—the men and women who explode fortunes, topple governments and steal billion-dollar companies in the high-stakes gamble called "takeovers"—politely known as mergers and acquisitions. All the glamour, the treachery, the insatiable passion for the best—in bed and in the boardroom—are richly exposed by the writer who knows this world from the inside out.

Veteran reporter Barney Leason has brilliantly portrayed the elite worlds of the rich, privileged and powerful in his best-selling novels, *Rodeo Drive*, *Scandals*, *Passions* and *Grand Illusions*. As a writer, roving correspondent in Europe, and West Coast bureau chief for *Look* magazine, Leason has seen, heard, and once again tells it all. *Advertising Age* calls Leason's books "steamy, sexy and successful." He's won rave reviews from Sidney Sheldon and Harold Robbins. Now Barney Leason creates the business love story of the century, where companies are mated overnight, where a man and a woman discover in each other the ultimate prize of America's dreams—passion, power, wealth and . . .

FORTUNES

FORTUNES

BARNEY LEASON

PUBLISHED BY POCKET BOOKS NEW YORK

Distributed in Canada by PaperJacks Ltd., a Licensee
of the trademarks of Simon & Schuster, Inc.

This novel is a work of fiction. Names, characters, places and
incidents are either the product of the author's imagination or are
used fictitously. Any resemblance to actual events or locales or
persons, living or dead, is entirely coincidental.

Another *Original* publication of POCKET BOOKS

POCKET BOOKS, a division of Simon & Schuster, Inc.
1230 Avenue of the Americas, New York, N.Y. 10020
In Canada distributed by PaperJacks Ltd.,
330 Steelcase Road, Markham, Ontario

ISBN: 0-671-50329-4

First Pocket Books printing June, 1984

10 9 8 7 6 5 4 3 2 1

POCKET and colophon are registered trademarks
of Simon & Schuster, Inc.

Printed in Canada

Chapter One

"THIS IS NORA ELLEN SWEENEY," SHE SAID INTO THE telephone. "Paul?"

His voice was as she remembered it, though a trifle heavier, more mature. She hadn't seen him in seven, maybe eight years. He chuckled; a smile seemed to ride toward her on the telephone line. "Nora, are you still blond and very earnest?"

Nora tapped a polished fingernail on the receiver; her shade was Natural Ice.

"You haven't forgotten me! Thanks for the note. You saw my name in the *Times?*" No, he wouldn't have forgotten her—how could he have? She smiled out the window of Diversified Towers, across Manhattan, possibly in his direction. "I should call you *Mister* Jerome. I didn't realize you were chief financial officer at Brown, Broadstairs."

"You have to stay in touch, Nora," he said modestly. He had always been that way, ever since she could remember. He was a dark-complected, handsome boy, as handsome as a movie star, but always self-effacing, even to her when she was young, seven years his junior. "What have you been doing besides Diversified? I lost track of you at Harvard Business School."

She tried to sound as casual as he. "I'm an MBA. I've been working for Diversified a couple of years now."

His voice soared a bit. "Thank God! Everybody I talk to these days seems to be looking for a job."

1

She studied the nail she'd used on the telephone. "And before I joined Diversified, I was quite seriously considering marriage to a non-Catholic."

"I'm *very* surprised to hear that, Nora."

She laughed self-effacingly. "You would be. Such a good Catholic, wasn't I? I still am. We wouldn't have married in the Church."

"So that would have been all right then," Jerome said, insidiously. "It wouldn't count. Who was he?"

"A Lebanese man," she replied. "I met him in Boston. He's an economist. Works for the Petroleum Institute. We were engaged almost five years, and lived in Washington. My plan was to do great things for the Middle East," Nora sighed.

"Missionary work," he suggested.

"Yes. But he wanted to stay in Georgetown."

Before she could elaborate—fortunately, for she'd already told him more than was necessary—he said, "Nora Ellen Sweeney saves the world."

"Not so much anymore, Paul. Lately, I've been concentrating on saving myself."

"The saving *does* begin at home."

"I still have hopes," she said defensively, "but I've learned you can't save anybody or anything, until you've got power and influence."

"That's called a power base."

"Correct. Once you've got a power base, you can do great things. Fantastic things. You *can* help people, help the world."

He didn't respond immediately. His silence was weighty and in a way significant. "You're wonderful, Nora." His tone was affectionate. "I'd forgotten. You haven't changed. You're still a missionary. You *are* going to save us, after all."

"Well, that's worth having as a goal, isn't it, even if you don't make it?"

"You should've become a nun, Nora—like Mother Teresa. I always said so."

"Oh, no, Paul!" She'd already thought this one through, years before. "I must operate in a man's world. Being a nun would never have been enough for me."

Again, the laugh was soft, almost intimate. "Then you should've been born a boy—you'd be Pope by now."

How many times had she heard that? "Don't make fun of me, Paul."

"Did I ever, Nora Ellen? Did I ever dare?"

Before he could ask, as he must, she said, "Mother died last year. . . . I never told her about my engagement."

"How could you keep it a secret?" he asked slowly.

"Easily. She never left Paradise Point."

"And how is Father Foster?"

She paused. "Father John is a monsignor now. Very big. In charge of diocesan money. He's a financial officer, like you."

"Nora, I'm sorry about your mother," he interrupted. "I didn't know."

"Like you said, Paul, you have to stay in touch."

"I'm really a stranger to the old hometown. I don't even stop there on my way to Connecticut anymore. We have a factory up there."

She managed a sad sigh.

"Your mother was a beautiful woman, Nora. A sweet lady. She was very nice to me, always. And patient."

"Why? You weren't a bad boy. She loved you, Paul."

His laugh was skeptical. "I was essential, Nora, don't you remember? I was the only Jewish altar boy there ever was, before or since."

Paul Jerome had lived around the corner from the church with his father, a widower. When one of the regular, Catholic altar boys failed to show up on Sunday, Nora was always sent to get Paul. The irony of it never bothered anybody, not Father John and certainly not Nora's mother, the housekeeper at the parish house. Possibly, it had been Mary Sweeney who'd suggested it in the first place, being a woman with a practical mind. Perhaps the idea had been to convert Paul Jerome, for

Paul's father, Humphrey Jerome, was by no means a religious Jew himself, not at all. He had been a man of science who taught chemistry and physics at Paradise Point High School.

"Paul," Nora said abruptly, "let's see each other. I'm glad you wrote me the note."

"And I'm glad you called, Nora."

"After all these years, Paul, it will be the most gratifying meeting in my life."

It could also be very interesting, Nora told herself, that by coincidence she was speaking to the chief financial officer of Brown, Broadstairs and Dunn, known as BBD in the electronics and aerospace industry. BBD was a moderate-sized but fast-moving company dedicated to making missiles blast off and aircraft fly. The company Nora worked for was a multibillion-dollar company called Diversified Technologies, Inc. and, as Paul had read in the *New York Times,* her department was devoted to corporate financial strategy and planning. Nora's major assignment was to keep a running brief on the aerospace industry in general and in particular on smaller, well-run firms that might be vulnerable to takeover.

"Acquisitions" was the polite term used in business circles for what Nora did.

Chapter Two

NORA ELLEN SWEENEY HAD ALWAYS BEEN A SHINING, OPEN-faced blonde and, if anything, she seemed even blonder now. Was that possible? Yes, her hair was like white gold, almost platinum, and looked as heavy as precious metal.

It had been a while since Jerome had seen her; he recognized her instantly, even though in one way she had changed completely. She had matured. She was slimmer than she had been at twenty-one or twenty-two, pared down. Fighting weight, he thought, as she paused for a moment in the low doorway into the "21" bar. She was tall and elegant, even though very casually dressed, the belt of a suede trenchcoat tied carelessly at her waist. Her cheeks were rosy from the November chill and her eyes even bluer as they found him at a small table always reserved for him in the horseshoe facing the long curved bar.

Heads turned and conversations stopped. Eyes followed her as she headed for Jerome with purpose. Christ, he thought, she could have kept right on going, straight to Hollywood. She took his hand and held it, knowing the men were watching her, then leaned a little forward so he could kiss her on the cheek. She smiled.

"Paul, you look exactly the same."

"Well, Nora . . . how are you doing? Sit . . . what'll you have?"

She *had* matured. She had the self-assurance of a woman of nearly thirty, who knew she was not only beautiful but intelligent, a woman with a career, with promise. Slowly, she unwrapped the trenchcoat and sat down in the place next to his.

"Don't tell me," she said. "The last time we saw each other was in the summer seven years ago, or was it six? I was home from grad school."

"Is that right?" It was. His father had died around the time he'd seen her last, and he'd been married soon after that to Shelley, the perfect Jewish wife.

"Yes, you'd just gone to work for IBM," she went on. "I guess I'll try a glass of white wine, Paul." She smiled again and Jerome saw that, slowly but surely, the regulars were returning to their drinks. "Always dieting, you know," she said, moving her head negligently. "What're you drinking?"

"Too many vodka martinis."

Her nose wrinkled but she squelched the expression quickly. "You had just started at IBM. You'd been to the war . . ."

"My war, yes. Vietnam."

"And then back to school and got *your* Master's in Business Administration. You were an MBA and I worshipped you," she said gleefully, remembering.

"I was lost in a sea of accountants," he shrugged.

"But not for long. You soon found land, didn't you?"

The waiter arrived. "We'll take a glass of white wine for the lady," Jerome said, "and another one of these for me."

"Okay, Mr. Jerome."

When he'd gone, she said, "They know you at '21'."

"I'm here often."

Nora's blue eyes sparkled. She was slightly tanned, as if she'd been in the Caribbean in late summer, after the crowd, when the sun wasn't so bright and strong.

"You were my role model, Paul."

He snorted politely. "Thanks, but I don't accept that, Nora." He wanted to tell her not to go overboard. "We're a dime a dozen, we servants of the corporate machine."

6

"Oh, no," she said briskly, "don't you run us down, Paul. You're the number one financial man at BBD and I'm . . ."

"Yes? And you?"

The blue eyes fired a salvo. "Me? Someday . . . I don't know. Just say . . . someday Nora will . . . *whatever.*"

"Someday Nora will *forever.*" Then he asked a serious question. "You're what they call a bottom liner, aren't you?"

"Strategic planning." Her smile held fast. "We squeeze the stone for the last nickel."

"Exactly *what* do you do, Nora?"

She looked at him steadily. "We're attached directly to the president's office."

Ah, yes, Jerome thought. Search and acquire, that was what financial planning really amounted to.

"Kurt Morgan is your boss."

"Yes. Well, actually, a woman named Helen Marconi. She runs the department. We all have our specialties and I—well, we're all fairly anonymous to Kurt Morgan. You know what he's like."

"I've met him a couple of times. I don't really know him."

She nodded, a little anxiously. "Sometimes he calls us his productivity task force."

"Are you happy with that? I can imagine the line engineers hate your guts."

"Yes." She nodded firmly, eyes moving around the room. "I'm proud to say they do."

Jerome chuckled. "Bottom-lining the poor bastards into ulcers, right?"

She shrugged coolly, unconcerned. "You appear to know just *a little bit* about Diversified," she observed.

"When I read about you being there, I did some research," he admitted. "But anyone in *our* business is bound to know about Diversified and Kurt Morgan."

"Maybe. I have to admit though," Nora said directly, "I know hardly anything about BBD."

"No reason you should. We're minuscule compared to Diversified."

"Also, you see," she went on hesitantly, "I was not very well informed about your industry until recently. Before I came up here, after . . . my engagement ended, I was in Washington in a very junior spot." She paused and drew a breath of resignation. "Where does the famous Buck Collins spend his time?"

"Ah!" he said. "See now—you know about Buck Collins."

"Collins is very well known, Paul. You don't have to be in business to know about Buck Collins. *Time* magazine calls him the whiz kid of aerospace."

"Not because he knows an awful lot about aerospace, or electronics," Jerome said flatly. He could afford to be realistic about Buck. He admired him enough. "He knows how to talk it up for BBD."

"Married about a dozen times," she reminded him playfully, her curiosity showing.

Jerome nodded. "They always say that—just because he was married to Martine Martin." Foolish Buck. He'd married Martine in a moment of weakness in Las Vegas that had lasted all of five minutes, as they said out West.

"He was a hot pilot, an ace."

"True, but there are a lot of hot pilots around. We've got them from every war. No, Nora, let me tell you, I like Buck and work for him. But we all know, including him, that Buck's main feature is making it sound like a computer gave him birth and a word processor taught him to talk."

"What you're saying," Nora observed slyly, "is that you *don't* absolutely worship him."

"Of course I don't." Jerome smiled. "Face it, beautiful —that's what he'd say—he's nothin' but a fuckin' good businessman. . . . Sorry."

She batted her eyes at him. He had forgotten. Nora didn't talk like the boys.

"You and Buck get along, don't you?"

"We'd better," he laughed.

Of course they got along. Buck didn't fool with him. Paul Jerome was in charge of the money, and anybody who stepped out of line got slugged, including Buck Collins. Jerome kept them all on a tight rein; that's why he had his job. These aerospace types knew how to spend it, high, wide, and handsomely. The founders, Brown, Broadstairs and Dunn had been of the same ilk as Collins—hot pilots, daredevils, war heroes. They understood each other.

"BBD sounds like a wonderful place. How did you get the job?" she asked frankly, obviously considering it curious that anyone so unimpressed with the romance of high tech had landed inside such a glamour firm.

"Pete Broadstairs likes me and he liked the fact that I viewed all those guys, like he does himself, as mere mortals."

"I see. . . ." But she didn't see.

"Listen, Nora, Buck is an absolutely marvelous man, but he's kind of a wild card. He's magnetic, he's got pure animal magnetism—and that's his weakness. He gets his way with people too easily."

"With you too?"

"Sometimes, yes."

"Well, you're magnetic too, Paul," she said smoothly, "in your own way." She inspected his face analytically. "You're quite attractive, even dangerous-looking . . . yes." She smiled brilliantly then; if her smile had been soprano it could have shattered glass. "Mr. Tall, Dark, and Handsome. Mystery man. Very enigmatic, aren't you?" She touched his arm familiarly; he could have been her older brother, from the dark side of the family.

"Yeah," he grunted, "Mr. Enigmatic, that's me." Jerome didn't feel any of the things she said, so he changed the subject. "Let's talk about you, Nora. You look gorgeous . . . very healthy, like you take good care of yourself."

"I'm wholesome," she grinned, showing her even white teeth. "That's me—Miss Wholesome. I go to the gym when I have time. Sometimes I jog in the park."

"Let me know when. I'll come and watch. Remember, I used to take you for walks on Sundays when your mother was busy . . . making lunch for Father John."

"I remember," she said softly. "That's when I was going to be a priest, like him. Remember? The voice? He was so handsome."

"Nobody could talk you out of it."

"I was only eight. They talked me out of it when I turned twelve," she said, with a chuckle. "Wasn't I stupid?"

"Well, not really." John Foster had been like her father—foster father was how he'd heard the relationship described.

"I adored him," Nora said. "Understandably, don't you think?"

"Of course."

Nora smiled inwardly. "So instead I became a high priestess of capitalism."

"Not so shabby, is it? Cheers." He lifted his drink.

"Cheers to you, Paul," she said. "It's wonderful to see you again. The years slip away."

"Sometimes I wish they would," he said soberly. "Sometimes I'd like to re-do the last eight or ten years."

"Well, you can't, darling man," she said cheerfully. "Besides, I have a surprise for you, something that will take you back. How long has it been since you've seen Father John?"

"I don't know, Nora—probably as long as it's been since I've seen you. After my father died."

"He's in New York," she said excitedly, "and we're all going to have dinner together. Father John and us . . . and, something really funny, John Joseph Gogarty's widow. Remember the castle? The haunted Gogarty place on the river?"

He smiled. "I couldn't ever forget that." As young boys,

they'd snuck up on the Gogarty property and peeked through the trees, trying to see past the heavy fence posted with No Trespassing signs and warnings that guard dogs patrolled the area.

"We're going to Côte Basque," Nora said. "Father John can't wait to see you. . . . How *could* you become such a stranger to us, Paul?"

"I don't know. . . . It happens. People move away, get married, get on with their lives." He shrugged indifferently; did it matter? "Who's the Gogarty widow? Did we ever know Gogarty was married? Did we know *anything* about J.J. Gogarty, except he owned that goddamn ugly stone barn on the river? Nobody ever saw him. I don't know anybody in Paradise Point who ever laid eyes on him . . . but everybody talked about him."

"He was married at least twice," Nora said. "Father John got to know him in the end, and a man named Oswald who took care of the place . . ."

"The scarecrow, I remember," Jerome grinned happily. "He used to chase us sometimes."

"This widow Gogarty is a *young* widow, Paul," she said.

"So?" Jerome winked an eye. "You're not trying to fix me up, are you, Nora? Better not—because if I suddenly decided I'd like to devote less time to drinking and more to the opposite sex, I'd do it with you."

"Do it? That sounds suspicious to me, Paul," she chided him prissily.

"I mean *devote time,* Nora." He felt silly, then irritated. "Don't get the wrong idea, Nora. I'm not going to make a pass at you."

"No, you're not, are you, Paul?" She blinked. "Just as well. I wouldn't sleep with you."

"Nora, I wouldn't ask you."

"I *couldn't,*" she repeated stiffly. "You shouldn't be surprised. You know what I'm like—I'm . . ."

He leaned back, fondling his drink for reassurance. "Wait a minute, Nora. Do I recall you telling me you'd been engaged for almost five years?"

"Yes, but . . ."

"But what?"

"It never really worked out, *that way,* Paul." Her expression became evasive. "We could pay the bill, couldn't we, and go on to the restaurant?"

"Yes." Jerome considered what he would say next, but Nora beat him to it with another leading question.

"Were you married? I never heard," she said sorrowfully. "Or *are* you married? God, I never thought to ask! I'm sorry—I'm so self-centered."

Mea culpa, mea culpa. Was she self-centered? He tried to remember. And then suddenly, all he *could* remember was that one time when she'd been about fourteen, he'd been back home from the army or school and passing by Father John Foster's parish house where Nora lived with her mother. They'd gone for a walk down by the river, and suddenly this nubile adolescent, with gleaming, excited eyes, had stopped, turned, thrown her arms around him and pressed her full young body against his. Next she kissed him and then turned and fled. He wondered if she remembered that, along with everything else.

"Yeah," he said haltingly, "I was married for about five years."

"Was? What happened, Paul?" Nora's face wrinkled with concern, lines drew her eyes together at the forehead, as if she'd been told he was mortally ill.

"Nothing really. Her mother always wanted her to marry a doctor and I was only a lowly accountant. There were no children. She ran away with a dentist finally."

"How awful."

"Why? Her name was Shelley. Should I be sad a woman with a name like Shelley took off?"

Chapter Three

THE WIDOW OF J.J. GOGARTY WAS NOT IRISH AT ALL, thank God. The man people had called Black Jack Gogarty—who had once controlled the beer and the slots and the road-building in upstate New York—had evidently come across her some ten years before while attending one of his frequent papal audiences in Rome.

Lucia Gogarty was a woman of no more than thirty-five, a creature the Italians and anybody else with heart would have described as *stupendo*. Her skin was dusky, almost Sicilian. She was not very tall but was fully and succulently formed, like a flawless piece of fruit. Shaking her hand, Jerome was pulled toward cleavage falling into a delicate, pale-blue silk dress that clung to her figure. Her hand was so soft he wanted to chew on it, to suck on the long fingers with his lips. Dark eyes danced at him; her hair was as black as a gypsy's.

"Paul," John Foster was reproving him gently, "I'd given up on you. Where in the world have you been all these years?"

"Underground, Father . . ." Father Foster? Father John? John? What was he to call him now?

Foster was no different, his face possibly a little longer, the classic forehead bonier, eyebrows shaggier, the eyes slightly more weary, more understanding, forgiving; in a way Foster looked surprised you were no worse than you seemed. He was as elegant and imposing as a mandarin.

"It is a delight to see you, Paul. It is *wonderful* to see

you two together again." Foster's baritone vibrated and he laid his waxy fingers on Lucia's forearm—fingers softened by years of wiping the chalice. So sensuously he had done so, Jerome remembered. He thought about the fleeting little smiles on Foster's face as he caressed the gold-plated receptacle containing the unleavened wafers which Foster turned into the Body of Christ, and which Jerome had never tasted.

"Seeing these two together," Foster told Lucia, "is moisturizer for my cracked and wrinkled soul—God bless you both, Nora fair as the dawn and Paul black as the night."

Jerome smiled at Lucia Gogarty, trying to let her know she shouldn't take any of it, or them, very seriously.

"Paul . . . Paolo. An Italian name."

Foster chuckled magisterially. "Paul is Mediterranean. There's not much difference between any of you."

Jerome glared at him snidely. "He's telling you I'm a Jew, Mrs. Gogarty."

"Ah, good," she said, "I'm tired of Italians." Her bosom seemed to swell with boredom.

Foster went ahead. "I wanted you all to meet. Jack Gogarty, God rest his soul, has gone to meet the same . . ." Lucia's eyes dropped. "Lucia is going to be living in New York for a while and we mustn't let her get lonely. She could stay upstate, but the castle is so desolate . . ."

The widow was anything but desolate. "I also have my business."

Foster explained, "Lucia collects and deals in art."

"Yes," she said, "you must come to my apartment and see my collection. We will have dinner. . . . My cook is excellent."

Foster said, "Lucia has a big place on Park Avenue."

Jerome had never been interested in little dinner parties, especially since he'd been free of Shelley. She had been very big on *intime* candlelit evenings. "I . . . my problem is I'm up in Connecticut many evenings at the factory."

For just a second, Lucia looked hurt. What had he done? He hadn't meant to insult her. "Of course . . ."

"Now, come, Paul. You're not going to give us the slip again. You haven't been in Paradise Point in years."

"I know. Not since my father died."

Foster's eyes softened significantly. "And he is roundly missed." To Lucia, he said, "Paul's father was one of the most beloved of our high school teachers." He strained with sympathy and sadness, so much that Jerome wondered how he was bearing up under the loss of Mary Ellen Sweeney.

Foster murmured, in addition and amendment, "As Mr. J.J. Gogarty is also missed in Paradise Point."

It was silly of him to try to flatter Lucia Gogarty. Surely she would know—or would she?—that Gogarty had never been seen in Paradise Point. No one would even have been aware of his death.

Lucia paid no attention. "The way of the world . . ."

"You think death is the way of the world?" Jerome asked innocently.

"Well, yes," she said. "Death is the end of life and so part of life, *young man.*" Her eyes said something to him that made Jerome tremble.

Foster corrected her, or tried to. "Many of us believe, my dear, that death is the beginning of life."

There could be no doubt about Lucia's view. "Not I. I believe death is the beginning of being dead. Gogarty used to say that dead is for a long time."

Foster's sad eyes dilated. "Jack Gogarty was one of a kind."

Jerome challenged him mildly. "You think they threw away the mold?"

Foster didn't look at him. "Yes," he said, "J.J. Gogarty was unique." He drew a long breath. "As you should know, Lucia."

Lucia didn't answer.

Over dinner, she told them about her art business. Based on what she said, they could assume she had many businesses, including a gallery in Rome with branches in Milan, Venice, and in the ritziest resort on the western side of the peninsula, Forte dei Marmi, where such as the great English sculptor Henry Moore had a home and studio. Of her past life, before and with J.J. Gogarty, she said there was not much to tell. Lucia had been happy enough in her job at the Vatican Library, a post found for her by a relative highly placed in the Church hierarchy. Yes, she agreed with Father John, she probably knew more about the workings of the Church than many American bishops, and was in no way intimidated—although she might be bored—by discussions of doctrine.

Jerome decided he liked her. Lucia had a hardheaded view of Father John's and Nora's sacred Church, in reality a powerful, rich, rather efficiently run institution.

Yes, it was true what Father John said. Lucia's family was related to Pope Pius XII; her mother was first cousin to a living cardinal, Avia of the Curia. But it was not unusual, Lucia said. Most Italians were related to one cardinal or another, or had a pope somewhere in their families. Lucia joked that she was a Daughter of the Vatican Evolution.

Jerome liked her even more. He listened intently to her voice, her soft Italian accent. A sense of alliance built, crested, receded, then came again, and he wondered if he was confusing empathy with desire. He hoped. Desire was preferable in these dark days of loss and lack.

Lucia would be staying in New York through the winter, she told them, and then going back to Rome for Easter. She wanted Father John to visit her then, and it was understood, with glance and smile, that Nora, and Paul—yes, certainly, Paul—would come too.

Foster warned Jerome with his eyes not to say anything untoward; he was apprehensive that Jerome, with his flippant humor, might point out how unseemly it would be for her to invite one of the race of Christ-killers to Rome to celebrate the Resurrection.

But the ascetic and gauntly handsome priest should have known better; Paul Jerome was not a boor or a peasant. He understood what Lucia, the money, and the big house upstate would mean to a practical churchman like John Foster.

Lucia was speaking directly to him. "Paul," she said, nothing backward or falsely modest about her, "please set aside those days for a visit in Rome. A friend of Father John's is a friend of mine."

There was an ancestral *palazzo* overlooking the Roman Forum and a house, even older, on the Appian Way.

"Lucia," Foster said effusively, ignoring the fact her invitation was as much Jerome's to answer as it was his, "it's up to the bishop, really. I don't know how long I could go away."

"But surely, you are entitled to a vacation, Father."

Innocently, Jerome said, "What's the problem? It'd be a business trip, wouldn't it?"

"Now, Paul . . ." Foster held up his hand.

Jerome grinned at him and then looked at Nora, who beamed happily at the two men. Seeing Foster again was like running into an old college professor, one you'd respected very much and feared a little, and now had the liberty to tease in a careful way. "A business trip back to headquarters. The bishop would go for it like a shot."

Lucia was quick. "Of course. And we will arrange your ticket, Father John."

"Oh, but I could never accept—"

"No *buts*," Lucia said warmly.

"Dear lady . . ."

Foster was a *rascal;* had Jerome always known that? The priest's face was set in a humble smile. He bathed Lucia in it, the balm of love and affection and fondness for all creatures, living and dead. Slyly, Jerome winked at him, and Foster's lips cornered with a nervous twitch. He was conning Lucia, and he almost burst into laughter realizing that Paul had caught him at it. Good thing Foster was not a Jesuit; he was knowledgeable and he took advantage of his openings, but with all that, Jerome conceded, he was probably not cynical in the Jesuit manner. Perhaps he was too obvious. He never would have made it as a member of Christ's own army, the Household Cavalry of God.

"You are a very dear lady," Foster murmured, repeating himself.

Then Lucia rather surprised them. "No, I am not a very dear lady, Father. You would not say that if you knew me better." Her voice was sharp and her look at Foster more irritated than grateful.

"Now . . ."

"Father John," Jerome interrupted him.

"Yes?" His voice licked Jerome.

Jerome shrugged. What was he to call him, after all? Father John sounded right, but funny in his mouth.

"Should I call you *Monsignor?"*

"It's not required," Foster said frostily. "But you certainly may if it makes you feel better."

Chapter Four

Riding north in the cab, Nora very deliberately took Jerome's hand in her own and brought it to her lips.

"Well, darling man, are you happy you had dinner with us?"

"Uproariously."

As if puzzled, she said, "You devil—Lucia fell for you."

"Hardly."

"Not *hardly*," she said cleverly, "*hard* to get, *hard*, that's what you are."

He shuddered silently. Was that a double entendre? No, she didn't realize what she was saying. Of course, he was happy to have had dinner with them. The question recurred: How had he gotten so far away from John Foster? Foster could have been a help when Jerome had badly needed it, but he had not thought of seeing Foster then. No, Jerome knew, or thought he knew, it wouldn't have worked. He'd have been too embarrassed to confess to a fugitive wife and shattered marriage.

Now that he thought about it, how good would Foster be in death-bed scenes? The man was a mystery himself, a research project. Scattered, indistinct memories had come at Jerome all evening. Had he known that Foster was such an ambitious man? Yes, Jerome couldn't remember how, but he had known. Father John was vain, too, and this was probably more obvious now, to Jerome's more experienced eye, than it had been to Jerome the youth. And he was conceited. God, yes, Jerome thought fondly, the *monsignor* was enormously conceited. He had enough going for him right there to be declared *persona non grata* in the Garden of Eden.

Jerome reversed Nora's grip on his hand, carrying her fingers tentatively to his lips.

"Oh, Paul," she sighed, "it's nice to be together again." Her chest seemed to fill. Did she expect that he was going to make a pass at her after all? Softly, she said, "You were the first boy I ever kissed."

"I was?" He sounded dull, he knew. So she had remembered what had happened that day.

"Yes. We were walking by the river and you grabbed me . . . I was so scared . . ."

Oh, he thought, *her* version. He laughed sardonically. "I might kiss you again before the night's over."

"Well, I hope you'll give me a good-night kiss."

Oh, Jesus.

She went on, sounding old, memory-laden, like a flat tire. "I'm less sad now when I remember the past."

"That's good. Being sad is very counterproductive."

She turned to him sympathetically. "I can see you're still a little bitter. Were you very broken up when she left you?"

"I guess . . ."

"Why did she do it? It's hard for me to imagine a woman leaving you."

"I told you," Jerome said, "she met a dentist. Didn't you know dentists have a very high sex-success quotient? They're irresistible to Jewish women. I don't know—it's got something to do with the twentieth century. Maybe they like to sniff Novocain. . . ."

"Oh, Paul," she admonished him, "how you joke." She stared out the window of the cab for a moment, then spoke moodily. "I was sadder about my mother dying than I was about breaking off my engagement."

"I believe you," Jerome said pointedly. "I admired your

20

mother, but . . . how can I say it? I always thought there was something . . . you know, unfulfilled about her life. Am I right?"

"Yes . . . in a way, I suppose."

His thoughts boiled over. Nora's mother had lived her most fruitful years as housekeeper for John Foster. Somehow, there was something inexorably sad, tragic, in that story, but Jerome had never known quite what. Nora's father had gone the way of the Irish lush, or so it seemed. John Foster, temperamentally more of an Anglican than a Catholic priest, had been quite unable to understand the phenomenon of the Irish, that despair, depression, hate, and vindictiveness that sometimes seized those people and led to self-destruction. But in his unsuccessful attempt to save Nora's father, Foster had become well acquainted with Mary Ellen Sweeney. Not long after Mr. Sweeney's lamented—or maybe not so lamented—farewell, his widow, not at all well-provided for, had moved into Foster's parish house.

Foster, said the gossips—including, and possibly especially, his Catholic parishioners—had been in love with Mrs. Sweeney for years. The affair could now be consummated, if ever it was to be, under the roof of the house next to St. Mary's Church, perhaps aptly named.

But who could know the truth? On balance, Jerome didn't believe that anything of a carnal nature had happened between them, aside from sharing the ritual Sunday roast beef.

Nora leaned forward to speak to the cab driver. "Stop at the next corner, please." To Jerome, she said, "Come up for a minute."

"I'll see you to the door."

"I mean upstairs. We have a doorman, Paul. Besides, I think I can defend myself. I took a karate course at my gym." Her tone hardened. "I pity the mugger that comes after me."

"He'd have to be a madman, Nora."

21

Her building was twenty stories high. Air conditioners stuck out of the windows above them, all the way to the sky. Inside, a sturdily built doorman cracked the legs of his chair to the marble floor and, groaning, got up.

"Good evening, Mr. Fiorello," Nora said.

"Evening, Miss Sweeney."

This man looked suspiciously at Jerome, as if he might have had a gun stuck in her back. But he let Jerome pass without a search.

Nora smiled silently in the elevator until it jerked to a stop at the tenth floor. Her key was ready and Nora shoved it into a door two apartments down the hall.

Not a bad place by New York standards, Jerome thought. The hall carpet was clean and the walls had been freshly painted. His own place, off First Avenue, was bigger, older, scruffier, but had more character.

Nora shut the door and dropped a safety chain into place. Jerome noted she'd also installed one of those iron-bar arrangements linking door and floor—hell, it was like getting into a fortress, Fortress New York.

A tiny foyer led into a small, squarish living room; to one side lay a dining alcove containing a small table and a sort of midget armoire. The place was as neatly organized as a furniture showroom on Fifth Avenue.

Nora pointed at a highly varnished wooden cart which served as divider between living and eating areas.

"Make yourself a drink, Paul." She smiled, too cutely. "I'll be right back."

Did he want another drink? Christ, yes! A short, straight, unmerciful brandy, out of a well-dusted bottle.

Water gushed in the next room. She would be washing her hands, cleansing herself of all frightful little scents, making herself all neat and proper again. Such a shame that people like Nora had to go to the bathroom at all. Still, what was it they said about her in Paradise Point? Nora Ellen Sweeney shit ice cream and pissed ginger ale.

When Nora returned to the living room, all smiles, she nodded approvingly when she saw him with the brandy.

"Could I have a light film of that on the bottom of the glass, darling man?"

Returning to the cart, Jerome considered having a talk with her. It would not do for her to keep calling him darling man. It was out of character for both of them.

Jerome handed Nora a snifter with just a fingernail of brandy. Naturally, she would hold the glass up in a toast. He *would* have to talk to her.

"*My role model,*" Nora murmured effusively.

She backed up to sit in an armchair; Jerome placed himself at the far end of the couch so there was no way their knees could bump.

Nora tasted the brandy and cleared her throat. "Wow!" Shyly, she went on. "I guess there's a big difference between somebody like Lucia, and me," she probed, looking away from him.

"Why's that, Nora?" He'd give her an answer without prompting. "You're more reserved, I suppose."

"Colder you mean?"

"No, just reserved."

"Icy," she said tartly.

"Not at all. She's Italian, and you're Irish. The Irish are not an especially warm-blooded people."

"Not so," she said. "We can be very warm-blooded. There's a lot of Spanish in the Irish. . . . You think Lucia is very sexy, don't you?"

"She's what we call zaftig. It means tasty," Jerome said ironically.

He studied the nubby, dark red upholstery. Above the couch hung a splotchy modern painting apparently chosen to coordinate with the fabric. He wondered if the apartment had come furnished.

"I don't think I'd be classified as tasty," Nora said thoughtfully. "My former fiancé thought I was ice cold and unapproachable."

Jerome spoke up daringly. "The Lebanese have the itchiest crotches in the Middle East."

"Paul!"

He laughed at her shock. "C'mon, Nora, what do you want me to tell you? The last time I saw you, your only worry was how to get to heaven."

Nora nodded vigorously, and laughed. "You're right, of course. I was a very religious girl. I'm still extremely religious. I believe very strongly," she said. As if the one followed the other, the words prompted her to slide around the corner of the coffee table to sit beside him. Forcefully, she pressed the round base of the brandy glass down on his thigh. "Men are so brilliant," she said enviously.

"Nobody ever said you're a dope, Nora."

She nodded, seemingly far away. "Pete Broadstairs hired you personally, you said. He's retired now, isn't he?"

"He lives in Palm Springs," Jerome told her. "Talk about role models and hero worship. There's the man for you to idolize. Pete was the youngest of the founders. Brown died and Dunn's had a stroke. He can't even steer his golf cart anymore."

"Growing old is awful," Nora said. "Although inevitable . . ."

"But Pete has managed it pretty well. He's seventy-five and every once in a while he'll take a plane up. . . . He was with Doolittle when they bombed Tokyo in the forties."

Nora beamed merrily. "And I read that he just got married again to a much younger woman."

"Of about your age, Nora," he said dryly.

"That is young—what a relief. I still have a chance."

"You've got a few years yet, Nora." He touched her hand and felt her flinch. She was tied up in knots. "Her name is Connie," Jerome told her. "She's tall, skinnier than you, not brilliantly blond. A bit giddy, if the truth be known. She's always been crazy about Buck; they had an affair a few years back."

She thought about that. "But she married Mr. Broadstairs. Why?"

"I think Buck told her to. Buck wanted Pete to have a happy third act. Buck says everybody, no matter how old, is entitled to a satisfying sex life and if we couldn't arrange that for one of our founders then what the hell kind of guys were we?"

"My God!"

Jerome was pleased to throw her further off-balance. "The fact is, Pete's family is furious about it. He's got a couple of sons from early marriages."

"Good God!" she said disgustedly. "How many times has the man been married?"

"Six times, I think. He's had a very satisfying sex life, I'd say. Wouldn't you, Nora?" he asked her engagingly.

"The family must be worried about what'll happen to his share of the company when he dies. I'd be worried too, if I were them."

"That's right," Jerome said. Weighing his words as if they were gold, he continued, "There's talk, and this is strictly between us, that Pete's sons would like to straighten it all out before Pete buys the farm and little Connie inherits his whole estate."

"Buys the farm?"

"The hot dogs—surfers, skiiers, pilots—use that expression to describe their final crash and burn."

"I see. Well," Nora said emphatically, "that'd be my advice, were *I* their financial advisor. Is that what you've told them, Paul?"

"No, no, I have nothing to do with Pete's personal finances. But naturally, I hear things."

Her smile switched on, positively electric. "You must know *everything* that's going on, Paul. What about Dunn?"

He shrugged. "His financial affairs are tied up beautifully. No worries there." Jerome pushed himself forward to leave. "Well, Nora—"

"No! Have another drink, Paul. Give me just a little more. Good, isn't it?"

"Too good, Nora." Had she so easily, instinctively,

25

discovered his weak point? "Nora," he murmured, mocking her openly, *"darling girl.* Have you found the chink in my armor? If you've found him, get him out of there, please."

"Oh." Her lips pursed. "You *are* still crazy, aren't you?"

"Nora, I was *never* crazy."

She accepted the freshened drink and patted the couch. Jerome sank down, feeling he was falling into a bottomless pit. "Paul, between them, the three families must *control* BBD—it's not a very broad-based company, is it?"

"Right again. It's no big secret they own over fifty percent."

"And their fortunes are entirely tied up in BBD," she said. "Dangerous."

"Why? We're a sound company."

"No." She shook her head impatiently. "You should broaden the base. Better protection for everybody. Don't you have a piece of it, Paul?"

"Sure, I do. A very, very small piece."

"Yes, I'll bet. Small to you would be huge to me." She smiled at him and put her hand over his when he placed it on her knee. "You're pawing me, Paul."

"C'mon, that's not a paw. Don't worry, I remember what you said about karate—I wouldn't risk a broken arm. You're comfortable, Nora. Nice." He was teasing a little, but in a way he was serious too. "You smell good."

Her cheeks flushed just enough to be visible, like a light being heightened. She suddenly smiled. "You have options too. You're probably worth millions."

"No, not millions," he said sardonically. "You know we aristocratic types become highly embarrassed when you discuss money."

"It occurs to me," she said firmly, "that Diversified Technologies is always on the lookout for worthwhile companies—with whom to merge . . . or is it *with which?"*

Jerome laughed, as if at an outlandish joke. "Sure,

Nora. Make us an offer. Hey, have you been trying to pump me? You can't repeat *anything* I've said."

"You haven't said anything I didn't already know."

"Good."

"But maybe you've given me an idea." Shrewdly, she said, "I'll just ask you one direct question, Paul. Okay?" He nodded. "Well, is there any reason *anybody* at BBD would be unhappy if a merger took place? Just nod or shake your head."

"Hell," he scoffed, "I can talk. The only guy who might be unhappy is Buck. What would happen to Buck?"

"You mean he doesn't have a golden parachute?"

"No way. Pete and the boys always felt anybody who's any good can fend for themselves."

Nora's eyes glittered. "The world can't stop moving for the sake of one ambitious man—particularly if Buck's as conceited as you make him out."

"I didn't say he was conceited. He *is* ambitious."

"Sure." Was it his imagination or was she breathing faster? "It could be exciting, Paul. It could be good for all of us." Her body shifted closer to him and he felt the swell of her breast against his upper arm. "It could be *very* good for you, Paul."

"Oh, hell."

"Our chief financial officer—"

"Gerald Ball."

"Yes." Her intense expression blurred a little. "Gerry Ball, I hear, is going to retire soon. If BBD came into Diversified, you'd be a natural to take over his job, Paul."

"Jesus, Nora," he protested. But, in fact, he hadn't known Ball was prepared to leave. "I didn't think he was old enough to retire."

"Well . . . it *could* happen, Paul."

Everything was so logical to her, wasn't it? Unconcerned, he said, "We'll see."

Nora's warm lips closed on his jawbone and, not thinking, without really wanting to, Jerome turned his head. She kissed him carefully, as though making a promise, opening her mouth to his tongue. A puff of hot breath lit his skin and Jerome was aware of a sexual tension building in his loins. As impulsively as she had started the kiss, Nora stopped and hurled herself back against the cushion.

"God, I'm awful," she whispered blackly. "I couldn't help myself. Don't frighten me."

"Why would I? *You* kissed me, Nora."

"You pushed against my breast."

"No, not so. I was sitting quietly—you pushed me."

She stared at him, stricken. "When you did that, it made my blood rush, violently."

"A kiss does that sometimes. It shows you're alive." Christ, he told himself, he would just play along. Desire was already hanging by its thumbs.

Intensely, Nora said, "Do you want me to get undressed? I will if you say so."

Jerome shook his head. "No, I'm not asking you to do anything. Just let me drink this little brownie and get out of here, safe and sound."

"You make it sound like I'm threatening you."

Uh oh, he thought, this was where he came in. He did not need, or want, another chaotic, irrational relationship. He had to get out of here. "I've got to go, Nora."

She clapped her hand on his thigh and squeezed. "No! Don't you see I'm trying to work through my neurosis? Can't you help?"

"Nora, what the hell can I do? I wasn't very successful last time I tried to help someone."

"If you don't do what I say, you're not a friend."

She didn't give him a chance to reply, just disappeared into what he'd deduced was her bedroom. He didn't know what she intended and didn't care. As soon as she was gone, he went for the brandy bottle. Whatever happened, he would be relaxed.

He'd barely sat down again when she hailed him softly.

"Turn out the light, Paul."

Oh, shit! But he switched off the lamp. She giggled. Then, dimly, he picked out the white ghost of her facing him over the coffee table.

"Where are you?"

"Right here, Nora."

She crept toward him, located him with one hand, and flopped down. She was in a half slip; he was sure she hadn't taken off the brassiere.

"Will you kiss me again?" she pleaded, voice small.

"Okay."

While he was pondering her craziness, Nora found his hand and slapped it on her left breast. She whispered in his ear, "Will you remove my bra?"

The catch gave easily and Jerome pulled the white undergarment away from her. He sensed, more than saw, the zoom of her chest toward him. Carefully, he put his hand back where it had been. Her flesh was warm, the breast full and firm. He stroked and her breathing hastened to labored and hoarse remonstration. No, she didn't; yes, she did. Her mouth yawned open and inarticulate little cries nipped at him. Finally, she got out what she wanted to say.

"Paul, promise you won't put it inside me. I couldn't allow that."

The remark was enough to make him rigid. "Nora, I wouldn't!"

"Paul . . ." In a rush of passion, she didn't hear him. "It's only our first date."

"Goddamn it!" Anger and frustration swept him. "I'm not your enemy, Nora."

"I know, Paul." An apology. Despite her protests, she pressed the whole length of her body against him and when she felt the bulge of him against her she almost screamed. Her belly trembled, but recklessly he pressed her until she burst out in alarm.

"Oh, Paul!"

"Nora, listen . . ." He was beginning to feel a terrible lust.

29

"I won't let you!"

"I know. I'm going."

"No, you can't."

"What the hell are you saying, Nora?"

Her voice broke in a sob. "I'm still a virgin," she cried out passionately. "I have never . . ."

"Now you tell me." He couldn't believe it.

Jerome felt her wet face against his. "Don't worry, I won't make you suffer. I know how, Paul."

"Nora," he cautioned irritably, "you're teasing me."

Unbelievably, her fingers plucked at his trousers, pulled at his belt, groped for his fly. Thus stimulated, he thrust his hand between her legs. She seemed to jump a foot off the couch.

"Nora, I don't get you," Jerome said grimly. "There's got to be a first time."

"Why? Why does there have to be?" she demanded feverishly. "I could die as a virgin if I chose to."

"Yes," he urged, "but you'd miss a lot of fun in the process."

"Fun!" she scoffed. He could practically feel her lip curl.

Jerome struggled to get away from her. "Goddamn it, I can't be responsible if you keep working me over."

He remembered her again, as the adolescent blonde who'd kissed him so yearningly that day by the river. And now this? She was a stranger, he realized with a shock.

"Paul," she said heavily, "I can't. You see . . ." He had the impression she was thinking fast. "I had an operation. It's impossible for me to—"

"What?" he cried. Christ, anything for a little levity. "They didn't sew it up? Don't tell me that, please."

"No!" she yelped. "You fool! It's . . . something else. Somehow, you see, I'm inverted . . . the pelvis."

Caustically, Jerome said, "As long as you're not perverted."

"Don't talk like that!" she cried. "I know—it's all my fault. You're tense. I'll relieve you."

"Relieve me? What? A massage? Nora, cut the chatter. I'm going home."

Amazingly, she had opened his trousers, this blonde who was no longer an adolescent, and even as he squirmed to escape what all the devout Catholics at Paradise Point would have agreed was a mortal sin, she had withdrawn his pecker from his pants. Before he could fully absorb what was happening she began applying her form of first aid for the tension-ridden while making cooing sounds like a lovebird. Jerome understood finally that this little girl from his youth was treating him to something very special.

He didn't dare ask, but could not help wondering whether she had taken a course in fellatio at Harvard—Fellatio One would do a lot more for a woman's career than two years of accounting.

The incredible thing was not the Nora Ellen Sweeney method, but the fact it was Nora Ellen Sweeney of Paradise Point doing it.

Absently, quite lovingly now, Jerome stroked the spinal ends at the nape of her neck, then ran his finger down her back. He slipped the flat of his hand under her white panties, just there, where the rear-running gulch began. There was a shallow pool of perspiration and he dipped a finger and brought it to his nose. The odor was of sweat, pure human sweat, a little sour, a little animal, but very fertile. Right there, he thought, he could have grown a geranium.

Chapter Five

If Kurt Morgan of Diversified Technologies, Inc. had ever expressed interest in Brown, Broadstairs and Dunn, it was really only a symptom of normal predatory appetite. For a man like Morgan, BBD was merely one more of many morsel-sized bites which lay before his ten-billion-dollar-a-year giant.

Diversified, and perhaps the industrial system itself, had grown to a point of saturation at which further expansion was no longer simply a matter of producing more, selling more, and thus making more money for thousands of shareholders.

Diversified had attained capitalism's hated plateau and for the future had a restricted number of options open to it—living with a slow-growth economy, more emphasis had to be laid on bottom-lining, that is, living by the balance sheet, leaving no stone unsqueezed for more profit outside of huge new capital investments. Costs must be cut, worker productivity maximized, retirements forced, unions fought, expenses curtailed.

Alternatively, greater emphasis could be put on research, new products, on the unexplored industrial regions where initial large profits went to the fleet and daring.

But for a monolithic, industry-bridging conglomerate in Diversified's category, the most dramatic way of stimulating—or simulating—growth was to engage in corporate imperialism, gobbling up smaller cash-rich firms occupying stranglehold market positions—a firm like

BBD, perhaps, unassailable in strategic aerospace-vehicle development.

Diversified had begun life as a New England manufacturer, Peabody & Sons, maker of fine looms for the cotton trade. During World War II, Peabody exploited its precision engineering expertise and bid low enough to win contracts to produce gunsights for the U.S. Navy. In the fifties, the company was renamed Peabody Technology and committed itself to that fascinating new industrial form called electronics.

The Peabodys were long gone. The last to leave had been the youngest grandson of the founder, and he had departed for Florida with his cash and stock on the very day Peabody Technology had been renamed Diversified Technologies. The same day, Diversified laid the keel to its first nuclear submarine.

Thus, Diversified had become a conglomerate whose holdings spanned aircraft, missiles, and nucleonics; hotels, insurance, and banking; resort communities and nursing homes; and thousands of consumer products everyone took for granted.

Kurt Morgan was fond of telling people that this was called putting your financial eggs in many different baskets, that "When Madame Inflation sits on American industry, there's no way she'll smash all Diversified's eggs!"

Some people said if Kurt Morgan had lived in a different time and place—say, in the Caribbean—his name would have been Captain Henry Morgan, cutthroat of all the Antilles.

Nora preferred to think of Kurt Morgan as a gentle man trapped within an ungentle system. He certainly did not look like a pirate. In his late fifties, Morgan was more bald than hairy, slightly stooped in the shoulders of his six-foot-two frame. His blue eyes were large and world-weary, or at least skeptical. Morgan was a quiet, husky-voiced man, and to some observers he seemed lonely. Or perhaps he was merely a loner. In those rare moments when Nora mustered the nerve to say something at one of their acquisitions meetings, she loved him for being so patient and so unfailingly courteous, even when she wasn't sure of her ground.

Nora's purpose now, she had decided after the evening with Paul Jerome, must be to get her findings about BBD directly to Morgan—that is, without going through Helen Marconi's department. Ordinarily, all paperwork went to Kurt Morgan's office with Miss Marconi's initials at the bottom.

Morgan was a man of legendary work habits. He had a family in Scarsdale. During the week, he usually stayed at his *pied-à-terre* in the city, working from seven in the morning until seven or eight in the evening and then going on to business dinners, receptions, or banquets.

Nora had easily adapted to arriving at the office at six-thirty each morning, and someday, just in the normal course of human events, Kurt Morgan was going to notice that Nora Ellen Sweeney arrived at Diversified Towers before he did.

The Brown, Broadstairs and Dunn intelligence report Nora prepared was as professional as she could make it, including the expense of having it typed outside the office. The report was based on information any secretary could have obtained from the *Wall Street Journal,* various business journals and reference books, and bits and pieces of the usual industry gossip. The meat of her report was the information from Paul about the families and Buck Collins, *plus* her own interpretation of Paul's information. Nora had dressed carefully this particular morning in November, in a cream-colored long-sleeved silk blouse with a single gold chain at its chaste neckline. The full skirt Nora had chosen was a soft, green tweed which touched, precisely, the middle of her knee; if asked, she'd say it was Sweeney Green and dedicated to the luck of the Irish. Nora always wore practical shoes. Being tall, she had no need of high heels. Low-heeled Italian loafers covered her feet and sheer pantyhose provided her with a snug self-confidence.

Before leaving home early that morning, she had drawn her heavy hair into a knot at the nape of her neck, and then applied just a shadow of lipstick.

Quickly, she wrote the *pro forma* note to Helen Marconi: Helen, here's a little something that might interest the boss. Don't ask me about my confidential source at BBD. Nora.

She slipped the memo into an unmarked folder and strolled in the direction of the coffee machine, located in a room down the main corridor, next to the ladies room.

The forty-fourth floor was Diversified's nerve center. Here were located the communications room, accounting and legal departments, computer systems and conference rooms. Facing the bank of elevators, the reception area was furnished like Morgan's mind—logical, simple, and spartan. Functional but plush furniture rested on a deep carpet. A single, abstract painting of great space and endless time hung behind the reception desk, facing the elevators. Arriving on forty-four, you recognized you had come to the right place.

Nora stood very still, folder in hand, and glanced at her tank watch, a copy of the Cartier original she'd bought for herself the previous Christmas.

It was almost seven on the dot when she heard the approaching rumble of the elevator. Nora waited a split second to make sure it stopped at forty-four, then turned and hurried down the corridor to the ladies' room. Morgan, she knew from careful observation, invariably dumped his briefcase on a desk in his outer office and headed for the coffee machine. He often boasted that he was in so early every morning that he often brewed the first pot of coffee of the day.

Inside the ladies' room, Nora pressed her ear to the crack between door and casement. The carpeting was so thick it would be impossible to hear him approaching, but she would catch the clunk of his heels against the tiled floor of the coffee room.

Yes, yes, he'd come. It *had* to be him.

She opened the door a sliver and listened. When she heard him leave the coffee room, she charged out into the corridor.

Morgan saw, but not in time. He halted, his hand jerked up, and a plume of coffee flew. Nora lifted her folder in an instinctive gesture, the black liquid slapped against it and ran inside, onto her memo.

"Hell!" Morgan's eyes jumped with alarm. "I'm sorry. Did I—"

"No, no," Nora cried. *"I'm* sorry. I should watch what I'm doing." Her face was red, she knew; she was, in fact, very flustered. She shook the folder. "A little coffee on it, that's all . . ." She laughed nervously. "It was for you. I'll have it retyped."

"Don't be silly," Morgan said.

"It didn't spill on you, did it?"

"No, no. I'm fine, Miss . . . sorry. I do know your name."

"Nora," she said instantly. "Nora Ellen Sweeney."

"Of course, you come to the meetings with Helen . . ."

"Marconi," Nora supplied the name.

"And you're Nora Sweeney. I won't forget, I promise." He glanced at the folder, still up like a flag between them. "You're in early, aren't you?"

"Catching up, that's all."

He held out his hand. "You might as well give me the folder, Nora."

Done. Gently, she handed it over. He passed her his coffee cup to hold and flipped it open, scanning quickly, first the note to Helen Marconi.

"Ah," he muttered, "so you have a confidential source at BBD, do you?"

Nora didn't answer since it was more of a statement than a question. Morgan began reading the report, nodding, turning the pages impatiently until he reached the information from Paul. She saw that he was rereading the last page. Abruptly, he slapped the folder shut.

"Well, okay, Miss Sweeney," he said noncommittally.

"It doesn't amount to much," she stammered. "I just thought it might be interesting."

"If it doesn't amount to much, then why put it down on paper?" he demanded, then skeptically added, "and get it to me at seven in the morning? I like your initiative, Miss Sweeney."

Oh, God, he had caught on. She looked stricken. "Oh, please don't think . . ."

He smiled at her inquiringly, those liquid blue eyes droll. Maybe it wasn't going to be as bad as she thought.

Retrieving his coffee cup from her limp hand, Morgan said, "I'm going to fill this up again, Miss Sweeney, and maybe you'd like coffee, too." He peered at her and continued briskly, "Then we'll walk to my office and discuss this BBD business more."

Nora's heart leapt. She knew then that she had a chance. At least, he was not dismissing her out of hand.

"Well, come on," he said impatiently. "I've got phone calls to make, Miss Sweeney. London first; I've told them never to go out to lunch before we talk. I'll carry the folder, Miss Sweeney."

Nora had never been in Kurt Morgan's private office, which seemed bigger than his conference room. The wall behind the long wooden desk was one broad window, a suicide's view of the whole southern portion of Manhattan.

Belgian and Oriental rugs, about a dozen of them, floated on the deep-pile carpeting. The inside walls were crowded with art. Morgan, Nora had heard, collected abstract paintings, like the one in the reception area, but there were other more classical styles included here. The one of most significance to her was a painted icon, a portrait of a long-faced and soulful Virgin holding the child, both protected by heavy gilded halos. The brilliant deep red was almost blazing, the tones achieved only in pre-revolutionary Russia.

She gazed at this picture. To her, it was so much more impressive than anything modern art had to offer. "It's beautiful, Mr. Morgan . . ."

"Yes," he said somberly, "it is wonderful. *The Virgin of Novgorod.*"

But he was already behind his desk, punching out a number on the telephone. Nora told herself she must remember to tell Lucia Gogarty about Kurt Morgan. He would be an important customer for her.

"This is only a small portion . . ." Nora heard the trans-Atlantic connection clicking and buzzing as it ricocheted off a satellite. "Johnny . . . morning! Kurt."

So as not to seem to eavesdrop, Nora went to the far side of the room to study a gold-leafed Giotto. She'd thought Giottos were all in museums. Morgan was complaining that he had to deliver a speech that night, and hadn't any idea of what he'd say. Abruptly, he said good-bye to Johnny.

"Well, Miss Sweeney," Morgan recalled her, "you heard. You're good at writing a report—how are you at writing speeches?"

Timidly, she approached his desk. "I've never really . . ."

Morgan stopped her by unsnapping his briefcase and pulling out a yellow legal pad. "I scribbled a few notes last night. Do you think you can decipher my scrawl?"

Accepting the pad, she felt something like an electric shock transmitted across it, from him to her.

Morgan stretched backwards in his leather swivel chair, legs extended under the desk. "Normally, Joe Fenton writes these things, but he's out of the city handling a PR problem." He remembered something else in the briefcase, dug into it again and handed Nora a stapled sheaf of paper.

"Here's one of my last efforts, for a group of Pentagon

guys a couple of weeks ago. That's the style." He chuckled dryly. "I gave 'em a little jolt, you see. Now they all think I'm a terrible un-hawkish person. I don't believe in nuclear arms, Nora," he said darkly. "I'm for the freeze."

She stared at him, wondering if she'd missed the point. It had never occurred to her to consider his politics.

"So, Nora, tone it down a little. I am *not* saying we should surrender but I do believe the bomb is its own deterrent—we really don't need ten thousand of the goddamn things to destroy the world."

He stopped abruptly and smiled up at her. Clearly, she was supposed to say something.

"That's fascinating," she said shyly. "I happen to agree with you, Mr. Morgan. I'll give it a try."

"Do better than that, Nora. There's no time for anybody else to tackle it." He glared at her. "Now, I hope you're not going to withhold who your confidential source is at BBD. . . . Sit down, for God's sake."

Nora wilted. "Would it be absolutely between us, Mr. Morgan?"

"You have my word." He frowned and clasped his hands into fists under his bony chin. "It's not, I take it, Buck Collins."

"No."

His expression became intense. "I'll tell you something, Nora. One of the reasons I'd go after BBD would be to get Collins for Diversified. Let me tell you, Nora . . ."

He'd forgotten the question. Nora relaxed a little, crossed her knees, modestly pulling down the green skirt. She couldn't believe it had worked so well.

"Buck Collins is a star," Morgan mused, talking to himself. "He's brought BBD out of the woods. The three old guys, they were fine for their era, the spit-and-polish days of transition from prop to jet. Today, they couldn't make it. . . . Well, maybe they could. They'd be different though. Collins, he's the new breed."

"Like you are," she said.

"Me?" he echoed her. "I just jolt along. Buck Collins is

a major talent. I've seen him in action. He could charm the balls right off a brass monkey."

The words slipped out of his mouth and Nora assumed he was unaware of what he was saying. Inwardly, Nora flushed. But she didn't move, didn't change expression. It would be stupid to say anything. The tenor of business conversation was constantly deteriorating and it was often the women, Nora noted, who outdid the men in vulgarity.

"Of course," Morgan debated himself thoughtfully, "you'd have to watch Buck like a hawk. He knows where all the aerospace bodies are buried. And he's ruthless. Let down your guard just once and . . . whammo!"

Nora tried to remain objective. So far, she had not received a very flattering picture of the great Buck Collins. Paul Jerome had hinted that Collins was not much more than an opportunistic blowhard, and now Kurt Morgan was saying that though he'd like to have Collins at Diversified he wasn't sure he'd ever trust him.

"Mr. Collins *sounds* brilliant," she said cautiously.

"Oh, yeah?" Morgan frowned skeptically. "Well, Miss Sweeney . . . Sweeney, isn't it? Well, *you* be brilliant with that speech. I need it by five o'clock tonight."

Chapter Six

As she'd promised, Lucia Francesca Saltimbocca Gogarty pulled up at Jerome's place on East Sixty-second Street at precisely 9:00 a.m. that Saturday morning. He tossed his overnight bag in the back seat and climbed in the front of the dark green Jaguar sedan.

"Hello, Paolo," she murmured warmly, smiling at him with her brilliant black eyes as if they were already old friends.

"Well, good morning, Lucia. Rainy weather agrees with you."

The downpour had been heavy overnight, knocking into the gutters what remained of the autumn, and it was still drizzling. Lucia set the wipers on slow.

"Moist air is good for the skin."

She pulled away rapidly, then braked hard at the corner.

"Would you like me to drive?"

"Why?" She glanced at him amusedly. "Maybe you don't trust my driving, Paolo?"

"I trust your driving," he answered. What could he say? That he didn't fancy thrills so early in the morning?

Lucia bit her lip, then said, "Sorry Nora Sweeney could not come with us today."

Unconcerned, Jerome glanced out the side window. A woman with wet shoes and an umbrella over her head stood on the curb, glaring at them. "Yes," he murmured, "there is the intriguing matter of Nora Ellen Sweeney."

"Intriguing?"

"She had to go out of town this weekend."

"So she told me," Lucia muttered, whipping the car around the corner, headed for Madison Avenue. Quickly, he looked at her face. Concentration set her chin, gave her a stubborn look. Her skin had such depth to it, such resonance.

"Nora has gone to California with her boss, Kurt Morgan. Morgan is a very powerful man. Did Nora tell you he's also an art collector?"

"Yes, she told me, Paolo." Lucia was not impressed. "He buys abstract art—which is not of much interest to me."

"You prefer . . ."

"Classical—and Impressionists."

"I see. I don't know anything about art. Was Mr. Gogarty a patron of the arts?"

Lucia laughed swiftly. "In no way, Paolo!" The mere mention of such a thing seemed preposterous to her. "The castle has second-rate paintings, all fortunately dirty and dimmed with age. You will see."

It was in fact toward Gogarty Castle that she was driving. Jerome was still wondering why she'd invited him and Nora. It was an ironic fact that at last Paul Jerome, local boy possibly made good, was to see the inside of the granite pile.

"I've always wondered what the place was like," he mentioned.

Lucia shrugged slightly. "It's true that my husband never invited the local people to his home?" She glanced at him.

"I never heard of anybody going there."

She made a face. "A very strange man, wasn't he?"

A strange question too, coming from Gogarty's widow. Surely, she'd have known whether he was strange or not, and how.

"He told me," Lucia continued, "that he built the house for his first wife, the sainted Gladys. He said he chose the

42

location with the greatest care . . ." She chuckled rather spitefully. "Putting it as he did on that finger of land, like a veritable penis plunged into the flooded Hudson River. I should probably sell it soon. I keep it for Oswald, the man who served Gogarty for so many years. Oswald will die one day or sail away. Then I may give it to the Church— Father Foster believes it would be perfect for a cloistered order of nuns. How proper that would be—J.J. Gogarty would roll in his grave."

"A splendid write-off," he commented dryly.

"Ha! Yes." Amused, she took her eyes off the road to look at him and smile. "Should I be looking for write-offs? It seems to me that is all you Americans talk about—taxes and write-offs. It's much easier in Italy merely to cheat." She laughed aloud at his reaction. "Father Foster will join us tonight for dinner. Too bad not Nora as well. She is a beautiful creature, royal almost . . ." She turned again. "Are you in love with her, Paolo?"

The question surprised him. The possibility of falling in love with Nora had never occurred to him. If he were, wouldn't he be feeling jealous that she'd gone off with Kurt Morgan and angry with her too? That answered the question.

"No," he said. "Why would you think so? I hadn't seen her in years until that night we had dinner."

Nonetheless, he was annoyed that Nora had used him so blatantly to call Pete Broadstairs in Palm Springs and arrange a meeting Sunday so Morgan could test the old man on a merger offer.

It was not nice, or even ethical, to line up your employer for such a corporate chop-chop as Nora had in mind. Still, Jerome thought, let her think that she'd used him. On the surface, it was all very innocuous . . . so far.

"How old is Nora?" Lucia asked next.

"Just about thirty."

"Ah," Lucia said sadly, "so young. And I am thirty-five —so old."

"*Not* old, Lucia."

"Yes," she disagreed impatiently, "and I would like to have a child—almost too late, already."

He kept his eye intently on the street, wondering about that old goat Gogarty, whom she'd married. "You know something, Lucia," he said, risking the remark, "people in Paradise Point always called Gogarty Black Jack. I have no idea why."

She tossed her fine shoulders, snug in a black turtle-neck cashmere sweater. The movement seemed to set off a fresh, clean and flawless scent.

"I know that as he was dying Gogarty kicked the attending priest in the stomach and refused the sacraments or any attempt to console him. He was dragged to death by demons," she said solemnly. "Gogarty did not want to die, I can tell you."

Jerome said, "But I thought he was a *very* religious man."

"Oh, yes, I know—he had his audiences with the popes. He should have owned an apartment in the Vatican he was there so much."

"But then—kicking a priest in the stomach."

Lucia laughed shyly. "Black Jack Gogarty did not like priests and toward the end he was convinced the Church was too interested in his money, that the Church would strip me bare after he was gone."

"Which they wouldn't have done," he said simply.

"Oh, yes? Are you so sure?" she challenged him. "They want it still. Father Foster wants to arrange everything. You will see. He will discuss it tonight at dinner. He wants me to create a John Joseph Gogarty Foundation with a mission to help deserving Catholic scholars and to finance missionary work in far-off places, such as filthy Africa. Oh, yes," she grimaced, "they have their plans."

"I know—the one thing the Church has is plans. But I wouldn't know. What am I, Lucia? A mere Jew, caught in Father John's intricate web."

Lucia scowled at him. "More than that, I hope, Paul."

They had cleared the northern slums of the city and

44

were on the parkway at last—the way Lucia drove, another half-hour to Paradise Point.

After a few moments' silence, Lucia warned him, "Paul, don't misunderstand me. I trust Father Foster. He is a good man. But I would appreciate you, perhaps, advising me on some of his proposals. You could be my second opinion. You would be neutral, would you not?"

"I'm obviously not under any sort of Church discipline."

"Paul!" she barked at him, "no thoughts like that! Catholic . . . Jew . . . it is all the same to me."

"You're a strong Catholic, Lucia," he pointed out.

"I am an Italian Catholic, Paolo. That is what you must understand."

"All right." He had one observation to make. "From what you tell me, J.J. Gogarty might not have approved of this foundation in his name."

"That is very true. You know, Paolo," she said, "he was one of the black Irish. I was told by Oswald once that Black Jack was suspected of killing Gladys and burying her under one of his highways."

"Do I remember that story?" Jerome asked himself, aloud.

"Do you?"

"I'm not sure. I know the castle was supposed to have been built of loose pieces of granite he trucked in when he dynamited through the Catskills."

"No trace was ever found of Gladys Gogarty," Lucia said playfully. "Fortunately, he never tried to murder me."

"You? The man would have to be insane to want to murder you."

"He was a little insane, I'm convinced," Lucia said. "Well, we will never know the truth until Judgment Day."

He laughed. Yes, he liked Lucia. She was by no means an unhappy widow, deep in mourning, clicking her rosary. "May I say, you survived Mr. Gogarty very nicely."

She nodded happily and took one gloved hand off the

steering wheel to tap his knee. "I tamed the wild Gogarty, Paolo. I formed him into a gentleman and made him the elder statesman of highway construction."

"I'm sure you did, Lucia." He hoped she would go on. He enjoyed listening to her.

"I am a fabulous woman, quite fabulous," she said frankly. "I hope you will appreciate me."

"I do," he murmured, "more and more."

Chapter Seven

IT WAS NOVEMBER WEATHER IN PALM SPRINGS—SUNNY, warm, and turbulent enough over the airport to make the landing a rough one. But what a break the crystal clear air was, Nora told herself gratefully. She had never been to California before.

Kurt Morgan had changed his clothes on the plane from his conservative business attire to a golf shirt, light windbreaker, and red golfing trousers. As soon as the plane rolled to a stop, he was on his feet.

There were just the two of them and to Nora's disappointment Morgan had spent the entire flight working out of his bulging briefcase, pausing only to nibble at the lunch the stewardess had served.

But, never mind, Nora told herself, she was incredibly lucky to be along for such a ride and was not going to allow so much as a cross thought to dirty the rarefied air inside the plane. Hadn't her plan come up roses? Not without a few hitches, of course, but what in life went any more smoothly? Morgan had liked the speech and thanked her for writing it. But then he had seemed to forget about her existence. Helen Marconi's nose was out of joint as a result of her initiative, and Joe Fenton hated her guts just for being there to step into his spot, no matter how briefly.

Then, just a week before, the office environment had flipped from negative to positive in a matter of minutes. Mr. Morgan wanted to see her immediately. In his shirtsleeves, tie askew, even stained at the bottom, he looked so very tired and harried that Nora wanted to hug him.

"Nora, I want you to use that contact of yours at BBD," he said when she entered his office. "We're flying to Palm Springs on Saturday, the thirtieth, and I want a date arranged for us to see Pete Broadstairs Sunday morning. Arrange all that, will you?"

Nora nodded. "You and Mr. Ball—"

"No, no," he said. "*You're* coming with me since this was all your bright idea. It'll be good experience for you—I've read that report a couple of times and it's damn good. So was the speech you wrote." He looked at her irately. "You see, I believe in bringing good people along . . . and up, Nora. As of now, I'm assigning you to my office as one of my personal assistants. You get one of the empties down the hall and half a secretary. She'll bring your things over."

Nora wet her lips nervously. "May I sit down? I'm overwhelmed, Mr. Morgan."

"As you should be," he said curtly. "Congratulations. Although you may come to hate me for it—I'll tell you up front, Nora, you're going to be working your ass off."

The tone of his warning didn't register. She'd have to adjust to his use of swear words. Helen Marconi would be livid, Nora knew, absolutely livid. And she was. Even after the announcement had been made of Nora's promotion, Helen couldn't accept it. One day they were alone in the same elevator. Not even looking at Nora, Helen sneered, "How'd you do it, Sweeney? Not from the speed of your shorthand, that's for sure." Nora knew what she was hinting and what other people would be thinking. But Nora would always know that she, for one, had achieved her promotion by working hard and not, like Helen Marconi, by carrying on a long-running affair with an executive vice-president, namely Rustford Lancer.

But it was easy now, waiting to alight from the company jet, to forget about Helen Marconi and practically everything else. Nora stood behind Morgan, while the attendants opened the door. He'd given her his heavy briefcase to take to the hotel. He trusted her totally, she told herself warmly.

He glanced over his shoulder. "Nora, I'm going straight out to Tamarisk. We're teeing off at two-fifteen. Where do I go then?"

"We're staying at the Hotel Sunset Spa, Mr. Morgan. Just tell the driver."

He was on the steps by now. "See you, Nora."

She watched him go. He walked purposefully across the steaming tarmac toward a long black car drawn up a distance from the plane. The driver saluted him and Morgan nodded back. Nimbly, he jumped in the car. Why this great show of athletic vim and vigor? Was it to impress her?

It didn't bother her that he was leaving her in the lurch. It was her job to take care of the cumbersome, perhaps annoying details. Why should she suddenly feel so left out because he was going to a country club to play golf with business cronies? Nora had never even held a golf club in her hand.

Besides, it was her first time in California and she was going to make the most of it.

The Sunset Spa was a city-block sized pink adobe refuge not far from Palm Canyon Drive, which Morgan had told her was Palm Springs's main street. But the hotel could have been miles out in the desert, built as it was around a quiet, pool-filled inner courtyard, a spa within an oasis. The palm trees looked unreal, so motionless in the still, sunny air. Bodies filled most of the lounges around the pool, waiters scurried to and fro bearing trays with drinks and food.

Heavenly, Nora thought. To think that most of the world knew nothing about places like Palm Springs. In season, it seemed warm, friendly, and relaxed. She could adapt to this life very nicely.

The heels of Nora's sling-back shoes tapped the broad tiles of the lobby floor. Above her, a beamed ceiling was lit by skylights. A mezzanine floor soared through space, seemingly unsupported. Nora felt suddenly awkward, foreign, as she made for the front desk; she was dressed in a heavy suit made of a dull gray wool, while all about her women were practically undressed in colorful light fabrics, or bikinis and open robes, thonged sandals, crazy sunglasses. And she hadn't even brought a bathing suit.

Nora controlled the flow of impressions and announced herself and Kurt Morgan to a young blond man behind the desk. He scanned the reservations and, hardly interrupting his smile with a show of white teeth, spoke and pointed at the same time.

"That's two-sixteen and two-eighteen. Straight across, past the pool, second floor, overlooking the interior." He motioned for a porter. "Joe will show you, Miss Sweeney."

Did he leer at her? Two-sixteen and -eighteen? Was that a suite? She hadn't ordered a suite. Too late now. The porter had the bags on a cart and she was following him.

Outside, the sun climbed on her shoulders. Incredibly, it was actually *hot* when you left the air-conditioning, first of the car, then the hotel lobby. She definitely had to shed her heavy suit. Fortunately, she observed, there was a woman's boutique to her left.

"Joe." She handed him two dollars and pointed out Morgan's bag and hers. "Give me my key. I'll be along in a minute."

Inside the shop, Nora found what she needed for the next few days—a simple, well-cut red dress, a two-piece bathing suit that would have shocked her mother but which was like long underwear compared to what she'd seen outside, then quickly, in case Kurt Morgan called from the country club, a pair of red sandals and a hip-length kimono for poolside.

Nora didn't even look at the total. She signed a credit card slip for a purple-haired saleslady, then stuffed receipt and card into her purse. The saleslady thought she was easy, a perfect size six.

Probably a month's salary, she thought, as she continued on to the room. But, really, when in Rome . . .

The bathing suit was tighter and more revealingly cut
than any she'd ever owned. But, whirling before the
mirror, she decided she looked good. Self-consciously, she
covered herself with the kimono and went downstairs to
poolside. But no one paid her any particular attention;
why should they? There were any number of women,
blondes like her, brunettes, even a redhead or two,
stretched out for inspection, all pretty and with the same
pert noses. Through the afternoon, Nora swam several
times, napped a little, and soaked up the benevolent sun
under a moderate coating of sun block. She watched the
mating ritual indolently. The men, she judged, were
handsome in their brief bathing costumes. Everybody out
here seemed to believe in displaying themselves *au natu-
rel.* The men's suits hadn't any interior support. Whatever
they had showed and you couldn't avoid seeing it unless
you closed your eyes.

By the time she went back to the room, feeling vaguely
baked, Morgan hadn't called or left a message.

It *was* a suite, she now discovered. The extra door she
hadn't wanted to open led into a living room. On the
opposite side was another door, and she knew this would
be Morgan's bedroom. Firmly, Nora returned to her own
room and closed the door.

At seven o'clock, he still hadn't called, so she went
across the quadrangle to the restaurant for dinner. There
wasn't any trouble about a table; the place was only half
full. Everybody probably went out to local restaurants—
who wanted to eat at the hotel, after all? She did. She
hadn't any choice. But even so, alone was not bad. Nora
was used to being alone.

She was back in her room by eight-thirty and Morgan
still had not called. Her bed had been turned down and a
chocolate mint in a foil wrapper had been placed on the
fluffed-up pillow. The door to the other bedroom had been
left open. Nora went through the living room and peeked

into Morgan's quarters. The bedside lamp was on, the bed turned down, the mint in position. But no sign of Morgan.

The phone rang. She was startled, yet pleased. At last he was calling.

"Mr. Morgan's suite," she announced.

The grunt at the other end of the line was not masculine or pleasant. A fuzziness indicated a long-distance call.

"Who's this?" a woman asked.

"Nora Ellen Sweeney. Is there a message for Mr. Morgan?"

"Yes." The voice sounded droll. "Tell Mr. Morgan his wife called."

"Oh. Yes," Nora said. "I will. Thank you. He's out at a business meeting."

"I'm sure." Mrs. Morgan hung up.

Oh, blast. She might have known. Now his wife would hate her, when she was just doing her duty. At the moment, that entailed answering the phone, didn't it? Who could have known it was not Mr. Broadstairs wanting to change the time of their meeting the next morning? No, she was reacting foolishly. Mrs. Morgan was not going to think Nora Ellen Sweeney was in California with Mr. Morgan for anything but the most upright reasons. Was she? Then, Nora reminded herself that innocence was its own reward and evil was in the eye of the beholder.

Quickly, she returned to her room and closed the door. Should she lock it? No. She went into the bathroom. The beautifully tiled tub was huge, with a Jacuzzi spray positioned in the sides. Twisting a gold-enameled faucet, Nora started the hot water, tested it, added cold, and undressed. She slipped out of the green blouse, pulled down the black silk slacks which were perfect for Palm Springs, folded them and laid them across the foot of her bed. Then she shed her underthings and looked at her body in the full-length mirror alongside the bed.

Just looking at herself gave her something of a thrill. She was faintly narcissistic, she'd admit that. The breasts were wonderfully firm, she decided, for a woman of twenty-nine, and full enough for now. Nora believed that when a woman began to indulge enthusiastically in love-making, as she fully intended to do—someday—they would grow larger. Yes. Her belly was just a little rounded, not unlike Venus's as she tottered out of the half-shell, and, below that, her pubic patch looked fluffy, like a little pussy, unstroked until the man who was worthy of such an unspoiled treasure came along.

Nora made a face, then laughed at herself. She was pretty silly, indeed, for a brilliant and mature woman, a Harvard MBA, author of an economics thesis that had been praised by a former professor who was now an advisor to the president of the United States.

People did call those things pussies. Quite extraordinary, she told herself introspectively, how such a thing had the capacity to drive men so wild. Silly of them, wasn't it? Even Paul Jerome, and he hadn't even been given the chance to touch—though he hadn't asked if he could. Probably because she'd paid him so nicely for his information, though he wasn't aware that he was being paid.

It didn't really matter what you did with your mouth, she thought, for the mouth was made to deal with ugly things—to eat sloppy and disgusting food, or to suck on fat cigars, or to spout swear words.

All she had done, really, was to relieve Paul of all the tension and pressure that had grown to such explosive force inside his testicles. She thought about all of that fluid hitting the opening to the womb. A woman could not avoid getting pregnant. But Nora Ellen Sweeney could. She laughed to herself. Paul would have been surprised if he'd known what had happened to his *fluid* that night when he'd reached his *spending*. She'd kept it in her mouth, leaped up and dashed into her kitchen and spat it into a jar she kept in the freezer for just that purpose. She believed the protein-laden stuff was a stimulant for the skin and its hormone-content a deterrent to the sprouting of facial hair. Without even knowing it, Paul was helping Nora keep her eyelids and face smooth.

Feeling very pleased with herself, Nora tested the water with one foot. Perfect. She stepped in and knelt, thinking she would try the Jacuzzi jets on the back of her thighs. The water streamed toward her, water within water and, crouching, she realized she could arrange herself so it whirled against her most guarded place.

The sensation made her suddenly weak, pumping life-force up her legs from her toes. Quickly, Nora flopped down in the tub. She must deny herself any such suggestive stimulation, she cautioned, for surely it was a prelude to masturbation. The clitoral button inside the labia of her vagina tingled with heat but that must be merely a sensory failure. On her finger, it was merely smooth and quite at body temperature.

Not to touch. She dwelled instead on dear, dear Paul Jerome. So beautiful. How would he look, Nora wondered, in a modeling strap, the sort of immodest garment men wore at the pool in Palm Springs? He'd hold his own, she remembered, closing her eyes. What Paul had was soft, though not soft, and so long that she couldn't imagine how it would fit into anything but an outsized Amazon.

But she definitely must not think about it. Plenty of time for that sort of thing, after she was on the fast track.

But, Paul would be rewarded, that she promised. What he'd done to help her had not been strictly ethical, but wasn't it ethical to help a friend? Without Paul, Nora told herself, she would not at this moment be in Palm Springs, reclined in a shaped bathtub waiting for her genius of a boss, who in her most lavish fantasies was a bald-headed Western hero.

Nora was in her white silk nightie and long robe at ten o'clock, and was beginning to worry about Kurt Morgan. Suppose he'd had a seizure or died on the golf course? Tragic things happened all the time.

At ten-thirty, finally, the door slammed on the other side of the suite. Nora remained where she was, sitting in front of her TV set. Next she heard the flushing of a toilet.

Next he was in the living room; she heard him whistling.

Had he come back with one of his cronies in tow? Nora got up silently and looked through her door, opened a crack. Morgan's back was turned to her. He was bent over, switching the channels on the TV set in the main room.

Her voice was like a whisper. "Mr. Morgan . . ."

He didn't move. "Yes, Nora."

She murmured, "Your wife called."

"When?" he asked. "What did she want?"

"I don't know. She just told me to tell you she'd called."

He wheeled and gazed at her, his eyes bugging slightly at the sight of her neatly bunned hair and the robe.

He frowned. "You were embarrassed?"

"I didn't know we'd have a suite, Mr. Morgan. I *had* to answer the phone. It could've been very important."

He seemed annoyed with her. "Listen, Nora, no sweat. So she's suspicious . . . jealous. What the hell do you care?"

She faltered. "I have a reputation," she said weakly.

"So do I. So what?"

She realized he really didn't care. His power was unassailable. It didn't matter what people said about him; he'd always win. Nora backed toward her room and she would have gone there and hidden if he hadn't stopped her.

"What about something to drink? There's a bar over there." He pointed. "I'm having a beer. What about you?"

"I'll get it," she said.

"No. Sit down, Nora."

"Could I have a little brandy? I guess they wouldn't have Irish whiskey."

"Probably not," he grunted. He banged open the small refrigerator and extracted a beer which opened with a heady belch. Then he rattled miniatures until he found a brandy which he emptied into the first glass his hand touched. "Here's to it, Nora," he said. He handed her the drink and flopped down beside her on the far end of the couch. "I did okay today. Anybody else call?"

Nora shook her head.

"Then I assume we see Broadstairs at brunch. You better confirm it early tomorrow, Nora."

"Yes, sir."

He grinned at her happily. "You look serious enough to bust a gut. I think you do take yourself very seriously, don't you?"

Cautiously, she said, "If I don't, who does? I guess . . . I'm very impressed, that's all."

"With what?"

"Everything," she replied. "Making this trip . . . being here with you . . . it's all new to me, Mr. Morgan."

"Holy Christ," he marveled, playing with the beer bottle. "You're very intelligent, Nora—despite the little-girl act you put on all the time."

She smiled anxiously. It would be easy to say the wrong thing. "I'm sorry. I don't mean . . . I'm just not very worldly, I guess."

"Oh, shut up," he said pleasantly. "Be anything you want, kid. You don't have to convince me of anything. Christ, I've been around the block a few times. You're smart, Nora. Clever. You don't have to hide it."

"Mr. Morgan," she exclaimed softly, "you make me blush. I try, but I am very innocent. I admit it. I . . ."

"Bullshit," he sighed, just as easily as before. He was a little tipsy, she realized. "I reserved the suite, you know."

Genuinely shocked, she said, "Why?"

He sounded totally cynical. "So you'd be here to answer the phone, kid. Why do you think?" That wasn't what he meant, she knew.

"Deliberately!" Her voice shook. "Why me?"

Morgan shrugged scornfully. "To keep her off-balance maybe. Let her think I'm playing around." He laughed. "She knows I'd dump her if I could afford to. Obviously I can't split everything with her. I'd end up a goddamn pauper. No—let *her* take a walk. If she does, though, she knows she gets fuck-all from me." His expression was fierce, ruthless, almost murderous. Even in such exalted places, men behaved like this. It was sickening. But he hadn't finished. "I thought of having her bumped off. She's got a boyfriend in New York. I know all about it. He's a TV actor, does commercials when he gets work, which isn't very often. He's an Italian import. . . . Someday," Morgan said poisonously, "when I'm ready, I'll get him too. I could leak an item to the press right now if I wanted and he'd never work again. But why should I? It'd cost me. *She'd* give him money." He was glaring. "Do you understand . . . *Nora?*"

She paled, nodded, not daring either to sympathize, or disagree. She stared down at her glass.

Her silence had served its purpose. He sounded miserable but contrite. "I'm sorry. No reason for you to hear such stuff, Nora."

"Poor man," she whispered, looking at him, her robe wrapped about her knees. "I'll fetch you another beer."

She went hastily to the bar. She opened the bottle and carefully poured the beer into a glass. She was still pouring when she handed it to him.

"I used to do this for my father," she said.

"Did you?" He accepted the glass. As he did, he touched her hand, and awkwardly stroked her knuckles with one finger. "You're okay, Nora."

She didn't budge. She stood beside him. He moved his hand to her forearm and pulled her down on the arm of the sofa next to his shoulder.

"What'd your father do?"

She didn't miss a beat. "He was an engineer."

"Dead?"

She nodded sadly. "He died of a brain tumor when I was twelve."

"Poor kid. Your mother?"

"Also dead, Mr. Morgan. She was a nurse."

"All good people, Nora," Morgan grieved. "What happens to all the good people?"

"There are some still around, Mr. Morgan."

"Very goddamn few and far between, Nora."

"No," she cried, "you shouldn't say things like that, Mr. Morgan. Most people are not bad—they're basically good. You're a good man! Right now you're unhappy, but it'll work out. You'll see."

He looked at her sourly. "Don't hand me that 'Somewhere Over the Rainbow' bullshit, Nora."

She laughed, then impulsively grabbed his hand and pulled it to her lips.

As she'd expected, he was surprised. "Nora, I . . ."

Clutching the hand, she pressed it to her breast, feeling the hard knuckles. He shifted sideways and pulled her down beside him. Nora wasn't caught unaware by his kiss. He pushed his mouth against her cheek, then caught her lips. He smelled of beer and the hand she had introduced to her breast now cupped it, then groped inside her robe.

"Black underwear!" he exclaimed gutturally.

She gushed. "I forgot to pack anything else. Oh, Mr. Morgan. Please."

His voice deepened in lust. "What's the matter?"

"Mr. Morgan . . ." She ducked her head away from him. "I'm not . . . I'm surprised. Please. I don't know what to say. Oh! Be gentle!"

"Trust me."

More controlled, he decided to loosen the sash of the robe instead of trying to tear it to pieces. He jammed his left hand between her legs. Nora slapped her thighs together.

"Oh, please," she groaned heavily, "I wish you wouldn't. I'm ashamed. I think . . ."

"What?"

"I'm getting my period, Mr. Morgan. Oh, I'm sorry."

"Oh, shit."

"When I get excited, it brings it on with a rush, you see."

"I see, goddamn it," he cursed. "You might know—the luck of the Morgans."

58

"I'm so sorry," Nora said softly. She prayed she hadn't ruined everything. "Are you . . . very *tense?*"

"Tense?" He blinked, almost tearfully.

As if to reply, Nora tentatively placed her hand on his red pants and, feeling his muscle jump, spread her fingers over the place she knew would be in an absolute uproar.

"You are tense," she decided.

"Yes." He sounded bitter, as if he'd been let down by the whole human race.

"Poor man. It's all my fault."

He nodded violently. "Yes, it is your fault."

"I feel terrible."

"You should."

Nora cast him a sidelong, guilty look. "Tension is very counterproductive."

"Yes, that's true," he growled. "My doctor told me to avoid tension at all costs."

His genital was about to burst the seams of propriety. She had known all along that Kurt Morgan was a man of vitality and virility, the two characteristics that together spelled power. This, she thought, proved it. She now understood the ultimate aphrodisiac: power.

"A man like you should never be denied relief from stress and tension," Nora said.

He was watching her very carefully, warily, like one predatory animal of the jungle watching another.

"Lean back," Nora said, "and don't look."

He didn't question the command. He slumped to the side, his body loose. Nora very carefully undid the bright red golf trousers. She chuckled when she found pink boxer shorts underneath.

His hand infiltrated her robe, going behind her to the snap on her black brassiere.

"You're going to remove my top?"

"It's not going to hurt you."

"My breasts are very tender."

He didn't have a chance to hurt her though. His hand fell away and he sighed when she began to relieve him of the bad tension and stress. His fingers kneaded the nape of her neck and then found the intricate whirl of hair wound into a bun at the back of her head.

"Nora, your hair is so thick . . . it's so smooth, so slick . . ."

She didn't answer; let him go on. She could feel the tightening of single strands of her hair as he clasped the bun, tangled his fingers in it. He squeezed it, pulled at it spasmatically as he began to relax. Then his belly tightened, the root quivered, and she was aware he was about to spend his life-force.

Suddenly, roughly, unexpectedly, he yanked on her bun, pulling her lips away, wrenching her head to the side. Nora cried out, alarmed, and then realized he was thrusting into her thickly massed hair, crying out angrily and releasing himself into her blondness.

He was an animal, she told herself. But such an animal.

Chapter Eight

THE HOUSE THAT GOGARTY BUILT WAS AS GRAY AS ITS
granite. It was a rough, crude edifice which looked like it
had been blasted, already cast, out of a hillside, and
unceremoniously dumped at the side of the Hudson River.
But Gogarty Castle was much like the man who had
ordered it built—dark, brooding, enigmatic, not kind or
sentimental. The house could have been brought over
from Scotland, or from some dank moor in England,
hundreds of years old, as old as broadswords and boiling
oil.

Deceptive. The place had actually been thrown up
during J.J. Gogarty's road-building heyday in the mid-
thirties, when Federal money was dedicated to keeping
out-of-work muscles occupied. It seemed to have been the
fruit of Gladys Gogarty's imagination. She had been a
great fan of Sir Walter Scott and might even have fancied
herself, before disappearing, as a will-o'-the-wisp Lady of
the Lake, or River.

Once off the potholed macadam, the road was very
bumpy. It had never been paved, Lucia said, because
there was no purpose in paving it. Winter ice and snow
cracked any permanent surfacing in the north of New York
State.

The first glimpse of the castle viewed through the array
of pines, hemlocks, maples, birches and oaks, was of a
pillared *porte-cochère* big enough to accommodate a

double-decker bus. Lucia ran the green Jaguar under it and honked loudly.

"Oswald," she explained. "Gogarty's man—and a little deaf. From listening to foghorns, Gogarty said."

Also a little old, Jerome discovered, so old that he insisted on carrying the two overnight bags into the house himself. Oswald was dressed in a black tailcoat with a stiff collar and white bow tie. His trousers were unpressed gray bags. Jerome tried to remember—was this the same scarecrow?

"Madame Lucia," Oswald bowed, once they were in an echoing, marbled foyer, "a delight for my old eyes to see you. And *this* be?"

"This be Mr. Jerome," she replied.

"Ah, 'tis Mr. Jerome, I see," Oswald exclaimed cordially. "Welcome to ye, sir."

"Thank you," Jerome said.

"Leave them there, Mr. Jerome," Oswald said. "I'll carry them up later. There's hot coffee in the library, Madame Lucia."

Oswald's hand indicated a stone stairway without a bannister, so wide and gently pitched they could almost have driven the Jaguar to the second floor. Inside an open double door, Jerome saw a room so long it could have been foggy at the far end. Logs were in flames in a huge, rough-stone fireplace.

Lucia stripped off her driving gloves and put one warm hand on Jerome's forearm, drawing him with her.

"Oswald is of the old school," she whispered, "Gogarty's old school. They went to Notre Dame together."

She told him why heating, as one could imagine, was a problem, an expensive one, in a building this size. "In the very dead of winter," Lucia said, "we close most rooms. Oswald's apartment has its own heating system."

"Don't forget I come from this part of the world—it's *cold.*"

"I would never come here in the winter. My blood

would freeze. I go to the sun. We will have coffee, Paolo, and then I will show you your room and after that we will walk by the river."

Jerome's guest room was heavily draped and deeply carpeted but smelled moldy or mildewed. He pretended not to notice. He knew it was a function of disuse, not something evil or revolting.

An oversized four-poster dominated one whole side of the room's thirty-by-thirty dimensions, facing another fireplace. A dark, smudgy oil painting hung above the mantel, and after they'd left him alone, Jerome was able to identify it as the portrait of a heavily black-bearded man in a full suit of armor. Behind his right shoulder was the depiction of a medieval fortress; across his left shoulder was slung a double-edged battle sword. A red pennant flew off the turret of a fortress.

As Lucia had directed, Jerome had brought with him a pair of heavy shoes. He sat down on the edge of the bed—lumpy he feared—to put them on, then standing again, gazed out the deep-set window across the garden wilderness toward the swiftly flowing river. A lone man dressed in a brilliant blue warm-up suit pulled a scull upstream against the wicked current. Jerome remembered how fast the river flowed in spring and fall, and realized he was being overtaken again by the mournful recollection of the past. Gusts of wind raised rivulets on the river's surface, rattled the bare branches of the trees. Nonetheless, the lone man pressed on, bending his back against the southward force of the river.

Red and yellow leaves, surely the last of this year's harvest, flew past the window, and Jerome sighed deeply. If he were Lucia, he wouldn't wait until the dead of winter to seek the sun. Already he'd be on his way to the South Seas, or at least California.

He turned to his bag for a red pullover and slipped into it and then back into his Harris tweed sportcoat. With gray flannels, he looked quite the country gentleman. And here he was, outlandish as it seemed, standing in the midst of magnificence, at least what he, as a youth, had considered magnificence.

When he headed downstairs, Lucia was talking with Oswald in the black and white marbled foyer. Her voice echoed into the second floor corridor off the ceiling vaulted like a cathedral's. She was telling Oswald that there would be the three for dinner—Jerome, herself, and Father Foster.

"Also, please, you'd better prepare a room in case Father Foster decides to stay the night."

"After the Port. Yes, Madame Lucia, I know only too well about the padre's drinking habits."

Looking past Oswald, Lucia saw Jerome on the stairway and her smile intensified. Did she always smile so brilliantly? Did her eyes *always* sparkle like that?

"Let us go then," Lucia said.

At the door, Oswald passed her a wooden walking stick. "Against the wild dogs," he muttered.

"Wild dogs?" Jerome repeated. He'd never heard of the wild dogs. Watchdogs, yes, not *wild* dogs.

Oswald looked very grave. "Indeed, Mr. Jerome, the forests are full of wild dogs. . . . You'll be hearing them barking tonight."

Lucia accepted the stick and went down the front steps. Jerome wanted to say something about being a native of these parts and never hearing a wild dog bark. But he kept quiet.

Lucia took his arm, swinging the walking stick in her other hand. When they were a safe distance, she laughed. "Mr. Oswald has a wild imagination, Paolo. He's alone too much, but he is such a good cook. You'll find out tonight."

Jerome, again, didn't say anything, but he didn't much like the idea of having a meal cooked by a delusional butler.

It was fall, the dying season, sky dark, a feel of moisture in the wind. Thank God for Lucia—otherwise coming back here was almost too much for him to bear. Lucia was wrapped in a calf-length wool cape. She wore a fur beret on her head and a pair of crushed-leather boots. She walked with vigorous strides. Nonetheless she kept to his arm and accepted his help over jagged logs and rocks. Actually, as his blood warmed, Jerome decided it was a nicer day outside than it had seemed from inside the gloomy castle.

Lucia seemed to perceive what he was feeling. She pulled him against her; that by itself was enough to make his spirits bound. She stopped to look back at the house which showed in sketchy outline through the bare trees.

"It is a strange thing, isn't it?" she asked rhetorically. "It is not something an Italian would have built, I can tell you."

"We used to think it was haunted," Jerome murmured. "Now I see it was—by Mr. Oswald."

"Soon, you will see the water. It is said locally that this spot to which we are going was the place where your General Benedict Arnold once ate a picnic luncheon."

Jerome could feel her softness. He wanted to put his arm around her and squeeze until her juices ran. "Locally? I'm from here and I never heard that, Lucia."

"Such information is passed down," she chuckled.

Under their feet, leaves rattled and rustled but the elements were already reducing them to earth. Winter was just around the corner.

"Where are you planning to go this winter?" Jerome asked.

"Oh, miles away," she said breezily, "somewhere to put great distance between me and my shadow."

"Ah, memories, sure. You miss him."

"Oh, yes, a little. But other memories too." She smiled at him shyly, at his look of inquiry. "Oh, yes, I have several memories, Paolo. You assume because I have my connections with the Church and Vatican Library I have no . . . *memories?*"

"Well . . . yes."

She laughed loudly, causing a squirrel to chatter back. "Do you know in which department of the library I worked?"

"No."

"Ah, ha!" she chortled, "I was on the curatorial staff of the *forbidden* department. Do you know what is the forbidden department, Paolo?" Again, he shook his head. "It is," she whispered in a confidential tone, "that place where the popes have collected all the world's production of profane art and literature."

"You mean pornography?"

"Yes. Are you shocked, Paolo? That *is* where I worked."

"And I do not believe that," he said.

Lucia shrugged delightedly, grinning at him. "Believe or not. I am more expert in the profane than in the sacred, Paolo. Come, here we find the Hudson River."

"The Hudson River," Jerome said threateningly. "Cold and dark and wet, Lucia."

He felt her shiver. "You would not throw me in there, Paolo."

"Only if you tell me lies, Lucia."

"What I say is true," she cried passionately.

She turned away from him and walked ahead to a sandy estuary, stopping with the toes of her boots precisely at the spot where water met gravelly sand.

How serenely she posed by the water, head back, dark hair short and wavy under the beret and over the wide collar of the loose cape. He began to feel something was happening to him—like a stroke or heart attack.

Suddenly, she turned to look back at him. Softly, she said, "You are very nice, Paolo. Will you come here and kiss me?"

"Lucia . . ." Why did he hesitate? She was so beautiful as she appealed to him, so vulnerable as he stared down at her. "Yes, I will," he said, and he jumped off the bank.

She was short, the size of a teenager. Carefully, he bent his head and touched her lips with his own. She was even more astonishingly soft and insubstantial than she looked. Her scent was as clean as a knife and cut into him. Her kiss was eager. She breathed voluptuously, pressing at the small of his back, pulling him to her.

"Paolo," she sighed.

He hadn't bargained for this, not at all. The weekend had been billed as a quiet one in the country with a proper widow, and he was on his best behavior. But he wasn't sure now where best behavior would lead him.

Lucia cocked her head, studying him inquisitively. She opened the edges of her cape and wrapped him with her inside the garment, pressing them together so he could feel all the roundness and warmth of her.

"You see, it is big enough for the two of us," she murmured. "Paolo, why do we do this? Tell me."

"I don't know."

"Don't try to escape," she said. She tilted up on her toes to kiss him again, to introduce the point of her tongue to his lips. She breathed deeply. "It is I who have done it, not you, Paolo. It is because of Gogarty."

"Lucia . . ." He tried to stop her. He was sick of hearing about Gogarty.

"He was a beast, you see," she said darkly.

"Now, I'm sure he wasn't!"

"True!" she whispered intensely, "an insatiable beast. He should have been sold into stud like a racehorse and sent to the service of Long Island matrons." She licked his chin mischievously. "I'm exaggerating a little. Do not tell Father Foster what I said. He sees Gogarty as a saintly person, like Gladys."

Glumly, Jerome stared over her head at the rushing river. A heavy branch, broken off during a storm up north, rolled past them, heading for the ocean.

He couldn't think of anything to say to her. Dismally, he felt all hope begin to collapse. But Lucia pressed against him all the more demandingly. The arching hardness of her pelvis trembled against his thigh.

"Paolo, hug me under my cape . . . please." She

opened the cape for his hands and then rewrapped them in it. She was warm, Jerome thought. Her back was firm under the black turtleneck. He knotted his hands and pulled her close, making her strain for breath. She sighed again and said, "Paolo, it is six months now. I have *need*. Will you come to my aid?"

"Lucia, it's cold. We should go back," he said uneasily, wondering if he was understanding her correctly.

"You like me, Paolo, I know you do."

The tip of her tongue challenged him gently. Her lips were soft.

"We will make love in the forest," she said.

"Lucia . . ." He was embarrassed. "You'll catch cold."

"And not you?" She laughed merrily. "I know you want to, Paolo." She pulled him away from the water, toward a clump of delicate birch trees. "Yes, there, so beautiful . . ."

"I think you're nuts, pretty lady," he muttered, but he didn't resist.

"Paolo, it is only that I cannot wait," she explained simply. "I must have you, now."

"Must?"

"Yes. Must. I need you right now, Paolo," she said earnestly. Her upper lip was trembling, her eyes misty with desire. Desire? Yes, he thought. What else could it be if she needed him right now? Needed *him?*

There was a tree stump in the middle of the little birch grove and Jerome wondered if she'd been here before, with Gogarty. Was it possible?

Lucia placed her hands under her skirt and pulled, standing on one foot, then the other, then handed him a pair of sheer pink panties. "Here, put these in your pocket, Paolo. Now then, warm your hands before you touch me."

"Lucia, how the hell are we going to manage this?"

But they would. Somehow. Lucia pulled his hands inside the cape again, pressing them on her breasts, down her belly and under the skirt, on her smooth bare thighs and buttocks. Impatiently, she reached to unzip his trousers, the gray flannels which would probably be ruined.

"Ohh . . ." Her voice was a moan. "Sit down, let me sit on your lap," she pleaded.

"Yes. All right," Jerome said.

He squatted on the stump and, smiling as if in a delirium, Lucia lowered herself on him. She was warm there, very very warm, and fit over him like a glove. She sighed deeply, pressing down, squirming a little on him. Her eyes drifted shut, her head fell back and she groaned as if in torment. Then, her movements became erratic, hasty, uncontrolled. She was climaxing. Her eyes flew open and she stared at him as if he were a stranger. Her gasp was hoarse. She cried out loudly.

In a moment, she was very calm. "Paolo, that was a good and kind thing you did for me."

Father John Foster appeared to know as soon as he walked through the wide portico of the castle that something had happened between Paul Jerome and Lucia Gogarty. If he had meant to intervene, he was too late. A knowing but pious smile oiled his face all through dinner and even the expected speech about the great gift of the J.J. Gogarty Foundation was muted.

Lucia was in a euphoric state—and when Jerome chanced to say a word, no matter how inane, she gave it her full attention.

Foster, like Lucia, regretted that Nora couldn't be with them. Nora had become so successful, Foster intoned smugly as proudly, as if he had been her father, smiling paternally into his Port. "Nora called to tell me she's on Mr. Morgan's personal staff and had to go away on business. Diversified is a huge company."

He sounded almost as though he envied her the job. Foster had always had a fine talent for money management. During recession years, when the normal Catholic parish was broke, Foster's in Paradise Point always had plenty of money due to his ability to parlay the proceeds of the occasional bingo game and the Sunday collection into much bigger money. Finally, it seemed, the diocese had caught on to Foster's exceptional ability.

"Diversified does about ten billion a year," Jerome said.

Foster took this information as a cue to turn to Lucia. "You see, my dear, after the foundation is established and funded, we'd want to invest in companies like Diversified. It pays a high return—true, Paul?"

"*Tax free,* you mean?" Jerome said pointedly. "Sure—you'd be getting the equivalent of eighteen or twenty percent on your money."

"Ah, you see?" Foster murmured, then smiled a saintly smile. He was no fool. He'd seen how the land lay. "You know, my dear, we could do worse than having Paul Jerome take an active hand in administering the resources of the J.J. Gogarty Foundation."

"No," she said, surprising both of them, "Paul would be bored. He is an entrepreneur, not an administrator."

"I already have a job, John," Jerome added. He thought he should be allowed a sly smile. "You know how it is. We Jews are so good with money."

To Foster's embarrassment, Lucia giggled. His face crumpled like paper. "You could never accuse me of being a bigot, Paul Jerome! I didn't say that." Foster's face flushed.

"Just a little joke, Father."

Foster turned down the offer of a second Port. He reminded them that Sunday was a work day—even though he was in high finance now, he still had to say Mass every day.

Truce declared, they walked Foster out to his car, a modest Dodge. Modest, yet on closer inspection they could see it was fitted with stereo sound—Foster liked to play church music when he drove—and a telephone, in case some poor soul needed instant help and advice.

Foster lifted his hand in a gesture of benediction and drove away down the bumpy road.

Chapter Nine

THE HOUSE WAS QUIET NOW. OSWALD HAD CLEARED THE dining room and put fresh coffee in the library while they were outside saying good-bye to Father John, and then disappeared into his own distant part of Gogarty Castle.

They sat on a low and creaky couch in front of the dying fire. As the heat receded the room chilled, and Jerome became more and more aware of Lucia. She was sitting very close to him, holding his hands, her legs curled up under her.

"Paolo," she murmured, "tell me—you did not want to be a part of Father Foster's tiresome foundation?"

"No. Definitely not. Thanks for getting me out of it, Lucia."

"He is a very intelligent man," she said thoughtfully. "Only sometimes you would not know it—he is mad to have this foundation."

"The money, Lucia. The Church gets their hands on your money—"

"Gogarty's money," she said, "not mine."

She stated the case so realistically. She heard what he'd said and didn't take offense. It pleased him that they understood each other.

Lucia rubbed his hands briskly and held them to her bosom. "We are getting cold, Paolo," she said wistfully. "It is so cold in this part of the world."

"Well, it gets very damp and chilly in Rome in the winter too."

"Yes, but it never seems *cold*. Do you know what I mean?"

Jerome nodded. "Anyway . . . Lucia . . ." He wanted to call her something else. There had to be another name. Fragrance. No, too Chinese. Soft lips, smooth skin, sparkling eyes. No. "Anyway, you'll be leaving soon and you'll be warm again. And me—I'll be in the North, freezing, all alone."

"All alone, yes," she said sadly, as if he'd just made the most tragic remark since Shakespeare. "What would I do without you, Paolo?"

Her voice was so quiet, so troubled, he wanted to say, I'll come with you, Fragrance. Lightly, he answered, "You'll do fine, I'm sure—it's just a passing fancy."

"Passing fancy?" She turned almost fierce. "You believe I make love in the afternoon on the bank of the Hudson River as a passing fancy?"

"Well, Lucia, you surprise me so much. I never know what you'll do next. . . . I don't know what you feel."

"Silly boy," she cried merrily. "We met over a month ago . . ."

"Three weeks."

"So how is it a passing fancy?" she demanded delightedly. "And Father Foster told me you were married but . . . not anymore. Is that so?"

He nodded. "How did Foster know that?" It was obvious. Nora had told him. "Yes, I was. Her name was Shelley and she ran away with a dentist."

"Ah, no!" Lucia exclaimed. Her eyes danced. He realized she wanted to laugh. "A dentist? So romantic!" Then she did laugh.

Jerome felt flustered and realized that he should have been laughing too, perhaps all along.

"I am so sorry, Paolo," she gasped. "It is not a laughing matter, I know that."

"Lucia," he said solemnly, "*you* are a devil. You are not serious."

"I know. I am clownish, I have been told. Mostly by my mother, who says I am a silly goose. This woman who ran away, she must have been a very stupid person."

"When I married her, I thought she was very bright."

"And there were no children?"

"No, there weren't any children, thankfully. She had too many other things to do."

"Such as?"

"Little dinner parties."

"No! Nothing else?"

Jerome shook his head. "That's all I can remember. Funny, isn't it? That's all I can remember, the little dinner parties."

"And love . . . passion?" Lucia asked cautiously. She held his hands tightly, studying his fingernails.

Frankly, he said, "She wasn't the passionate type, if the truth be known. At least as far as I was concerned. Maybe the dentist was better."

Lucia shook her head. "I am not fond of dentists."

"Good—you're different, like me."

"It is the Mediterranean in you then."

"And the Mediterranean in you too?" he echoed.

"Yes, I have the Mediterranean in me, or the boot of Italy in the Mediterranean . . . Paolo, it is very cold."

True. The fire was in swift decline. Oswald was not extravagant with his wood.

"Time for bed," Jerome murmured.

She clung to him as they climbed the long, open staircase and paused at the top, breathing hard. "I have a heart murmur," she told him, unbidden. "It beats harder coming up steps. I need much love and tenderness."

He held her close. "I'll buy that," he said. He didn't know how to handle her, and that was the fact of the matter. He wanted her. But she was so ready it was almost embarrassing.

"I want to show you something," she said, "in your room."

He didn't want to be alone either. A dismal light burned at his bedside. Lucia laughed huskily and he saw she was pointing at the grimy picture over the fireplace.

"You know who that is there in the finery of the Knights of Malta, Paolo?"

"One of your ancestors?"

"No. It is Gogarty. Take care—he will be watching you. He aged the picture artificially."

"My God—I thought it might be him when I looked at it before."

Even in the smoky portrait, Gogarty was a disturbing, wild-eyed man. One might be concerned that he would come flying off the wall at them, the broadsword flailing the darkness, and suddenly Jerome accepted the truth of it—he was very happy, very pleased that he had never known J.J. Gogarty, member of the Knights of Malta.

Lucia seemed determined to shock Gogarty into action or a retreat to final blackness. She pressed against Jerome, her breasts surging eagerly.

"Paolo . . . Paul . . ."

Impulsively then, she withdrew and began to take off her clothes. He reached to caress her but she shook her head. "I like to undress myself, Paolo, and you do the same."

In the afternoon by the river, Jerome had experienced his first yet incomplete knowledge of her. Now she was naked before him but only for a moment. Then she whipped back the covers and jumped in bed and, in the dimness, her smile was expectant and moist.

"Come in bed immediately. This is more comfortable than in the afternoon, no?"

"Warmer," he mumbled.

He dropped in beside her and she squirmed, pressing herself as closely to him as possible, skin to skin. "But I was so hot, I was afraid you would get away—like a fish leaping."

"Get away? You're mad—why would I want to get away?"

74

"Who knows? I was afraid I would frighten you."

"No, I am a very brave man, Lucia. Now, quiet, because I want to make love to you."

Under the heavy covers his mouth found the small, dark nipples of her dusky-skinned breasts, the flesh tone that drove him wild. She was like the universe; the depth of her was infinite. The nipples rose to his lips, pointy and puffy, the breasts not too large, rolling easily to his mouth, as insubstantial as her lips. She sighed and moaned to his touch as his lips moved across her belly to the place between her legs which seemed to grope to meet him. He kissed her there and she wept.

She pulled him up and then into her. He entered with a long, silky movement, reaching toward that fleshly infinity. Her body grew to him, into him where they met. Her only sound now was a whispered "Yes." And then, too quickly, he was aware of a spinning in his brain and the blood roaring to the place where they were mated, a perfect fit, then of earthquake, as his stroking quickened. He thought surely the room must be rocking, even in this granite fortress, or perhaps the solid rocks were coming apart and he could not hold himself back. She was too sensual for him, too warm, too liquid, her interior muscles grasping. Jerome gasped loudly enough to wake Gogarty, as life rushed from him and into her, more, still more, draining him. Now she was pulling at him, wanting also to climax, but panting so hard that finally she stopped.

"Lucia, you didn't. I'm sorry."

"Never mind." She closed her eyes tightly and he kissed the lids.

He knew. It was because of that hot-eyed Irish asshole staring down at them from the wall. They never should have done it in here.

"I'm sorry," he said again. "I'll do better next time. I couldn't hold back. It was so—"

"It doesn't matter, Paolo," she whispered. "It's not so important for a woman. The rest of it is so peaceful making."

Beside her, his head against her bare shoulder, he said, "I don't know anything about women . . ."

Bitterly, he thought of the wife who'd deserted him. One of the great failures of his life, which Shelley had never tired of telling him, was that she *couldn't come.* And the harder he tried, the more she couldn't. Eventually he couldn't either and finally couldn't even bring himself to try. Recalling his marriage made him shiver the whole length of his body and soul, as if a dark, wet cloud had descended upon him.

"What is it?" she whispered sleepily.

"Nothing." He studied her ear with his mouth. It was delicate, very like the proverbial piece of Dresden china.

Her body stirred but only to creep even closer to him, her fingers splayed across his back, digging at his spine. She was so trusting, open, so uncomplicated, he felt like he'd been here forever. Another definition of infinity. Her throat was exquisite, and her shoulders. No wonder sculptors had trouble with shoulders, such an intricate inventory of bones, muscles, and joints all managed by a particular knot of nerves located somewhere in the left hemisphere of the brain—exactly where, nobody was quite sure yet. Christ, he thought, tears coming to his eyes, the wonder of her, of life.

Sunday dawned beautifully on the Hudson. The sun trickled out of the east and into his room. At seven Lucia took up her clothes and fled down the corridor to her own suite of rooms, leaving him behind, on his back, hands clasped on his chest, to consider all manner of things between now and the time he would join her for breakfast.

But there was only one thought in his mind. It required an hour to digest, and even then he hadn't finished with it—he was in love with Lucia Saltimbocca Gogarty.

At eight, the first sensible thought came to him. He had to shave and dress, and he'd forgotten to bring a razor. So he merely showered under an ancient, half-rusted fixture and dressed in corduroys and a wool plaid shirt.

Thoughts of a razor forgotten in the city reminded him of Nora Ellen Sweeney, she of the razor-sharp mind. Ambitious Nora played her own game. Jerome smiled to himself. So did he. What was it she'd promised him? That he wouldn't come out a loser for arranging Kurt Morgan's *chin-wag* with Pete Broadstairs. Jerome stood for a while, staring out at the sunlit river. He'd get Gerald Ball's job? What made her think he'd want it? From what he had learned about Diversified Technologies, a successor to Gerald Ball would be nominated from an unexpected but tremendously powerful quarter, and once nominated there wouldn't be a vote.

Buck would come out fine. He was well-known to Diversified's merchant-banking advisors, Hazard Sons, and to the twenty or so institutions which underwrote Diversified's line of credit. This, of course, was thanks to the financial acumen of Paul Jerome.

Lucia's door was open for him.

"Mrs. Gogarty?" he called.

Lucia's laugh was jolly but when he was inside her big bedroom—nicely decorated in bright fabrics, unlike the dingy drabness of the guest room—she said, "Such an ugly name, Paolo. Only my mother hates it more than me. But then the Princess Saltimbocca hated Gogarty."

"I see," he said indifferently. But he didn't and didn't care to see. "I'll call you Shorty."

"All right." She beamed. She'd dressed by now, in the same black turtleneck she'd had on the day before and a pair of tight black slacks replacing the tweed skirt she'd worn to the river. "And I will call you Big Boy, for you are my lover now, Paolo, and I am *not* leaving you ever."

Jerome felt like genuflecting before her. She was a thing of delight. How did you thank a person who pleased you so?

"I feel wonderful," he said, staring at her, smiling, wanting to laugh aloud.

She kissed him quickly, saying Oswald would be coming with breakfast, putting her hand to his cheek.

"I forgot my razor, Lucia."

"Your beard is not heavy, *caro*. But you want to shave? I will fetch you Mr. Gogarty's razor. Can you use a straight razor?"

"I might cut my throat," he said.

"His beard was rough enough to grate a lemon and by now, just think, it must have grown enough to strangle the rats that would dare to enter his coffin."

"Whew!" Jerome whistled. "Jesus, little love, I don't know where you learned to talk like that."

She chuckled merrily. "From J.J. Gogarty, a terrible man, Paolo. Florentine in his ruthlessness. Follow me, *caro*."

Crossing the hall, Lucia entered a white-tiled room filled with antiquated exercise machinery. Next to it a steam room and shower stall big enough for an army platoon and a wall of closets. Dangling from a hook by the sink was a thick, black razor strop.

She pointed to another enamel receptacle next to the sink. "Gogarty's vomitorium. Every man should have one."

"Yes, very handy, I'm sure."

Lucia's mouth twisted in distaste. "Gogarty did not take stomach remedies. If something did not agree with him, he came in here and stuck a finger down his throat."

Jerome nodded. "No-nonsense sort of gourmet guy. My type."

She pulled open a protesting cabinet. Inside she found a silver-encased straight razor.

"There," she said.

Jerome pried open the razor. It was an instrument of some importance. The steel glittered like new and he could tell without trying it that the edge was as sharp as it had ever been.

"If you like it," Lucia said impulsively, "you may take the razor with you."

"No, no, according to ancient lore a friend does not give a friend a blade. It's supposed to be terrible luck."

"Then I will loan it to you."

He closed the razor and put it back in the cabinet. "I'll just skip the shave today unless you've got something less lethal."

"One for legs."

His chest constricted. "For shaving the legs?"

"Of course," she said. She knew, watching his eyes, that it didn't take much to arouse him. "You would not want to be scratched, would you, by my legs around your back, your bare body?"

He laughed uneasily. "I don't know, Lucia. I might like that."

"Oh, you would, would you? Paolo, are you a decadent man, then?"

"No more than the next guy." A good question, Jerome. "I don't run to whips and chains, but a little leg-stubble scratch could be pretty exciting. I mean, unless you thought you'd like to draw blood."

"Oh, you!"

"Hey, listen," he said. "I've got an idea. I'm hungry. Do you think we could get something to eat right away if we go downstairs?"

She put the back of her hand to his cheek. "You have no beard at all. Scratch me somewhat and then we'll go down."

Jerome put his cheek to hers, rubbed gently. "Feel it? Rough stuff, right? Get your shoes—is there anything you'd like in the line of shoe fetish? I mean I could—"

Lucia put the palm of her hand over his mouth. "Quiet please."

Breakfast was gigantic, the best meal likely to come out of Oswald's kitchen—eggs, meat, toast, rolls, butter, jam, coffee. Oswald said he believed in serving a big breakfast, especially since humanity worked so hard during the night—sleeping, not easy work, Oswald said.

But he would be going off to church now and then wouldn't return to the castle until about four in the afternoon. He had somebody to see in Paradise Point.

"Say a prayer for us, Oswald," Lucia murmured. Smilingly, she told Jerome, "Oswald is an expert at praying."

A smile passed across Oswald's face. "I'll say a Hail Mary for you, Madame Lucia, and one for Mr. Jerome too. I remember you as a boy, Mr. Jerome, sneaking around in the woods out there."

"No!" Jerome was astonished. "You couldn't . . . Lucia told you!"

"Not on your nelly, you little rascal." Oswald wagged a horny finger under his nose. "You little rascals used to shout at me—you used to call me Scarecrow, you all did."

Embarrassed, Jerome laughed. "If we did . . . I don't remember . . . If we did, I apologize now."

Oswald glowered menacingly. "I'll get you yet, I will, you little rascal, before I sail away, around the world."

Lucia put her hand on Jerome's arm. "Oswald has his jokes." She grinned at the old retainer. "Have a nice day, Oswald."

Oswald left them, finally, but Jerome was shaken. The old man had sounded like he meant what he said.

"He just scared the living shit out of me, Shorty."

"Don't be silly, lover, he is harmless."

In the distance, a car started with a long grinding of ignition, a roar and explosion.

"Oswald's Studebaker," Lucia said. "A relic. He has had it since World War Two. You should see his sailboat."

"It makes as much noise as a bomber."

"Still going strong," she murmured. "Like me."

"Of course," he said, sarcastically. In fact, she was at the height of voluptuousness. There was about her a physical opulence almost too lavish, like a baroque church, and a hint of buried treasure as if by digging he could unearth a fortune in jewels. She was perfect, down to skin texture, the grain of her pores, the depth of her eyes—a fragrant machine, engineered by those with the greatest experience, the Italians.

Once more, gazing at her across the breakfast table, he was swept by a crashing, crushing need, more than a poor sentimental emotion. Rather, as the poets said, it was a craving, a hunger for her skin.

She dashed head-on into his musings. "What are you thinking?"

He didn't pause. "I'm wondering . . . what's happening."

"We are eating our breakfast," she said calmly, "absorbing protein which you have need of after last night . . . and today, if you are not too tired."

Chapter Ten

Sunday, the fourteenth of November, also came up bright and clear in Palm Springs, California. The rising sun could have shattered the sky, it was that brilliant.

Kurt Morgan had mumbled before falling asleep something about a golfing date at eight. He'd be finished eighteen holes by eleven and back in plenty of time to shower and shave and take her off to the brunch with Pete Broadstairs and his wife.

Nora set her alarm for six. Up before dawn, she showered and spent a long time shampooing her hair. See how it gleamed now, she smiled, humming happily to herself under the rushing water. Everything was coming up roses after all. She'd had her doubts. Morgan was abashed by what he'd done and rather on the defensive. He'd tried to beg her pardon, but Nora pretended she didn't know what he was talking about. What a strange man he was, she reflected, finally exercising her facial muscles violently in the cold jet of desert water. There was no accounting for the peculiar tastes of men, she remembered her mother telling her. The only man she'd ever known who behaved in a consistently normal—or one might say, logical—manner was Father John Foster. And, of course, he was a rarity.

Nora was ready with orange juice and coffee when Kurt stumbled out of his room dressed in the same golf outfit he'd been wearing the day before.

"Nora! What the hell! Don't you ever sleep?"

"The early bird . . ."

"Yeah?" He glared at her stolidly. "The early bird gets eaten by the worms, don't forget that."

"Here," she said, undeterred by the heavy sarcasm, handing him the juice, "this will make you invincible."

He looked at his watch, wanting to resist her but not knowing how.

"You've got plenty of time to drink it," she told him primly. He gulped it down. Nora handed him the coffee. "And this." Next she handed him vitamin C pills from her own ever-ready supply. "And these . . ."

"Jesus Christ, Nora."

But he did as she told him, swallowing the pills with the coffee that was unfortunately lukewarm.

"Now you'll be a star," she said. "Except, I think you could've brought another golf outfit with you. If I'd known, I'd have bought one yesterday. I stopped in the store downstairs for a dress. I hadn't counted on such wonderful weather."

"What'd you buy?" he asked sharply.

"A nice dress to wear to brunch."

He nodded, almost wearily, as if he'd expected it. "I'll pay for it. Don't ever put a thing like that on your expense account."

She was genuinely shocked. "I wouldn't, Mr. Morgan! I know I'll be wearing it again on summer vacation in France."

"In France? You're going there? Who with?"

"My boyfriend, of course," Nora said modestly.

His eyes narrowed. "You've got a boyfriend? Is it that guy from BBD?"

"Oh, no. *That's* business . . ."

"The other is pleasure? I get it," Morgan muttered.

"Now, Mr. Morgan, let's not get things confused," Nora said cheerily. She looked at him frankly. "I gladly offer myself to your . . . relief. You're older so you can understand these things. It's a physical thing, the way I look at it, like a trigger that has to be pulled. Not anything deep and binding," she finished reasonably.

He stared at her, aggrieved. "Yeah. Well, I better get going."

"Have a good time."

"Yes." He tossed the plastic coffee cup in the trash. "Nora?"

"Yes, Mr. Morgan?" She held the smile, brilliantly.

"We must be careful, Nora," he said in a low voice. He didn't give her a chance to answer. "I'm going. Check with Broadstairs that it's okay for twelve-thirty. Call him around nine."

"On Sunday?"

"Naturally. This is important business, Miss Sweeney."

The Broadstairs residence looked like an authentic *hacienda*. Long sweeps of red-tiled roof surrounded an interior patio, where a fountain bubbled quietly with the sun. The central wing of the house was white-washed with high, cool, dark-beamed ceilings—like a church, Nora thought. The furniture was appropriate to the architectural theme—long heavy oak tables, outsized chairs and sofas upholstered in stiff tasseled damask and leather.

Pete Broadstairs was a small, muscled man, quick of step and extremely alert for someone his age. His eyes were like black jumping beans, his face tanned and firm. However old he was, one would have said he looked younger. He was in remarkable shape, especially when you consider that one of his original partners was dead and the other totally incapacitated by a stroke.

Pete was pretty much what Nora had expected. He was a fighting cock, a maverick who'd always gone against somebody's grain, defied all the rules and regulations. If it hadn't been for the Second World War, Pete Broadstairs would have gone nowhere in the military—he was too undisciplined and undisciplinable. The War was made for people like Broadstairs. If you won, nobody cared how you did it. If you lost, you were dead. Everybody knew of his exploits with Jimmy Doolittle. Before the war, Pete had been constantly in trouble with his barnstorming stunts—flying under bridges, buzzing cows in the American heartland, landing on city streets. He'd carried the mail and raced experimental planes. He'd escaped death and disaster by the skin of his teeth more than once.

Connie Broadstairs was head and shoulders taller than the little man, but seemed modestly spoken, maybe because she had an unmelodious Midwestern accent. She was so soft, so misty-eyed, Nora wouldn't have been surprised if Connie had run and hid from them.

"So you're Kurt Morgan," Broadstairs said briskly. "I've heard a lot about you, son. Welcome to our *casa*."

Nora thought Morgan sounded just right. "Sir, the pleasure, believe me, and the honor, is all mine."

Broadstairs smiled appreciatively. He was old enough to be pleased when a junior-in-age pledged to him that he hadn't been forgotten.

"Funny our paths never crossed, Kurt." Broadstairs's face knotted up like a fist when he grinned. "But anyway, here we are. Come on in and have a Bloody Mary." He dropped Connie's hand and took Nora's. "Come with me . . . Nora. You drag Connie along. Absolutely the most bashful girl—ain't she wonderful!"

Connie blushed. How in the world had she ever hooked Pete Broadstairs? Or Buck Collins?

As they trooped across the living room toward the patio, Broadstairs turned his head to roar in the direction of the kitchen. "Maria, *por favor,* bring the Bloody Marys. . . . Some Spanish, hey?"

Outside, Broadstairs placed them around a glass-topped wrought-iron table firmly anchored in brick, then sat himself down and gratefully lifted his face to the warming sun.

"Getting cool," he growled. "In the summer, when it's boiling, we're stuck inside with the air conditioner on. Maybe we shouldn't try to live in this place year-round.

But Connie likes it, especially in the summer when there's nobody here."

Broadstairs obviously adored her; he doted on her. Connie smiled at him shyly.

Nora thought she could be allowed a comment. "It's a lovely place, Mr. Broadstairs. It's so peaceful."

"Yup . . . yup, so it is," he agreed.

Maria ambled out of the house with a tray of glasses, a bottle of vodka, Bloody Mary mix and an ice bucket.

Beaming, Broadstairs said, "Go ahead, Connie, mix 'em up. . . . She used to be a bartender."

Nora remembered what Paul Jerome had told her. To wit, Connie had met Pete Broadstairs while mixing 'em up on the BBD jet. Nora tried to recall whether she'd passed that along to Kurt Morgan with all the other information. Morgan said nothing. He smiled mutely as Connie expertly put the Bloody Mary ingredients together.

Broadstairs held up his glass. "Here's to it, boys and girls! Good, huh?" He smacked his lips. "What'd I tell you?"

"Delicious," Nora said quietly.

"You said it!" Broadstairs looked inquisitively at Morgan. "So, tell me—what brings *you* to this neck of the woods, Kurt? You and Nora Sweeney here?"

Morgan lied easily enough. "I'm en route to Los Angeles for a business meeting. Nora's got an old friend who works at Brown, Broadstairs, a high school sweetheart." He smiled comfortably, as he might have, much her senior.

"Sure, sure," Broadstairs exclaimed. "Paul Jerome. An old boyfriend of yours, huh?" he asked Nora. "Paul is a sweet guy. *And* plenty smart, Kurt."

"So Nora told me," Morgan said, not as comfortably as before. "Anyway, since we'd never met, I took advantage of him for an introduction. You get the picture, Mr. Broadstairs."

"Sure I do," Broadstairs said smoothly. He got the picture all right, Nora decided. He saw right through it to the canvas underneath. "Hey . . . Kurt. The name is Pete. And we sure are glad you stopped by." He patted Connie's hand, then, hardly finishing the drink, he scraped his chair back and stood up spryly. "Lunch'll be ready in about a half hour, Kurt. Why don't you and I take a little walk?" He told Connie, "We'll be back in twenty-five minutes, on the dot." Then he and Morgan strolled amiably through the gate.

"Mr. Broadstairs is a marvel," she said warmly.

Connie nodded. "One of the wonders of the world," she agreed. Nora didn't object when she refilled her glass. Then, Connie glanced at Nora sharply. "I suppose you think it's funny I'm married to him."

"Why?" The question was very direct, so Nora didn't feel backward about answering it directly. "It's always pleasantly surprising to me when two people of different ages—"

Connie stopped her. "I wouldn't have married him if I hadn't loved him, you know," she said defiantly.

"So?"

"So that's why I married him."

"Well . . . good." Nora had the feeling that somehow Connie suspected she'd been told about Buck Collins.

"But I may be missing something," Connie murmured. "I envy you, I think. You're out in the world, with an interesting job, marvelous opportunities."

Nora nodded. "I *am* lucky. I work for a brilliant man. Mr. Morgan is a marvel too, in his own way."

"Diversified is a very big company, isn't it?"

"We do ten billion a year," Nora stated frankly.

"I do envy you," Connie said again. "It can be a hell of a bore being stuck down here, I can tell you."

"I wouldn't mind it for a couple of weeks," Nora sighed. "The weather is magnificent, compared to New York. It was cold and windy when we left."

"Yeah," Connie scoffed petulantly, "you could take it for a week, maybe two, and then you'd be up the wall."

"Maybe . . ."

Connie Broadstairs laughed wryly. "I'll tell you what—we'll trade places. I'll go to L.A. with Kurt Morgan and you stick around here with Pete."

Nora smiled. "Great idea."

"I know what you're thinking," Connie charged irritably. "You're thinking you couldn't lay an old man like that."

Nora froze. *"I was thinking no such thing."*

"No, that is what you were thinking, I know it. When you saw us together that's the first thing that came into your mind—how can that girl fuck that old man?"

Nora pushed her glass away. If she'd had gloves, she'd have gathered them up preparatory to departure. But she was stuck; she had to wait for Morgan.

Coldly she said, "Actually my first thought was what a mild and retiring woman you are." She glanced crossly at Connie. "I see I was *not* on target."

Connie laughed carelessly. Her tone was crude and cheap. "Everybody gets me wrong. I hate it when people are so obvious about it—Good God, that old relic with this young chick."

Nora folded her hands in front of her. "I think I've heard enough. You needn't haul me over the coals, my dear," she said harshly. "Personally, I do not care a smidgeon."

"Sorry," Connie said, not put off at all. Her next question was just as forward. "How old are you?"

"Going on thirty."

"I'm twenty-four."

"Congratulations." Nora reached again for the drink, thinking a crisis of sorts had passed.

Then, also, the sound of the front-door chimes helped break the impasse.

Connie scowled laconically. "I wonder which one of our geriatric neighbors this is?"

The man who strode out to the patio, however, was so vital, handsome, and so un-geriatric, that Nora's pulse missed a beat. This man was an inch or two taller than Morgan, broader at the shoulders, and younger. His face was lean, hungry as an animal's, and his eyes blazed like fires. Moreover, he had a full head of close-cropped, graying blond hair.

Connie jumped to her feet. "Buck!"

"Hello, sweetheart." He grinned at Connie, obviously an expert at flashing his white teeth.

Buck Collins, Nora thought in panic. So this was Collins the star, and what in the world was he doing *here?*

Connie ignored Nora now. She flung herself wildly into Collins's arms, lifting her face to him. Laughingly, Collins dropped his head and kissed her on the cheek, at the same time cleverly disengaging himself.

"Easy, Con . . ."

His look carried over Connie's shoulder to Nora, eyes drilling right through the red dress Kurt Morgan had promised to finance, into her body.

"Hi. I'm Buck Collins."

Nora nodded, and slowly said, "So I gathered." She would keep her cool.

"And *you're* a Palm Springs lady, I guess, one of the leisured class . . ."

Nora scowled, hair-triggered. He'd better get this straight. "My name is Nora Ellen Sweeney. I'm with Diversified Technologies. Kurt Morgan and I . . ." She stopped to choose her words carefully. "Mr. Morgan is passing through town and he wanted to pay his respects to Mr. Broadstairs."

"Kurt Morgan? You don't say," Collins drawled. "Great. I'm for the whole world paying their respects to Pete Broadstairs. He deserves every respect he gets, the grand old man of American aviation!"

Boldly, he winked at Connie. Grand old man? Well, it was so, wasn't it?

"And you?" he asked Nora. "What do you do for Kurt Morgan? Secretary, pilot, what? You know, sweetheart,"

Collins mentioned scornfully to Connie, "Morgan is boss of a company like Diversified and he can't even fly a plane . . ."

Nora could feel her bones rattling inside her skin. She didn't like Collins. He was everything she had heard he was—brash, overbearing, arrogant. There was nothing subtle about him. He was the personification of the rogue-capitalist; he was everything that was anathema to the Harvard Business School.

Collins might very well have jarred the confidence of a lesser being. But Nora wasn't just anybody, she reminded herself, and she wasn't going to be intimidated by this man hinting she was Morgan's traveling playmate.

Slowly, as if she were dictating an inviolable rule to a backward student, she said, "I'm on Mr. Morgan's personal staff, attached to the office of the chief executive officer of Diversified Technologies. Mr. Morgan happens to be a qualified pilot."

Collins's smoky green eyes didn't blink. "Do tell . . ."

Something clicked angrily inside Nora. "I *do* tell," she said evenly, her own eyes making incisions on his face. "Furthermore, Mr. Morgan is not *allowed* to fly the company plane. The insurance people won't have it."

"All right," Collins buckled carelessly. "I take it back. I'm sorry. I cheap-shotted him." He tried to make her smile. "How come I don't have a personal staff like you, Miss . . ."

"Sweeney," she said decisively. "Nora Ellen Sweeney."

Connie mumbled, "I thought you did, Buck."

"Nothing like Miss Sweeney, sweetie," he said. Nora's eyes held him. He couldn't stop looking at her. He probably hadn't been verbally humiliated all day.

Sadly, Connie gazed at him. "Don't tell me you flew down here by yourself, Buck."

He grinned sheepishly. "She's at the hotel, Con."

"Redhead or blonde?"

"Redhead," Collins chuckled. He squinted. "She's sort of a mix—redhead and brunette."

Nora was not about to react to that suggestive statement. Her gaze remained steady.

"Oh, Buck!" Connie cried out, more in admiration than admonishment.

"Hey," he exclaimed, "do I get a drink? I haven't had one since breakfast—breakfast yesterday, that is. I never drink before I fly," he informed Nora. "Safety first."

"A Bloody Mary?" Connie asked woefully.

"Nah, sweetheart. Just make it a vodka on the rocks, about a triple. Mind if I take off my jacket?"

"Be my guest," Connie said.

They were now supposed to be diverted from his impressive physical configuration to his sartorial splendor, Nora realized. He was a truly impeccable dresser, she admitted, the clear winner if he'd been competing with Kurt Morgan's rumpled, creased, and spotted look.

Collins slipped off a lightweight gray herringbone-tweed jacket.

"Vicuna," he said, flipping the coat tail at Nora. "Go ahead, beautiful, touch."

She was confronted by her first confusion. She didn't know how to react to this approach. "Very nice," she said.

"See," Collins yelped, "she's not so bad after all. Nora Sweeney is a *feel* person. She likes elegant threads."

Wryly, Connie said, "You're eyeballing the best-dressed man in the aerospace industry."

"Hoorah," Nora said.

"Now, sweetie," Collins protested, "I am merely the man that the designers love to dress. This shirt," he explained, putting thumb and forefinger to button-down collar, "is a classic." He tossed his jacket on the back of an empty chair and twirled on his heels like a model. "The trousers, a wonderful light flannel, are made for me in Hong Kong by a gifted Chinese tailor. He will be blinded when he has finished working on my wardrobe so there can be no copies."

Nora became aware of a rising gorge, conscious of her burgeoning dislike for this boor, this conceited fool. She yearned to say something harsh and fatal. But, as always, she controlled herself. It was enough that she *knew* Kurt Morgan was ten times the man Collins was. How was it possible that such a self-involved buffoon could be the chief operating officer of a high-flying firm like BBD? There had to be something good about him that wasn't showing. Paul Jerome, she sensed, had his reservations about Collins, but on the whole he seemed to respect him. But how? Why?

Suddenly, Collins stopped playing the clown.

"Here they come," he said. "The grand old man of American aviation and that modern-day mogul, Kurt Morgan."

Collins projected his long, lean body toward the gate. "Allow *me,* gentlemen!"

Broadstairs guffawed. "Buck! You bastard! What the hell are you doing here?"

"Flew in only this morning, Pete." Collins put his arm across Broadstairs's shoulders and hugged him to his chest. "Kurt Morgan, I presume."

Whatever it was Morgan had said to Pete Broadstairs, it had not gone down well. Broadstairs motioned for Morgan to sit down at the table again and lowered himself broodingly next to Connie.

"Shall I make another pitcher, honey?" she asked.

"Sure . . . anybody want another one?" Broadstairs looked lopsidedly at Morgan. "You, Morgan?"

"I wouldn't mind."

Broadstairs's eyes were red and rheumy. Had he been crying? Had Morgan upset him so much? Why? How? If Broadstairs went for a deal, he'd find himself richer in ready cash and his estate much fatter than it was now.

Broadstairs turned to Collins and softly said, "I see you already got your belt in hand, son."

"Yes sir."

Collins was disturbed by the same thing Nora had seen in Broadstairs's face.

But Morgan didn't give any of them a chance to ask

about the old man. "What've you been up to lately, Buck?" he demanded. It was a question seriously asked and Collins had to answer it. Waiting, Morgan leaned back in his chair as if he were the most relaxed man in the world; here they were, all of them, in God's country.

But Nora knew *this* was not God's country. This was only a way station.

Unhappily, Collins muttered, "Spending a lot of time in Washington."

"Yeah," Morgan agreed sympathetically. "Me too, half my time testifying on one thing or another. Nora can vouch for me on that."

"Yes . . ."

Collins leered at her, cutting across her reply. "God-damn budgets are so huge. Everybody's scared to death."

This was one of Morgan's pet topics. "We're going to defend ourselves straight into bankruptcy," he said darkly.

"Nah," Collins said, "just one more round, that's all. *One more round* and the Russians are finished."

Morgan shook his head sorrowfully. "We can't handle the deficits, Buck."

Collins grinned cockily. "Sure we can, Kurt. *We got to.* I'm convinced we can whip their ass right at the starting gate *if* we're willing to fund the new bomber and the Heartland missile."

"What about it, Pete?" Morgan asked politely.

Broadstairs looked at him balefully. "I agree with Buck. We *can* whip their ass—if we invest in heavy throw-force."

In somber tones, Morgan said, "Nobody can convince me we'd survive a full-scale exchange."

Even more bitterly, Broadstairs grunted, *"We will."* He glared at Morgan. "You know why? Because we're *us* and they're *them.*"

Such an unthinking statement would ordinarily throw Morgan into a fit. But, out of respect, he merely nodded and said faintly, "I'm glad you've got faith, Pete."

"Jesus Christ, Kurt," Collins blustered, "Diversified by itself makes enough tonnage to wipe them out."

Morgan grimaced. This was true, but it was not the way Morgan wanted it. He had confided in Nora that his aim was to reduce Diversified's reliance on defense contracts. It was, therefore, perhaps illogical that Morgan should be interested in acquiring BBD which, by all accounts, was even more aligned to weaponry than Diversified.

Morgan's reasoning, however, was quite simple. He hoped that with BBD leading the way, Diversified's aerospace effort could be optimized, thus turning loose research personnel and cash for work on consumer-product development, that great area Morgan was convinced the country was losing to the Far East and Europe.

Grudgingly, Broadstairs said, "I admit it ain't like the old days, Morgan, when you loaded the bombs, flew for eight hours, dumped 'em and then flew home. Jesus, half the time you weren't even sure where you were. It was like taking a cross-country bus. And now! *Now* some whacko presses a button and it's all over in five minutes."

"Yeah," Collins agreed morbidly, "and the trouble is the goddamn whacko's in Moscow. They shoot first and we're up shit creek—excuse me, ladies—and I mean with no paddle."

Broadstairs approved ferociously. "Goddamn Russians! I used to think people were nuts in nineteen forty-five when they said we oughta give the German army a new pair of boots and turn 'em around for Moscow again . . . maybe we *should* hit 'em first."

Visibly, Morgan winced. Finally, he could not help it. "C'mon, Pete, talk sense. A preemptive strike? No way!"

Broadstairs's nubby face turned red. "Don't you like realism, Morgan?"

"I *am* a realist and therefore don't believe in the first strike—for the simple reason that it won't be the last strike."

"Bullshit!" Broadstairs's fist came down hard on the glass table; a little more force and he could have shattered it. He was really angry with Kurt Morgan for other reasons, not because they disagreed on nuclear strategy. "Goddamn it," Broadstairs yelped, "let's talk turkey and stop beating around the bush." He glared at Collins as if he too were a deadly enemy. "Buck, Morgan here has an idea BBD belongs in Diversified . . ."

Collins grinned wolfishly. "I *wondered* what the hell he was doing here, Pete. I kind of figured Kurt didn't show up in Palm Springs to look at your cactus plants."

Kurt Morgan didn't like to be fooled with. Stiffly, he said, "Our idea is that BBD would be very comfortable inside Diversified. BBD would top up our aerospace companies which, frankly, have turned stale . . ."

Broadstairs appealed to Collins. "Why should we jump into the big pond, Buck? We're happy."

"Yeah," Collins agreed, "we are. BBD's in a very healthy niche. We're not the biggest fish, but what we do, we do well and we make money at it."

"I *know* that," Morgan snapped. "And you're not going to be a small fish in a big pond if you come in with us. What I've got in mind is that you'd be BBD Aerospace, a division of what we'd rename Diversified Industries. Autonomous. Buck would be running the whole aerospace show at Diversified. Like I say, I'm trying to jack up our aerospace companies. . . . Besides—"

"Money? You're going to talk about the money?" Collins said. "How are you thinking, Kurt? Stock plus cash?"

Swiftly, Morgan shook his head. "No. I'm thinking a straight stock trade. You want your shareholders to pay big taxes on a cash deal? If we throw in cash, it would cost Pete a lot of money. You're better off with a stock trade."

And another thing, Nora knew, was that Morgan wasn't in the mood to squander Diversified's own cash reserves on a merger.

"What kind of trade, then?" Collins demanded.

"I'm thinking of two of yours, one of ours," Morgan replied.

"Hey, nix," Collins growled. "Don't forget we've got five hundred million sitting in the bank, Kurt—*and* a three-billion-dollar backlog of orders."

"Right, goddamn it!" Broadstairs sputtered. "And there's more to it than the money, boys. We built this goddamn company with our bare hands—me, Brown, and Dunn. Why *should* we throw in the towel?"

Patiently, Morgan said, "Because the time has come to do it, Pete. If it's not us, it'll be somebody else. Buck knows I'm right."

Broadstairs looked at Buck. Buck frowned but he didn't disagree. "Fuckin' hogwash!"

Morgan said firmly, "You know we could take it, Pete, Buck . . . even if you don't go along. We've got the cash in the war chest to do it."

"And pay for it with your five hundred million after it's done," Nora interjected.

"Buy us with our own goddamn money!" Broadstairs bared his teeth, "Buck, this blonde is a killer."

Morgan smiled thinly. "That's not the way I'd put it. But Nora's right. The point is, why should we both squander our cash fighting it out?"

"Goddamn pirates," Broadstairs exclaimed.

Morgan asked the salient question. "If you go along, Pete, hypothetically, is there any reason your sons would disagree?"

Broadstairs shook his head. "No. The little bastards have been after me to make some kind of an arrangement. They're scared Connie is going to inherit the whole thing when I kick off."

"And the Dunns?"

Broadstairs shrugged. "No reason they wouldn't go for it. They'd like the extra protection they'd get under the big umbrella. Right, Buck?"

"Yeah." Morosely, Collins said, "To be honest about it, we're in almost over our head with the bomber *and* Heartland—*almost*, I stress." He grinned at Morgan.

"Don't break my heart, Buck. I know exactly where you're at. If Washington goes for both the Century bomber and the missile, BBD will be in clover."

Broadstairs burst out again. "Son of a bitch, that's why you want us. Because you know we're going to score."

"*We* could score," Morgan said quietly, "because together we could afford all the research. *If* we don't shoot all our cash fighting each other."

"Shit!" Broadstairs snorted.

But he knew Morgan was right and that it was already decided—Morgan and Collins were in agreement so it didn't really matter what Broadstairs thought, or how much he might protest.

Quietly, smoothly, Morgan said, "I don't know why in hell you guys haven't named that bomber the Broadstairs-Century."

Connie tittered. "B.C.," she said, her voice reaching at them through her nasal passages. "Let's hope it doesn't help set us back to Before Christ."

What a silly, inane thing to say. Morgan fixed her with a sterile smile.

"You don't really mean that," Nora said.

"Don't I?" Connie grinned wistfully. "No, I probably don't. What the hell do I know about guns?"

Patiently, Nora said, "Mustn't be gloomy about *guns*, dear. They exist. The whole purpose of the exercise is to make sure they're never used."

Broadstairs was still indignant—the whole system was unjust. You build something and *they* take it away from you. Nora knew the argument. It was a very old one.

"Sure," Broadstairs said. "Yeah, name the plane after me. So what? Why don't you call it the Broadstairs Wheelchair . . . or the Senility Express? Jesus Christ!"

Angrily, he stood up and stomped his feet.

Collins intervened. It was up to him, after all. "Come on, Pete. Kurt makes sense. I don't like it any more than you do, but it does make sense."

"What don't you like about it?" Morgan asked.

Collins showed the classic poker-face. "Tell me about a contract."

"How long do you want?"

"Five years."

"You got it."

Broadstairs listened to this exchange with something like horror in his face. But Morgan had a comforting word for him. "And Pete, whatever your present arrangements are with BBD—consultancies, travel, remuneration—they go on without a break, as long as you want. The connection will be seamless. Any discussion?"

Broadstairs grunted, "I'll talk it over with my lawyers." He glared at Morgan. "You are a straight-ahead son of a bitch."

Morgan shrugged. "I like to think so."

"Well," Collins exclaimed, all smiles, "do we got a deal, guys?" He stuck his hand into the center of the table. Morgan laid his atop it. They looked at Broadstairs. Slowly, he extended his own hand and slapped it down on the other two.

"Okay," he almost snarled. "I suppose it was inevitable this would happen once I was out of the day-to-day picture."

Collins glanced at Morgan. "We'll discuss the details in New York. When do you go back?"

Morgan turned his eyes swiftly at Nora, then away. "Early tomorrow. I want one more game of golf."

"With me . . . this afternoon," Buck said. "That's a good chance to let our hair down. . . . I've got some excellent ideas."

Morgan nodded at him fondly.

Nora was thinking how unlike Morgan it was to linger an extra hour. The Diversified plane was refueled and ready to go whenever he said the word. What it meant was that they were staying here, together, one more night.

"Let's have lunch," Broadstairs finally said, breaking up the meeting.

Broadstairs seemed to have grown older in the last five minutes. Morgan put a hand on his shoulder. "I'll walk in with you, partner."

Broadstairs didn't acknowledge the gesture. Nevertheless, the two of them crossed the patio together and went into the house.

Buck Collins, in a jocular gesture, threw one arm around Connie's waist, and pulled Nora to her feet with the other. "Come on, beautiful."

She wasn't prepared to be this close to him. His arm circled her; she felt his broad and heavy hand under her ribs. She glanced briefly at his hand and observed that the hair on his wrists was golden and thick.

Connie scowled jealously, then pressed against Buck, trying to smile. Nora hoped Pete Broadstairs would not turn around.

Chapter Eleven

"You were really brilliant, you know," Nora told Morgan when they were on their way back to the hotel.

He shrugged. "All in a day's work, Nora." Deliberately, he ignored what she said, thinking it was flattery. But she was not trying to flatter him; she meant it. They'd all had a lesson from the master. "I just laid out the facts to Pete. He knows what the score is."

"It was something to watch," she insisted.

"Bull . . ." He winked. "We'll take Buck to dinner tonight."

"Yes, all right," she said hesitantly.

He seemed to understand what she was thinking. "Listen, Nora, you're in on this. We're going to have a lot of paperwork to complete and you'd better know everything that's going on."

"All right." Soberly, she said, "I felt sorry for Pete Broadstairs. Connie says BBD kept him going."

"Sure." Morgan pursed his lips impatiently. "I understand that, but guys like Pete have got to learn to let go. Me—I'll walk away without looking back. Off fishing. So long, folks!"

Nora wondered if he would actually be like that. They promised themselves it would be that way, but when the time came it was often very different.

"What about Buck Collins?" she asked. "He seems very conceited."

He glanced at her inquiringly. "He's got a right to be conceited." Then he chuckled. "Maybe he won't be so conceited when I'm through with him. Do you think he's obvious?"

"Not to everybody. Connie Broadstairs is crazy about him," Nora said.

"I could see something goes on there, yes." Morgan shook his head. "I wish that Buck would stay away from it, if he can. Don't you think it would kill Pete? She'll be about all he'll have left, after we finish with them."

But Morgan was too preoccupied with the mechanics of the merger to devote much sympathy to Pete Broadstairs. Now he was saying that the following March thirty-first would be the date for finalization. It was a date fiscally convenient for both companies. "Consummation . . ." He smiled. "A lovely word, don't you think, Nora?" Smugness worked one corner of his mouth.

She overrode the suggestion. "Mr. Morgan, we'll have to make an announcement right away. Rumors will be flying."

"We'll talk about that with Buck," he said. "There's no big rush. Nobody knows we were out here talking to them, do they?"

"No. Just us, them, and Paul Jerome."

"Oh, yeah. The little *sweetheart* who arranged it. Isn't that what Broadstairs called him?" Morgan asked nastily.

"Paul *is* a sweet man," Nora murmured.

"I'll bet he is," he grunted.

Nora realized he was jealous, good God, jealous of poor Paul Jerome. It was peculiar, she thought, that Kurt Morgan didn't ask how Buck Collins had found out they'd be in Palm Springs. It was extremely unlikely that Collins was in the habit of falling out of the sky every weekend. And, unless there was a leak so bizarre it was not to be credited, then Collins, she assumed, had had to find out from none other than Paul Jerome.

But she didn't say anything. Let him think she was close

to Jerome. In a way, she was. She'd always be close to him.

"Mr. Morgan, you know how word gets around." She repeated the caution, gesturing with a raised eyebrow toward the driver in the front seat. For all they knew, he worked for the Russians—or at least the *Wall Street Journal.*

"Yes, yes. All right," he said irritably.

"We'll call it merger, not takeover, right? They wouldn't like *takeover.*"

"Yeah, don't rub 'em the wrong way, not yet anyway."

Smart girl. He could have said, *smart girl.* He could also have said, *call me Kurt.*

Food was not something that interested Kurt Morgan very much, or Buck Collins for that matter. They were both straight American fare. Both ordered T-bone steaks that night, both wanted them cooked medium-well. For starters, both decided on shrimp cocktails. Morgan wanted a beer with his meal. Buck asked Nora if she didn't want to share a bottle of wine, proving a degree of sophistication. Out of the corner of his mouth, he told the waiter to bring them a bottle of California *cabernet sauvignon* and he didn't care what brand.

Morgan had grown up a poor boy in the Pacific northwest. His education he owed to World War II and the GI Bill. Morgan was entirely self-made and he had grown up tough. Of tenderness, he'd learned very little and that from his wife, Hazel—who, he said, cheated on him and whom he would dump given the opportunity. Obviously, he had outgrown Hazel, and now there was nothing in Kurt Morgan's life but work. His was not an unusual career pattern. Nora had studied such case histories in business school.

That night, Nora learned only that Buck Collins was from a different background; he'd been brought up in an Eastern college town. Buck had known about button-down collars and vicuna sportsjackets long before Kurt Morgan ever knew they existed. Buck, she calculated, was ten years younger than Kurt. His war had been Korea, his planes jets, not the propeller-driven antiques of World War II.

They didn't discuss how many times Buck had been married, though Nora would have loved to know about Martine Martin. He had a son, it seemed, but not with Martine.

Sitting there, listening to the two of them talk, these men who were different yet basically so similar, Nora thought about herself—that curious new creature, the female corporate being. She monitored the conversation, but really was thinking about how much smarter women were, how one woman was smarter than ten men put together. These two, did they appreciate that Nora Ellen Sweeney was responsible for their being here discussing merger? No, it was beyond them to appreciate that Nora Ellen Sweeney had manipulated Paul Jerome, and then Broadstairs, Morgan, and even the egotist Buck Collins.

She felt sorry for them, yes indeed. Baldheaded Morgan with his woeful, hound-dog eyes, what kind of a life did he have? Or Collins, twisted in ego knots. No telling how much they could have accomplished if they'd ever been set free of the tether of their own vanity.

Was this her avocation, after all? To be brilliant, yet humble. A genius hidden under a facade of femininity? To be brilliant, but quiet? To be brilliant, yes, but to serve poor, downtrodden men? Well, yes, she would give of herself generously, every last cell of her brilliant, clean, efficient, computer-swift mind.

"Could I just say one thing?" Nora interrupted them. By now they were talking golf and fishing.

"Sure, Nora," Morgan said.

"I've been thinking that Diversified Industries is going to be just about the most illustrious conglomerate in these United States."

"Jesus . . ." Collins winked gleefully.

Morgan chuckled. "Nora has a habit of saying these things, Buck. Sometimes she scares me."

Collins said flippantly, "We're just out to make a buck, Nora."

Severely, Nora slapped him down. Why should he be allowed to get away with saying such childish things? Collins infuriated her.

"You know there's more to it than the money!" she exclaimed. "Don't tell me money is the be-all and end-all. Don't forget what else you're doing. You're making this country prosperous! You're providing jobs! You're making a vital product that we need if we're going to defend ourselves! My God!" she almost shouted, so ecstatic was her fury, "men like *you* should be running the country, not the politicians."

As unexpectedly as she'd been set off, she stopped, laughing anxiously with the embarrassment of one who'd made a fool of herself. She blushed hot and dropped her face into her hands.

"Jesus . . ." Collins' exclamation dropped dully. He didn't know how to respond to a message from the heart.

"I'm sorry," Nora said, "but I am *not* going to apologize. I believe every word of that—whether *you* believe it or not."

Morgan's expression dared Collins to make a sarcastic remark. "Say what you believe, Nora. It's refreshing to hear people say what they think. *Isn't it, Buck?*"

"It sure as hell is," Collins agreed emphatically. His eyes sought out Nora's, still not believing her. "Man, we are surrounded by phonies, especially in this business. It's wonderful to meet a real person."

As all things must, dinner had to end. Buck asked to be dropped at his hotel where, evidently, he was to meet his redhead who was also a brunette.

Morgan put on a brave show later of carefree man-on-the-make with a few hours between planes. He hummed a tune without melody in the elevator, tried whistling in the hallway, and after he opened the door of the suite and banged it shut, he sang out, "Nora, what a hell of a day! But it's done and all done in one goddamn day. Outstanding!"

"Surely," she said noncommittally, as she didn't want to begin another painful and embarrassing scene, "it has been a very long day. I'm for a hot bath, Mr. Morgan."

"You know," he said haltingly, "you *could* call me Kurt, especially when we're alone."

"Yes, sir . . . Kurt. God, there's been so much talking, nonstop talking . . . *Kurt.*"

"Nora, for Christ's sake, that's what a *chin-wag* is all about. Don't you think we ought to celebrate a little?"

"I'll get you something," Nora said. "A vodka? One of those miniatures of vodka?"

"And *you,* Nora. Don't make me drink alone."

She felt his eyes on her back as she crossed the room. She appreciated the fact that he lusted for her, but his lust created an aura that was like a scorching odor. The feeling made her shiver, but not from fright. This was something she understood; it was not the unknown. It could be controlled, as man was able to control so many physical facts of nature by the exercise of pure spiritual and moral strength.

It would not be easy, however. This became clear when he grabbed her from behind while she was searching for a glass for his vodka.

"Goddamn it!"

"Oh . . . God . . . Kurt!"

Those powerful long arms crushed her waist, the virile hands swept under her red dress, and before she could respond he was tugging down her panties, baring her behind. His zipper rasped, and like a red-hot poker, his penis jabbed into the small of her back. If she hadn't known better, she'd have thought it was a pistol.

"Goddamn it!" he cursed. "You're teasing me, bitch!"

"Kurt . . ."

She would collapse now, Nora knew, she would faint

dead away like the heroine of a romantic novel. But if she had fainted it was for only an instant. He was dragging her backwards across the room toward the couch.

"Goddamn you, Nora."

She heard herself whimpering like a wounded animal. "Just throw me down . . . anywhere . . ."

He pushed her down on the couch. His hands were everywhere on her body, his fingers between her legs, and finally, he met the bulge of her sanitary pad—hadn't she warned him the night before about her period?

He roared a deep-pitched basso of disbelief. "Goddamn it!"

"Kurt . . . Kurt. I told you yesterday . . . my period!"

"Oh, yes, son of a bitch, I forgot."

"My poor man."

She put a hand on each side of his head, caressed the temples, feeling his racing pulses.

"Oh . . . to hell with it," he groaned.

Nora let out a tortured sob. "Why am I so bad?" she wailed.

"It's not your fault," he said viciously, as if to say it was her fault and that if he'd been king of France he'd have ordered her head chopped off. "Look—I don't mind a little blood, if that's what worries you."

Tears ran down her face. She reached for that part of him which he had himself taken out of his pants to stick into her back.

"Nora," he exclaimed churlishly, "I don't want a blow-job. I want to get laid like a normal American boy . . ."

"But I can't!"

He sneered at her hatefully. "You wouldn't, even if you could. You're a cockteaser."

"*I am not,*" she cried loudly. "You're insulting me and that's not called for. I can't help it if I have the curse."

"Bullshit," Morgan raged. His face was insane; his eyes bulged psychotically, lips frothed at the corners. "Spread your legs. I'm going to eat that bloody hamburger."

"You can't!"

"I'm going to chew it up, I don't give a goddamn, Nora. Merger hours are over. You're on your own now."

He fell on her rapaciously. First to go was the top of the red dress, because he couldn't wait for even two buttons. He ripped the fabric. Surely, she thought, nauseated, he would have to pay for the dress now since he'd ruined it. And then, he was venting her brassiere and whipping her breasts into the open.

Nora did not stop tugging on his distended genital, hoping she could get it to her mouth, for that, she was sure, would quiet him. She twisted herself and the reddened, throbbing thing slid between her breasts while his lips sought her most private part.

Morgan cried out; the sensation was overpowering. He was at a physical disadvantage and Nora pressed her breasts around the purply phallus; she joggled him between the two enlarged, now aching, glands and Morgan wheezed once and ejaculated. The powerhouse of clear, milky-clear fluid hit her forehead and ran into her hair. She didn't care.

"Jesus Christ!" Morgan was panting stertorously, not believing it. But he'd better believe it, Nora told herself, for it had happened.

Slyly then, he opened his eyes to look at her.

"Goddamn, goddamn," he gasped, "someday, Nora . . . someday I'm going to bang you properly."

She stared up at him anxiously. "Kurt, please don't rob me of my self-respect."

"Don't worry about that, Nora."

She shifted him away from her sensitive breasts, the poor things used for *that,* leaned forward and kissed his lips solemnly, even hungrily. She tasted herself on his breath and was not displeased.

"Nora, you need relief yourself. Sex is not a one-sided thing. . . . Tell me you want me to and I'll go down and eat your bloody snatch."

"Oh!" Her cry was faint. "Please . . . Kurt . . . my darling. Don't say such things. I would never ask."

He turned his eyes downwards and at the same time laid the palm of his hand over her pelvic area. "I'd do it," he said determinedly. He patted her. "You've got a sparse blond patch, Nora."

She chuckled bashfully. "Did you think I wasn't a sincere blonde?"

"Nora," he said, voice taut, "you're probably the most sincere woman I've ever met. Hands down!"

It sounded like a command. Faithfully, Nora wrapped her fingers for a moment around the flaccid remains of his erection. His penis was still wet and sticky. She hated to think what condition her cleavage was in.

"Hands off, toots," he muttered, showing all his false bravado. "I've got to go take a piss."

Oh, nice, Nora told herself. She always associated with such quality people.

He clambered away, stood up. "This couch has seen a little action, hasn't it, Nora?"

"Oh, yes," she said faintly.

What was *she* supposed to do? Nothing much. Nora lay where she was, like a comatose victim of an automobile accident.

When Morgan came back, he was undressed. For his age, he was still a fairly athletic figure, and clearly this was a fact Nora was supposed to observe and remark upon. He flexed his muscles, a Charles Atlas of the aerospace industry.

"I feel pretty good, considering everything," Morgan said, his long, usually sepulchral face wandering between smugness and smirk. Then he betrayed his guilt, his discomfort. "Nora, I'm sorry. I feel I've taken unfair advantage of you."

"In what way?"

"Well . . . you couldn't . . . you know . . . because you've got the rag on . . ."

"God! Kurt!" There was no reason for her to keep disgust from her voice. She was more sinned against at the moment than sinning.

He tried to make a nonchalant smile but didn't succeed. "Well, you know . . . Nora. What the hell . . ."

"Yes. I know," she muttered.

"Now, look, kid," he said peremptorily, "no regrets, right?"

"No," Nora said. "No regrets." But she felt sad. "It's too bad, isn't it? Everything is purely physical. We could be a pair of animals. Too bad," she said steadily, "too bad, Kurt, there's not just a little love. A little? No. But just a little would make God feel a lot better."

"God?" Morgan's face caved in with skepticism, a near leer of sardonicism. "God doesn't give a shit, Nora."

"Oh!" A rush of tears, a wave of remorse and regret for everything swept through her.

"Love?" he repeated callously after her. "I haven't given that particular crime much thought lately. My marriage . . ."

"Without love," Nora summarized hollowly.

"Right."

"Which doesn't mean there's no love left in the world, Kurt."

"Don't lecture, Miss Sweeney."

Primly, she answered, "I don't wish to be damned, Mr. Morgan."

"Oh?" He considered that for some time. "Well, Miss Sweeney, maybe I can make it right . . . *somehow*. I wouldn't, if I were you, worry about being damned, Miss Sweeney." She waited, watching the smile broaden on his face. Was he going to promise to make her an honest woman? Mrs. Kurt Morgan the second?

"Remember, Nora, you're only doing what comes naturally. There's no sin in that."

Chapter Twelve

"HELLO, PAUL," NORA SAID. "I'D LIKE TO TALK BUT I can't . . . I've got to see you tonight. It's important." Her tone was brusque and businesslike.

"I know you're busy," he said. "Buck told me you're working on a release for the *Wall Street Journal*. Keep it short and to the point, Nora. All you need is a couple of sentences saying Diversified and BBD are exploring a possible merger. We aren't required to say anything else."

"I know what I'm doing, Paul," she said. "I've got to have it ready to show Mr. Morgan at four o'clock."

"We don't want it to go out until tomorrow after the stock market closes."

"Tomorrow. Why tomorrow? Why not *today* after the market closes?"

Jerome worked to hold his patience. "We want it tomorrow. The reason is—Buck is still working out his own deal with Morgan and he doesn't want to get undercut by any announcement, Nora. Is that clear?"

"It's clear," she snapped, "but I don't agree. I'll ask Mr. Morgan."

"Yes, you ask him, Nora."

"I will!"

"Then do it, goddamn it, and he'll tell you what I am trying to tell you myself."

"Paul . . ." Her voice rose. "You're not my boss yet."

"And never will be, I devoutly hope," he barked back.

"Don't patronize me, Paul!"

Evenly, he said, "I wouldn't dream of it, Nora. I am trying to save time, that's all. If you don't want to believe me, then don't."

At last, he got her to stop to think. "I'm sorry, Paul. I'm kind of nervous," she said apologetically. "So much work. I want to get this right."

"You will."

"I *must* see you," she said again.

"All right. I've got an hour. Six o'clock."

"At my place, all right?"

"All right, Nora."

She was so tense, he might have assumed the merger scheme had somehow misfired. But he knew from Buck that everything had gone very smoothly indeed, better than they'd hoped for. Collins had told him earlier they had to their credit a good weekend's work. Pete Broadstairs had been floored, but there was no other way. On this, Jerome and Collins agreed. The stakes had become too big, the required investments in missile and bomber development beyond a company of BBD's moderate size. So, it was on. Everybody had gone for it like a ton of bricks.

Collins, however, was very curious about Nora. "That friend of yours, Paulie. She's smart as a fuckin' whip and very good-looking. Tell me something—what the hell's going on between her and Morgan? By the looks of it, she's got a grip on his nuts."

Jerome chuckled. "I wouldn't be surprised. Old Kurt must wonder where Nora's coming from. He thinks she's brilliant. She put together the whole merger idea and brought it to him on a platter."

"Yeah." Collins laughed hollowly. "Didn't she ever? Lunch, Paulie?"

"No thanks. Sandwich. I've got to put our papers together."

He spent the afternoon briefing his executive assistant. Most of the company's financial material was at their fingertips but everything had to be copied and arranged in

111

neat portfolios for the board of directors, bankers, financial houses, and the most important shareholders outside of the three founding families. This all had to be done with great care because Morgan would have his search teams drawing another corporate profile of BBD, and the two had better match up.

When he arrived at her place, Nora was waiting, pacing the apartment in her baggy terrycloth robe, tied loosely at the waist. She'd cleansed her face of makeup and, as always, managed to look fresh, newly minted.

"I wonder if you'd like a martini," she said briskly.

"Since when?" he inquired. "I thought you never drank anything heavier than white wine."

"I sometimes have been known to have Irish whiskey, Paul. . . . Do you want it on the rocks, with a twist?"

"Yes, please."

"Kurt and I celebrated in Palm Springs yesterday with vodka martinis," Nora said significantly.

"So, I take it . . . things are going forward."

She smiled knowingly. "Of course, you tipped Buck off we'd be there."

He smiled back. "You got it!"

"Well, actually, that worked out very well. Kurt was able to tie down the whole thing after Buck showed up. You were *very clever* to do that, Paul."

"Thank you." He accepted the drink.

Nora sighed, focusing on her glass in a way that was unreasonably mournful if they were supposed to be celebrating. Then, abruptly, she said, "I'm having an affair, Paul."

"So I understand," he muttered, "with Kurt Morgan."

Her lip trembled. "How do you know that?"

"Buck told me Morgan was all hearts and flowers with you that day."

She smiled silently.

"Nora," Jerome said slowly, "you're playing with fire. Surely, you learned at Harvard that's a no-no."

"Yes, yes, quite right, Paul," she agreed vehemently. "But it's not a serious affair. You know I'd never, never go so far as to have a serious affair outside marriage. The poor man—he's very unhappy."

Jerome shook his head. "He's doing the unforgivable, Nora—fucking around with the help. That just ain't done, no how."

Nora blushed fiercely. "I'm not . . . exactly . . . help. I'm his executive assistant."

"I don't care how you explain it, Nora. It's no good."

She stared at him as if she knew something he didn't. Which she did. "He's very jealous of you. He thinks you're my boyfriend."

"I see. That's marvelous, Nora. That's going to really boost my career. Morgan will be out for my ass."

"No, no, nothing will happen. If it turns nasty, I'll step in."

Jerome scowled. "Nora, you've got to stop using me like this."

"Using you? What do you mean?" she exclaimed, insulted.

"You used me to arrange the date with Pete."

"Yes, but *you used me* by telling Buck Collins." She compressed her lips sternly. "So? So far we're even."

"Well," he said irately, "you can just clarify matters and tell Morgan that we're old childhood friends and that's it."

"Oh?" Nora took a tiny try at the vodka and gagged. "I seem to recall something more *intime* than that, my dear."

It was his turn to be embarrassed. He'd hoped that somehow Nora would forget that insignificant episode, or perhaps not mention it or remind him of it. He looked at her grimly, not able to decide whether she was capable of blackmail or was just taunting him. It would be disastrous if she told Lucia Gogarty. But how could she? Why would she? It would make her look like an absolute fool.

Christ, he wished he hadn't come here. Why hadn't he gone straight to Lucia's? She'd been alone all day. She was lonely, she complained, she needed him, to hell with business. She was right—to hell with business. Lucia's face came up, as if backlighted, between him and Nora.

"You're not answering me," Nora interrupted his regrets sharply. "I suppose you'd deny that you were my childhood sweetheart, Paul, that you kissed me and tried to seduce me by the river . . ."

"I did?" He was amazed. She was talking about *that*? He studied her eyes, her expression, for some sign of what she was thinking. Yes, then he understood—not everything, but more than he had. She *had* put it out of her mind, that impulsive act; she *had* erased it. Yes, and even more astounding, Nora was pure again, that was it. Whatever she did, the act of self-purification followed automatically. She was like a self-cleaning oven. All this effort of hers to preserve her virginity was meaningless. She was a self-regenerating, vestal virgin.

"Yes." Moodily, she tried the vodka again. "I remember that you wanted to touch me and I wouldn't let you."

"I'm sorry. I'd forgotten," he said humbly. It was not impossible that such a thing had happened. He hoped it had. But the truth was, he'd forgotten it entirely.

"So you see . . ." She smiled at him distantly. "I have a loyalty to you. I didn't tell Kurt Morgan that you double-crossed us by sending Buck Collins to Palm Springs. But he guessed it by himself. It was *quite* obvious."

Thankfully, Jerome accepted the non sequitur. "You agree, though, that it served a good purpose. Besides, Nora," he argued, "I think I was bound to tell him. Isn't my loyalty to BBD and Collins? I don't work for Diversified . . . or Kurt Morgan."

"I know," she said, then added cleverly, "I'll just tell Kurt our love affair has cooled down."

"Nora . . ." Jerome was on safe ground now. He grinned at her sardonically. "Are you playing with a full deck? Maybe you should switch back to white wine on the rocks . . ."

"Now, Paul, no need to be mean," she said. "I have

some right to your concern, don't I? Just for old times' sake, if nothing else."

"Nora," Jerome said impatiently, yearning to be gone, "I don't want to embarrass you but . . ." He couldn't resist saying it. "One swallow doesn't make a summer."

"God! Vulgar!" she cried hotly. He thought she could easily have burst into tears. "What *do* you think of me?"

"That you're a great mystery, Nora." He laughed softly. He was right; she would never acknowledge that moment of truth. They could have boiled her in oil. Maybe she'd confess it to a priest, but to no less a soul. "Buck thinks you're quite a lady, by the way."

She snorted indignantly. "Conceited man. I don't care what he thinks. I suppose *you* had a marvelous weekend with Lucia."

"Yes. Spectacular, Nora."

"Paul, there *is* something between us, you know. I look upon you as sort of a . . . I don't know. I've never really had a father, you know, anybody I could go to and—"

He interrupted her. "Kurt Morgan is much better qualified to be a father figure than me, Nora."

"My would-be lover?" she mused.

"Would-be? No, don't explain, please. I don't want to know." Jerome took a deep breath. "Nora, what is it you want from me? Some kind of blessing? You won't get it, not from me. Word is bound to get around that you're Morgan's mistress, his traveling piece of ass—whether you are or not. Did you stay in the same room?"

"No, no. It was a suite."

"Christ! That's just as bad, or worse."

"Paul!" Her voice jumped an octave. "We were on business. Why does staying in a suite have to mean that we were up to . . . no good?"

"Because people have dirty minds, Nora. They'd rather believe the bad than the good."

"Too true," she agreed grimly. "Dirty minds is right. There have always been dirty minds at work—the things they used to say about my mother and Father John. Yes—what would people say if two men shared a hotel suite?"

"Maybe that they were gay," he suggested drolly.

"No, no, not if it was somebody like Kurt Morgan and Buck Collins."

"For sure," he said, "they wouldn't say it about those two, at least about Buck. I don't know about Morgan."

"No!" she squealed. "He's not like that."

"How can you be sure, Nora?" he needled. "Since you haven't . . . being the good Catholic girl that you are."

Nora blushed again, ruddy Irish color filling her face. "You are *so* bad, Paul."

Jerome put his fingers over his eyes. He wanted to laugh, but he also thought that he possibly wanted to cry.

"Break it off, Nora, before you get too involved. If you don't, you'll have trouble. Someday, somehow, Morgan could land in an embarrassing spot—with the shareholders, or his own opposition inside the company. Every man in his position has that to contend with. If he does, he'll throw you to the wolves. You'll be the ritual sacrifice, believe me, and you'll have trouble even finding another job. There's not a company man alive who would dare introduce you to his wife, not with the reputation you'll have."

"Yes," she said bitterly, "and a reputation based on nothing but lies and slander—"

"Whatever, Nora."

"He as much as said in Palm Springs that he'd leave his wife, Paul."

"Yeah? Good luck," he said laconically.

Her eyes shone stubbornly. Nora Ellen was nothing if not determined. "I could take him," she said thoughtfully. "I could mold him." She stared past Jerome, as if into the uncharted future. "I could change Kurt Morgan. I could direct his energies. Right now, he's chief executive officer of Diversified Technologies, a company employing tens of thousands of people, turning over billions of dollars a year." Jerome nodded, thinking she could spare him the recital of Diversified's might. But she continued. "He's big now, Paul, but I could make him *bigger*. We've got the company in our hand. Look!"

He looked. She extended the fingers of her right hand and slowly closed them into a grasping fist. She set her glass down and did the same with her left hand.

"In one hand, the company," she growled huskily, "and in the other one public opinion. I could make him into anything I wanted, Paul. I could make him president, Paul!"

"He's already president. He's chairman too." Jerome groaned to himself. He knew what she was leading up to.

"I mean *of the country,* Paul! The whole country! Kurt Morgan has imagination and charisma and awesome energy."

Jerome would not have agreed on the charisma part. Energy and imagination, yes. Charisma, no. Morgan was a dull man.

"I admire him," Nora exclaimed, "and I think it's about time this country was run by a good businessman."

Jerome disagreed. He was not impressed at all, neither by the sermon nor her delivery. "Bullshit," he said. "My opinion is that the country should be run by somebody whose first public office was dogcatcher. That should be the major qualification."

"Or *she,*" Nora cried passionately. "Why does it have to be a man?"

"It can be a baboon for all I care, as long as he's, or she's, been dogcatcher."

"You are not amusing," Nora snapped. "You refuse to talk seriously. You *always* refused to talk seriously."

Chapter Thirteen

KURT MORGAN'S NEW YORK *PIED-À-TERRE* WAS A HAVEN, Nora soon learned, more than simply a place to park one's bones for six or seven hours of sleep between long business days. She wondered why a man with a place like this ever bothered to go home to the country.

It was a small apartment, with a moderately sized living room fitted out like a ship's library, a dining alcove that could seat six comfortably, one large bedroom, and a smaller one furnished with bunk beds.

Every inch of space was employed to perfection in this expensive bit of real estate at the corner of Fifth Avenue and Sixty-second Street. The decor was neat, not fussy. The remarkable thing about it was the art—and this was only part of what Morgan had acquired since he'd begun earning the money required for such an expensive appetite. Only in this one way did Morgan exhibit acquisitiveness, and this one, Nora thought, was highly permissible. Morgan intended to leave the bulk of his collection to a museum in a small town in Oregon. The scheme was typical of him. Morgan was a lone wolf, not a team player, she'd decided. It was doubtful he could have made it to his present exalted position if he'd had to start over; the team would have chopped him up along the way.

Hazel Morgan was to get practically none of the art. Bitterly, Kurt had told Nora that his wife couldn't tell a Picasso from a pisspot.

And there was another thing he warned her about. He

didn't like, or want, his art talked about around town. It was too dangerous. People, including potential art thieves and various white-collar swindlers, shouldn't know what he owned, he stressed ominously, making the point by aiming his finger at a well-lit work over the drinks cabinet. It was a genuine Picasso, but no one knew it belonged to Morgan. When strangers came to the apartment, he put the picture against the wall in a closet.

At Morgan's direction Nora came to the *pied-à-terre* most nights when he stayed in town. She'd bring paperwork assembled during the day for his attention, and, while Nora listened, Morgan would sit in his paisley robe and dictate notes, letters, and memos for his secretaries into a recording machine. He could go on for hours, disposing of the work of a dozen people in a single evening. And Nora listened. She realized there was nothing she would not, in due course, know about the inner workings of Diversified Technologies. When he'd finished the paperwork, he would analyze the day's transactions, discussing any number of problems out loud. Now and then he would allow her to make a comment; once in a while, he might accept what she said.

Why was he doing this? It seemed to her at very hopeful times that he was molding her into his alter ego or surrogate in the business world. It occurred to her that Morgan was capable of retreating to the *pied-à-terre* and staying there.

The normal routine was for them to have a light dinner about eleven, and then Nora would simply leave, as unlikely as this might have seemed to the suspicious minds which overpopulated the world.

Nora was feeling very satisfied with her accomplishments thus far as she bucked a northerly wind up Fifth Avenue on this damp evening in December. "Her" merger, as Morgan referred to it now when they were alone, was as good as completed. Although the idea of a merger might have seemed extraordinarily exciting to an outsider, it mainly involved a mass of boring details. Beyond the personalities, there was nothing dramatic that a headline writer or business analyst could seize upon for more than dull, dry exposition. The preliminary work had all been done. It was a matter now of the experts meshing BBD into the Diversified system and coming up with a new entity to be called the Broadstairs Aerospace Division of Diversified Industries, Inc.

Kurt Morgan had told Nora expansively one night that had she been an outside company doctor, or corporate marriage broker, or merger midwife—such were the names—she'd have earned a hefty fee for coming up with the idea of putting BBD with Diversified. She didn't tell him that she understood now how it had worked—BBD had arranged it, using her, to fall in front of the Diversified juggernaut.

Money, Nora had decided, she didn't need, not as much as she thirsted for recognition. She'd received the recognition, but on a narrow scale, so far only from Kurt Morgan. She was immensely grateful to him.

And so, for this and other reasons, it didn't matter to Nora what anybody said about her. Rumors! Nora Ellen Sweeney was putting out for Kurt Morgan. Lies! She hadn't and she wouldn't. Ever. That is, until . . .

Nora knew that most of the lies and dirty talk originated with Helen Marconi, and she suspected that Helen's boyfriend, the bland-faced hatchet-man Rustford Lancer, encouraged it. Nora remembered Jerome's fateful warning —every chief executive had within his own firm an opposition waiting to destroy him. Nora hated Lancer and Helen Marconi. It was a wonder to her that Helen dared spread her slander when she was just as vulnerable to gossip, or more so. It was common knowledge around Diversified Towers that Lancer and Marconi went to a cheap hotel room for lunch three or four times a week, and sometimes had fivesies before Lancer caught his evening train to Connecticut.

It was a disgusting fact, if true, and the more so because Helen was such a *dirty* and foul-smelling individual. The dumpy and ugly wage slave had been with Diversified for twenty years, she and Lancer having joined at the same time. Lancer had worked his way up in the consumer divisions. At one time, so Nora had been told, he'd sold women's toiletries. He'd brown-nosed and made it, dragging Helen along. Helen's job as head of the financial research department was a fabrication. The department hadn't amounted to a hill of beans, had it, until Nora Ellen Sweeney arrived?

Nora laughed scornfully into the wind as she thought about Helen Marconi, really not an opponent at all, not a worthy one anyway. Let Ms. Marconi rust and rot. But, on the other hand, perhaps it was time for Ms. Marconi to take the plunge back into the real world. Nora wondered if she had the clout to get Helen fired. Would Kurt force Lancer to dump his paramour? It would be an interesting experiment, a trial of strength, would it not?

Clutching her Gucci business portfolio to her chest along with a bulging envelope of confidential papers for Kurt Morgan, Nora ducked out of the wind into the sheltered entrance of the apartment building. The security arrangements here were far more elaborate than Mr. Fiorella's up on Madison. Nora was sure the guard who sat at this desk, really a command post with a dozen TV monitors spread before him, had a gun or two under there with him.

The guard nodded impassively at her. She was known here. Then he punched a line into the telephone upstairs.

She heard Morgan's voice crackle.

The guard said, "Miss Sweeney's here, sir."

Morgan's reply sounded scrambled but the guard nodded approval for Nora to board the elevator. It hissed nonstop to the twelfth floor, thudded open. The apartment door was heavy, oak panels with a steel plate in between. She tapped lightly.

"Nora?"

She knocked twice more, the signal, and he opened the door a crack. When he saw she was alone, he took a chain away and opened the door just long enough for her to come inside.

"Hello, Kurt," she said self-consciously.

A revolver hung in his right hand. The door relocked, he shoved the snub-nosed weapon into the pocket of his robe. He wore it open and he was not dressed underneath. His genital was puckered, she saw, not lethal like the revolver but, in its own way, just as much an instrument of aggression.

"What'a'ya got?" he asked.

She could tell he'd had a couple of drinks. His voice was slurred.

"Last minute things," she said brightly, "and me . . ."

"You." He stared as if he hardly saw her. "The cold makes your skin rosy, Nora. Are you freezing?"

"No," she said. "It was just very bracing."

She stepped carefully past him. He didn't touch her, or press his sex upon her. He left it up to her now, and contented himself with an occasional show of flesh. Did he think the sight of that ungainly chicken-neck would send her wild? No. What Morgan got from Nora was respect and attention. She was his angel of mercy; yes, that was it.

A blue gas-fire leapt in the fake fireplace and she saw that places had been set for two at the dining table.

His hands came down on her shoulders, but their purpose was to take her wool-lined trenchcoat. She shrugged out of it and at the same time unpinned a black beret from her hair.

His breath for a second time came close to the nape of her neck.

"A vodka martini, Nora?"

"Oh, yes, please. What did Mrs. Werth leave for dinner?"

"Roast beef, roast potatoes, roast carrots," he said.

"Yummy," she sighed, ignoring his sarcasm, "just the meal for wintry weather."

"Yeah." Then he yelled, "Goddamn it!"

"Oh, what's wrong, Kurt?"

"I cut my finger. I cut the end right off it."

"You didn't." She looked, then wrapped the bleeding finger in the bar rag. "That'll stop it in a minute."

He waggled the knife under her nose. "See how sharp this goddamn thing is? I ought to stick it right in your gizzard, Nora," he said darkly.

"Why?"

"For making me suffer, you bitch," he grunted. "I don't know why I put up with it."

"Please," she said, "we agreed that you wouldn't expect me to *cheapen* myself, Kurt."

"Did we? Goddamn it, did we?" He jerked his hand away from her ferociously and jammed the finger into his mouth.

"Let me," she said.

"Let you . . . *what?* Nora, the time has come—what the hell is this all about? What the hell do you think I am?"

She turned her back on him. "I don't know. I'm sorry about me," she whispered. "I shouldn't come here, if it hurts you so. I don't know why I do . . . maybe because I'm afraid you'd fire me if I didn't."

Such a remark was bound to have a terrible effect. He grabbed her shoulder and whirled her around.

"Goddamn you, Nora, I will fire you if you ever say a thing like that again. I wouldn't take sexual advantage. For Christ's sake, that's why I haven't thrown you down already."

She gasped and felt the blood leave her face. "I'm sorry. Oh, God, I'm sorry. I didn't mean that . . . darling. Forgive me."

"Maybe." He was shaking. "I'm not made of iron and steel, you know."

"I know. I just wish I were more human." She slumped down on her knees in front of the fire. "I see it won't work," she whispered agonizingly.

"It'll work, goddamn it. Can't you see I'm nuts for you?"

She shook her head forlornly, gazing at the flame. "No, it won't work. I promised myself. I couldn't . . ."

"Nora," Morgan pleaded, dropping beside her. "This is not the fucking nineteenth century. I don't know what the hell you're saving it for—"

A wracking sob tore at her. How he talked! "Please . . . you know as well as I do. You're not a cruel man."

"Son of a bitch," he grated, "I'm going to get a divorce. I am. I promise."

"Don't promise what you're not going to deliver, Kurt."

"I am. Next month. It's too late for this year."

"Taxes," Nora murmured wanly, "of course."

"Goddamn it. Why do you doubt me so much?"

"Please . . . don't swear, Kurt. Never mind. It doesn't matter. You don't have to lie to me."

"I'm not lying to you, you stupid bitch," he said. He was so abusive when he'd had a few drinks and the frustrations closed in on him. "Stop torturing me."

Nora's face tightened. "I am *not* torturing you."

"We're getting married," he declared. "As soon as I work things out."

She said nothing and his mood blackened even more.

"That's if *you* want to, Nora. I know what the problem is. It's that goddamn Jerome. You're in love with him. Goddamn it, you are, aren't you?" he said viciously. "I'll get him, that's what I'll do," he threatened.

"No," Nora exclaimed. "I'm not in love with Paul Jerome. I swear to you that's not it at all. *If* I love, Kurt, it's you I love. It's just that . . . well, you know me, I have to be sure of you before . . ."

"Jesus Christ, Nora, I'm going to divorce her, I'm telling you. What about Jerome then?"

"Paul?" Nora laughed shakily. "You don't know—Paul is head over heels in love with an Italian girl. Her name is Lucia. You should get to know her, Kurt, she's in the art business. She imports pictures and sculptures from all over Europe."

The mention of art diverted him so easily that Nora told herself to remember it for another time.

"Lucia . . . what?"

"Lucia Gogarty," Nora said. "She's the widow of a crazy old man called J.J. Gogarty."

The name meant nothing to Morgan.

"She's a broker? Well . . . shit . . ." His mouth closed grudgingly. "Good for Jerome. She could probably come up with some rare pieces," he mused. "You know, Nora, a lot of European families are liquidating their collections. Afraid of taxes, or the Socialists. There's art in private houses in Europe many collectors think disappeared a hundred years ago. Some of that stuff . . . Jesus!"

"Kurt," Nora broke in, "if it happens . . ."

"What happens?"

"Us. Wouldn't we be a great team together, Kurt?"

At last he remembered his other preoccupation: her. His eyes lit and, going on his knees beside her, he kissed her hungrily on the mouth. The talk of art had excited him so much she couldn't hold him off. His big hands drove at her breasts.

"We'd be a team all right, Nora, but you've got to let me fuck you before I go crazy. If I go crazy, there's no team, no nothing. There! That's reality, Nora. How does that sound?"

"Oh, Kurt . . . darling. I wish you wouldn't say things like that. When you do, it hurts me . . . here." She pressed the pit of her stomach.

Furiously, he swept his loose robe aside. His genital was stiff, pointing at her, like the revolver he'd put in the pocket and which dragged the robe down on one side.

"And if you won't let me, it gives me a pain *here.*" He grabbed the roughened sack of his testicles. "I get a horrible pain in my balls when I can't fuck you, Nora," he added grimly.

"Oh . . ."

With a moan, Nora toppled over on the soft carpet,

125

thinking she had performed a classic swoon. But that didn't stop him. He jerked her around. She tried to clamp her legs together but he wrenched them apart, and the next thing she knew he had grabbed the top of her white panties and yanked. The elastic gave and then his fingers were at her threshold.

"Nora!" he bayed. "Nora!"

"Oh, darling . . . God."

"Oh, Jesus!" The panties came over her hips. She was too exhausted to resist any longer. He lunged at her; she felt his genital prodding her opening.

At the imminence of the threat, a crazy hysteria gave her strength. "No!" she cried shrilly. "No . . . no . . . no!"

Each contained shriek drove him back.

"Goddamn you!" he bawled. "What's wrong with you? You don't have the rag on again, do you?" She thought he would take her by the throat and throttle her.

He continued to push at her but she was aware his steel was melting, and when she stifled a louder scream he quit and rolled backwards on his heels, glaring wildly.

"I can't, Kurt. I can't!" she sobbed. "I'm afraid of hell—don't you understand?"

Slowly, he got to his feet. He looked away from her dishevelment and bareness, defeated. "Fuck it!" he muttered. "What's the use? Forget it, goddamn it!"

"I can't forget it," she wailed, from her position of extreme inferiority. "I don't know what to do about it."

"*I* know what to do about it," he stormed. She had never seen him so angry. "I'm going to hire some big goddamn stud to come here and jab that cherry of yours right through the heart!"

"Oh . . ." Her voice was a moan and she closed her eyes, crying bitterly.

"You think the whole world revolves around *that thing!*" He pointed, sneering, at her midsection.

"I feel so horrible," she said woefully. "Can you bring yourself to understand?"

"No! I can't make out if you're just a cockteaser or if you really do have a religious hang-up."

"The latter, I assure you. Please . . . forgive me. Just kiss me once more."

Unwillingly, he knelt again and Nora raised herself to reach his mouth. She laid one hand on the paisley robe, over his lank buttock.

"Nora . . ."

"Just the kiss, please."

She touched his gums with the tip of her tongue, exhaling into his mouth softly. As she did so, she slid her hand across the silk and eventually reached the limp genital.

"Nora . . ." He wanted to struggle but he was helpless, like putty in her hand. But then the putty began to harden.

She gasped slightly, thinking how wondrous a muscle it was, constantly in a state of growth and recession, then growth. She stroked the fineness of it with her fingertips until Morgan gasped, the signal that his stress quotient had dropped. She tried to catch the fluid in her hand but some slipped through. She didn't think it would stain the carpeting.

When they sat down to eat the modest dinner his housekeeper had prepared, Morgan was ready to talk about anything except sex and frustration.

He launched into a long discourse on Washington's reaction to the proposed merger of BBD and Diversified. There was very strong argument, according to the business section of the *Washington Post*, echoing what had already appeared in the *Wall Street Journal*, for applauding this new combination. In the arena of high tech, international competition was at its fiercest and most ruthless. The only answer was a consolidation of America's science-based industry. The newspapers pointed out that the Japanese trading companies had already streamlined their industrial system to maximize research investments. Similar things were happening in the rest of the world, and it was, therefore, no more than logical and sensible that American business leaders should also mobilize their industrial system for a prosperous future.

The government could have disapproved of certain elements in the merger on anti-trust grounds, but Diversified's lobbyists saw no danger of that. In this case, everyone seemed to agree that what was good for Diversified and BBD was also very good for the country.

"Thrilling to think it's being discussed in the highest circles, Kurt."

"Nothing new about that. They watch us like a hawk in the best and the worst of times."

"The beef is delicious, Kurt," Nora said, hoping to cheer him.

"Yeah." He didn't care. "The fucking *Journal* was going on about how Collins and I complement each other. Do you think *he* complements me, Nora?"

She didn't answer directly. "What do you *really* think about him?"

Morgan replied hesitantly. "He drinks a lot. Not *necessarily* so bad, as long as he controls it. He's smart and he's highly visible. He hates to be desk-bound—he's around the country and he spends a lot of time in Europe. He's a member of a couple of hush-hush NATO committees to do with research. Yes, Buck's got deals going everywhere. Hard to nail him down, Nora," he said, his mind wandering. He was talking to himself, as usual bouncing the thoughts off her. She made a better sounding board than she did a mistress.

"But he's a *star*."

"True," he nodded. "I've seen him in action in Washington. He's a whiz. He leaves 'em gaping—provided his guys give him good briefing. Your *friend* . . . Jerome. He's good at that."

He glanced at her for a reaction. She realized he was still not one hundred percent convinced there wasn't something between them. But there was hope he was beginning to accept Paul Jerome, perhaps give him credit for more brains than he did Collins.

"Paul *is* good," she commented. "I know it's not up to me . . . but you know when Gerry Ball retires Paul Jerome could step right in there."

"Yeah, sure he could. But he won't."

"Is it . . . you wouldn't have him?" she asked timidly.

"No, it's got nothing to do with me, Nora. You don't know anything about Ball. He swings a lot of weight. His powerbase is built on several very powerful entities."

"Entities? Commercial entities?" She didn't know what he was getting at.

"Sure, call them commercial entities. Banks. Big ownership interests. I'm positive they wouldn't accept Jerome."

"Because he's a Jew?" she asked cautiously.

He shrugged and laughed. "Nah, *shit,* he could be a Moslem for all they care. It's just he wouldn't be *known* to them, Nora. It'll be somebody who's known to them, okay?"

So he didn't want to talk about it anymore. If he wasn't ready to listen, there was no way she could persuade him any differently. Morgan, as always, would do precisely what he wanted to do. But she could underline *one thing*.

"Kurt, what I said is true—Paul was the boy next door and he was older than me. We were not even high school sweethearts. I was only in the fifth grade when he graduated from high school."

"So?" Morgan said capriciously. "That didn't mean he didn't drag you into the bushes behind the school and slip it to you, Nora."

She scowled. God, he was such a mixture of man. "That's crude, Kurt."

"I'm a crude man, Nora," he said, inciting her. "A little crudeness is sometimes a healthy thing. It can serve as a release. You ought to try it sometime."

Deliberately, Morgan lifted the ruby-colored bottle of Bordeaux he'd opened for them and poured some in his glass. He held it up to the fireplace light.

"Like blood. If you want me to, Nora, I'll pour some of this into your snatch and lap it out."

129

"God! Kurt!"

He grinned at her. "Never mind. About Buck Collins—I hope he learns to trim his sails to the facts of life in a big corporation. BBD is a popgun compared to Diversified. We're megabig, Nora—and hot-shot executives are a dime a dozen. They trim their sails to suit us, not vice-versa."

"He's a realist—with a five-year contract."

How cavalierly Morgan switched back and forth, from talking dirty to talking hard-nosed business. She couldn't understand why he did this to her.

"He better be. Otherwise, he's out on his ass, baby, with his nuts caught in the revolving door. I don't care what kind of a contract we give him."

"But surely . . ." she began to object.

"We pay him off, that's all," he snorted. "On the other hand, Nora, if he learns to sway like the bamboo tree, the sky's the limit. In another five years or so, he can have the whole ball of wax."

"What do you mean?" she asked, suddenly fearful.

"What do I mean? What I mean, Nora, is I'm going fishing. In another five years I'll have had just about all the bullshit that I can tolerate. I'm going to walk away while I can still walk . . . and get it up." He smiled at her daringly. "But only when I find the guy to replace me."

"You couldn't *not* work," she protested.

"That's what you think."

"You'd be bored stiff," she said. He was only trying to push her off-balance again.

"I might be stiff once in a while, but not from boredom, Nora. You might get bored with *me* though," he observed shrewdly, "if I didn't have all this, and the fat perks, people flying my airplane and waiting on me hand and foot."

"Never," she said faintly.

Morgan chuckled. "Thrown naked out of the corridors of power, Nora—think about it. That's why I've got to be careful about this divorce, don't you see? I want something left so I can buy a rowboat and the six-packs."

She looked at him worriedly. "You're not serious, are you?"

"I am." He did sound serious. "I've been putting it off long enough. I guess you get credit for waking me up to that. I let it drag on because I didn't give a damn." He glowered at his wine. "But, enough is enough. So I give her fifty percent. Isn't that worth it, just to be free again?"

Now was not the time to say anything. Let him talk it through.

"Well, Nora? Isn't freedom worth whatever it costs?"

"I don't know what to say. I don't want to influence you."

"Bullshit. I want input, Nora," he said stridently. "I buy her off with a couple of million. Would she take a couple of million?"

Nora found a way to answer the question. "I would hope . . . if I were ever in her position, that I'd never have to make a choice. I mean," she smiled bravely, "you're worth more than two million. On the other hand, I hope I'd never stoop to that, trading a man's freedom for mere money."

He laughed mockingly. "Quite the heroine, aren't you?"

"Well," she defended herself, "it would lessen a person, don't you think?"

"Come on, Nora," Morgan guffawed rawly. "I bet if I rolled up fifteen or twenty thousand-dollar bills and shoved 'em up your snatch you wouldn't piss 'em out."

"Oh, God!" She covered her face with one hand. "Kurt, there you go again! How can you say such awful things?"

His expression was nothing less than what she had to describe as malevolent. "Bullshit. Stop playing goody-two-shoes. Just because you won't give it to me doesn't give you a pious license. Let me ask you," he said tauntingly, "doesn't Hazel deserve something? The fat little pain in the ass invested a certain amount of time in me."

131

Nora understood he was getting back at her now. He was having his revenge. "I'd just point out that she's got a boyfriend. She hasn't been faithful to you."

"So what? I haven't to her either. I couldn't blame her for that—she probably needs reassurance that she's still worth a poke. So she picks up this Italian bastard—he's a lot younger than she is and every woman, especially when they hit fifty, want to get a good screwing as often as they can. You know, every one might be the last."

Nora's eyes faded shut. God, she couldn't stand it. "You're so kind. Maybe you should reconsider leaving her."

"Oh, no," he said. "My mind is made up. Life is too short. I want you, Nora. I'm determined to climb in those pants of yours. You're not easy, God knows, but I have a feeling if a guy could get there you'd be wild."

She knew she was blushing. People did not talk to her like this. "Do you think so?" She tried to sound removed, far away, unimpressed by his directness. "But what if I wasn't . . . wild?"

He poured wine in her glass. "I'm cutting loose, one way or the other, Nora. With you—or without you."

She must show that she might believe him. "Yes . . . *with* me, then."

"Good. So, it's settled. I'll make an honest woman out of you. But to be made an honest woman, first you have to be a dishonest one—right?"

"Wrong," she said sternly. "I want everything clean and aboveboard."

He frowned, foiled again. "That means you don't trust my motives, Nora, goddamn it."

"There's no need for you to keep using the Lord's name in vain like you do, so habitually."

"Holy smokes," he sneered at her.

"Not funny." Tersely, she said, "I don't want people talking about me, saying evil things. They already are, but I know what they're saying is lies. That makes it *not* so bad."

His voice jarred, sounding like he was chipping ice. "Who's talking?"

Nora laughed shakily. "Well, it's somebody in the office. Your fault, really. You practically flaunted me in her face."

"Who?"

"Helen Marconi," Nora said.

Violently, he cursed. "That fat-ass. She's got b.o., bad breath, a moustache, and Lancer fucks her in the ear!"

Carried away, Nora laughed raucously. "Yes, yes, how well you put it." God, he was right! There was a certain psychological relief to be had in using vulgar words.

He considered the matter. "I'll take care of that twat. I'll force Lancer to fire the bitch. . . . Have some more wine. Forget it . . ." His mind drifted and Nora knew he was working out how he would get revenge for her, for them.

Morgan got up, gathering his robe modestly at the crotch, and went into the kitchen. He stooped and looked back at Nora through the hatch over the breakfast counter.

"I'm going to open another bottle of this crap," he said.

He popped the cork on the second bottle and came back to the table.

"I think I'll transfer her to Alaska. We've got a satellite ground-station up there, just outside Nome. It'll be a big promotion for her—a job she can't refuse." He smiled thinly. "If she did, she'd have to resign. How do you think Rusty Lancer would like them apples?" He paused. "On the other hand, he might be pleased to hand her over to the Eskimos."

"One way or the other . . ."

Morgan rolled the wine on his tongue. "'Course, she's liable to melt the permafrost," he muttered, smiling complacently. "In the interim, there's something important I want you to do for me."

"Kurt . . . don't play with me, please." She couldn't take much more of his cruel jesting.

"I'd like to, Nora, but I'm serious now. For real."

It must be so, for he pushed himself back in his chair and put two reflective fingers under his chin, pulling at the loose craw of skin—not one of his most attractive characteristics.

"Certain people down in Washington," he said quietly, "would like to see Diversified extend its European interests. You know, we've already got three or four subsidiaries over there, including the chemical and synthetic divisions in northern Italy." Yes, she knew about that. He went on, "It seems, without it becoming public knowledge now, that because of the rotten state of the international energy market, our friends in the south would like us to have a stronger position in Europe. They feel we could help stabilize the market in petroleum and petroleum products. I've been prompted to look into a possible deal with a conglomerate, might as well call it a cartel, by the name of Eurochemie S.A.—financial interests throughout Europe, probably including Moscow," he added sourly, "judging from what they tell me."

"I know the name. Powerful. They do a bigger volume than ours. The ownership is very tight, also very secret."

"Right. Their volume, in fact, is about double ours, if you can believe the figures. We're talking about an outfit with megaleverage. Now, Nora, what I want you to do is to begin pulling together every available scrap of information on Eurochemie—who really *does* own it, plants, *complete* product range, table of organization, and then as much *personal* information as we can get. In other words, *dirt*. Who belongs to the Communist Party, and who's screwing who, and how and where . . . and when."

"Not so easy."

"No. We know they've got a strong electronics group, and they're mixed up in the European space program and nuclear energy research."

"Okay." She was breathless. God, what a challenge, what a project! "You're way ahead of me."

"My tentative plan would be to use BBD—and that

glad-hander Collins—as sort of point-man to get our foot in their aerospace group. Maybe they could use a technical agreement with BBD—BBD is too thin to feed a bomber *and* missile program. They need more base. We can help but maybe it would make sense to spread the bomber program into Europe—if we could get the goddamn NATO bastards to buy the thing once it's built. Build it here, and build it there. We dilute the development costs. Do you understand me?"

"Yes." She nodded.

"The idea ought to please Collins," he said sardonically.

"I should think so," Nora said. "It'd put him in a power position, though—would you want that?"

He grinned. "You think he might overshadow the mighty Kurt Morgan, Nora? You want it all for me, don't you? Look, it doesn't matter. It's important—Eurochemie supplied piping and construction materials to the Soviets for the gas line out of Siberia into Western Europe. The *boys* are scared the Soviets could use this to establish their powerbase in Eurochemie. We've got to prevent that, head them off at the pass, Nora."

Morgan put down his wineglass and rubbed his face with those big bear-paws. Nora waited for him to proceed. What he said next surprised her. More than that, he astounded her.

"Nora, I'm going to make you a vice-president of Diversified, I think as of January first."

"I . . ." Her mouth must have gaped, for he held up his hand.

"Don't come in your pants," he cautioned. "It's no big deal. You'll be one of the least important vice-presidents. But I've got to do it because I want you to have the clout to do this project. People pay attention to title."

"I'm flabbergasted."

"Well, don't be. I want you to get in touch with a firm of private eyes in Washington," he said coolly. "An agency I use from time to time, run by a couple of ex-CIA agents. One of them was mixed up in Watergate but he's very quick and smart. They're called Eagleye, Incorporated. Ask me tomorrow for the phone number. Strictly on the QT, understand. They've got sources in Europe and everywhere else. They'll be able to get you inside information on Eurochemie. Cross that with what's public and available, and we'll have a pretty good profile. Does that figure?"

"Yes," she said.

He yawned tiredly. "Pooped," he summed himself up. "I'm thinking if I can put all this together, it might be the last big deal. About time to call it a day, don't you think?"

"No . . . darling . . . I wish you wouldn't talk like that." A dire and rather frightening thought struck her. "I want to ask you something," she said. "Is the BBD merger *part* of this bigger picture?"

Morgan chuckled. "Well . . . *I wonder*. The BBD idea certainly surfaced at the right moment, that's for sure."

"But, you had no plan to take over BBD, did you . . ."

"You mean, before that morning when you bumped into me?"

"Yes, that is what I mean." Although she'd just been made a vice-president, she felt curiously deflated.

Morgan shrugged. To him people were always little cogs in the grander scheme. "You were a catalyst, Nora, one of many, I suppose. You put two and two together and got four. I don't know for sure, but probably somebody else must have been doing the same addition."

She shook her head. "Great minds . . ." Right. Might as well smile about it.

"Nora, it's never mattered *how* these things come about. The important thing is that in our system they do come about." He smiled at her benignly. "Tell me, Nora, now that you've got the title and the money, doesn't it change your mind about giving old Kurt a little bang?"

She wanted to blush scarlet but couldn't anymore. His profanity, his lust, was becoming too commonplace.

"You keep hurting my feelings, Kurt. You talk about something so important, and then you say *those things*."

"Right," he said. "I shouldn't make jokes."

She shivered, her backbone chilled by the timbre of his voice. "Was it the president who asked you to do this?"

"You know I couldn't answer that, Nora."

Her eyes moistened. "Kurt . . . promise me one thing? That you'll remain strong, just like you are now."

"You bet, little Nora, you can count on that."

"You're brilliant," she sighed, "absolutely brilliant."

"Okay," he muttered. "Being brilliant doesn't help get your rocks off."

Chapter Fourteen

CLEARLY, KURT MORGAN DID NOT LIKE HIM, PERHAPS BEcause he had tried to give Nora Ellen Sweeney the moral strength to steer clear of deeper entanglement with her boss. But it seemed to Jerome that Morgan's hostility had to be rooted in something more than personal dislike. Obviously, Morgan still couldn't believe Jerome was not Nora's lover.

During the weeks leading toward Christmas and closer toward consummation (as Morgan preferred to describe it) of the merger, by his pointed and heavily patronizing treatment of him, Morgan made it clear he'd rather be dealing with anybody except Paul.

However, the fact was that there was no way Morgan could avoid sitting down with Collins, Paul Jerome, and other BBD advisors. BBD didn't have a big superstructure, Collins was fond of repeating in a derisory sort of way; it operated like a fast gunboat while Diversified waddled around like an oversized and top-heavy battle wagon. BBD, Collins would stress, making the odious comparison, had always been able to turn on a dime while Diversified needed a half dollar to perform the same maneuver. If a question came up during their negotiating sessions, Collins and Jerome were able to answer it on the spot. Morgan had always "to consult," perhaps with his board, possibly with his merchant banker-advisors, or maybe with his computers.

Morgan had begun to look across the conference table warily, as if they were amateurs. One day, he said irritably, "Sometimes, Buck, I wonder if you understand what all this is about—in plain old dollars and cents." Morgan pointed at Jerome. "*He* does. We're going to have to do a stock issue to buy out you bastards," Morgan went on. "Appreciate something—it's more trouble for us than it is for you."

Collins nodded steadily. He smoothed the soft cashmere sleeve of his blazer, whose gold buttons he wanted them to believe had once graced one of Commodore Vanderbilt's yachting coats.

"Paulie is a financial genius, Kurt," he murmured. "I'm just a broken-down old helicopter pilot."

"Even so, Buck, you've got to understand that Diversified can't move as fast as you're used to doing at a little pisspot company like BBD—"

"I *beg* your pardon," Collins said, exaggerating insult.

Jerome was left to smooth their feathers. "I think we're straying off the subject matter, if I may say so."

Soon after, the final agreement was completed. The share exchange would be two BBD for one Diversified or, if a BBD holder unwisely chose to sell, then Diversified would pay fifty dollars for each BBD share surrendered. The proposal was accepted on the market as a fair, if not excellent, trade. Over the year, BBD had swung between thirty and forty. After the announcement, it went to forty-five. Diversified closed that day at one hundred and two and by the weekend had dropped to ninety-five.

The *Wall Street Journal* acclaimed the merger agreement. Both companies, the financial paper said, were well run and as Diversified Industries they could look forward to a bright future in aerospace, as well as in Diversified's consumer-goods groups. The *Journal* described Morgan as one of the ten leading American industrial figures—hardworking, imaginative, and well-liked by his peers. Collins, however, was viewed with less enthusiasm. He was younger than Morgan and had a reputation, whether deserved or not, of being brash and opinionated, with a tendency to shoot from the hip.

Collins complained to Jerome about the article, wondering whether Morgan for some reason had leaked his views of Collins to the *Journal* writer.

"Whatever you *are*, or *aren't*," Jerome counseled him, *"you'll* sign the formal agreement, you and Morgan."

"That's true, Paulie," Collins said. "He may not like the color of my hair—"

"Or the fact you have hair."

"Yes," Collins chortled. "But he's got to put his John Hancock alongside mine."

And so it was done in the big boardroom at Diversified Towers.

Kurt Morgan shook hands with Buck Collins. Buck gathered Paul Jerome in a brief bear hug, and Jerome shook hands with Morgan and his advisor and next-in-line, Gerald Ball.

"Good job," Morgan grunted.

"Thanks," Jerome replied. "From you, that's a real compliment."

"Don't cream your jeans," Morgan sneered. He pressed an intercom button. A second later, the big oak doors to the conference room swung open and white-coated waiters began wheeling in food and drinks.

"It's a quarter to twelve, Buck," Morgan remarked. "Is that close enough to noon for a belt?"

"Not a moment too soon, Kurt."

Collins should be overjoyed, Jerome told himself. Buck would come to Diversified Industries at a salary double what he'd had at BBD and job guarantees that stretched almost into the next century.

"You know what this whole deal is worth?" Morgan asked them rhetorically. "You're talking thirty, forty, fifty billion dollars, boys. Kind of scares the shit out of you, doesn't it?"

"Not me," Collins joked. "I'm used to big numbers. Like on my expense account."

Morgan didn't think that was very funny, and Jerome didn't either.

Morgan suddenly grinned. Staring past them, Jerome realized, he'd spotted Nora Ellen Sweeney hovering in the doorway.

Morgan mumbled, "I thought it'd be appropriate to invite Nora to join the festivities. As you know, she was the inspiration for the piece of paper we signed today. *Over here,* Nora," he said loudly. "She's a V.P. now."

People moved to the side to let her pass; they moved gladly it seemed. Executives smiled and nodded at her, but as she cleared them, and Morgan's attention was elsewhere, Jerome noticed several raised eyebrows that could only be knowing looks.

He frowned to himself. Goddamn it, Nora had it coming to her for being so stubborn and careless about appearances. She was in for it. These guys would cut off her arms and legs, and chop off her balls if she'd had any—and didn't they actually resent her the more for not having them to chop off?

Nora didn't notice, or at least she didn't appear to. Her face shone with such enchantment you'd have thought she was going to be awarded the Nobel Prize for Merger-Making.

"Well, gentlemen," she said happily, "do I understand we have reason to celebrate?"

"Tell those guys to get the champagne open," Morgan barked to an aide.

"Hi, Paul," Nora said. She looked at him self-consciously. "Hello, Mr. Collins."

"Call me Buck, beautiful."

Popping corks made Nora smile all the more. In a moment, waiters passed through the crowd with silver trays laden with champagne and hors d'oeuvres.

Morgan was gauging the room. When it seemed like

everybody had a glass in his hand, he called for attention. Everyone became quiet, quickly.

"While we're all here, people," he held his glass high, "I want to toast everybody who's worked on this. I toast Buck Collins for coming with us. I toast *Diversified Industries!*"

Collins was not to be outdone. Taller beside Morgan, he lifted his glass. "I say, *Hurray* for Diversified Industries! And here's to Kurt Morgan!"

Well done, Jerome told himself. Both men smiled like they'd been boyhood chums, slapped each other boisterously on the shoulders, and laughed too loudly.

Morgan turned toward Nora. His eyes, for once, were not guarded and wary. He looked happy, satisfied. Nora's head inclined forward. It was obvious she expected Morgan to peck her on the cheek. But Morgan was not going to kiss her in public. Never. She should learn that lesson then and there.

"Done," Morgan muttered. "Signed, sealed and delivered. Your *boyfriend* here did a good job."

The remark, very impulsively made and one Morgan obviously regretted, nevertheless angered Jerome. He'd had just about enough of this charade Nora was playing.

"Thanks," Jerome snapped. "It was a pleasure doing business with you."

Morgan's eyes tightened. *"Was?"* he repeated coldly.

"If for some reason you don't feel comfortable with me around, Mr. Morgan, just say the word. I'm sure we can settle what's left of my contract."

"Hey . . . hey!" Buck exclaimed. *"Cut that shit out!"*

Morgan eyed him calculatingly, seemed to circle looking for a vulnerable spot. "I don't intend to start settling contracts at this point in the game, Jerome," he growled.

"You can have my resignation on your desk the day the merger is effective if that's what you want," Jerome muttered, even more angrily than before.

"Paulie!" Buck hissed. "Cut it out, goddamn it."

Jerome stared straight into Morgan's eyes which dulled

lethally. Morgan hated any form of opposition. But he wasn't ready for a showdown, particularly in front of all these people, on a day, at an hour, which should have been so corporately joyous.

"Forget it! We're celebrating," Morgan murmured.

"Yeah and here's to it," Collins cried. He forced them to lift their champagne glasses to each other, draining his own. He grabbed a waiter by the arm. "Bring me a Scotch and water."

Jerome waited uncomfortably, sorry now he'd reacted so strongly. There'd been no need. Let Morgan stew— what the hell did he care if Morgan suspected Jerome was banging his sweetie?

Nora didn't help things; she moved closer to Jerome and whispered, "Sorry." Morgan watched her kiss Jerome on the cheek. Perspiration broke out on top of his bald dome.

Jerome felt like pushing Nora away. What she was doing to the poor bastard was cruel.

Morgan stared at them blindly. Bemused, he mumbled, "We want everything ready to go out to the shareholders before Christmas, Buck. My suggestion is that our Gerald Ball and Jerome coordinate it."

Buck interrupted pointedly, "What about Nora?"

Morgan glanced irritably at her, then at Collins, and finally at Jerome. He shook his head. "No—I've put Nora on another project. It's an . . . international matter," he said cautiously. They were still comparative strangers, despite the piece of paper they'd just signed. "It's an . . . um . . . energy thing. Interesting though—isn't it?" he demanded of Nora.

"Very."

Poor Nora, Jerome thought. Deeper and deeper into the soup.

But there was no good reason Paul Jerome should have felt responsible for Nora Ellen Sweeney, not at all, he told himself remorselessly. She was old enough to know better and she was in no way defenseless. And now he was uncertain she was also as innocent as she pretended. She had ignored his warning to steer clear of Kurt Morgan and now she was closer to him than ever—*and* a vice-president of Diversified. Jesus!

This was heavy and not very digestible food for thought, but on his way to Lucia's that night Jerome decided he'd mention none of it to her, or to John Foster, who was in the city overnight, and would join them "at home."

Lucia, Jerome had learned early, was not a woman who showed much interest in or tolerance for other women, especially one like Nora. Lucia was completely male-oriented, and, in fact, she admitted she did not feel very comfortable in the company of other women. She wanted Paul for herself; she'd made that clear and he was flattered. She was jealous of Nora, with as little reason as Morgan had to be jealous of Jerome. Lucia appeared convinced that he and Nora were bound together by hometown connections. How wrong she was.

Lucia lived in a small and deceptively inelegant apartment house on Park Avenue in the sixties. But the exterior of the building was, he had decided, deliberately seedy and unprepossessing, the theory in New York being, unlike in California, that if you've got it, *don't* flaunt it.

The downstairs lobby was very small but manned day and night by guards who looked like they'd been trained in the Green Berets. The elevators too seemed to be designed for little people but they moved through the shafts as fast as bullets. From the elevator, one stepped directly into very large and airy apartments with mirrored walls and arched ceilings, with enormous, over-sized kitchens and huge bedrooms that were once the norm in this city.

Lucia's place was cluttered with art and there was more art in unopened crates. Her collection began at the front door and continued into all the rooms, bathrooms and kitchen included. Lucia even stored lesser works in the closets. She dealt in every sort of masterwork—paintings, lithographs, watercolors, sketches in pen, pencil, and crayon, sculptures in every material man had ever worked. On one wall, Jerome had idly counted three Degas, a Renoir, three Miros, a large Dali, three Pompas and a Picasso; on another a collection of primitives, Gauguin, Grandma Moses and Sister Garish and here and there, pedestals holding sculptures by Europe's finest, living and dead.

J.J. Gogarty, as she'd told him already, was not interested in art beyond advising Lucia to cut up a Picasso and sell it by the square foot. Only once had he shown any interest in art: Gogarty had financed a black and white movie and this was how she had met him. He had been given special permission to do research in the Vatican's forbidden library to prove his theory that permissiveness in a society, that is the loss of inhibition and fear of damnation, led directly to decline and fall.

"In this," Jerome told her, "I see an element of truth. These freedoms should not be extended to the masses. For us, they're okay, Lucia, but not for the masses."

She'd agreed with a smile and pinch but said this was not the whole story because Gogarty was actually doing research for an erotic movie, called *Where the Sun Don't Shine*.

"Lucia, I don't believe this."

He had better believe it, she told him. "Do you know what Gogarty said? He was taken with my body." She pondered for a moment. "And that is not all. My foot appears in the movie. Gogarty thought it would be a big joke on the Vatican. He whistled with laughter . . . you understand why? My position, my relatives . . . the juxtaposition?"

"What was your foot doing in this movie?" he asked.

Lucia chuckled with embarrassment. "There was a peasant lad, the hero, a lad of great . . . what should I say? Dimensions. In one scene, a foot, toes, fondle him. It is my foot—only my foot."

"Jesus, that's disgusting," Jerome said.

"I was very young. The movie made a great deal of money and if we establish this foundation of Father Foster's, it will be partially supported by the profits of *Where the Sun Don't Shine*. Do not tell poor Father Foster. He would have a seizure."

Weakly, he said, "I don't understand . . . your foot, the peasant lad."

"The youth. He was called the Youth."

"And you . . ."

"It was only through a curtain. I did not even see it. They needed a foot and Gogarty said I had a nice one."

"I don't like it," Jerome said blackly.

"Oh, Paolo, you are so much better than any Irishman. It is the Mediterranean people who are the children of God. God had given them—the Latins, Greeks, Jews, and Arabs—the quickness of mind, the scientific bent, and the genius for art that would have put them in the forefront if they hadn't quarreled so much among themselves."

Lucia employed, at the Park Avenue residence, a Chinese couple who had worked for her since she'd first come to this country with Gogarty. They were Catholics, having been converted to the faith in Shanghai before the revolution. Now they were stronger Catholics than Lucia. But, the crucial point was that her Chinese couple, although more Catholic than the Pope, took an eastern delight in the fact that Jerome more often than not slept overnight with the bereaved Lucia Gogarty. As far as Paul and Lucia knew, the couple had never squealed to Father John Foster.

This night, while at dinner, Jerome thought Father John had grown gaunter since they'd last seen him not so many weeks before. His face was grayish and unhealthy looking. Even his earlobes seemed to have lost weight and were so distended one might suspect that when he was alone Father Foster hung heavy ornaments on them.

Jerome thought the explanation for his pallor was to be found in the money Foster dealt with. Some men took money too seriously and he feared Foster was one of them. All that money earning money was making Foster look less and less like a peaceful priest and more like a wizened John D. Rockefeller. Jerome thought morbidly that money, if handled or loved too much, could confuse one's mind, turn one green in skin tone, and transform red blood to quicksilver. In short, money was a dangerous matter.

Foster was always ready to put aside his financial and worldly preoccupations for a meal of won-ton soup, egg rolls, noodles *al pesto,* crisp and crackly Peking duck, spumoni ice cream, followed by espresso.

"So, children," Foster said languidly, heavy eyes drooping in their baggy anchors, "how is everything?" He lifted first the small coffee cup to his mouth, and then the glass of sticky old Port.

"Paolo has finished buying Diversified Technologies," Lucia informed him chattily.

"Ah," Foster said merrily, "the gigantic entity for which the beloved Nora Ellen Sweeney works so diligently."

"Of which, yes," Jerome said mockingly, "I was informed today she is to be a vice-president come the new year. There now. News?"

"No!" Foster beamed. "The clever duck!"

"Clever, yes, but much bigger than a duck," Lucia said spitefully.

"Now, Lucia," Foster admonished her, "don't begrudge the child her victory." He threw her a sweet smile, then smugly added, "BBD—high for the year, thirty-eight, low thirty, presently going to forty-five on the strength of the merger announcement. Congratulations, my dear Paul."

"The financial mind never sleeps," Jerome muttered.

It was unwise to discuss the situation. Unfortunately, because of his position, he hadn't been able to take advantage of the increase. With the BBD stock he owned, and by trading in his options, he could have cleared a neat six figures.

Lucia seemed absolutely thrilled. She played excitedly with a heavy gold Bulgari chain from which hung a stone-studded cross. Laughingly, she announced, "I wish to inform you that the finance ministry of Lucia Saltimbocca Gogarty has purchased five hundred thousand shares of your BBD."

Both looked at her with puzzlement and deep curiosity, as if she had just come to the door a total stranger. Then, Jerome thought he might black out.

"Lucia—*before* or *after* the announcement," he asked slowly.

"*Before,* of course. We got it at thirty-two a share. Big block trading, you see," she said proudly.

"Lucia! Good God! Why?" Foster asked. His face had turned ashen.

"Because it is Paolo's company and I knew some time ago that he would merge with Diversified Technologies and the share price would rise . . . and I love him, that's why!"

"I'll be put in jail," Jerome said.

He wouldn't, would he? No. Yes. It could happen. This was called dealing on inside information.

"How else to show my adoration, Paolo?" she demanded teasingly. "Should I sell and take my profit?"

She was trying to drive him crazy. She knew the answer.

"No, please, don't sell, Lucia."

"If you are not nice to me . . ."

He stared at her, not believing it. "Devil! Blackmail. Did you hear her, Father John?"

Foster nodded speechlessly and Lucia said, as if it were the simplest thing in the world, "The holding is in Italy. It will come over here to help fund the J.J. Gogarty Foundation."

"How?" Jerome hardly dared ask.

She shrugged, smiling fixedly at him. "Diversified is offering fifty dollars a share if I cash them—eighteen dollars profit per share. That is nine million dollars. Not bad, eh, *caro?*"

Jerome groaned as if he had been stabbed. "Jesus Christ! Sorry, Father John."

Foster's face underwent several drastic changes and reversals. On the one hand, he was shocked and horrified. On the other, he saw nine million for the foundation. He said nothing.

"Lucia," Jerome murmured, "you can't. You absolutely cannot. Have you ever heard of the Securities and Exchange Commission, S.E.C. for short?"

Placidly, she sneered. "They have nothing to do with me. I am a foreigner and the shares we purchased do not come near five percent of BBD equity."

"All right, all right," Jerome said nervously, "but that is nonetheless a huge block of shares and questions could be asked. If questions are asked, my ass is in the fire!" He was angry now, seeing himself victimized once more by a scheming female. He glared at Foster. "That little trick would be typical of your friend Nora."

Lucia sat up straight, back stiff; now she too was angry. "Do not compare me to Nora!" she spit. "It is a pure business transaction. I am no fool," she went on haughtily. "And how is it, do you suppose, that my Venetian and Florentine ancestors made their fortunes? They were making money while your ancestors were crawling around in animal skins. By buying low and selling high!"

"All right," Jerome said again, bitterly. "All right—do as you please. I'll deny I ever met you. Goddamn it!"

Foster muttered automatically, "Language . . . language."

"I thought I knew you," Jerome said, ignoring him, "art collector, patron, Italian cook, porno librarian . . . and now, goddamn it, if I don't find out you're some kind of big financial adventurer . . ."

He scowled at her.

"You could flee the country and we will live on the nine million . . . in Brazil." Her eyes danced with an almost indecent hilarity, then sobered. "All right, I will not sell. I will take the new Diversified shares. I will accept the dividends. I will be nice . . . and patient." She shook her finger mockingly at Jerome. "But I warn you, Paolo— make a profit, or else!"

"Or else what?" he growled. He was relieved, but not relieved to discover this new dimension of cleverness. He realized she was going to be hell to live with.

"Or else," she said merrily, glancing once at Foster, "I will do very bad things to your body."

Foster blinked. "Children . . . children. You're going too fast."

"I love you," Jerome said, before he knew he was speaking. "As an accountant I love your figures, as a man I love your figure."

Foster's face flushed. "What!"

"Ah . . ." Lucia's face shone, the black eyes jumped at him. "You should know my bank, Father. It is the much-esteemed Banco of the Sacred Heart of Jesus, of Milano."

"Good God," Foster yelped. "You're compromising the Vatican's most faithful and *beloved* bank!"

"Bosh, Father John," she said, annoyed and showing it, "the Banco Sacre deals with industrial clients whose portfolio spread is very similar to the new company, Diversified Industries."

Jerome's voice cracked. "Now what are you telling me?"

Calmly, she replied, "I am saying *our* investment in your company may only be in the beginning stage. My *finance ministry* and certain friends are very interested in your company, Paolo."

"Lucia, I don't like this very much."

"Lucia," Foster said sternly, "you're jumping around too much."

"No, no, you understand me. You are a fox," she flattered him.

"A fox?"

"A sly financial fox," she said affectionately, "and together we can manage anything."

Foster, naturally, tried to look very sly. "If you're telling me your bank is The Bank of the Sacred Heart of Jesus, then you're saying Vatican money was involved in this huge purchase."

"You have said it . . . not me," she murmured.

Jerome smiled edgily. "Forgive me, but why would a bunch of Italians put money into Diversified Industries in order to earn money to support a J.J. Gogarty Foundation? Especially when none of them even knows who the old son of a bitch was? Isn't Gogarty's money going to be used for the same purpose? Or—is all his money in Italy?" He finished pointedly. "That is to say, out of the reach of the Internal Revenue Service?"

She smiled at him. "I do not understand. That is too complicated for my mind."

"Liar," he exclaimed. "You are a cute, sweet, little liar. *You understand*—and so do I. Lucia, you're a crook. The foundation would be a very convenient way to get money out of Europe, wouldn't it?"

"Paul!" Foster exclaimed. "A terrible thing to say. The J.J. Gogarty Foundation will be the soul of financial propriety, a paragon of probity."

"You have said it, not me," Lucia said again, to Jerome. "But please, my beloved one, do not call me a crook."

"No, don't," Foster agreed.

Jerome sighed deeply. "Lucia, I'd like a double brandy."

"Of course, my lover," she gushed. "Ah, Paolo, you are my delight, my companion in ecstasy . . ."

These were words Father Foster could understand better than all her financial flights of fancy.

"What are you saying to this man, Lucia?"

She was on her feet. "You know that I am an impetuous woman."

"I know it better tonight," Foster observed anxiously, "than I did before."

She didn't give him a chance. "You know I am a warm-blooded Italian widow, the widow of an *older man*."

She flashed a smile at Jerome; he began to enjoy *this* performance.

Foster squirmed. "Lucia . . ."

"You must know that I cannot bear to be alone, Father, that I need someone in my bed . . ."

"Good God, Lucia . . ." Foster couldn't look at her.

"The physical," she said, "it is—"

"The animal!"

Lucia turned stubborn. "Humans are animals."

"Of a higher order," Foster blustered. If Lucia blushed, Foster seemed to turn absolutely purple. "Human beings do not behave like animals, Lucia." She tried to reply but he stopped her with his hand. "There is no argument to that, Lucia! And you should know it too, Paul Jerome."

"Me?" Jerome demanded. "I know something, but not what you're saying."

"Father," Lucia exclaimed, "Paolo did not seduce me. I seduced him."

Foster's face jerked disgustedly. "No more, Lucia. This is not the proper time!"

"No, not," she agreed passionately. Suddenly, Lucia let herself down on her knees. "Now, you can confess me." She clasped her fingers into a piety. "Forgive me, Father, for I have sinned . . ."

"Get up," Foster thundered. "Not now, Lucia."

"I will confess," she insisted, still on her knees. "Yes, Paolo and I make sweet love. I twine him in my limbs and we join—"

Foster jumped to his feet. "Lucia, two hundred years ago we would have tied you to the stake and burned you."

Chapter Fifteen

IT WAS INTOLERABLE TO NORA THAT A MAN LIKE KURT Morgan should, in effect, be blackmailed by a wife who carried on as she pleased with a gigolo actor, spending Morgan's money profligately while never intending to free him.

To Nora, the situation was more than exasperating; it was vulgar, even obscene, and it called for radical action. She realized that Morgan was too kind and honorable a man to defend himself, to fight fire with fire, and she admired him for it. Characteristically, he even nurtured a crazy loyalty to Hazel; never, Nora knew, would he be an active party to anything that could hurt her, whatever the provocation.

But Nora didn't have such qualms. When distressed, women operate outside normally accepted standards, she thought. This was one of the many things men didn't understand. The jungle had been created for women, not for men. Men had no idea of how to lurk and then leap and slash. Women made far better, more ruthless, terrorists than men.

For some time Morgan had known Hazel's lover's name. Joe Mercury was an Italian actor whose knowledge of English was so poor that he supported himself, when he worked, in thirty-second non-speaking TV commercials for Italian wines. In other words, a hunk.

Nora was in Washington a week before Christmas to consult about Eurochemie with Eagleye Inc., Morgan's favorite detective agency. Thus, she first met Eagleye's head honcho, Vincent Norman, sometimes called Norm Vincent. She waited for him at the bar of the Jockey Club in the Hotel Ritz-Carleton, and the man who approached her had to be the ex-CIA bag-man Morgan had described.

Norman, or Vincent, looked the part precisely because he *didn't* look the part. Dressed in a loose tropical-weight suit, button-down-collar shirt, and regimental striped tie, he sported a Hitleresque black moustache, closely cropped black hair, and wore wing-tipped cordovan shoes. Norman looked strictly Princeton University. Perhaps the moustache should have given him away; it looked phony, like a slash of black shoe polish. But this man had to be Norm Vincent or Vincent Norman because over his left arm he was carrying a brand-new trench coat.

He headed directly to her. "You're Miss Sweeney." He didn't even wait to hear the fact confirmed. "I recognize you from Morgan's description. He told me to look for a beautiful blonde sitting at the bar of the Jockey Club." He glanced around warily. "One of my favorite watering holes, Miss Sweeney."

"Brilliant," she said, smiling coolly, as she thought one should at an ex-CIA man, "since I'm the only blonde sitting at the bar."

He laughed heartily, sizing her up, and down, with dark eyes spaced perhaps too close together over an insubstantial but straight nose. A sprig of black hair curled down his forehead, crossing a pronounced widow's peak, like an arrow pointing into his head.

"You're a wit, too," he said, "and what're you drinking?"

"A white wine."

"Yes. With a twist. I see." Vincent crooked a finger at the bartender as he slid up next to her. He folded the trench coat over once and put it across his knees. "I wouldn't have come had Morgan not called me personally."

"Oh? Why would that be?"

"I'm about to go on a mission . . . to Italy."

"Italy? That's perfect," Nora said. "That's the part of the world we're interested in." She opened her purse. On a small bit of paper, she had printed the name: Eurochemie S.A., Milano, Italia. She slid the paper at him. "Did Mr. Morgan explain any of this?"

Vince ignored the paper. "I wasn't going to Italy on business, Miss Sweeney. I was going over to recharge the old batteries. I worked there once. I am crazy about the food. Also I'm getting over a love affair. My girlfriend married a wrestler. For a while, I was thinking about terminating the son of a bitch. On the other hand . . ." He laughed self-mockingly. "On the other hand, there's guys who'd like to see me vacationing at the bottom of the Potomac."

Nora nodded, drawing him out. "You're a complicated person, Mr. Vincent."

"Norman, call me Norman," he said, honking a laugh. "Okay, then, what is it you want to know about this Eurochemie thing?"

"We want inside info—about their directors, who owns the stock, family histories—"

"I get it." He sounded bored. "You mean who's doing everything to everybody."

"Exactly. The . . . dirt," Nora said, slightly flustered.

At this statement, he warmed a little, or seemed to become less distant and more tolerant of her presence. Smiling blandly, he pulled the ashtray toward him. When he struck a match Nora assumed he was going to light a cigarette. But he just blew it out, after watching it burn down to his fingertips. He threw the charred stub into the ashtray and struck another.

"I understand," he said absently. "Morgan always likes to be completely briefed before he moves. You think this company has got any anonymous owners, such as Vatican City?"

"Well . . ." One had to be realistic. Nora smiled frostily. "We know they own points in just about every major company in Italy, don't we?" He nodded. "So," Nora added, "we'd like to know how much and who pulls the strings."

"Sure," he said sarcastically, blowing out a third or fourth match, "you just want me to bust into the Pope's office and study his bank statements."

"I'm sure you could manage it, if necessary."

He bared his teeth in a smile; they were short and straight, like his nose. "Tell me I'm good, Miss Sweeney . . . I love it!" He lit another match and stared at it. "There's a cardinal. He happens to be one of the cardinals who manages Vatican City investments."

Nora didn't notice for a second that he was holding the flame under the palm of his left hand.

The sickening smell of singed flesh invaded her nose. She watched in horror. She had never seen a man deliberately burn himself.

Vincent Norman chuckled morosely as if it didn't hurt, or not as much as he'd hoped. He turned his hand so she could see the blackened skin, the emerging blister. Nora could've thrown up. She had a strong stomach, but not for self-immolation.

"Pay no attention," he said carelessly. "I do that once in a while to remind myself I'm a man and a hard nut, and life is a game of hard ball. Morgan knows if anything goes wrong, Miss Sweeney, I take the rap. I've told him several times—anytime he doesn't think I'm doing a good job or that I ratted on him, I'll supply him the name of a hit man to take me out."

She was speechless. In confusion, she reached for her glass.

"That's right, Miss Sweeney," Norman Vincent said, *"there's looking at you."*

Nora gulped. "We need . . . the information as soon as possible."

"Sure thing. Why? Morgan gonna buy into this Eurochemie thing?"

"Why do you say that, Mr. Vincent?"

"Norman," he corrected her again. "Why else would he want such deep research, Miss Sweeney?" He held his glass up again.

"Shouldn't you . . . uh . . . put something on that hand?"

He shrugged. "Nah. Just a little of this." He dipped his forefinger into the wine and dribbled some of it on the burn.

"Doesn't it *hurt?*" she asked, wincing.

"Sure. But so what? Hurt is manageable. You just project yourself into a state of self-hypnosis." He made a fist over the burn. "See these knuckles? Every one of them has been broken one time or another." He nodded proudly. "I've had fingernails pulled out too. You can't see—they grow back if you've got the will to make 'em."

Nora nodded. "I need another drink, Norman. I have to admit you scare the daylights out of me."

"Out of *you?* Don't make me laugh. Morgan told me all about you."

Nora grinned shyly. "What'd he say about me?"

"Well . . ." Vincent appraised her sardonically and Nora grew wary of what he'd say. "Well . . . Morgan told me, Miss Sweeney, that you like sucking cocks," he said slowly.

"What!" She swayed. If he hadn't put his hand behind her, she'd have dropped off the barstool. "He didn't!" she cried. "He wouldn't. Why would he tell you a thing like that?"

Norman Vincent answered as if it were the most obvious thing in the world. "Because Morgan knows that when I'm doing business with people, I always like to know something extra about them. That's for a double reason, Miss Sweeney. First, to protect them from weakness, and second to have something significant to use on them if they get funny."

"But I don't believe it," she insisted. "Kurt wouldn't make up a thing like that about me."

"Ah-ha!" Vincent chortled, "small victory, number

157

one. So it's true? *You do?* You're right—Morgan didn't tell me. I made that deduction myself, Miss Sweeney."

She stared at him angrily for a long time before she decided how to answer. If she hadn't been sent here by Kurt Morgan, she'd have walked away without answering at all. "You're a pig."

"I'll betcha Sherlock Holmes himself couldn't've figured that out, Miss Sweeney. He was good on soils but he didn't know shit about lipreading."

"Really," Nora said disgustedly, "don't repel me, Mr. Vincent."

He grinned. "I'm telling you I can read it in the lips, Miss Sweeney. Yours are sort of puckered in the middle, a little notch there, usually a tip-off that these lips like fastening on to a good healthy joint."

She decided she *would* leave and never mind about the Morgan mission. "I guess I've heard enough. I'll report to Mr. Morgan what sort of man you really are," she said as icily as she could.

"Hey! Sorry. Cross my heart, I'm sorry, Miss Sweeney." He put his hand on her arm to stop her. "I'm just kidding, sorry. What else was it you wanted to ask me?" He flung his hand up. "Barkeep!"

Before Nora could object, Vincent had ordered two more drinks and she decided that when in the company of reptiles, one had better grow some kind of a snake skin.

She had a second scrap of paper in her bag and she now pushed this toward Vincent. On it, she'd written the name Joe Mercury.

Vincent reacted foggily. "Who's this—a guy or a car?"

"A guy. He's an actor. He's blackmailing Mr. Morgan."

"Hey, that shit don't go!"

Nora ignored his grasping, caressing hand. Or tried to. His hand was on her knee, squeezing her kneecap, making her toes leap in nervous reaction and, strangely, projecting a stab of dark pain up her thigh to the pit of her stomach. Vincent seemed to know a lot of tricks.

"This man," she said nervously, "has wormed his way

into . . . shall we say the *confidence* of Kurt Morgan's wife."

"Into the confidence?" he repeated. "What do you mean *into the confidence?*"

Nora felt bashful saying it. "He's her . . . lover."

"Oh," Vincent said, "you mean *into the panties* of, not so much the confidence of . . ."

"Yes." Nora nodded. "Don't ever tell Mr. Morgan that I told you this—please!"

She placed her hand on top of his on her knee.

"Mum's the word," Vincent said heavily. "My mother's name was Mum, Miss Sweeney."

"It's . . . the company that's worried, Norman," Nora lied. "The company is concerned with the embarrassment that would ensue if the story got into the gossip columns. We want proof to confront them, to bring pressure to bear."

"Sure. I understand. To get her loose without Morgan paying through the nose, right, Miss Sweeney?" He smiled. "And then what? *You* step in. Am I right?"

"No, not at all," she exclaimed softly. "You're jumping to another conclusion, Norman."

He shook his head. "I dunno. Eagleye doesn't ordinarily do divorce stuff. It's too sordid for my men."

Nora didn't believe that. He was playing hard to get. "Just consider it a side order, Norman. A footnote on the big picture. Besides, you *can* see the ramifications, can't you?"

"Yeah, I see, I see all right. Pictures, you want pictures."

"They'd help, wouldn't they?"

Vincent sighed. "Well, you know what they say—one picture's worth a thousand words, Miss Sweeney. Sometimes it's easier to advise this guy to skip town or he could wind up looking like the Hunchback of Notre Dame on camera . . ."

"Oh, no," Nora said, "no violence. Mr. Morgan is not a violent man."

"Hey! Who is?" Vincent protested, then agreed. "Okay, I'll put somebody on her tail, so to speak. One of my neophytes most likely. The hot-beds detail is a good way to blood the kids. Where's this all supposed to be happening?"

"I gather they meet somewhere in New York City."

"So I'll need the home address and all. She'll have to be tailed from doorstep to downfall. A camera oughta do it. I wish all my assignments were so easy, Miss Sweeney," Vincent said professionally. "The deal in Italy now—that's a tough one."

"But you're the man for it, according to Mr. Morgan," she said generously. "Were you . . . uh . . . with the CIA a long time?"

He looked over his shoulder before answering. "Twenty big ones."

Again, Nora felt she must ignore the pressure of his fire- and battle-scarred hand which was creeping matter-of-factly up her leg. Norman Vincent paid it no more attention than she did; it was as if his hand was someone else's property. His face remained disinterested. But he was undoubtedly going through the motions of feeling her up and despite herself Nora was aware of the tumble of excitement in her solar plexus. Adventure—meeting a strange man in a faraway city where no one knew you. All the rules slipped into neutral or hold. She decided then that Norman Vincent was not an unhandsome man. Moreover, there was about him the virility of the man of action, a trained killer.

"What about I buy you dinner? You're not going back to New York tonight, are you?"

She spoke uncertainly. "Well . . . I was going to catch the shuttle after we finished."

He nodded knowingly. "Only trouble with that is we're not finished yet, are we, Miss Sweeney? We haven't even started yet, have we?"

"I . . . what do you mean?" She didn't know how to respond,

He squeezed her leg. "I mean we're probably starting up a fine love affair . . . Nora."

In a low voice, she said, "What are you saying, Norman?"

"Hey, call me Vince, Vince Norman. Say, Nora, let's get out of here. Let's go back to my office. Everybody'll be gone home by now so nobody's going to spot you coming in. I wouldn't want to compromise you that way. I've got to write down some of the particulars."

"Well, I don't know," she said uneasily.

He chuckled kindly. "Listen, Nora, don't be afraid of me. I know it's easy for me to scare people to death but, actually, down deep, I'm a pussycat."

"What are you trying to say, Vince?"

"That you've got quality, Nora . . . Miss Sweeney. But I don't know yet about the quantity. That's why I want to weigh you very carefully."

"I don't understand you," she said frankly.

Again, he stared at her as if everything was so very simple—which it was not.

"Stay over, Nora. Christmas is coming—want to come with me to Italy? You could be my assistant."

"I've got to get back to New York," she said quickly. "I've got to report to Mr. Morgan."

He laughed. "Well, I tried."

He was scary, she told herself. Not so much because of the way he acted; it was the disjointed way he talked.

But she could have stayed with Norm Vincent or Vince Norman in Washington or gone with him to Italy over Christmas for all the notice Kurt Morgan took of her when she returned to headquarters.

Christmas day was to fall on a Wednesday and, thus, the eve of Christmas on Tuesday, so naturally nobody was going to come to work on Monday. In effect the year came to an end December twentieth, Friday afternoon, at the Waldorf Bar.

Since her return from Washington this was the second

chance she'd had to see Kurt alone and he was taking the train up to Scarsdale. She wanted to throw herself into his arms and hug and kiss him, but of course she couldn't. She knew he was trying to keep his mind off the fact that he was deserting her through the holidays and felt guilty about it. But his kids were coming home, one from college, one from California. She didn't like it but she did understand and she wouldn't want it any other way.

They were sitting at a little table in the bar, inhaling the smell of soggy clothes, wet shoes, and too much cigarette and cigar smoke. Morgan put his hand over hers and looked at her sincerely. "Nora . . . next year . . . I promise."

She shook her head stoically and remembered what her new friend, Norm Vincent, had taught her. Life is a game of hard ball and you've got to be disciplined enough to stick your hand in the fire without screaming. Yes, Nora told herself silently, on Christmas morning, when all the happy, American families were together, she'd practice burning her hand. Then she'd burn down her Christmas tree—except she hadn't even thought to buy one for herself, only a tiny one for Morgan. He wanted nothing bigger. "For the *pied-à-terre*, a mere *pied-à-tree*," Morgan had smiled over it, and then presented her with a Christmas gift, a small gold chain with a little gold heart hanging on it. It looked like the mate to a friendship ring, those awful things girls used to give each other in high school.

Nora fingered the chain as she smiled at him bravely. "You are not to worry about me. I'll be fine, Kurt."

Last year had been better, but her mother had been alive then. Now her mother was dead and Nora Ellen Sweeney was alone. She should have taken Norm Vincent up on his invitation, she told herself forlornly.

Uneasily, Morgan asked, "What do you think you'll do, Nora?"

"Well," she said matter-of-factly, "I'll be in the office Monday."

He shook his shoulders dispiritedly. "Christ, there's not going to be anybody around."

"You won't be around until after New Year's," she said. "But that's fine. You deserve the time off, Kurt."

He knew he did, but he was not going to say so, not now. "You know where I am—if anything comes up, I can be down within an hour. You know that, Nora."

"Kurt," she said, "I know that. *Not to worry.*"

His eyes burned. "Why not . . ." He paused and drew breath. "Why don't you call your old pal Jerome?"

"Now Kurt . . ." But she softened her reply. "He's going off to Europe."

"What? *Leaving now,* at this juncture?" This did not please him. After all, she knew he'd be thinking, these were tenuous days. The BBD-Diversified deal was proceeding smoothly, but you never knew . . .

"He's sort of down, you know."

"Down? Why should he be down?" Morgan demanded.

"He's not sure of his future with us," Nora said frankly. "He's still feeling hurt the way you talked to him. Your apparent attitude. I don't know . . ."

"Hurt!" he exclaimed scornfully. "He's a grown man. You don't get *hurt* playing the corporate power game."

"Yes." She nodded mournfully. "That's what Norm Vincent said. Hard ball, play hard ball. That's what he said."

"Norm Vincent?"

"Your man at Eagleye."

"Oh, yeah," Morgan chuckled. "Jesus, Norm Vincent is one of the world's A, number-one nut cases. Didn't you think?"

"He seems to know what he's doing. Isn't that why you sent me to him?"

"Yeah, I guess," he admitted grouchily. "So he lectured you, did he?"

"On playing hard ball."

"Well, he's right. So," he muttered, "Jerome thinks he can just trot away, huh?"

163

"Mr. Ball and he discussed it, apparently. Paul has gone off to Italy with the lady I was telling you about—Lucia Gogarty, the art dealer."

"Yeah? Well, in that case, I approve."

"Kurt . . ." Her voice dropped. "You and Paul should be friends. You *know* we are *not* having an affair."

A shadow of a smile crossed his face. "I'll say one thing for him—he's damn good on the fine print. If that's supposed to be the basis of a friendship, okay. But you know, I don't really have any friends, Nora. Except for you." He stared at her intently, his light blue eyes watering as they did when he became slightly emotional. "And the reason we're friends, Nora, is you won't let me make love to you properly."

"Oh, Kurt . . ."

"I mean, in the New Year, now, you've got to resolve that you're going to spread your legs for me. Right?" he asked cheerily.

"You're going to be alone with your wife," she reminded him cruelly.

"Yeah, I know. Most likely, *she'll* be coming down to the city to meet that Wop of hers."

"No," Nora said, "I'll pray that you make it up, Kurt. That's the only possible thing for a Christian person to do. But, on the other hand, I *hope* that you won't."

He scratched the baggy skin under his left eye and, God, Nora thought, how tired he seemed.

"All right, Nora, I know. I don't deserve any sympathy."

"Kurt," she protested, "I am going to be in church over the weekend and I *am* going to pray that you reconcile with Mrs. Morgan. *I want you to be happy.*"

A frown a foot long fell off his forehead and onto his full lips. "Fuck that, Nora! I'm finished with Hazel. Leave me out of your prayers."

Sometimes Nora was convinced he was not in love with her, that he had never been in love with her, that he had merely been using her. She remembered what Norm Vincent had said Morgan had told him about her and suddenly she wasn't so sure Kurt had not told him. But why? He was not a vicious person. Saying a thing like that to Norm Vincent would have been purposelessly cruel.

Her misery must have transmitted itself, for without warning he said, "I was going to call you but I see that I'd better tell you now, up front—I'm going to Texas for New Year's. Buck Collins and me for a big blow-out at Deke Watson's ranch. You know who Deke Watson is."

Nora was miserable before. Now, her body turned cold. She should have expected the worst. Of course she knew who Watson was. Watson was going to run for the Republican presidential nomination in two years and there was an even-to-good chance he'd get it. He had money and influential people behind him. She felt destroyed. Why didn't Morgan have the guts to tell her everything? That it was all over?

"I know—don't tell me. Hazel's going with you." She could easily have screamed in pain.

Morgan's eyes dropped. "It's a command performance, Nora. You know, I have to keep up appearances, at least for the time being."

What was it Paul Jerome had told her? He'd warned her, yes he had. Beware, Nora, you'll be burned and she was and it was hot.

"Well . . . what is it they say? *C'est la vie.* . . . You don't always get what you want." Her voice was a wretched whisper. She hated herself.

"Ain't that the truth?" He brightened, in the hope she wasn't going to take it too badly.

She shook her head despondently. "Buck—he'll probably bring some hooker with him." A saving thought burst inside her. *"I'll go with Buck. I'll be his date!"* she said.

This idea shook Morgan to the depths. *"With Buck?"*

"Well, why not?" Nora demanded excitedly. "Who's going to object? It's proper he should bring *one of us*. It's a business gathering. I mean, you're not going down to Texas for a New Year's orgy, for God's sake. You *know* I can get you in Watson's cabinet!"

"Jesus, Nora . . ."

"I promise I won't embarrass you. I won't even look in your direction."

"Nora, the plan is for us to fly down in the Diversified plane. Hazel will be on the plane. She'll get the picture right off the bat. She's no dummy. Nora, I *can't* run the risk of her making some kind of a scene at Watson's." His face was drawn, fearful. "The board would never forgive me."

Angrily, Nora let go. "How would she *dare* make a scene? I mean for God's sake, Kurt, you even know the name of her lover."

Again, he registered deep anxiety. "Nora, I couldn't use that!"

Nora nodded, but she was not defeated. If only Norm Vincent could get those pictures *before* New Year's. "Kurt," she said, "it makes me sick with disbelief that you're the one on the defensive, afraid *she'd* make a scene. I cannot believe you!" Let him think what he wanted. So she was pushy, forward, asking too much. His eyebrows rose ominously.

Sarcastically, he said, "It'd be just wonderful if she did what she *shouldn't* do at Watson's—started screaming and yelling at you? Wonderful, Nora, just wonderful." He glared. "I'm surprised at you. I thought you'd know better. I didn't pick you for my executive staff . . . *and* make you a vice-president *to be* because I thought you were an irrational person."

"I see," she said, just as roughly. "What you're saying is if I make trouble, then I'm not going to be a vice-president and I won't be on your personal staff any longer. All right, let me tell *you* something. I'm very rational and I know best what I can do for you. I know *better* than you do, or are willing to admit, Kurt, how *good* you are. I certainly

166

know that better than Hazel Morgan," she blurted contemptuously.

Her voice had gotten loud enough for him to say, "Take it easy, Nora." He looked around charily. In his own way Morgan was afraid of her. If this was so, then the time had come to give him a real test.

"You know, Kurt," she said levelly, her voice under control, "if somebody didn't know us and saw us together, they'd never suspect from the businesslike way in which I behave . . . that we'd been intimate . . ."

Her voice was raised again. He looked worried, glancing this way and that over his shoulder. Sure enough, four men at a nearby table had paused in their conversation.

"Nora, goddamn it!" he hissed. His face was red.

Quite distinctly, she said, "Nor would they suspect, Kurt . . ." She was about to pronounce his last name but thought that might be going too far. As it was, the four men would spend the holiday guessing; probably guessing right, too, if they gave it enough thought. Watching the flush drain from his face she said, "They'd not have any idea, would they, that I'd sucked your cock."

She was in shock herself just saying the terrible words. It had the desired effect. Two of the men turned to look at Morgan, whose eyebrows twitched under the bald head.

He wet his lips rapidly, in a fit of embarrassment. She was about to say more but the murderous look on his face stopped her. "That's *enough*, Nora."

What was he going to do now? Fire her? No, there was nothing he would dare do to her.

"You're not really worried how I'd behave, are you?"

"No," he grunted.

"Well, then, if I can talk Buck into bringing me, will it be okay?"

"Yes."

"I'll make some excuse and fly commercial. That'll spare one scene, anyway."

He'd turned away, putting one hand up against his face

so the four eavesdroppers would have a difficult time identifying him.

He was in a fury now, but in the end, Nora knew, he'd forgive her. She spoke back to him softly. "I'm only trying to help, to be at your side."

He merely nodded. She knew she had gone too far. She had been confrontational in front of witnesses.

"I know now," she addressed his hostility, "I'm nothing to you. Just an extra motor, in case one conks out. I'm going now . . ."

Nora pushed her chair back, gathered her coat around her, set her feet to get up.

"You're going to walk to the station with me."

"What good would that do?"

He stuck his face across the table. "Shut up, goddamn it. Let me pay the bill and then we'll go. If you say one more word, I'll kill you. I swear I will."

"I've got it coming too," she replied.

Morgan slammed a twenty dollar bill down on the table and got up, his face blazing. He couldn't get out fast enough.

Chapter Sixteen

As she walked away from Grand Central Station, it seemed to Nora that she was walking away from a chapter of her life. Things between her and Kurt would never be the same. She knew too much about him.

Despite his reputation as a corporate swashbuckler, Morgan was weak. He might force a financial opponent to walk the plank, but in personal matters he was indecisive. He'd come up through the ranks, clawed his way through a corporate jungle where men led the lives of killer tigers and piranha fish. And now, he was weary of the struggle, and even wearier of going home, although she knew he wanted to be with her, not with Hazel.

What if Buck Collins was a conceited ass? Ignoring the rainfall, Nora shook her head fiercely. Didn't any of them care about her plans? Deke Watson had a very good shot at the nomination. If he got it, what he'd need immediately was a well-known industrialist to be his advisor and spokesman on defense. Whoever got that job would be in line to be President Watson's secretary of defense. Kurt was that man.

Who better, really, than Kurt Morgan? What exposure! In four years Morgan would be ready to make *his* move. He'd still be only in his mid-sixties, a youth in politics. The sky was the limit.

What a campaign slogan for him: *The Sky's the Limit!* Nora became warm inside her fur-lined trench coat thinking about it. She admonished herself for thinking Kurt was weak. He was nervous and wary of women, but he was not a milquetoast.

Lost in her thoughts, she was home before she knew it, standing in front of Mr. Fiorello, her clothes a mess and her shoes ruined.

"Hey, Miss Sweeney," Fiorello laughed, "you look like you swum the reservoir."

Nora stepped out of the shoes. "You can throw these into the garbage, please."

His olive complexion creased. "You had a visitor—the priest."

"Where did he go?"

"He went next door to Ryan's, for a drink, he said."

"Look," she said, "I've got to get out of these clothes. Duck next door . . . No. Call Ryans, will you, and tell him I'm home?"

"Okay, Miss Sweeney."

Father John to the rescue, the dear man. He always knew, he sensed when she was feeling low. Good. They'd have dinner and talk about everything. Father John and Nora Ellen Sweeney, the straight-A student, and the servant of Jesus and the Virgin Mary.

Nora hung her coat in the kitchen to drip into the sink and then hastened to the bathroom to strip off her wet clothes. She was standing there, rubbing the soft terry robe into her skin when the buzzer rang.

"Darling Father John!"

"Hello, Nora . . . I hear you finally had sense enough to come in out of the rain."

"It was *so* wet!" She kissed his satin-smooth cheek and he stroked her back through the robe. "Let's have a warming drink, Father John."

He was as jolly as old Saint Nick. "That's the spot to hit in weather like this, little Nora."

She bustled around him as her mother used to do, pulling off his coat and scarf, taking his black hat from his fingers to hang on the back of the door. She massaged his hands in her own briskly and, if he'd asked, she'd have taken off his shoes, washed and kissed his feet. That's how happy she was to see him.

"I didn't know I'd be free tonight, Nora, that's why I didn't call. I came around, hoping you'd be here. The archbishop stood me up," he explained proudly. He'd come a long way for a modest parish priest.

He was precisely the antidote for her present unhappiness. Should she confess to Father John, she wondered? High time, but what had she to confess? There *never* had been anything.

Foster stood limply, shoulders sagging, staring. "You look dazzling tonight, Nora, amazingly like you mother just now."

What, she wanted to cry out, like this, in the robe? But she couldn't hurt or revile him. He seemed sunk under a ton of sadness.

"You've been thinking about her, haven't you? I have too, Father John. All day. I was just remembering last year, we were together up at the Point. And this year—" She intercepted a sob before it reached her throat.

Oh, God, was this a flight of fantasy? Was there lust in his eyes as he stared at the robe? He turned away, tottering stiffly into the living room, and sank into an armchair.

"The weather for aches and pains," he sighed.

"I'll make you a Scotch, Father John." She was flustered. The room was too hot. "And one for me too. Strong," she exclaimed, cheerfully, putting evil thoughts from her head. "You seem distraught, Father John."

"*Actually,* I should be feeling pleased with myself. I'm off to Rome for New Year's—didn't Paul tell you?"

"No." She poured Scotch into two glasses and put the bottle down, again out of sorts. Damnation! Everybody was going somewhere except her, unless she could talk Buck Collins into taking her to Texas. "Good for you!" she said faintly. "Paul . . . and Lucia, they've already left?"

"This evening, Nora," he said. He smiled fondly. "Those two are really in love. It gladdens the heart."

She handed him the drink.

"Lucia gave me the ticket to Rome as my Christmas present," he said, somewhat bashfully. "I'll probably go over at Easter too. The J.J. Gogarty Foundation is all set now, finally. Lucia's putting up one million dollars seed money." He held up his glass in a toast. "Here's to you, Little Nora."

Little Nora, indeed. She wished she'd put arsenic into his drink as a reward for all his good news. Father John had always called her Little Nora as a child. Pathetic thing, like Little Nell. Little Nora, the Ice-Woman Cometh.

She shivered so obviously Foster said, "Have you caught a chill, Little Nora?"

"No, I was thinking of something."

"Oh? What?" he asked solicitously.

She laughed provocatively. "Couldn't tell you *that*, Father John. Wouldn't want to shock you."

"I'm sure not, Nora," he said primly. His smile said Little Nora could take communion right now, if she wanted to, she wouldn't even need confession.

Indeed, something kept pushing inside her, to tell something, to remove the burden of being good all the time, or leading people to assume she was good. "Where will you be Christmas?" she asked, staring at the amber Scotch.

"In Albany," he said. "I've got meetings with the state treasury people on Christmas Eve, would you believe it? You know, we could meet for lunch Christmas Day, Nora. That'd be nice, like," he added sadly, "old times."

"You did love my mother, didn't you?"

He looked at her for a second, then abruptly nodded. "Yes. You're old enough now, Nora, to absorb this, and, hopefully, to understand. I'll confess something to you." His face lengthened. "I should have resigned my priesthood and married her, Nora. And I regret it."

"Surely not!" Nora exclaimed in alarm. "You couldn't have done that. *She* wouldn't have accepted that."

"Well, maybe not. And then, anyway, it was too late."

Once again, she remembered all the poisonous gossip. "What's the difference?" she asked sheepishly, "if you loved her? And I know she loved you. What difference would it have made if you married her?"

He frowned. "I don't know. I'll leave that to you to figure out, Nora. Enough! Will you come up Christmas Day? Lucia says I'm to have Christmas lunch at the castle, so Oswald won't be lonely."

"Yes." Change the subject, Nora thought. "So, Paul and Lucia are madly in love?"

"Very much so. But Paul was not happy with the way Kurt Morgan treated him, Nora. Partially, he feels, it was your fault."

Her irritation with Jerome grew. "Really? What he's referring to is that Kurt is jealous. Kurt has the idea that Paul was my boyfriend."

Foster's eyebrows rose, though he did always attempt to be worldly. "And this made Morgan jealous? I see," he said ponderously. "Nora . . . are you having an affair with Morgan?"

Nora cried out, "Did Paul say that?"

Foster shook his head, his eyes closed sorrowfully. "No. But one would have to be a fool not to deduce it from what you said."

"Well, I'm not. That's the truth, Father John." She smiled. "Of course, Mr. Morgan tried to seduce me . . ."

Foster's face dropped. "He didn't!"

"Yes, men on his level do that all the time. He tried to get me to take my clothes off."

"But you didn't!"

She dropped her eyes. Her hands were clasped together in her lap on the white robe, fingers twined inwardly.

"I was a little rash," she admitted. "I . . . I don't know how to tell you this . . ."

"Tell me," Father John said, leaning forward.

"Well, I let him see my breast, just one, not both. I hoped it would satisfy him . . ."

And did it?

"Yes. I let him touch the nipple." She raised her eyes, looking directly at Father John. His face had turned beet red. "I let him touch the nipple . . . with his mouth."

"Oh, Nora!" Was that sheer horror in Foster's tone?

"But, Father John, much worse things happened during my engagement."

"Oh, God, did they, Nora?"

"Yes," Nora said tortuously. "He forced me to do unnatural things."

Foster faltered. "Unnatural . . ."

"Yes, he only wanted to make love unnaturally, Father John. Do you understand?"

"I . . . yes, I think so, Nora." He was stricken, as if he didn't want to believe it, was afraid to hear what she said.

"Father John," she confessed, tears forming in her eyes. "He only wanted to . . . do it from behind . . . in my . . ." No, she could not finish. She could not bear it.

Foster trembled. "The savage!"

"And so I broke off the engagement," Nora said, shrugging.

Foster pulled himself together. "I am your spiritual advisor, Nora," he said, seized by an evangelical fervor.

"I know you are," she said meekly, "and my father as well, Father John." Her lips quivered. "Best not to talk about these things," she said firmly. "Tell me . . ." She changed the subject again. "Do you think Paul and Lucia are . . . lovers?"

Reluctantly, he nodded. "I'm sure they are. I'd be naive if I didn't think so. Lucia is very open about it. It's difficult to believe her many Church connections the way she talks." He clucked despairingly. "She had the nerve to ask me for a dispensation so she could sleep with Paul."

"No!" Nora was shocked, and more shocked to hear him say such a thing. "You wouldn't."

174

He snorted. "I *couldn't!*"

Nora exhaled, "Whew! Will you stay in Rome . . . with them?"

Foster nodded. "At the Princess's house on the Via Appia, won't that be lovely? The historical thoroughfare of the pagans."

"It sounds wonderful, Father John," Nora said. "I wish I were going with you."

"Wouldn't that be nice, though, Nora?" Of course, he needn't worry about that. She hadn't been invited for New Year's, had she?

"The Princess . . ." Royalty, too.

"Saltimbocca," Foster pronounced carefully. "She was married to a commoner, as I understand it, a meat distributor who eventually owned the best and most expensive fine-food store in Rome." He chuckled. "Elena is the total opposite—a minor poetess, I gather, and something of a Red."

"You're really in for it then, aren't you?"

He laughed comfortably. Father John was becoming perhaps too serene, Nora thought. There had always been an element about him of vigor, or fervor. By itself the voice was enough to fire a girl's imagination, and that ascetic, monkish face with the cynical, yet loving smile was captivating. Perhaps it was his eyes that were losing their intensity.

He was staring at her now, almost as though he had forgotten who she was. She felt as though pins and needles were sticking in her legs. Nora shifted her position, crossing one leg over the other beneath her robe. His eyes widened.

The phone rang then, just at the right moment, considering the exotic thoughts racing through her mind. It gave her hope that the weekend might yet turn up roses. Kurt? He'd changed his mind and was coming back to the city to be with her.

But it wasn't Kurt.

"Hello . . . Mr. Collins!"

"Yeah, old Buck, who don't give a fuck."

"Mr. Collins!" Obviously, he had only called because he was drunk.

"C'mon, Nora," he said impatiently, "don't give me that shit. You've heard all the words. I don't want to take a lot of your time—you're probably balling or something."

Her lips tightened.

"I'm looking for Paulie," Collins said. "Has he left for Rome?"

"I believe so."

"Shit! How'd *you* like to make a trip to Italy then?"

"Italy!" Everybody was going to Italy! *"With you? I couldn't. Besides, you're going to Texas."*

"Not with me," he barked. "I'm not going to Italy. You! I need some important paperwork delivered to Jerome, and since he's already gone . . ."

Severely, Nora said, "I knew he shouldn't have gone away just at this moment."

"Bullshit."

She ignored that. "Mr. Morgan wasn't very happy about it either, I can tell you."

Collins's voice stung. "Listen, beautiful, you tell Kurt Morgan to shove it. Tell him to quit laying it on Paulie. Paul did a goddamn good job on this—"

"I know that," Nora said faintly.

"Just because Morgan thinks Paulie laid you when you were kids . . . no reason to have it in for him."

"Mr. Collins, please!" She glanced at Father Foster.

But Collins was racing on. "If Morgan tries to get rid of Paulie, you tell him it'll be our first test."

"First test? What do you mean?" Now, she knew he'd been drinking.

Collins snarled, "You don't think Morgan and I are going to live in perfect harmony, do you? A gladiator like me and him, the aging emperor?"

"Aging!" How dare he say such a thing? "You're out of order, Mr. Collins!"

"Didn't I tell you to call me Buck?" He stopped and, sure enough, she heard the tinkle of ice and then swallowing. He *was* drunk. She shook her head helplessly at Father Foster. "Listen, beautiful, you really don't wanna go? It's a free plane ticket to the Eternal City."

"You could air courier as fast," Nora suggested.

"Oh, no. I don't trust this to no commercial courier!"

Suddenly, the solution occurred to her. She smiled at Father Foster.

"Buck . . . I know the most reliable man in the world to carry a package to Italy and straight to Paul Jerome." She nodded at Foster. "Our friend, Father John Foster, is flying to Italy, the day after Christmas . . . aren't you, Father John?" she asked in an aside, and chortled at Collins, "He'll be happy to take the package."

"What!" Collins said jovially. "A priest? Can I trust him?"

"Don't be silly!"

Collins was silent for a moment. Then he said, "Okay, sounds good. No Italian customs guy is going to check a priest's luggage, are they?"

"I hope it's legal, whatever it is," she joked.

"It's legal, all right. Just . . . uh . . . highly confidential so I hope your priest is not going to open it out of curiosity . . ."

"Don't be ridiculous!"

"I'm not ridiculous, Nora," he said curtly. "I'm careful. Where can I find him?"

"He's here with me, right now."

He chuckled. "Then I guess you're *not* balling."

"No." Nora shook her head. "Where are you?"

"I'm up in Connecticut . . . I could bring it down to the city, I guess."

Nora had read a magazine article about his place in Connecticut. It might have been transplanted from the English countryside, with stables, barns, and guest houses on several hundred acres, complete with its own stream and a fish pond which Collins supposedly stocked with trout. And the girls. Three or four female artists or actresses were always supposedly in residence.

"I have an idea," Nora said thoughtfully, for in the end the purpose of the exercise was to go to Texas with Collins. "I'm supposed to go upstate for Christmas lunch with Father John. I could stop in Connecticut to pick up the package and then swing over toward Albany."

"No, beautiful," Collins's voice crackled, "too complicated. Here's what we'll do. I'm coming down for a meeting with Gerry Ball and the Hazard boys on Monday. I'll chopper you back with me and then we'll fly over there Christmas Day. How's that—you're not all booked up, are you?"

"I'll cancel," Nora said. "That would be a very exciting thing to do."

"Hey, good! You're alone and me—we'll have a quiet Christmas Eve here. My kid is with me. Pete and Connie were coming East but they canceled. Pete's feeling lousy, Connie told me today. Dunn finally died. You probably didn't hear yet."

"I'm sorry."

"Don't be. Dunn didn't want to be alive. He was a vegetable but not enough of a one not to know it."

"I'll plan on it then." She smiled at Foster. "It'll be nice to meet your son."

Obviously, nothing inappropriate was going to happen with a child in the house.

He told her he'd let her know when and where to meet him Monday and then hung up.

Nora turned gleefully to Father Foster. Things were definitely going to work out.

"What is it I'm supposed to carry to Paul?" Foster asked.

"Some documents to do with the merger."

"No problem, Little Nora," he said.

"Father John, will you do me a favor? Please don't call me Little Nora anymore."

He looked hurt. "Well, all right . . . Nora."

Her glass was empty. She had drained it while talking to Collins. She hadn't noticed either, that while talking her robe had parted slightly in the middle.

"You're empty too," she said, reaching for his glass. The movement of her legs twisted the robe and she knew that for an instant Father John had seen her shining blond pubic hair, at the soft place where her thighs met. His hand was trembling violently.

Impulsively he stood, threw his arms around her waist and pulled her toward him, thrusting his face between her breasts with such force she nearly dropped their glasses. She felt his cold nose between her cleavage.

"Oh, Father John . . ."

He wept. "Nora, I miss her." His tears were warm against her skin.

She was transfixed, paralyzed, unable to move as he rubbed his smooth, thin cheek on her breast. What he did frightened her, yet it made her so happy that she was almost delirious.

Chapter Seventeen

THE NEXT FEW DAYS RUSHED BY, AS IF NORA WERE ALREADY on holiday, a holiday from reality.

She would never have guessed that Father John Foster had been so distressed by the death of Mary Sweeney until that night, when he submitted himself to Nora's tender sympathy. It had been, she told herself later, close to a religious experience spending all those hours together, praying and talking. And, in the end, Nora felt almost like a sacrificial being, an unbloodied lamb led toward, then away from, the slaughter.

Nora felt good about everything, although she knew there were many people who would have thrown stones at her or branded her a witch and unclean person. But there was so much more to it than that. After all, at stake was the well-being of Father John. And when he'd finally gone back upstate, he'd actually seemed himself again, and better. So, Nora assumed, he had felt good about it too, the poor man, and was now able to bear the loss of Mary Sweeney.

It seemed, as far as Nora could determine, that Foster's relationship with her mother had been totally platonic, regardless of the gossip. But it also appeared that this was something Foster bitterly regretted. Why? Why such a sudden disillusionment with his priestly life? Nora suspected she had somehow served as her mother's proxy; thus, the intimacy, if one would call it that, had been of an ethical sort.

Nora had shown Father John her body, grown now to a splendid maturity that surprised him. As if he were one of God's artists, she had posed for him like the figure of Minerva or Athena or Venus, the goddess of love, upon whom, as Father John had gently speculated, the Catholics had based the purest of them all, the impeccable Virgin Mary.

She and Father John had visited St. Patrick's Cathedral together Saturday night and she was going there again this morning. Until now, it had never occurred to Nora that she could be like the Virgin Mary. Wasn't it true that Mary had never been touched? And wasn't it true that whatever might have happened to her, she had never been physically intimate with a man?

Nora had draped herself in a black, hooded duffel coat for the early morning walk to St. Patrick's. She was so exhilarated she could barely contain her energy. She could not recall a time she had felt so whole, a rampant being far removed from the crowd. People scurried past her against the wind and snow flurries, but Nora did not feel the elements. She blessed the people with her heart and made a mental sign of the cross over their heads in the cold air—God's air, God's people.

Everything was in clear perspective now, all her life, love, ambition, success and all her accomplishments. Not that any of it mattered. For it was now obvious to her that vanity was merely the dynamic of striving.

Nora allowed herself to believe for a few moments that she was the incarnation of the Virgin. Coming into the cathedral, she did not genuflect but went straight to the pew where she and Father John had huddled together. Ahead of her at the high altar a young priest was in the middle of Mass; she watched him critically, following his words, the argument of the Mass. Did he *really* know what he was saying? Probably not.

Above the altar was the cross from which hung Everyman, the spikes in his hands and feet. Nora shivered jealously, the pain of the wounds vivid in her mind. Tears ran down her cheeks. How sad it had been, how awful, how obscene.

Nora gathered her heavy coat warmly around her and abruptly left the church to walk back home. Her head was clearer than it had been before.

Monday was another day, a wonderful day for work since so many people had not come to the office. Nora arranged and carefully studied all the material she'd assembled so far on Eurochemie S.A. Before they were done, she'd need a special secretarial assistant just to deal with Eurochemie. In addition to information available in New York, Eagleye had begun shipping material from Washington—various government reports to which Eagleye had access. It was not her purpose to ask Norm Vincent how they had acquired excerpts from secret congressional hearings and copies of documents which appeared to have originated in Langley, Virginia, home of the CIA. Eurochemie tentacled into every continent and most countries around the world, and what began to emerge was a confirmation of Eurochemie's growing association with the Soviet bloc, through the intermediary of Moscow's faithful Bulgarian satellite.

When the phone rang it was already 5:00 P.M. and Nora had forgotten about Buck. At least, that's what she would have liked to tell herself.

His voice barged out of the phone. "Hey, beautiful, it's too late to fly tonight so what about tomorrow morning early? About seven A.M. at the East Side chopperport, downtown."

"I'll find it," Nora said quickly.

"Every cabbie knows where it is. We could have . . . uh . . . dinner."

"No," she said, lying, "tonight is taken. I'll meet you in the morning." She laughed breezily, the way he'd like it.

* * *

The next morning was cold but not as windy as it had been the previous week. So, Nora thought, Buck shouldn't have any problems about clearance to fly.

At 6:20, Nora was ready. She'd put some things in a Vuitton garment bag the night before; most vital was a festive holiday dress for Christmas Eve in Connecticut. She wondered if Buck had invited some of his rich country friends for drinks. The difficult thing had been to decide what presents to buy Buck and his son. Finally, taking the route of busy people, she'd stopped in Doubleday's on Fifth Avenue and purchased a couple of books, a science-fiction fantasy for the boy and a business manual for Buck. She put the books in her *New York Times* totebag, slipped on her leather boots, and left.

The cab buzzed through deserted streets, reaching the terminal at ten minutes to seven. Nora tipped the driver five dollars and told him Merry Christmas; she called this ransom to the Gods. Nora strolled back and forth, waiting. Buck's hand came down on her shoulder at two minutes before the hour. "You're under arrest, beautiful."

Naturally, his broad face was split by the cocky, big-toothed grin she found so hard to accept.

"I'm crazy about your beret," he cried, "and I'm nuts about you, beautiful. I have a feeling this is where Kurt Morgan gets his."

She smiled silently. What did he mean by that?

"We can go," Buck said. "They just finished gassing her up." Collins picked up the bag. "Let's get the hell back to God's country."

Buck swept her across the icy tarmac, pushed her into the passenger seat of the small helicopter, and leapt in beside her, blowing and puffing steam. He rubbed his hands, waved the ground crew out of the way, and started the ungainly machine.

"We warm her up a little bit," Collins said loudly, as he

studied the dials in front of him. He turned and grinned. "You want a drink?" he yelled.

He was joking; it was much too early and against the law for him to drink when he was flying a helicopter.

The cockpit warmed up quickly and Buck tapped her knee, motioning for her to strap herself in.

It was very exciting, the more so as gravity lost to the engine and the flimsy craft jerked off the ground, hovered for a moment, and then nosed toward the river. Wonderful, how much simpler it was than following a highway. Like a crow flying, Collins would head straight north, up the East River and then, she supposed, when he reached a certain point he would turn right for Connecticut. Just now, the dramatic United Nations complex loomed to the left. Looking back, Nora could see the twin towers of the World Trade Center and, further west, the spike of the Empire State Building and the greenish tint of the Chrysler Building. She spotted Bloomingdale's as they reached the Roosevelt Island tramway.

When Collins looked at her, Nora nodded and beamed.

"Some bird, huh?" He put his mouth next to her ear to make himself heard.

Bird. Chopper. Helicopter. Call it what you wanted, it was a marvel of engineering. Even Leonardo hadn't conceived this flying object, but then maybe he'd never seen a hummingbird.

His head bobbed toward her again. "I said, some bird, ain't it?"

She agreed, nodding violently, but then, in a fright, she realized that what he meant by bird was not chopper or helicopter. Buck had unzipped his trousers and his genital stuck boldly up through the opening of his crisp gray flannels. Her eyes must have bugged in consternation, for he smirked at her and once more yelled in her ear.

"I hear you give the best head on the island of Manhattan, beautiful."

Nora wanted to throw up.

She clamped her eyes shut and jerked away from any

body contact. Tears too heavy to hold back forced themselves past her eyelids. She put her forehead against the cold of the side window and remained like that until he put his fingers under her chin and pulled her head around. He was still grinning like a fool.

"Pig!" She formed the word with her lips, not even taking the trouble to try to make him hear her.

His grin lifted at one side of his mouth. He made no effort to cover himself. It might have been an accident, zipper giving way under the pressure of that thing, but since he didn't show any modesty, she could only assume he'd done it deliberately, to test her somehow.

Trying not to pay any attention to the heavy, arrogantly preening genital, Nora stared at the floor of the helicopter, carpeted around the mysterious pedals and levers. Too bad there wasn't a trapdoor he could drop her through if she didn't do what he wanted. Collins was wearing highly polished leather boots, pointed like cowboy boots, pointed like his head, she thought spitefully. Finally she had to look at him again.

His face was impassive, eyes fixed on the dials on the dashboard where needles fluttered and then, so suddenly her stomach went loose, the helicopter dipped and rolled into turbulence. Nora screamed. Buck looked at her askance.

What did he mean by this? She had to . . . or else? He couldn't be serious, she thought, not while he was flying such a tricky vehicle. Nora frowned stonily and shook her head. Men were such children.

As if he didn't care one way or the other, Collins guided the chopper northward. His mouth pursed in a whistle she couldn't hear above the whirling rotors, the rattle and roar of the engine. Then once more, the machine wobbled. Collins pulled and tugged on the controls to steady it. It seemed to her that he let it yaw and pitch more than necessary. But there was one thing she knew—he wasn't wearing a parachute either, and if they went down, he went with her.

Still, to her puzzlement, Buck made no move to return his genital to where it was cozier, even after it was obvious she was not going to do what he said he had heard she was so good at. And where could he have heard such a thing? He didn't know Norm Vincent.

Nora's heart sank. It must be Kurt who was telling these stories about her.

Nora put her face next to his fat and ruddy earlobe. "Kurt thinks you should take me to Texas with you for the Watson party," she said.

Collins looked astounded and Nora smiled, as if to say, hey, not my idea, buddy. She put her hand on his thigh, close to but a light-year away from the exposed genital.

A sullen pout crossed his face and he half nodded. "Be careful of my pants. I don't want 'em spotted."

She hadn't heard, yet she had heard. She screeched at him, "You *are* a conceited bastard!"

He howled with laughter and sang out so loudly she didn't have any problem hearing him. "Up . . . up . . . and away . . ."

Suddenly Nora sensed the crazy power pulsing through Collins's blood. His face was all hard angles and scowls; then he grinned.

He pointed at her head and howled, "Catch it in your beret, beautiful."

Whatever else happened in the next twenty-four hours, Nora was not going to let Collins forget he'd promised to take her to Texas.

As he cut the motor on a snowy field in Connecticut, Collins sighed, "They're right, Nora, it is the best head in Manhattan."

She didn't even ask who *they* were. She started to say something irate but then decided it would serve her purpose better to be distant. "Please don't mention it. Pretend it never happened, Buck. Say that I was afraid for my life and had no choice."

"Yeah." He laughed and nodded. "Next time . . ." He

pushed open the door on her side. "I guess you're coming to Texas with me, right?"

"Oh—that's nice. Yes, I'd like to very much."

"Yeah," he said glumly, "so you can be up next to Morgan, as usual."

"No. Only for the politics and the good of the company, Buck. I'm just worried . . ." She teased gently, feeling she had the drop on him now. "You never know what clangers you and Morgan might drop. You need somebody with you who's smart enough to catch them before they hit the floor."

"And that's *you?*" he sneered. "Listen, I don't fuck up when it comes to the big deals, Miss Smartass."

"You tend to drink too much." Morgan had made the comment.

"Says who?"

"Says me, and a lot of other people, Buck. For your own good—"

"Hey!" He glared. "Cut that shit out, Nora. Get out of the goddamn plane. I'll show you around the place, if you're interested."

Angrily, he jumped down and came around to help her out. The wind had completely died, and the country air was still, crisp, and clear. Two sides of his landing spot were the neatly trimmed edges of forest with evergreen trees and the deciduous whose branches were bare and spindly and appeared to be freezing. The ground crunched under her feet.

"Beautiful," Nora said. "Brrhhh!"

"Yeah," Collins said, "just like the fucking Holiday Inn, isn't it? Ever seen that old turkey-movie with Crosby?" He turned toward a long, low colonial-style house with white-painted clapboard sides and green shuttered windows. "Is smoke curling out of the fucking chimney? Yeah, and it better be or my housekeeper gets a kick in the ass."

In fact, smoke was curling out of both chimneys, one at each end of the house.

"Come on," he said. He took her arm above the elbow,

so firmly she could count the fingers pressing into the bone, closing off an artery, tingling her nerves. But his touch did not revolt her now, as she had once expected it would. Instead, she sensed the brawn, the power, the ruthlessness.

"C'mon," he repeated, "and we'll take care of the *brrrhhh* with a good stiff one. Drink, I mean." He stopped. "And, listen, no more lectures, Nora. I know I hit the bottle but so would you if you'd led the sad life I have, victim of run-away romance and collision on the road to happiness." His expression became comical. "The way people talk, you'd think I was falling-down dead-drunk all the time. And that's just not true. People say the godamnest things . . ."

That she could sympathize with. "I know. I won't mention it again."

Collins pointed toward other buildings—stables and, to the side of that, a classic barn. "We used to have horses but they eat too much and I couldn't afford 'em. Besides, I don't like the bastards, they're so dumb."

"Yes," Nora said cheerfully, "according to the stories, you moved out the horses and moved in the girls."

He laughed unhappily. "More bullshit . . ."

"Not true?"

"There's been a couple of women living here but they were artists, and that's the God's honest truth, Nora. The last one was named Violet Epstein but she's gone to Europe to research baroque architecture, whatever the hell that is." Just then across the hedges a door banged. "That ought to be my son."

A tall, skinny young man dressed in a long-sleeved shirt ambled toward them. Nora saw that although he was much slighter in body, his face might have been taken from a mold of Buck's. It was square, and the hair, blonder now, would mature into a darker brown like Buck's, and extremely disheveled, which Buck's would have been too without the close cropping. The boy had the same arrogant blue eyes which seemed not quite securely tacked down at the corners.

"This is Josh," Buck said briefly. "Miss Sweeney. . . . Why don't you put some clothes on, for Christ's sake. You're sixteen now. Wake up, kid!"

"Hello," Josh said to Nora.

"Hi." Nora had never decided what she really felt about children. She did know she was happy she wasn't a teenager again.

"Miss Sweeney is a business associate of mine."

Josh blinked. "You had a few phone calls. Nellie wrote them down."

Collins glanced despairingly at Nora. "Nellie is what keeps body and soul together around here."

"One of the calls was California."

"So?" Collins said.

"You don't want to know?" Josh shrugged. He tried to smile at Nora but his lip trembled. "I was going to pull the sled out to the plane so you wouldn't get your feet wet. But you're already here." There was something so plaintive about his voice that Nora felt sorry for him.

"If you'd move your ass faster," Buck growled, "you'd of made it."

"I have my boots on," Nora said brightly. "I'm not wet. Thanks though."

"Well . . . come on in," Josh said. "It's cold out here."

"You noticed," Buck said sarcastically.

Josh spread open the back door for Nora, and, as she passed him, he pressed forward for an instant, bumping her in the boobs.

Nora entered into the smell of cooking, the smell of meat, vegetables, spices and sugar bubbling, a melange of holiday odors. The creator was a big woman in a white uniform leaning on the sink.

"Nellie," Buck said warmly, "meet Nora Sweeney and goddamn but it smells good in here!"

Nellie wanted to know if they were hungry. Buck said

no but they'd go for some coffee and Danish and have it in the library by the tree. Buck was already on his way upstairs to answer the phone calls when Nora shook hands with Nellie and they exchanged a few words about the weather, Christmas, and what she was cooking.

Josh couldn't wait to lead her into the hallway to the other end of the house. "I'll hang up your coat, Miss Sweeney."

"Call me Nora, Josh."

As he lurked behind her, she unbuttoned the duffel coat. Quickly, he lifted it from her shoulders and hung it in a closet next to a door which opened to the library.

This was a lovely, low, beamed room, lined with bookcases. The fireplace was cheery with flame and next to it stood a moderate-sized tree, decorated lavishly, little electric lights twinkling.

"Now that is a beautiful tree," she said. "And you decorated it, didn't you?"

"Yes." His head hung bashfully, then came up. Buck's eyes danced at her. "You're beautiful," he stuttered. "My dad told me you were beautiful. He said if you get the chance, always pick a blond girl."

"Did he now?"

"You know what else he said?" he asked.

Nora shook her head. "No, how could I know."

"He said you should pick 'em built for comfort . . . not for speed."

Nora turned away. "I think I'll sit down for a while." Carefully, not looking at him again, she chose one of the easy chairs next to the fire. It was upholstered in blue and white plaid. Should she be flattered by what Josh said? Was it better to be comfortable than fast?

Josh was still staring at her, totally agog, Nora thought. "I hope . . . please . . . don't tell him I said that," he mumbled. It was barely possible he didn't realize what he had said. But not likely. Kids knew at age sixteen today what she hadn't learned until she was twenty-five and, maybe, hadn't learned yet.

"A beautiful room," Nora observed. She ignored his plea that she not tell on him. That was his problem.

"Shall I bring you something?"

"Isn't . . . uh . . . Nellie getting coffee?"

"Maybe something else. I know how to make you a drink if you want one. It musta been cold in the bird."

By that, she told herself acridly, young Josh surely did mean chopper, not something else.

"The bird was warm enough," she murmured.

No, she didn't want a drink. She'd wait for the coffee. Nora smoothed down her rust-red tweed skirt. Josh had perched on a little wooden stool opposite her and if she didn't arrange herself carefully, he'd be able to look right up her skirt. Were boys *supposed* to be like this? Nora had thought they were merely clumsy, that they tripped over their tongues in sheer terror when they met someone like her.

He turned his face away, blushing. Yes, in fact, he was dying of embarrassment.

"You're good looking," she murmured, smiling at him. She was his friend, that's what she wanted to tell him. "Tall, with lots of muscles."

"Oh . . ." He hugged his knees, perching like an awkward stork on the stool. "I'm wrestling this year in school. They say that's good for your muscles."

"I'll bet it is," Nora said companionably. "I was a tomboy when I was your age. I wrestled all the time."

"I suppose you don't anymore."

"Why, I'm too old?" she teased. "I could still arm-wrestle you, Josh."

"Oh, yeah, I'll bet you couldn't."

"Move your stool over here," Nora said, turning sideways, planting her elbow on the arm of the chair. He placed his elbow next to hers and they clasped hands. Josh smiled and pressed. She could hold him all right, but he was strong. She tried to force him the other way, with a groan of exertion, then chuckled and laughed.

His eyes gleamed. Strange, Nora thought, he was such a

child, but according to the textbooks at this age he was supposed to be at his sexual peak. If they dared, women would all take sixteen-year-old lovers, so innocent, so wholesome, so pure. She could almost taste him on her lips, his scent like raw milk, as voluptuous as freshly turned earth.

The hands wobbled between them. Josh was winning. He slowly pushed her hand downward. She resisted as best she could. She had to turn more in her chair and before she realized it, his taut knuckles were pressing on the downward roll of her breast. His eyes flicked up at her; in them was elation and fear.

Nora laughed, as if nothing was happening. Josh's grip faltered. His strength ebbed and he sighed. Nora took advantage, pushing his hand the other way, over her breast again in a backward caress. She held it there, laughing, her eyes sparkling at him even when she felt his fingers trying to clutch at her soft flesh.

"Josh . . ."

"What?" he said dully.

"I win," she cried. Daringly, she leaned forward and kissed his cheek, then playfully, she thrust her tongue into his ear.

"Oh . . ." What came out of his mouth this time was a full-fledged moan.

Recklessly, wildly, he turned his head and pushed it at her chest.

She could not ignore this. "Josh!"

"Sssh! Sssh!" he whispered frantically. "I didn't mean . . . I only wanted . . . oh, I just want to touch you once . . ."

"Bad manners, Josh," Nora said.

"Now, you're going to tell on me, I suppose." He moved the stool out of range, holding his arms at his waist, hands between his legs.

"No, I'm not going to tell," she said. "I don't understand you."

"I told you—I just wanted to touch one of your . . . you know."

"No, I do not know."

"Tits!" he babbled.

"Oh, my God!" Nora exclaimed softly. "That's what you wanted?"

He stood up. "And I did, didn't I?"

He backed away. He wasn't exactly sure what had happened. Clumsily, staring at her as if she were the life-force, he bounced out of the room and she heard him pounding up the steps, then Buck's voice.

Nora smoothed her skirt and sat back, composing herself. To think, she was going to spend the night in the same house as these two mad creatures.

Collins came into the room, ducking at the threshold, his head barely clearing several of the lowest-hanging beams.

"What the hell's Josh running around for?" he demanded. "Sometimes I think he's hyperactive, the little bastard." He flopped down on the other side of the fire.

"He's just . . . high-spirited," Nora said.

"Yeah, he's like his mother," he said, lowering his voice. "She's nuts too. He goes to school in Boston—that's where she lives. He's supposed to be some kind of an electronics genius." He scratched his head and chuckled. "His mother doesn't know it, but the kid wired her whole house, including the bedroom." His face creased maliciously. "He's got a tape of her balling some Harvard egghead and she doesn't even know it. The little shit!"

Faintly, Nora said, "You love him, don't you? He's precocious. Do you think he's wired this house too?"

"If he comes after blackmail money, let me know."

Restlessly, Buck got up and crossed the room to the liquor cabinet. He poured himself a thumbnail of Scotch, glancing at her, daring her to comment.

"Want one?"

"No. It's not even lunchtime yet."

"I just talked to Connie," he mentioned.

"Oh? How is she?"

He sat down again. "Pete's still feeling down and out. Can't blame him. He's the last of the Mohicans. The Three Mosquitos, they used to call them. They were crazy, Nora, *really* crazy. People say I was crazy as a pilot—but not like those guys. Never mind your astronauts—they're so well trained there's no life left in them."

"You didn't qualify, did you?" she asked frankly. This was not the flattering or perhaps judicious thing for her to say.

"Nope," he said, "I couldn't get in. You know why? I wasn't disciplinable enough—and it showed. I guess if I'd clipped my wings a little I might have made it. They want their astronauts slightly crazy but not really crazy."

"Well," she said, trying to boost his ego, "it certainly didn't hurt you. Their loss, I'd say."

"Would you say that, Nora?" He was not impressed.

Slowly, she inhaled. "Okay, so you have no use for my opinion."

"Did I say that?" he said carelessly.

"I can read you like a book, Buck."

He shrugged scornfully. "Then *read,* beautiful!"

She would make him pay attention. "Luck! If Broadstairs hadn't recognized you as a kindred soul, you'd be flying somebody's cargo plane right now. That's how you got to BBD, not because you understand one damned thing about business."

Buck tried to sneer, not liking her at all. "You hit a pretty long ball, don't you, beautiful?"

Sternly, she continued, "Just remember, *you're* playing with Kurt Morgan now and he's a man who *does* know business."

"Yeah?" His voice became gravelly. "And you know what I say to you, beautiful? Shove it! I can take care of myself."

Coolly, Nora said, "We shall see. One thing for sure—

you're lucky you've got Paul Jerome on your side. He thinks you're the cat's meow."

Collins grinned. "And he's right. Yeah, *what* about Paulie? How long does Morgan plan to keep *him* around? Morgan's got it in for him."

Nora corrected him. "Mr. Morgan is not a petty man and he does *not* have it in for Paul."

He didn't pay attention. "So, tell me, you think Morgan's planning to give me the works too?"

She shook her head. "No, he likes you. He thinks you're a *star*."

"Well, there you go. If Morgan thinks I'm a star, then I'm home free, beautiful."

"Yes, that's so," she agreed slowly, "and if it matters, I think you're really brilliant. You're intuitive—which even Harvard Business School admits has some value." She smiled provocatively. "You're a fast talker and people like being around you. People actually like doing things for you. I wonder why? Is it *charisma?*"

Collins threw his head back and roared a laugh. "Hey, beautiful, what else do I need?" He blew her a kiss over his fingertips.

"Yes, that's right, Buck. But . . ." Nora leaned forward and pointed her index finger at him. "But after you've said that, Buck, you've said it all." Coldly, she continued, "From what I've seen, you've got a short attention span. So when it comes to big negotiation, you're always going to need help."

"So? Do you know anybody that goes into the tiger's cage by himself?"

"Morgan," she answered succinctly. "You're a people person, Buck, not a detail or number person. You don't have the training to be a bottom liner."

"Bullshit. I know bottom liners in New York who talk to the telephone poles," he said. "That's when they're not talking to themselves or stopping traffic and walking on cars."

"All right, don't listen! I'm not telling you these things to be unkind."

"I can hire all the fucking bottom liners I'll ever need, beautiful."

"I'm trying to air out a little reality."

"Thanks a lot," he said irritably. "So I'm a good frontman, a bullshit artist and there's nothing, but *nothing,* behind the bullshit. In a nutshell, right?"

Nora grimaced. "I didn't say that. I said you've got charisma, didn't I? That's worth plenty. In a way, it's invaluable."

"Thanks so much, beautiful." She was dismayed by his look. He seemed so indifferent to her opinion.

"You're welcome. But I see it doesn't matter to you what I think. I'm trying to be a help—if you don't want help, say so!"

"Beautiful," he said, "of course I need help." He grinned. "Don't I need your help to cover up all my inadequacies? Morgan thinks I'm a *star* and with you on my side, I've absolutely got it made."

From dismay, she moved to shock. He expected her to help him, unquestioningly, like everybody who came into contact with him. An arid smile settled into the cleft of his handsome chin.

"I wouldn't go that far," she said tautly.

"You kidding? You've got Morgan wrapped around your finger like a piece of string."

"Not really," she objected.

"The hell! You're balling him—and *more!*"

"No!"

"Well, blowing him then—what's the diff?"

Again, as she had in the helicopter, Nora felt nauseous. It was difficult to find words that would be cutting enough.

"The *diff* is I don't talk in such vile terms, Buck. The *diff* is," she said emphatically, "that I'm not just a weak-willed female. You and all the other men think you've got all the sex drive, that we sit waiting like dumb flowers for some man to come along and sit on our petals." Her disgust boiled over. Nora couldn't remember ever having been so blunt about sex.

Collins didn't try to answer because he couldn't. He lifted his glass again, but it was empty now.

"Have another," she said.

"I will," he mumbled.

She smiled as he got up. He wasn't so bad, basically. He was just a blundering, stampeding herd.

"We *are* going to Texas together," she said, stating the fact.

Collins nodded wearily. Like she'd said, his attention span was short, thus his ability to maneuver severely circumscribed. He didn't understand exactly what had happened. All he knew was that Nora had won that round.

He tried boisterousness. "Hey! Are we going to Texas together? You bet. Nora, I'd sooner go without my asshole than go without you."

She groaned. "You think Junior got all this on tape?"

Chapter Eighteen

IF JEROME HADN'T KNOWN FATHER JOHN FOSTER WELL over the years, he'd possibly not have recognized the priest that morning at Rome Airport.

He'd been watching the arrival crowd off the Pan Am flight from New York for a thin and clerical man in black suit, black homburg and black shoes. But Foster was hatless, his thin gray hair parted neatly in the middle, and he was dressed in dark gray slacks and a blue blazer; an elegant, figured tie lay against a white shirt. He looked, for all the world, Jerome decided, like an itinerant tractor-salesman.

Seeing Jerome, Foster waved eagerly. Jerome took his hand. "You're in disguise, Father John."

"It's merely that I don't like all the attention people shower on you as a priest. People want to carry your bag. I don't need that. I can carry my own bag."

Showing how, he hefted a bulky old black Gladstone bag. It was battered, the smooth leather wrinkled like the skin of a prune.

Walking toward the baggage claim area, Jerome asked, "No problem with customs?"

"I just walked through. I have a feeling the Italians wouldn't take any notice of you unless you were carrying a gun over your shoulder. I hear," Foster murmured, "that the metal detectors aren't even plugged in. I know a priest who walked through wearing a metal brace and it never went off."

"Yeah, maybe," Jerome said. "But not everybody's so relaxed about it. Lucia's mother sent you her car, a Fiat slightly bigger than a soup can—nobody's going to know that broad has money."

"Ah, yes . . . Lucia's mother. What's she like, this princess?"

"She's something else," Jerome replied. "She scares me. She's royal and *very* artistic in temperament."

"A poetess."

"Yes. I can't figure it; the exact opposite of her daughter."

Foster nodded complacently. "Ethereal, I suppose. Lucia is the hard-headed businesswoman."

Not only that. The princess was a good deal taller than Lucia. She was not round like Lucia or as soft and luscious. She didn't look her age, though, which would have been in the middle fifties. The princess was slim and graceful. In her youth, she must have been something of a flapper, for even now, she had an archaic fondness for gin drinks and smoked too many unfiltered cigarettes.

"I guess," Jerome speculated, "Signore Saltimbocca must have been a short, and rather chubby figure of a man."

"Signifying?" Foster asked curiously.

"Signifying that alongside her mother, Lucia is a rank peasant."

"Lucia is flamboyant," Foster said fondly.

"Earthy."

Foster glanced at him amusedly. "Do you sound disenchanted? Why?"

"No, no, hardly," Jerome said. "I like earthy women. She's so unlike the one I was married to," he added. Disenchanted? Hardly. Lucia had breached all his defenses. "I'm completely hooked."

Foster touched his arm, just for a second. "Lucia is a wonderful, happy person, Paul, and you deserve each other. . . . What next though?" he asked.

"I know what you're thinking—we're living in sin."

"About that, I couldn't care less," Foster said, surprising him. "It's just that *eventually* it can be inconvenient. You're staying at the house?"

Jerome chuckled. "I told Lucia maybe I'd better stay at the Hassler but the old lady—I shouldn't call her that, she's like a kid—wouldn't hear of it. She doesn't seem to care either."

"A poetess." Foster sighed. "A free spirit. No, Paul, I really am not worried about you."

"Well, you must be worried about somebody—or something."

Eyes straight ahead, Foster murmured, "Everybody's got to be somewhere . . . in sin or in the faraway state of grace."

"The fifty-first state? You amaze me, Father J., you absolutely amaze me."

Foster laughed. "Nonsense." He tapped the Gladstone bag. "I have something in here for you, a package from Buck Collins."

Jerome nodded. "That figures. How did he find you?"

"Nora . . . found me," Foster said.

Jerome sighed. "Buck is scared to death of paperwork."

"So . . . Nora said. That's why you're such an invaluable man, Paul. To BBD, and next Diversified. And don't forget about the foundation. We'll be counting on you too."

The terminal was chaos. Crowds surged like tides.

Foster suddenly halted. "You know, Nora and Buck flew over to the Gogarty place in his helicopter to deliver me these papers," Foster said. "Oswald and I put a blue sheet out in the snow and they came right down. Wait till Lucia hears about it—she'll want a helicopter for herself. We had lunch and away he soared, like a young god."

"You were impressed with Buck?"

"I was and so is my little girl," Foster murmured. "Nora flew with him up to Connecticut so he could bring her to me in the . . . chopper, with the papers. It was the only convenient way for me to get them."

"Convenient? It sounds inconvenient as all hell to me, Father John."

Jerome *knew* there would be a lot more to it than that. Clearly, Nora had set in motion another of her devious plans. What about Morgan? Something must have happened to make Nora risk life, limb, and virtue with Buck Collins.

However disorganized the airport was, it *was* Italy. Foster gazed about, happiness in his eyes. "Dear boy, so wonderful to be here."

"I trust you brought your uniform," Jerome said. "Lucia and Elena expect to show you off at the Vatican."

"Could we swing by for a look on the way to the Via Appia?"

"We *could*," Jerome said. "It's still there, and the car is so small we could probably drive it right up to the high altar of St. Peter's without anybody noticing."

Foster had to collect only one suitcase, and after they'd gone outside and squeezed into the Fiat—faithful Bruno Belisario at the wheel—Foster clicked open his Gladstone bag and withdrew a heavily sealed envelope. He handed it up to Jerome in the front seat.

"I'd hoped to be spared all this, Father John."

Jerome ripped open the outer seal. Inside, there was a smaller envelope, taped and stapled shut. Obviously no one was going to tamper with this package. It contained legal papers, financial statements, computer read-outs, but strangely, nothing he hadn't seen before. At the bottom of the second envelope there was yet another, also tightly bound with tape. Now what the hell was this?

Tearing one corner, Jerome felt the unmistakably tattered corners of heavy banknote paper. But it was not money. No. He recognized them by weight and smell; they were bonds. But what in holy hell would Buck Collins be doing sending a stack of bonds to Italy?

Jerome smelled trouble along with the musty odor of paper and ink. He closed the envelope and, saying nothing more to Foster, watched the faded green of Italian winter.

Bruno drove fast but Jerome was too preoccupied now to be frightened, as he had been coming out to the airport.

Father John caught his attention. "Paul, do you realize there's a shotgun back here?"

Jerome turned his head and nodded with a smile. "Yeah. Bruno shoots birds. It's his sport. He goes out every Sunday morning."

"Today's Friday," Foster pointed out. "Is something wrong? Nothing bad in the package, I hope."

"Bad?" Jerome smiled back. What could be bad about an envelope full of bonds? "No, nothing bad."

"You're annoyed, Paul. I'm sorry I brought the package."

Jerome was annoyed. He was very irritated. What did Collins want of him now? There was a note there which he'd read later. "It's nothing important," he dissembled. "Some work for me and I'm not in the mood."

The little Fiat clattered over cobblestones alongside the River Tiber.

"Ah, glorious!" Foster's baritone hummed when he spotted in the distance the dome of the most famous cathedral of all. Then he began muttering in Latin, his prayers, no doubt. Foster had never much liked making the switch to English. Jerome watched the priest carefully. There was no way Foster could have gotten into that package ahead of him. What a terrible thought!

The Fiat crossed the river again and then a third time to pass Castel San Angelo, once the Emperor Hadrian's tomb, and raced into the chaos of Via della Conciliazione, built by Mussolini to celebrate truce between Rome and Vatican City.

"Such a treat!" Foster exclaimed. "My Father's house . . ."

Bruno's eyes jumped at Jerome. He was Roman enough to be very cynical about religion and its practitioners. He tooted the Fiat's squeaky horn viciously at a pair of Oriental nuns trying to get across the wide boulevard.

Foster stared quietly at the enormous dome, then said, "That's enough."

"You can go inside if you want to," Jerome offered. "We'll wait."

"No, no." Foster spoke quickly, with some anxiety. "We'd better go on. Lucia will be wondering where we are."

Jerome teased, "Are you afraid, Father J.? Is Big Daddy waiting to bawl you out about something?"

He might have slapped Foster. The smooth face was overcome by a most uncharacteristic blush. "Nasty boy!"

Jerome winked. "I heard you pray in Latin. Isn't that a no-no now?"

Foster frowned. "No, not if you want to, as far as I know."

"Well, let's go then. Bruno? To home!"

"Si," Bruno said, his first and last word on the matter.

Bruno's heavy arms compensated in clumpy muscles for what they lacked in length. He seemed to whirl the Fiat around in midair; in seconds they were clearing the environs of Vatican City. Foster twisted in the back seat to get a declining view of the massive structure, Bernini's colonnade and Michelangelo's wonderful cupola, likely to stand more militantly than ever, far above the muck and mire of the increasing ages.

Once back across the river, Bruno coaxed more speed out of the car than seemed possible. He whipped around the Coliseum and quickly reached the Porta San Sebastiano which opened the way into the old Via Appia. The car rattled on the cobblestones, shaking their teeth.

Fifteen minutes at top speed under the umbrella of stripped, wintry trees projected Bruno Belisario to the spot where he performed his astonishing, virtuoso left turn and stopped within inches of a heavy wooden gate. For one built on the shape of a cube, Bruno moved fast. He leapt out of the Fiat, pushed open the gate, and was back in the car, through the gate, out again and gate shut behind them. He had parked next to a sleek black Jaguar in the brick courtyard. And suddenly, all was silent except for a fountain whose water seemed to chime as it fell.

Foster smiled warmly. "Antiquity. Charming, Paul. I adore antiquity."

The new voice came from the staircase which led up to the second floor of the villa.

"If you love antiquity, then you have come to the right place. You are looking at her."

It was the Princess Elena Saltimbocca. She stood on the third step, fists on her slim hips, grimacing at them. Lucia was beside her.

"Ah," Jerome said. Elena still made him nervous. She was so imperious; she looked like a Roman emperor. "Here we are and this is Father John Foster—I always forget—Monsignor."

"But he is not dressed like a priest," Elena said suspiciously.

"He's traveling incognito," Jerome explained.

"Ha!"

"Hello, Father Foster," Lucia piped up.

"Where's the dog?" Jerome asked. He'd gotten used to Arturo, a hairless boxer with bulbous red-rimmed eyes and slavering slack red lips.

Elena said, with satisfaction, "Dead. He was run over this morning. Finally. Stupid beast, it serves him well, barking at wheels. When the gardener arrived and opened the gate Arturo ran out and attacked a bus. To his regret."

Foster glanced uneasily at Jerome. How could a woman be so heartless about a poor dog?

"The dog was a mess," Elena said, seeing Foster's worry. "He was one of Gogarty's granite dogs."

"How do you do, Princess," Foster finally remembered to say, ignoring the bit about the dog. "It is a pleasure to meet you. I've heard so much about you from—"

"This one?" she asked, jerking her thumb at Lucia. "And what lies has she told about me now?"

"No lies," Foster said warmly, "that you were a wonderful, kind woman . . . and mother."

"Ha!"

Lucia pushed past her. In tight black slacks, and a black sweater Jerome felt put too much emphasis on her breasts, she looked a picture of Via Veneto chic—not that that was so desirable.

Lucia put her hands on Foster's forearms and kissed him on both cheeks.

"Come! Upstairs! It is nearly time for our lunch."

Until he saw them standing next to each other, Jerome was unprepared for the uncanny physical similarity of Elena and Father John. They might have been brother and sister, he thought. He glanced quickly at Lucia to see if she'd also noticed. She nodded as though reading his mind. Her mother and John Foster were two string beans out of the same harvest.

Elena snapped her long fingers as if bringing Foster out of a trance. "This is our home."

"It's beautiful," Foster said. He stared at her as though trying to remember where he'd seen her before.

Elena's voice was deep and hoarse; this came from her smoking, nonstop from morning to night, cheap Italian Nazionales. They reeked and this was her single gesture to the masses, as far as Jerome could determine, though Lucia had told him that her mother often claimed to be a Communist.

"You will call me Elena."

"And you, Princess, I hope will call me Father John— *prego*."

The cornball, Jerome told himself. Did he have to try out his Italian already? Elena spoke English as well as she did Italian, with an Oxford accent. Openly, Elena studied Father John and eventually seemed to give him a provisional clearance. She smiled carefully. Elena's smile could be very dramatic. It accelerated slowly like a heavy car but in the end it was going a moderate speed. At that moment, she looked more like her daughter than she did the gaunt priest.

Both Foster and the princess possessed faces which would have been described as noble—deeply socketed eyes with a philosophical droop of eyelid and the quite distinctive nose of an emperor, Foster's straight like a knife, Elena's vaulted in Caesarean manner. Her mouth was far more sensual than Foster's; there was a tiny cupid's touch to the middle of it. But this was to be expected. After all, Foster had lived the abstemious life while Elena . . . well, there could be no doubt that *she* had lived.

Foster gaped at her.

"I have heard much about you too," she said, "from this one." She gestured at Lucia.

Lucia stirred irritably, moving closer to Jerome. *"This one* does have a name. It is Lucia."

"We know that," Elena said. She did not stop looking at Foster. She seemed to think she'd met him before, too. Without warning, she thrust her hand forward and Foster took it. Jerome would have sworn that volts of electricity passed between them.

"Come," Elena said, "I want to show you my garden."

Holding Foster's hand, Elena led him through French doors and outside to a terrace. The garden beyond was actually less a garden than a wintry forest of old, rotting trees, water-logged bushes, and frost-blackened greenery. Jerome imagined it had been this way since the century before or longer. Local lore had it that Caligula had weekended in a villa upon whose ruins Elena's was built.

"That one," Lucia said sarcastically, "has fallen under the spell of Father John."

"Yes," he drawled, "but much more vice-versa, don't you think? Come along—I have to open this envelope."

Elena's villa spread through several more reception rooms, a dining room, library, and into a modern wing where Elena had placed Jerome next to Lucia.

Her own apartment was in the old side of the house, for

206

Elena liked her privacy. Today was an exception. Usually, they didn't see much of her until dinnertime. Solitude, Elena said, was the jackboot of poetry. She spent the days by herself, reading, writing, and in contemplation.

Lucia adjusted the slats on her shuttered window and peered into the damp garden. "They are walking around the cyprus tree," she reported. "She is gazing at Father John . . ."

Jerome busied himself with the envelope. The bulk of it was nothing that couldn't have waited until he was back in New York. He spread the papers on the bed, then pulled the bonds out again.

"My God!" Lucia cried.

He looked up. "What's wrong?"

"Father John has just kissed my mother's hand."

"So? When in Rome . . ."

"The inside of her wrist!"

She was hysterical, Jerome decided. They were all hysterical.

"Come on, sit down. Leave them alone. You're imagining things."

"I'm not." Grinning, she did sit down though. "There will be trouble there," she said darkly. "*That one* takes delight in debauching priests."

"Ridiculous. Look!"

She looked. "Ah ha! What have we here?"

She watched as he smoothed out the crinkly paper. The bonds, each in a denomination of ten thousand dollars, had been issued by Brown, Broadstairs and Dunn when BBD had first gone public back in the fifties.

"What we have here," Jerome said unhappily, "is a whole stack of bearer bonds . . . and a note from Buck Collins." He read to himself. "Shit! He wants me to put these in a safe place. He says, with *your* connections, you should know where."

"The question is, where did they come from?"

"I haven't the faintest," he said, and began to count. He did them in groups of ten and ended up with eight piles. That made eighty bonds in all, he calculated dully, $800,000 worth. These could only represent money Buck had been squirreling away over the years and which, for some unknown reason, he didn't want in the country at merger time. It made no sense. Perhaps he was hiding them from one of his former wives—that made more sense.

"Well," Lucia shrugged indifferently, "we can give them to my . . . finance ministry, in Milano."

"Your Bank of the Sacred Heart of Jesus?" Jerome asked. "I'm telling you—I've never heard of a bank with a name like that."

Icily, she said, "Would you prefer something like the Vatican First National, Paolo?" She made a displeased face. "Mr. Collins trusts you enormously if he sends you so much money to hide for him."

"He does trust me. It's kind of nice to be trusted by *somebody.*"

She frowned. "Now you say *I* do not trust you?" Lucia stared at him. "You are sure you and Buck are not in partnership, swindling poor little old ladies?"

"Sure, sweetlips."

Impatiently, Lucia jumped up and went to the window.

"What's wrong? Why are you mad?" he asked.

Without turning, she said, "Who is this man that so easily passes over such a burden, such a responsibility?"

"Buck Collins," Jerome said. She was right and he didn't feel well about it. "He takes it for granted I'll take care of it. I'm sorry."

She shook her head, staring down into the garden again.

"My God," she cried.

"What now?"

"They are still walking around the cyprus tree," she said. "Is it not time for lunch? *Please?* I fear for Father John."

"It wouldn't be the first time a man of the cloth was led down the garden path," Jerome said.

"One does not have to be a man of the cloth to be led down the garden path, Paolo."

Depressed, he dropped back on the bed and put his hands over his eyes. "All right, Lucia. I know what you're saying."

"Yes. You let yourself be used too easily. How does this man have the nerve to think he has only to ask to use my connections to hide away his money? I have never even met Buck Collins."

"Lucia," Jerome said coldly, "forget it. Don't bother yourself about it. I wouldn't use your connections anyway. I have just a few of my own, you know."

"No! We will go to Milano. I must consult with Jean-Jacques Morel on other things and at the same time we will take care of Buck Collins, have no fear," she said.

"And who's Morel?"

"My man at the *banco,* an astute but decadent northern Italian. He was Gogarty's banker too, a master of the shady deal."

"He sounds wonderful," Jerome muttered, "just the man to pass some securities."

"He would not dare . . ." She flared. "His life would not be worth one penny if ever he played loosely with another's money. They would mercerize him—"

"Or vaporize?"

"Either . . . or," she said. "Good God! Now they are coming back and it is my mother I fear for."

"You needn't be worried about Father J. He's the soul of propriety."

"Yes, like J.J. Gogarty no doubt. Even in his Vatican regalia he used to pursue nuns. The German ones were best for him—you know how they love uniforms, Paolo."

"Lucia, forgive me, but why did you ever marry Gogarty, knowing what a horrible creature he was?"

"But that was *before* we married," she replied simply. Lucia then hurled herself on the bed, grabbed Collins's bonds and threw them into the air. She fell on Jerome, atop the crackling bonds. "Kiss me. You don't believe a thing I tell you."

She pressed him down with her body. It was like being crushed by a soft cushion. Inspired, Jerome forgot about Buck Collins, the bonds, Father John and Elena. He touched her caressing lips with his own and she went limp on top of him. Her mouth was warm and sticky, with an aftertaste of espresso. Jerome slipped his hand under the tight sweater; she wasn't wearing a brassiere. Lucia moved so he could stroke one breast, bringing the nipple to a peak. She breathed out slowly. He slid his hand under the elastic waistband of her slacks. No panties! His fingers slipped down the cleavage, feeling the dampness. He murmured to himself, in a half-daze. By the time he reached her crotch, the heavy black hair was moist, the inner lips wet and slick. Her belly jerked when he ran his finger over her clitoris. It seemed as though her eyes changed color, from serenity to desire.

"Take everything off, Paolo, quickly, now. I must—"

"No lunch?" he whispered. Pressing against the spot, she moaned and moved away, refusing to climax that way. Recklessly, she squirmed out of the slacks and, before he could move, unzipped his pants, yanked them down to his hips. With a frantic heave she took him inside. She crossed her legs over his buttocks, scissoring him tightly, catching his thrust. She took her pleasure quickly, lustfully, and Jerome was soon gone. A moment later Lucia cried out sharply.

Her heart was beating wildly, but slowly she calmed.

The scent of their coupling was strong, an exotically perfumed rawness, a rawness of creation.

Chapter Nineteen

THE ORGAN BOOMED, THE VOICES OF THE CHOIR RANG CLEAR-
ly, and a thunder of music seemed to take the nave of St.
Peter's by the neck and shake it. Clouds of incense
billowed up into the cupola two, three hundred feet above
the thousands of people in the Sunday morning congrega-
tion. St. Peter's held them all comfortably. Mass was in
progress, and down the main aisle, it might have been a
half-mile away, Jerome spotted the scarlet skullcaps of
several cardinals.

As he had before at the mere sight of the dome, Foster
sighed almost despondently.

"Paradise Point was pretty rinky-dink compared to this,
wasn't it?" Jerome asked.

Foster frowned as if he had a stomachache. "No one
ever expected St. Peter's at Paradise Point, did they?"

He was in his clerical garb, the first time he'd put it on
since arriving in Rome. Somehow, Jerome thought, Foster
didn't look comfortable now in the round collar and
dismal black suit. But one would have thought Rome was
the place where a priest would be happiest in proper dress.

The voices lofted again. Jerome could feel the music
reverberating against the ornamented stone, a complete
universe hundreds of years in the making, decorated and
redecorated by generations. It was a monument, and work
upon it could never end, for that would spell completion.
No, ever more piety, tradition, history would be layered

211

on like smoke from scented candles, new saints would be nominated, old ones busted, new popes voted and old ones laid away within the stone catacombs down below.

It had never been difficult for Jerome to understand that the Church was all about power, sheer rock-hard power; and inside the cathedral, buffeted by the music, breathing the incense, feeling the pulse of the faithful, this sense of power was very strong. It was a power without equal and whether you liked it or not, its basis was a people's faith, as strong as it had ever been, despite science, plague, and war.

"Well?"

"From here," Jerome said, "it looks like the main altar is on fire. You never used incense so lavishly, Father John."

Foster chuckled. "Never discount the show-business aspects, my boy."

There was little levity in his tone. Again, to Jerome it seemed that since arriving in Rome Foster had been at odds with himself. Meeting Elena had obviously not been a calming experience for him.

In a few minutes, they were to meet Elena and Lucia to pay a visit to Elena's first cousin, Cardinal Ottavio Avia, who lived in the Vatican. Jerome knew they wanted to look *him* over. Who was this Jew who dared to kiss the hand, and more, of the fair Lucia Gogarty? Was he man, beast, or devil that Lucia should be so enamored?

But it was Foster who seemed most nervous. He stared disconsolately down at the ancient paving stones, as if Ecclesiastes had just tapped him on the shoulder. Vanity: How many feet had trod on these and to what avail?

Jerome yanked him back to the present. "Tell me, Father, was J.J. Gogarty such a monster?"

Foster barked at him. *"In no manner.* J.J. Gogarty was an important man to the Church. Do you suppose the Pope, in all his wisdom, his God-given intuition, would make a *satyr* a Papal Knight?"

212

"It doesn't seem likely, does it, given that the Pope is infallible?"

Foster peered at him. "Not mocking, I hope, my son." He glanced quickly toward the altar, then admitted, "It is true Mr. Gogarty had need of a confessor." Finally, he admitted Gogarty was not a saint and felt awkward about it. "But he was human, after all, Paul, and he had human weaknesses." He stopped in confusion, then impulsively continued, "I must go home, Paul. I don't know what's happening to me—my spiritual resolve, it seems to be *waning*. And of all places, in Rome. It doesn't seem possible. The city of my dreams, the church of my fondest . . ."

Jerome considered what he could say. "Rome . . . it's always seemed to have a . . . pagan ambiance, even with the big church here. What . . . *has* happened to you?" Again, he knew. Lucia had already put it forthrightly. Elena was a dangerous threat to the integrity of John Foster.

The priest looked at him worriedly. "How should I explain? As you know, my son, our dogma is based strongly on the Platonic philosophy . . ." Thinking aloud now, he threw back his head and gazed upward at the dim vaults of the ceiling. "I . . . uh . . . don't know what to say."

"Hey," Jerome said playfully, "if it's philosophy, buddy, you're in the right place."

"No joke," Foster replied seriously. "Listen—in Plato's *Symposium* there's a discussion of the true aspiration . . . aim . . . of human love. The basic drive of the human spirit, love, is for completion. You see, the human being seeks, ceaselessly, for the other half of the whole. Seldom is this 'other half' found. When a man uses the expression 'my better half,' it's to this he's referring. That's the tragedy which makes for the 'human comedy,' since comedy is the other, perhaps better, half of tragedy. Do you see?"

Jerome nodded. "Of course. You're telling me that Elena is your other half."

"I feel so," Foster said.

"Lucia and I noticed as soon as you arrived. You two fit perfectly. You look alike. You were mated right there in the living room before our eyes."

Foster shifted uncomfortably. "Not exactly, Paul. It doesn't have to be sexual union. You realize that?"

"Sure, sure. But is this a reason to leave town?"

Foster's look was bleak. "Yes. I can't stand it, Paul. My vows . . ." He wrung his hands; knuckles cracked.

"But, as you say," Jerome offered unconvincingly, "Platonic love—"

"Yes, yes, but not enough, Paul! The thrust and drive is there. I can feel it very powerfully. So can she."

"My God." Jerome put one hand on Foster's black sleeve; he wanted to tear off the crisp white collar.

Listlessly, Foster shook his head. "That's why I've been so preoccupied the last couple of days." Jerome noticed there was perspiration on his forehead. "You knew about Nora's mother?" He laughed bitterly.

"I only know what people said," Jerome muttered.

"I told Nora I was sorry I hadn't resigned the priesthood years ago. I should have, Paul," he said miserably. "I'm a bad priest."

"No," Jerome said quickly, "you're a good priest because you're human."

Foster looked into his eyes. He wanted to be scourged, somehow punished.

Jerome glanced at his watch. "Come on. Let's go outside."

He turned to go but Foster grabbed him by the arm. "I want to tell you . . . wait."

"No! Come on! Don't tell me, whatever it is." He pulled away. "I know the answer anyway. *No* is the answer. Don't tell me otherwise."

Jerome headed for the light at the end of the cavernous church, the door which opened into St. Peter's Square.

Thankfully, he burst into the open air. Earlier, it had been gray and gloomy, a continental weather front submerging the peninsula, but now the sun was trying to slip through the curtain of damp mist.

Lucia and Elena were standing beneath the curving colonnade, waiting. Elena had the gift of absolute stillness; she stood rooted, at perfect rest. Not Lucia; she was restless, a fidgeter by nature. Mother and daughter were dressed modestly; the only touches of class were the Valentino scarves at their necks.

Now they clattered toward Jerome on their high heels. Foster lagged behind, not comforted or reassured. Jerome was sorry about that. But it was not in him to pass judgment.

A soft perfume seemed to surround them. Lucia shone; there were lights under her skin. And Elena looked golden and porcelain. There was much Etruscan here, Jerome thought.

"Hello," Elena said to Foster.

He seemed almost to melt physically. She touched his arm in greeting, and Foster reacted as if her hand had been a hot poker.

"So nervous, John, man of the Church?" she teased.

"We've been waiting for you," Lucia said. When she smiled at Jerome, he had to admit he felt almost as unraveled as Foster.

But he had the advantage. He already knew Lucia intimately, so he couldn't be intimidated by terrible want. He had lusted and been released, whereas it could be said that Foster lusted to no avail. Poor man. Jerome hoped that he would have the nerve to violate his vow.

The four proceeded to the left wing of the Vatican palace. Above here was the papal apartment and the window from which the world watched the Pope bestow his blessings. Other important Church officials and dignitaries lived here also, amid a maze of offices and reception rooms. It was a beehive, made for behind-the-stairs intrigue. Briskly, Elena led the way, Foster a step behind her, and then Lucia and Jerome, she with her arm boldly set in his.

"I am afraid for Father John. He looks miserable. Is he ill?" Lucia said.

"He's in love," Jerome muttered. "And you look like you're enjoying it very much."

"Should I be tearful then?"

Elena had no problem gaining admission to the inner sanctum. Obviously, she'd been here before. A fresh-faced monk escorted them along corridors and through courtyards, until, finally, they reached Cardinal Avia's quarters.

Given the apartment shortage in the Vatican, it could not be a surprise that Elena's cousin's place was small and overfurnished. Of two rooms, one was a bedchamber and the other a sitting room. The sitting-room walls were lined with a heavy red- and gold-threaded fabric; a stiff horsehair-stuffed divan was covered in a burgundy damask. Occasional tables were laden with newspapers, magazines, and books. The floor was bare stone, however, and on the opposite wall was a lifetime collection of papal portraits and photographs. Some were signed. And at one end of the room, a small dining table had been laid for five.

Cardinal Ottavio Avia was the very picture of a Curial cardinal. He was dressed in a stylish black cassock with the distinctive red sash at his waist, gold chain with cross on his chest, and the scarlet-purple skullcap atop his head, circled with a halo of white hair. His eyes were deep like Elena's and set in a long-suffering face.

Avia nodded first to Foster, who seized the cardinal's hand for the ritual kiss of the ring.

"Ottavio," Elena said.

"Yes, Elena," the cardinal said, in English.

"Father John Foster," Elena said. *"This one,* as you know, is my daughter, Lucia."

"Yes, yes," Avia said, "of course." His eye switched to

Jerome. It was *that one* he really wanted to meet. "Poor Lucia," he mused. "Widow of the Irish person who astonished everyone with the noises he made during the holy processions."

Elena laughed and nodded.

"Mr. Paul Jerome, the American."

The blue of Avia's eyes seemed to deepen as he extended his hand to Jerome to shake.

"It is nice of you to come," Avia murmured.

"I'm very pleased at the opportunity."

Avia smiled distantly.

"May I offer you a refreshment before we lunch, my friends?"

Promptly, Elena said, "A very dry martini."

Avia snapped his fingers and a boy-monk appeared. Avia took the rest of the drink orders. Except for Elena, vermouth was the drink of the day.

"May I smoke?"

"Of course. And I will join you," her cousin said.

Elena hauled out a pack of her vile brand and Avia's nose curled. He offered her a filtered Marlboro but she declined. A match was lit and their smoke spread through the little sitting room.

"Please . . ."

Avia was a completely self-assured man. Why shouldn't he be? He was one of the key men in the Vatican establishment. He had started his career as a Jesuit priest but nonetheless had remained a member of the conservative wing of the Church. Avia perched next to Elena on the stiff divan. He looked like a faded debutante when he drew on the cigarette.

"Cheerio!" Elena was making it very clear to everybody that she made no concession to her cousin's high office. And it was high. Avia was something of a Papal trouble-shooter, she had informed them, one of the Curia's main men on financial affairs. "Ottavio," she added in a spritely way, "it was so hospitable of you to ask my American friends today."

"Do you often come to Rome, Monsignor?" the cardinal asked.

Ah, Jerome told himself, the cardinal had been briefed about Foster.

"No, your eminence, unfortunately not more than once every five years. These visits are the very high points of my existence," Foster replied.

Elena looked annoyed.

"And now, my cousin tells me, you come with a view of establishing this—*John Joseph Gogarty* Foundation." He made no secret of it—Avia had detested Gogarty.

"Well . . . yes." Foster apparently hadn't expected to discuss his foundation today. "I had intended to make an appointment, to inform the Curia, the proper authorities . . . to ask for their opinion, advice . . . and blessing."

Avia frowned impatiently. "No need. I will speak *for* them. We will want a complete report on monies, financial planning, and projections, Father, and on a continuing basis."

Foster seemed confused. "Well . . ."

Avia leaned forward intensely. He looked at Foster, then at Lucia. "I believe your foundation will have considerable funds at its disposal."

"Oh, yes." Foster nodded uncomfortably. He seemed reluctant to commit himself to Avia. Jerome could understand why. The J.J. Gogarty Foundation had been Foster's baby and now an Italian cardinal, a total stranger—in fact, the Vatican version of bottom liner—was demanding to monitor the action.

"The foundation," Avia insisted, "it will be financed by investment dividend?"

"And bequests, yes," Foster muttered. "We will be a tax-free institution." He became more confident. "It is too early to say how big—or small—our annual disposable income will be."

Avia's face was even more lined and furrowed than John Foster's.

"I see," Avia said. "You must come to my office, Father

218

Foster. Tomorrow, let us say? Would ten A.M. be convenient?"

"Of course, your eminence," Foster replied. His head was high, but at the same time he was not ready to disobey a direct order.

It was Lucia who objected. "Cousin Ottavio, tomorrow we planned to drive to Milano for a meeting at the *banco*."

"Ah!" Avia's eyebrows were so thin Jerome wondered if he plucked them. They rose, as significant on his forehead as skywriting. "You will see . . . our *friend*, Jean-Jacques Morel?"

Lucia nodded. She had caught something in the manner of his speech, something not of a comfortable nature, perhaps, for Signore Morel.

The cardinal turned back to Jerome. "And you, Mr. Jerome, I'm told, will be giving Father Foster investment advice from time to time?"

Jerome shook his head modestly. "I'm sure that Father John is not going to need any help."

"Perhaps not help. But surely advice," Avia said. But again his expression took on a holy sourness.

"Paul is the chief financial officer of one of our major electronics companies," Foster explained.

Avia nodded. He seemed bored. "I know. Brown, Broadstairs and Dunn, called BBD, now in merger discussions with Diversified Technologies." He stared smugly from one to the other—see what a sly dog I am!

"I'd be happy to offer advice when asked," Jerome said, perhaps too stiffly for the occasion. He had the impression Avia was aiming at him. "But foundation work is not my forte."

"Of course," the cardinal said. He seemed to be considering another remark but repressed it. Back he went to Foster and then came the bombshell. "You would, of course, wish to be released from your diocesan duties, Father Foster."

Foster's face froze, his hard-earned wrinkles massed in amazement. He could not speak. Very obviously, he had not expected this. Why *should* he be released, Jerome thought, and Foster must have been asking himself the same thing. Foster turned his head to stare at Elena and she, uncharacteristically, lowered her eyes.

"I would be . . ."

Avia stared at him. Was this the perfect punishment Foster had been requiring for himself? "You will have the permission . . . the approval . . . of authorities here, Father Foster, if you wish to tender a resignation . . ."

"From the priesthood?" Foster stuttered, his voice a wheeze. "From my vows?" His eyes teared.

Elena's fingers were so tensely wrapped in each other, they turned white. She stared at them, absolutely still.

"Yes," Avia said simply, firmly.

"Have I somehow . . . offended . . ." Foster was tied in knots, his face quivering with emotion.

"No, no! It is to do with discipline, Father Foster. If you are to manage a large sum of money, it is best for you to be a . . . civilian," Avia said. "That way, there is no fear or favor on your part." Avia laughed like a mongoose. "If I told you to buy IBM, you would have to obey, were you a priest." He lifted his manicured hands, splayed the fingers persuasively. "As a civilian, you would say, Avia, crazy fool, please mind your own business! You see?" Avia laughed briefly, unmelodiously. Singing the Mass with him would be a job, Jerome thought spitefully. His laugh was high-pitched and cackly. "Yes, come in the morning, Father Foster," he said. "We will set it in motion." Briefly, Avia shot a look at his cousin and Jerome knew without a doubt this was Elena's idea. She wanted this poor priestly man for herself.

"Likewise, for you, sweet Lucia, a word of . . . a note of caution, an advisory. I do not wish to be definite. With Jean-Jacques Morel, *go carefully*." He smiled to himself, the thin eyebrows somehow set in a wavy motion. "I tell you no more."

Great, Jerome thought. Lucia had already admitted Morel was a master of the fast shuffle, and now a cardinal of the Church was warning them to go carefully with this servant of The Bank of the Sacred Heart of Jesus.

"And now, my friends," Avia said cordially, rising, smoothing his black skirt and adjusting the sash-of-office, "it is time for luncheon. Come, come, Father Foster," he chided, chuckling. "Why! The man is in an absolute daze!"

Chapter Twenty

THE JAGUAR IN THE COURTYARD OF PRINCESS ELENA'S house was the mate of Lucia's in New York. Not lingering to hear the results of Father Foster's meeting with the cardinal, Lucia drove Jerome to Milan the very next morning.

They arrived at the Principe i Savoia, a hotel of tarnished elegance down the boulevard from the monster railroad station, Stazione Centrale, in time for lunch.

"Here it is," Lucia told him, "where I played with the beautiful people, before I was given my position with the Vatican Library. We sat here so often, Paolo, joking, laughing, and gossiping."

"I suppose this is where you hung out when you were making your great movie," he said.

She laughed. "That doesn't matter. We were all so innocent."

"The hell you were," he said darkly. "You were decadent."

"No, no." The waiter saved her. "Let us order lunch, Paolo. I am very hungry. What will you have?"

"Veal *Milanese*," Jerome muttered. "What else?"

"Don't be rude." Lucia smiled at the waiter fleetingly. "I will have the same and spinach . . . *spinachi* . . . and some potatoes and bread and a bottle of Chianti. Yes?"

"Yes," Jerome said, "okay." He studied her. Then, acidly, he said what he'd wanted to say all day yesterday. "Your cousin, the cardinal, was a pain in the ass."

Momentarily, she looked perplexed. "I will not argue

with you. But he has an interesting side—he keeps a mistress in Salerno."

He couldn't hate her, could he? He couldn't but admire and love her, could he? When the wine had arrived and been tasted and poured, he lifted his glass. "I drink to you, Lucia Gogarty. I haven't asked you this before and I do so now with some jocularity, meaning I'm not altogether serious, but would you like to add another name to your string to make yourself none other than Lucia Jerome?"

"No . . . no . . . too many names," she said. "My suitcases, you see."

Elena had kept the flat in Milan for some years. It was the remnant of her marriage. The apartment was located in a modernized palace in the old sector of the city, roughly in the triangle of stone and rock formed by the Piazza Cavour, La Scala, and the Duomo, or main cathedral. A garage had been excavated from under the building without disturbing its ornate stone exterior. Appearance was only one-tenth of the battle, for behind the shutters and heavy drapes more than modest wealth was hidden. The place smelled desolate when they stepped inside, but Elena came here so seldom that no regular help was kept on the premises. Lucia opened shutters and windows on the interior court of the building, and cold fresh air blew away the staleness.

Jerome saw that the spacious rooms were nearly as overloaded with art of various types as Lucia's place in New York. There might be even more of it here, in fact, because the rooms were so much bigger.

He stared and Lucia chuckled. "It is . . . my business," she said rapidly. "You see, friends . . . well, they sell to me and then I bring the things out of the country, some to London for auction, to New York for private clients. It is not easy, you know, to get these things out of the country. Connections are necessary."

"So I've heard," he said.

"And the terrorists, so many, Milano abounds in them."

"I didn't see a single one at lunch."

"Ha! At the hotel. You are *kidding me,* no?" She pulled him along after her. "Don't look at these things. None are very good, or worth very much. You see . . ." Lucia stopped and faced him, breast rising and falling, face wreathed in a clever smile. "You see, it is a good market in America. If the picture looks old and is dusty and has a heavy frame, preferably gilded, then I can sell it for a great deal of money."

"Scoundrel," he said. "As I thought, you're running a racket, aren't you?"

She shook her head vehemently but didn't stop grinning. "I do not twist their elbows, Paolo."

He eyed her warily, not knowing whether he should approve of her cleverness or tax her for being a crook. "How many of your old masters were produced in the last twelve months?"

"Ah, do not ask, sweetheart," she cried delightedly.

"I'll turn you in, Lucia."

"No you won't, beautiful man." She tugged at him again. "Come along."

She showed him the rest of the apartment: another large reception room connected to the foyer, leading to a huge dining room, all furnished in an eclectic mix of heavy oak, blond veneered French-replica pieces, and overstuffed neo-Victorian armchairs, couches, loveseats, footstools, and antimacassars. The light fixtures must have been produced in the age of Edison, and there were hundreds of pictures and clocks of every description. Had *this* been to the Saltimbocca taste? Jerome asked her. Lucia laughed merrily, for the Saltimboccas had no taste. They'd been in meat since the days of Garibaldi. Her mother's family, on the other hand, went back forever.

"But you should not be impressed by that," she warned. "You must judge me on my own merits."

"I will. I'm watching you carefully and giving you marks," he said.

Eventually, they reached the bedroom. "The marital chamber of my mother and father," Lucia announced.

She squeezed close to him and kissed him on the mouth in such a way it seemed like the first kiss. And this made him realize for some reason that the marital chamber, unlike the other rooms, smelled faintly of lilacs, also of garlic. Perhaps not so oddly, it was extensively mirrored, a hint at the aspirations of Signore Saltimbocca, or the upper-class decadence of Elena.

"What did I say about the *dolce vita?*"

Lucia laughed unsteadily, as if smitten by his charge. She hung to him, pressing her softness the length of him.

"My father was a short man and short men love to see themselves in mirrors," she explained.

"Your mother, though, is a tall and handsome woman. She gave you stature."

"Yes." She shrugged. "Think how incongruous it must have been in this room. But with small men there *are* compensations, according to Mama. Small men, she told me, are very dainty and delicate. I think one reason Mama never became very fond of my husband was that he was by no means delicate in any way." She shook her head pensively. "But someone had to marry him so he would not become an out-and-out atheist and leave the papal knighthood and his money to another cause."

Jerome couldn't bring himself to answer at once. "I would like to talk to you, very seriously," he finally said. "There is altogether too much of a surrealistic feeling about all this."

"Yes, I would like to speak to you too," she said.

Just beneath the surface of her throat, a nerve of desire pulsed and throbbed, from deep inside her. She breathed so deeply that he put his hand on her belly, grateful for the reality of that. She sensed his concern, for her body shifted, reaching for him.

"Do you mind," he asked, "if I do this now?"

She gasped with pleasure. "Of course, anything you wish." Her eyelids dropped languidly, opened wide with anticipation, and then closed sensuously. "There is also

225

something I want you to do now. It is a thing of the utmost necessity, Paolo. Do you understand?"

"I think so," he said.

She seemed to recede to the bed. He sat down beside her and she leaned back. He kissed her solemnly on the lips, teasing them with his tongue. Lucia was actually transported by mere kisses, Jerome had discovered. All he had to do was kiss her.

"I seem to have something crawling inside my panties, making me very itchy. Do you think you could help me find it?"

"I think," he whispered, "that you would have to remove your fashionable clothes and accessories first, Mrs. Gogarty."

"Oh, yes, Paolo."

Jerome could not decide whether Jean-Jacques Morel was more or less sinister than he had expected. He did not detect death in Morel's handshake but on the other hand he could believe that here was a man waiting for death, a man who would not be surprised by death, and a man who might even welcome it.

Morel's voice was chipped, reedy. In Italian, it sounded whole enough as he ordered them aperitifs in the Savini restaurant in the Galleria. But his English had been cleaned of all unnecessary inflection. Jerome made a mental note to tell Lucia later that if a snake could talk he would talk like Jean-Jacques Morel.

When they were settled, Lucia said nervously, "Signore Morel is the man who will be in charge of the European side of the foundation. Some funds will be channeled through the Banco Sacre—"

"Of which I am vice-president for international," Morel announced.

"Yes. I understand," Jerome said.

But it had nothing really to do with Jerome. About bankers, or the care and feeding of same, he knew as much as he could ever want to know.

"Under my aegis," Morel added boastfully, "are investments in every foreign land." He smiled. "We have done some in your company, Brown—"

"Broadstairs and Dunn? Really?" Jerome interrupted quickly. He did not want Morel to know that he was already informed by Lucia. He didn't like this man. Intuitively, he didn't trust him, not because he spoke like a snake but because of the evasive eyes and the film of perspiration that appeared on his upper lip as he spoke about investments. Morel was up to no good; Jerome instantly remembered Cardinal Avia's not very veiled warning. The real question popped into focus: Was he to arrange to hand Buck's bonds over to this very greasy individual?

Uneasily, Lucia said, "Our plan was to have Father Foster with us today."

"No, not necessary," Morel said self-importantly. "I will see the priest in Rome, as ordered by Avia." He bobbed his head deferentially. "It is best we talk on neutral territory, if you take my meaning, Mr. Jerome. But it is a simple thing . . ." He stared past them, slyly, Jerome thought, as if to watch the promenaders in the Galleria. "J.J. Gogarty—one of my dearest old friends. *Such a man!*"

Lucia nodded.

"It'll be a handy little enterprise," Jerome observed, "tax free, don't forget."

"Oh, yes, the foundation. But not the supporting corporation."

"Also the corporation, in effect, if all the profit goes to the foundation," Jerome pointed out.

Morel smiled, and if a snake should chance to smile, Jerome thought, he would smile much like Morel did.

Jerome wondered again what this Gogarty Foundation was all about. Why did Lucia have to be so heavily involved? She'd promised Foster the seed money, yes, but after that? Why this pointless meeting with Morel without Father John being present?

About Morel there was only one thing Jerome had to decide. "Signore," he said slowly, "is your bank—hypothetically—able to dispose of American securities?"

Morel wet his lips and nodded, eyes darting. "But of course," he hissed. "I would handle such a transaction . . . personally. These securities would be . . . ?"

"*Possibly,* some bearer bonds."

"On which company?" Morel asked, voice oily. His eyes flitted, trying to measure Jerome's jacket. Had Jerome the bonds on him? Was there a gun at his armpit? His lips trembled, and Jerome realized that Morel would not have been very surprised either way, bonds or a .38. "I could accept them . . . tonight."

"I said *possibly,*" Jerome reminded him. "Would you have any problem selling them off, say in Geneva?"

Morel moved his shoulders in an unconcerned shrug. "Depending . . . on how much . . . in various places. For the usual commission." Again he licked his lips. "Would they be of the BBD variety?" he asked softly.

"That is also possible," Jerome muttered. To do, or not to do. "You would open an account to accept the proceeds?"

"Yes, of course," Morel said. "In whose name?"

"It would be numbered," Jerome replied. Saying this made him nervous. It was the first potentially dangerous thing he had said so far.

"Ah . . ." Morel breathed out dramatically, as if to say he'd gotten the message—that he would be dealing in problematic property.

"Nothing of an unusual nature, is it?" Jerome asked sharply.

Morel shook his head. "No, not in Europe. But not exactly . . . accepted procedure . . . for an American."

"The number holder would not be an American," Jerome said.

That was fairly simple. Morel would not know who held the magic number. His eyes flicked toward Lucia—was it to be Gogarty's widow? He came alive with curiosity. Was this the real reason they had come to see him? Jerome could almost see his mind ticking over.

"Ah . . ." Morel sighed again, turned his hands in a gesture of honesty, openness. "Then there is no problem whatsoever. But you must tell me—is much money involved? It is the variables that make the difference, Mr. Jerome."

"Yes, I realize that," he agreed. No, he dared not. To do or not to do? No, not to do. "I'll give you those details, *if* it's decided to go ahead."

Morel frowned petulantly and turned to Lucia. "The *youth* is in New York City now. He decided to make his career in America. Have you ever seen him there, perhaps on television?"

Lucia lifted her small aperitif glass and spoke impatiently. "No, never. Why would I see the youth? I did not know him then. So why now?" She turned apologetically to Jerome. "Signore Morel is speaking of the peasant lad called Mercutio. I believe I mentioned that he acted in Gogarty's pornographic film?"

Morel expressed great shock. "Pornographic? Oh, no, Lucia, it was an art film of the greatest virtuosity. The youth was magnificent!"

"No, Signore Morel! In fact," she said angrily, "the youth was a laughingstock then and must still be now, wherever he is." So it was Lucia who decided she'd had enough of Morel. She showed disgust, much deeper and more wide-ranging than warranted by anything that had been said. Lucia picked up her pocketbook. "We will be in touch in a few days, in Rome perhaps, Signore Morel."

"But Lucia, you agreed—we were to have dinner," Morel protested.

Thank God, Jerome thought to himself, she shook her head. "No, that was a misunderstanding. We must leave." Hurriedly, she looked at her wristwatch. "We are already late for another important appointment."

They had dinner at a small place near the Piazza Cavour and then walked back to the apartment. Jerome was troubled by what had happened. "You really got upset when he brought up this youth thing."

Lucia sniffed. "It *is* a thing of the past, Paolo. It all reminded me too much of that time. Gogarty leaping around like a madman. Morel, the disgusting man, playing to Gogarty's conceited ego, hustling him, stealing everything. All so disgusting a time . . . and even now, Morel asking me about the dear sweet youth."

"I'm beginning to wonder which one of you was in love with the youth," Jerome mused. "Maybe both of you." Lucia cast her eyes down, avoiding his. "Listen, Lucia, it doesn't bother me. I mean, I couldn't forbid you a love affair in retrospect, if that's what it was. It's not the first time a lady has fallen for a low-down peasant with a big roger."

Her tone was disagreeable. "You are what you Americans call a first-class son of a bitch, Paolo," she said, but there was not much fire in her.

"I'm sorry, Lucia."

She did not speak again until they were in bed. Lucia plastered her bareness on his, her face tucked into the hollow of his shoulder. Finally, she murmured, "It was only a small infatuation, Paolo. I could not help it, you know. He was a vile creature and I hate myself for it."

"We all have our ghosts. You yours, and me mine."

"Where is *she* now?" Lucia was glad to turn her memories aside.

"In Beverly Hills, California, with her new husband." He felt like laughing and then he did, raucously. "Beverly Hills. That's where all good dentists go with their lovely wives. I think she had her nose done too. Nose job in Mecca."

"Oh, Paolo, I *love* you quite desperately."

"That's good, Lucia, because it makes us even."

Her voice thickened. "I would like a small favor. Yes, if I turn just a little, this becomes a possibility, Paolo. Do you see?"

He flexed within her, straining for more and more.

The telephone rang.

Lucia would not release him. "Bastard telephone!" The first *brrr* caught him in mid-stroke, freezing him, like a movie in mid-frame. "Go on, *caro,* go on," she urged. Finally the raucous noise ended. Then he had to begin from the beginning. Lucia did love it, she loved it, yes. He watched her out of narrowed eyes, aware of her closeness and yet conscious too of how separate they were, even now, like strangers. He stared at her face. Even now, did he know her?

Her voice came from afar. "Paolo, isn't it wonderful? Wonderful?" And with that she climaxed.

She sighed. "All of you turns into one giant horn."

He considered needling her about the youth, but decided he had better not. She was sensitive on the subject, felt bad about it. Jerome was jealous, even of the time when he hadn't known her. And what did it matter? J.J. Gogarty had also intervened in the lonely years and he could not be jealous of Gogarty. But, of course, Gogarty was dead.

The phone rang again.

This time, he picked it up and heard the static and echo-like sound of an overseas connection.

"Paul!" How like Nora Ellen Sweeney.

"Hello, Nora."

At once, Lucia sat up beside him, pinching his arm.

"Bad news, Paul."

"Bad? How bad? *What do you mean?* Say it!"

Nora weighed her words for effect. "Not terminal. Buck's had an accident." She paused, but not long enough for him to interrupt. "He cracked up in his chopper, Paul."

"Oh." He'd always expected something like this to happen. "How bad, Nora?"

"He hurt his back, Paul. Where are you anyway?"

"In Milan, Nora. You're ringing Milan, Italy."

"All I know," she said, querulously, "is that somebody in Rome gave me this number. She didn't say where it was. For all I know, you could be on the moon."

"That was probably Lucia's mother."

"What time is it there?"

He looked at his watch. "Going on eleven P.M."

"Yes, that'd be right." Good, he thought, Nora approved of the time. "It happened this morning, a few hours ago. We were going off to Texas together to a party at Deke Watson's . . . oh . . . *damn it!*"

"Nora, one more time. *What happened?*"

"Buck is in the hospital." She was upset. *"Damn him!* They should have put him in Bellevue. He ran into a telephone pole."

Jerome made a perplexed face at Lucia. "How come? It's not like Buck to miss a telephone pole—was it foggy?"

"That's the trouble. He *didn't* miss it!"

"You know what I mean, Nora. I mean it's not like him to miss seeing something so obvious."

"Well," she groused, "he didn't see it and he's in traction and he's going to be stuck in the hospital for at least two or three weeks and maybe longer."

"End of January, you mean?"

"That's possible," Nora said.

For a second, he put his hand over the phone to tell Lucia, "Buck's had an accident." Lucia began caressing his leg comfortingly.

"Who are you speaking to?" Nora demanded.

"I just told Lucia what happened," he said.

"Oh?" Her voice was acid. "You're still . . . up? Well, you'd better get back here as soon as possible, Paul."

"Why?"

"You ask why? Well, don't you think you should? After all, Buck, the president of your company, is hospitalized. Aren't you *concerned?*"

"Nora," he said patiently, "I'm not a goddamn bone specialist or a nerve doctor. What can I do for him? New

Year's is coming up. Do you expect something earth-shaking to happen in the business world New Year's Eve?"

"All right," she said icily, "suit *yourself,* Paul."

"Where's Morgan? He's around, isn't he?"

"Mister Morgan has already gone to Texas, to Watson's."

"Well . . . how come you didn't go with *him?*"

Evenly, holding herself back, she said, "Mrs. Morgan has gone along, Paul. You see—"

"I see, Nora," he chuckled hollowly. "Look, nothing is going to bust loose. Buck's not in a coma, is he?"

"No. But he's doped up."

"Oh, yes? Is that doped up, as in before or after the accident?"

"Paul. Please."

"Was he drinking?"

"Paul, please! In the morning?"

Nora had that genius about her. If you told her the sun was hot, she'd say, the sun is *what?*

"Buck has been known to sip on a Bloody Mary, Nora."

Sternly, she replied, "I'm not informed about that, Paul."

"All right." He thought about it, not for long. "I'll be back as planned. Over the weekend."

Her voice pleaded, "Not until then?"

"You know where I am, Nora, if you need to get in touch. Either at this number or tomorrow afternoon back in Rome."

"New Year's Eve?" Her voice was sad.

"That's right."

"Father John will be with you?" She seemed ready to collapse. "Of course! But I'll be alone, as usual, Paul."

Jerome shook his head wearily. "Come on, Nora, don't start feeling sorry for yourself. Somebody's got to be the man . . . person . . . on the spot."

"Sure." He heard her stifled sob. "Yes, tomorrow night, though, I promise you, I'll be falling down drunk."

"Nora . . . we *all* wish you were here. Don't we, Lucia?"

Lucia stuck out her tongue.

"Never mind," Nora almost snarled. "I'll just let Buck know you're all informed on his condition."

"Say hello to him, Nora," he said cheerily. "Say hello to him from Milan. That'll bring him to."

"Good-bye, Paul."

The phone came down firmly, breaking the connection. Lucia's smile was like a victory flag. "She is not happy."

"She is definitely not happy. Buck had a helicopter accident and, therefore, will not be able to take her to a power party in Texas."

"A serious accident?"

"Not fatal. Anybody else, it would've been fatal. Buck has the luck of the devil."

She nodded disapprovingly. "Perhaps he has sold himself to that one."

"That is possible. What do you think Buck would sell himself for?"

"Power," Lucia said. "Opinion polls show that men sell their souls to the devil most often for power. Second comes money . . ." She paused. "Morel has sold his soul to various devils, Paolo. I am relieved you did not make a deal with him."

"I just didn't trust him. He's too slimy for me."

"What will you do now?"

Jerome shrugged. "I think I'll just give the bonds back to Foster . . . or to you. You can do with them what you will."

Lucia smiled brightly. "Perhaps they would be useful for the foundation . . . or whatever. Give them to Father John, you wise and clever man. Of what interest to you are bonds?"

"Of absolutely no interest in the wide world," Jerome said. He stroked her bare arm and kissed her shoulder. One breast came to rest on his chest. She lifted her lips to him. They were pouty, childlike. He kissed them.

234

"Lucia," he said, "to hell with all of them, right? I congratulate myself on being here with you, alone, in this big bed. I don't need anything else. I don't want anything else. Everything is here. You're like an oasis."

She trailed her hand along his body. "Then you better take some dates, Paolo, and taste from the spring that keeps this place fertile."

"And hope eternal?"

"That too."

Chapter Twenty-one

Since she couldn't be in Texas, and since all her plans had collapsed with Buck's helicopter accident, Nora decided on the morning of New Year's Eve that she might as well go to the office. There was always work to be done. Her preoccupation with Eurochemie had supplanted all other projects, and she could be rightfully concerned now that Paul Jerome was in Milan. She suspected he was there to muck around in that business, which was none of his. A good deal of info had already been collected by Eagleye, Inc. as to the plodding, secretive character of the giant cartel. She was amazed that the Europeans let companies like this achieve so much power; it couldn't happen here.

Morgan called at ten, still early hours in Texas. He sounded cheerful, though the cheerfulness might have been forced. He seemed pleased, but at the same time perturbed, to find her at the office. Well, she might have said, at least she wasn't in Texas to embarrass him. Hesitantly, he asked about Buck.

"He had a quiet night, Mr. Morgan." Actually, she had been just about to call the hospital.

He laughed gruffly. "A quiet night? That's something new for Buck, I guess, huh, Nora?"

"I wouldn't know," she answered stiffly, determined to keep her distance, some two or three thousand miles of it. "I called Paul Jerome in Italy and told him what happened."

"Good . . . good." She could tell he wasn't interested, not at all; that wasn't why he'd called.

"Paul doesn't think it's necessary for him to come back early."

Promptly, he said, "I agree. We're not expecting a crisis, are we?" She didn't answer. Awkwardly, he went on, "Nora . . ." He stopped.

"Yes, Mr. Morgan?"

His voice dropped. "I miss you."

She ignored the woeful statement. "I hope you and Mrs. Morgan are enjoying yourselves. I'm sure the party tonight is going to be absolutely smashing."

"I said I miss you, Nora."

"Well," she said mechanically, "thank you. But I'm feeling just fine."

"You have a big night planned?"

"Oh, yes. Two or three parties to choose from. But nothing like yours, I'm sure, partying with the man who may be the next president of the United States."

"Yeah." His voice dulled and she realized he was having a miserable time. "Too bad Buck and you won't be here, Nora."

"Well . . ." What should she say? Be magnanimous, Nora. "The main thing is Buck is alive and he'll be mended in time for the merger. As for the party, well . . . that's the way the cookie crumbles. People can't always have what they want, can they?"

"No," he said. "People should be grateful for what they do have. They don't realize how easy it is to lose *everything*."

"Exactly." She was too annoyed with him to be intimidated by such a pointed threat.

"I've got to go now, Nora," he muttered bitterly. "If I don't talk to you before that, I want you to have a *very* happy New Year."

It hit her then, the sensation of being alone, lonely and forsaken. She searched for a flip comment but it wouldn't come. Instead, a sob ripped through her nasal passage.

"Nora?"

"Happy New Year to you . . . Mr. Morgan." Her voice was shaking so much she hung up before he could reply.

Thankfully, she was alone in the office and the door was closed. Nora opened the drawer of her desk for a tissue, but not before a big tear fell on a Eurochemie financial statement. Clenching and unclenching her fingers around the tissue, wishing she could have a drink, Nora cried.

But when the phone rang again, she realized that all she needed, really, was to talk to somebody. Maybe it was Morgan again, calling to say how sorry he was and that he was coming back *right now* and to hell with Deke's party.

But the chirpy voice was not Morgan's. "Hey . . . wanna go to the movies, Nora Ellen?"

Norm Vincent arrived at Nora's place at seven bringing with him a small projector and, as he'd promised, the film that would destroy Hazel Morgan.

Norm had insisted he'd nothing better to do for the big night, and pushed all Nora's objections aside. No, he didn't have a date. No, of course, he didn't have a wife; he wouldn't, not in his line of work. No children, at least as far as he knew, or friends he cared enough about to stick around Washington for on New Year's Eve.

"I'm something of a loner," he told Nora on the phone. "You know the enemy never sleeps, nor does the rot which threatens the underpinnings of this great nation of ours."

"Norm. But Norm . . ."

"Whatever, I'm New York-bound and en route, you know—or do you?—to Milan, Italy, in due course."

When he was inside her door, he stopped dead in his tracks. "Something of the greatest import has come out of this investigation, Nora," he said curtly, noticing her expression, "if you consider the matter of industrial espionage worth taking notice of."

"I certainly do," Nora said. "But, my God, I thought it was going to be a straight case of . . ."

"Illicit sexual misconduct? By no means." He chortled. "I'll need a clean sheet."

"All my sheets are clean, Norm."

"I mean to show the film on. Perhaps it'd come out on the wall but better on a sheet. You're going to be nonplussed when you see this, Nora, and I hope not shocked. It's definitely X-rated. I have reason to believe this Joe . . . what's-his-face . . ."

"Mercury."

"Dodge . . . Lincoln . . . Mercury . . . whatever. I've got reason now to think he's a spy and that he deliberately cultivated Hazel Morgan, I regret to say, in order to get inside dope on Diversified Technologies."

"Sex for secrets?" She hadn't expected that.

"What's I just say, Ellen? He trades sex for secrets, that's it. We've got a good line on him already. He's Italian."

"We knew that," she said.

"And a Catholic."

"Which we could assume, couldn't we?"

Since it was the New Year coming up, Nora had bought a couple of bottles of champagne and slipped them into the refrigerator so that she and the head honcho of Eagleye, Inc. could celebrate as they worked.

Now was a very good time to lighten the atmosphere. "How about some champagne, Norm?"

Norm Vincent for the first time seemed to see her. "Hey! How are you? I forgot to ask, Ellen." He beamed. "You're beautiful, you know. Every time I see you, my sperm jumps, honey."

"Upstream?" she joked weakly.

"Wherever."

He stepped forward and put his left hand to her waist, pulling her to him. Then, boldly, not breaking the motion, he kissed her on the mouth, at the same time making a sharp Japanese-sounding exclamation. Just as quickly, he backed away from her.

239

"Gotta watch it. Gotta keep tight control at all times. Can't let yourself get sidetracked by quiff, Norm!"

She hoped she should not be insulted. "Quiff?"

He shot her a shy, brief smile. "Italian word . . . Where's that sheet now? I'll pin it up. You got some thumbtacks? Reason I want to show it on this white sheet is that the camera was placed behind a heating and cooling vent, so the effect is sort of venetian-blind stripes."

"But good enough?"

"Oh, plenty good enough. Important is we see her handing him the papers and him slipping her the payoff."

"Good God!" Nora turned in confusion to her linen closet. "I'll get the sheet. Champagne?" she asked again.

"One glass can't hurt me."

Nora chose a clean white sheet and found a box of thumbtacks. When she'd given him these things and had gone back to the kitchen to open the champagne, she was interrupted by a thump and an angry cry.

"Oh, shit!"

"Norm? What's wrong?" She was afraid he'd fallen off the stool.

"Son of a bitch, I had one of the tacks in my mouth and I think I swallowed it."

"Are you all right?"

That was a dumb question, she realized as soon as she'd asked it. Of course he wasn't all right. He'd swallowed a thumbtack.

"Fuck it," he growled, "it went down all right. I should worry about a goddamn little thumbtack? It'll work itself out okay."

The cork boomed out of her bottle and smacked the side of the stove.

"Hit the deck!" Norman shouted. There was another bump from the living room. "It's the goddamn film— how'd they find me, the lousy bastards?"

Nora laughed. "Norm, it's the champagne cork, you loon."

"Holy Christ, I thought for sure it was a frontal attack," he cried.

He limped into the kitchen and once more took her by the waist and planted a fervent kiss inside her mouth. His lips, Nora noticed, were hard and callused.

"You've hurt your leg."

"Why do you say that? Because I'm limping a little? Listen, sweetheart, one time I crawled five miles through the desert with a broken leg in five, six places. I should worry about a little sore leg? Bullshit, honey." He made a fist and smacked it down against the offending knee. "Go ahead, water! You son of a bitch!"

She was so alarmed for his well-being, she ignored his foul language. "Norm, don't hurt yourself deliberately."

He laughed scornfully. "It's downright impossible for me to hurt myself, Ellen. I've got perfect control over every one of my reflexes. You know, along with going to the Company's dirty-tricks school, I also took up Buddhism when I was assigned to the Far East, I won't tell you where. The Boods, as I call 'em, have a perfect fix on the pleasure-pain thresholds. Get me? *Pleasure,* as well as *pain?*"

"Pleasure," Nora repeated doubtfully.

"Right, pleasure, as in *sex-tasy,* honey. I invented that word. I could tell you stories, but first we've got a movie to see. Come on, fill those glasses and bring on the popcorn!"

Nora put the glasses and open bottle down on the coffee table facing the wall. Norm knew what he was doing, no question of that. He set the projector up quickly and fed in the film.

"Lights out!"

"Here's to us, Norm." She touched his glass with her own, then reached to the end table to turn off the lamp, dropping them into blackness. All she was aware of was his body next to hers on the couch.

"Where are you?" His voice seemed muffled by the dark.

"Here I am."

That hard hand found her knee and his fingers prodded her skin. It was the same thing he'd done the last time they were together. He had touched her, felt her legs, inch by inch.

She gasped, nonetheless. "What are you doing, Norm?"

"Reading you."

"I don't understand."

Her eyes were adjusting. She made out the white blot which was the sheet on the wall, and him next to her.

"Honey, you heard of phrenologists, guys who read the bumps on your head? I'm like a body-ologist. I can read you by touching places on your body."

"Listen, Mister," Nora said, "what about the movie?"

"Don't worry, I'm not going to do anything to you. I'm just taking your pulse."

Nora began to perspire, something she hated doing, especially on a cold day in New York. "Norm, I'm not in the mood, okay? Let's get to the film."

He was aggrieved. "You let me touch you down in Washington but not up in New York."

Nora groaned. "What have I done to deserve this?"

"Well, *didn't* you?"

In the dark, it was easier to say certain things. "In Washington," Nora said, "if you'll remember, I let you touch the insides of my thighs but only for a second."

"So what more do I want to do now?" he complained. "I can't figure you out, Nora. I never believed what Morgan told me about you before. But now that I'm reading you, I see it's possible after all."

She couldn't stop herself. Her body suddenly felt hot and itchy. "Listen, it so happens I'm a virgin and you shouldn't be talking to me like this."

"Oh, yeah, Miss Know-It-All, well it so happens that I'm a virgin too."

"You? In the CIA and all that traveling around, seducing the enemy, and you're still a virgin?"

He growled, "If I say what I said is true, then it's true and why shouldn't you believe it if I'm supposed to believe what you tell me?"

"*Touché.*"

He chuckled. "The French word for touch. I gotcha, baby."

But, why shouldn't she believe him when he said he was a virgin? She was safe with a fellow-virgin, like a colleague in innocence. They would, perhaps, experiment together, take it slowly, one step at a time, one day at a time.

He'd reached her thighs.

"I wonder what the New Year will bring?" Nora mused aloud.

"Peace and prosperity." It pleased her that his voice was choked up.

His fingers danced across her panties and his long middle finger wormed all the way under her, nudging that secret location.

"Yeah, huh. Huh," Norm grunted, "that's the spot, that's nerve-central, Ellen, the place that tells the story."

"What?" She didn't feel anything except a peculiar numbness.

"You're in good shape, Nora. You've got a good, healthy beat there, Ellen."

"*Nora Ellen Sweeney.*"

He yanked his hand away. Had she said something to offend him? The unexpectedness of the movement made her cry out.

"Sorry, honey." His hard lips emerged from the darkness to fasten on her cheek.

"You hurt me."

He laughed harshly. "I could hurt you a lot more than you know about being hurt, Ellen. I *could* make you suffer."

"Maybe you have already."

"Not purposely . . ." He seemed to pull himself together. "Hey, let's see a movie!"

He flicked the switch and the machine came on. A square of light filled the white sheet. Now Nora could see Norm's smile; it lit his handsome, broad face.

He was right about the quality of the film. It was fuzzy, grainy, and there were stripes across it. It should have been better given today's technology. The opening shot was long, of a blank front door of an apartment, Nora supposed, then a figure passed the camera eye.

"Hazel," Norman whispered.

"How do you know that?"

"Our guy tailed her from home," he hissed.

"She's so short. Why are you whispering, Norm? She can't hear us."

"And fat," he sneered. *"Somebody's* at the door."

If it was indeed she, Hazel Morgan had no waistline. Hazel put her hand on the doorknob and opened the door. Facing, in fairly good focus, was a tall young man with a thick, curly mass of black hair, which came close to making contact with the top of the door frame. The collar of a dark blue topcoat was turned up, and underneath he was wearing a wrinkled black satin shirt with no tie. He looked like he had just gotten out of bed. His face was swarthy white, puffy around the eyes.

"Joe Mercury."

"Yeah, the dirty, rotten bastard."

Joe Mercury, if it was he, stepped forward arrogantly, leering down at the dumpy woman. He leaned against the closed door and smiled, showing heavy white teeth like dabs of paint against his bluish skin.

Even in the film, Nora felt the distinct power of his presence. Although in only two dimensions, a sexuality surrounded him, and she could almost smell his cheap cologne.

Hazel fell on him ravenously, shoving and pushing.

"There's no sound," Nora said.

"You need sound when you get this kind of action?"

Hazel pawed Mercury. She shoved her hands under his coat, buried her face in his chest, too short to reach higher. Slowly, tottering with lust, the two figures edged closer to the camera.

"Camera two comes in," Norman muttered.

Camera two focused at an angle across the bedroom to catch a double bed upon which sheet and blanket had been neatly turned down. Portions of Mercury and Hazel Morgan came into view.

Hazel was already unzipping her skirt. Her hips seemed doubly bulky. Nora drew a deep and troubled breath. She knew she was about to see something horribly sordid. But that was part of life, wasn't it? She studied Hazel's face, as chunky as her bottom. There were red spots in the middle of each cheek which didn't come from rouge. Lust, that was it. Hazel's mouth gaped; she was laughing at something.

Languidly, Mercury unpeeled his topcoat and stood in his shirt, already unbuttoned almost to the belt. His body was well-proportioned but not strong. Nora was not impressed.

Hazel pulled down a half-slip and Nora was astonished to see she was not wearing panties.

Lazily, Mercury turned Hazel and undid her bra. The breasts rolled free, dipped. Nora looked away in embarrassment.

Hazel's eyes blazed as Mercury hefted one breast and then the other and let them tumble. Nora realized now, though the action was not in camera range, that Hazel was undoing Mercury's trousers.

Informatively, Norman said, "The cock is off-camera right now but wait till you see the concealed weapon this kid is carrying."

"Please! I don't want a travelogue." She could see for herself, couldn't she?

Suddenly, Hazel dropped out of the camera. Nora gasped, too loudly.

"That's right," Norman said smugly, "she's gone down—"

"I said be quiet, Norm!" Nora's face was hot.

Mercury's smooth face assumed a sorrowful pout. He looked as though somebody was hurting him and, after a moment or two, his hand closed into a fist in Hazel's hair and he pulled her to her feet. He moved her backwards toward the bed and now Nora finally saw what Norman had mentioned. She gasped at it.

"See what I mean, keed?" Norman asked loudly. "Call Guinness!"

It was the biggest one Nora had ever seen, extended straight at Hazel like a cannon. Nora gulped, shaken.

"Twelve inches that thing is, if it's a centimeter," Norman estimated. "You could measure real estate with it. You can see why he's popular. I'll bet he's serviced two or three dames by the time he even got to our Hazel."

"Will you, *please,* shut up?"

"See, he's all rumpled, like," Norman said. "He crawls out of one sack and into the next."

Nora felt weak. Her thighs trembled and there was a strange sensation in that part of her which Norman had touched. Her trembling thighs seemed glued together, so hard was she pressing them in response to Hazel's wide-open invitation. Nora knew she should turn away, but she couldn't. She was riveted; her eyes actually began to burn when Mercury manfully pushed Hazel backwards on the bed. But Hazel knew what she wanted. She hoisted her bottom toward Mercury, fists under her hips, and at the actual mating, left mostly to the imagination because of camera angle, Nora had to stop from catching herself between the legs in a sympathetic flash of lust. God, it was so evil!

"I've had enough, Norm, you can turn it off now."

Norman didn't hear. He was absorbed. "The wonder of it is, Ellen, that she can handle all that. It's hard to believe that's Kurt Morgan's wife, isn't it?"

"Please."

Nora stood up and tottered toward the bedroom to get away from the ugliness.

She heard Norman's shout. "Hey, thataway, Joe!"

Nora went into the bathroom and slammed the door. She sat down on the john, feeling nauseous. *Was* this life after all? So ugly, so terrible. She didn't want any part of this. Norman must destroy the tape. Yes, get rid of it! Nora's body was hot, almost feverish—the horrible effect on her of heinous sin.

Slowly, her nausea subsided. The light was on in the living room and Norman was sitting back on the couch, holding his glass, quietly waiting for her.

"Sorry, hon," he said. "I guess it is a little rough for a layperson to see stuff like that."

"Just burn it, Norm. I hate it."

"Aw, come on, it's all in a day's work. You don't have to see it, Nora. It's enough that I know what's in it. I saw her handing him the envelope."

"Money."

"No, documents."

"If you say so," she said meekly.

"We blew it up and made out Diversified letterheads, Nora."

"Okay, okay."

"So ends our entertainment," Norm said.

Nora nodded, still feeling queasy. "And so also ends Nora Ellen Sweeney," she said. "I feel so soiled."

"All in a day's work," Norman muttered. "All part of a game called hard ball."

And to think, she told herself, that at this very moment Kurt and Hazel Morgan were dressed in sparkling evening clothes, seated at an elegant banquet table at the home of millionaire politician Deke Watson. Disgusting when you thought about it.

"We got a line on this guy Mercury," Norman was saying. "He actually was in a couple of skin-flicks made in Italy for distribution over here."

"Must I hear this?"

"Ellen, there's things you've got to know," Norman

said. "What this is about is immorality. What happened in ancient Greece and Rome is going to happen right here, Ellen."

"What's happening here?"

"Decadence and defeat. One follows the other as surely as french fries do hamburgers, a planned foreign attack on our morality. The commies of course are planting the filth. We can't be too vigilant, Nora."

She nodded, convinced.

"Are you all right, hon?" His voice was solicitous. "Why don't you sit back? You'll feel better. Here." He patted up a pillow and put it behind her head, then moved so she could stretch her legs across the couch.

"Who do you suppose it is he's working for?" Nora asked, making herself comfortable.

"His employer, you mean?"

"Yes. His boss?"

He looked a bit flustered which meant, Nora decided, that he wasn't very sure.

"We got . . . uh . . . a line into Milan which, funnily enough, Ellen, looks like it might connect up with the other half of our project, the Eurochemie business."

"Mercury is a spy for Eurochemie? Oh, my God. How could I explain this to Mr. Morgan?"

Norman smiled. "You suppose this is why he wanted the investigation in the first place?"

She put her hand to her mouth. "My God! The man is *clever*."

"For sure," Norman agreed. "The line wiggles and waggles a lot, that's the trouble. It goes into the bank in Milan and from there into the Vatican, the cardinal I was telling you about, I'm not telling you who." Norman rewound the film. "I'm hoping this place isn't bugged, Ellen. That's why I never say certain things out loud and it'd take a torture squad of twenty-five hoods to deal with me and even then the secrets would die with me, honey."

Nora was ready to shriek by now. Why didn't Norm simply stick the film back in the tin can and shut up about it? All the while he babbled, she couldn't stop thinking about Joe Mercury, industrial spy, sex-for-secrets merchant, how horribly what he possessed could hurt.

Finally, the projector stopped and Norman did put the tape away and the little machine back in its carrying case.

Again, he asked her, "Feeling better now?" She nodded. "I was gonna say that it's a sad thing, indeed, when you see a woman like Mrs. Morgan fall for the wiles of a foreigner like this Mercury creature." True, she thought. Norman chuckled. "Funnily enough," he mused, "your guy, the BBD chief financial officer . . . Paul Jerome . . ."

Nora said, "Yes?"

"He's a good friend to an Italian woman who's a cousin of my friend in the Vatican, I won't say who, not loudly."

She smelled his Brut aftershave as he bent over her to whisper, "Cardinal Ottavio Avia . . . means bird in Italian."

The name was a new one. Also new was the feel of his rough lips on her earlobe. And then the next sensation arrived, that of the sharp tip of his tongue in her ear. Did he sharpen it? *Could* he? You weren't supposed to stick anything smaller than your elbow in your ear, Nora had always been told. Surely, though, a tongue couldn't hurt.

"Nuts about the taste of wax," Norman murmured.

But surely there was no wax in her ears. He'd be disappointed if that's what he was after.

"You know," he whispered, "it's possible to torture a person to death with a supple tongue."

Nora would never acknowledge such a remark. She pretended she had gone to sleep, her eyes rigidly closed. Whatever was going to happen, she didn't want to see. Seeing was half of knowing.

He finished poking her ear with his pointy tongue and pecked toward the corner of her mouth. The insistent tip of it, like a bird's beak, rapped on her lips.

Nora groaned.

"Okay . . . *hon?*"

"Oh, Norm . . ." She didn't dare move when he pulled

her lips apart with one finger and shoved the tongue against her teeth, trying to reach her inner mouth.

His breath was highly seasoned. "I like the taste of spit too," he purred.

Nora cringed. Why did her men always have to be so ugly with their language? How could a person like the taste of another person's spit anyway, like sewer fluid, that's what it was really. She began to think Norman was eccentric as a result of his years of training and experience in the world's sinkholes.

He didn't linger long at any one erogenous zone. The next thing Nora knew, he had dropped off the couch to his knees before her. The tongue dodged along her chin to her throat and then the cleft of her breasts. His mouth was wet and it served as an electric conduit. A shock of desire ripped through her, the same yearning she'd felt at the first sight of Joe Mercury.

Norman was clumsy. He fumbled with the small buttons on her blouse. He would have a tougher time yet with the brassiere, she decided. But he chose to leave it on and instead peppered sucking kisses on the cotton-stretch fabric, causing her nipples to ache.

The noises Norman was making stopped as he swung her legs off the couch, got between her knees, slid his hands up under her buttocks, lifted her, reached the panties at the elastic top and pulled. They tangled but he backed off enough so he could pull them past her knees and over her shoes.

"Norm, what *are* you doing?" She deliberately kept her voice unexcited, as if she'd just awakened from a sound sleep and discovered this weird situation.

"Nora, I want the following to be a reward for your kindness and personal consideration of me."

"Norm, what in the world *are* you talking about?"

"I want to put my tongue in there. I am very fond of the taste of vaginal secretions."

Oh God! She didn't know whether to scream or laugh. Surely, it was not so. Men didn't do *that;* they hated it.

But the force of his tongue made her realize he was indeed doing it. His tongue was rough, the point even pointier, and seemed burred with tiny hooks, which caught her tender membranes.

His voice was muffled. "Relax . . ."

"Norm . . ." Her voice rang. "Let me . . ."

"No," he slurred, "my treat."

"I'm a virgin," she reminded him.

He pulled back. "And remain so, Ellen. I do *not* go that far."

"God . . ." She moaned and squirmed but he held her fast. It didn't really hurt, but it was a sensation that made her feel uncomfortable.

Norman chuckled. "He can't help you now . . . *hon.*"

Later, after she'd washed herself carefully, powdered with a soothing talcum, put her panties back on, smoothed down her skirt and came out again, she found him leafing through a copy of *Time.*

"Hi," he said. He grinned broadly, catching that tongue of his between his teeth. "Tell me—*you like?*"

She nodded. "I . . . did. Norm, I've never let anybody do that to me before."

As impossible as it seemed, his boyish grin got even wider. "Really? I just figured that if you like going down, then you'd like being gone up on."

She blushed. "Let me ask one thing of you—please don't embarrass me by the way you talk. Everything else I can handle. Language really puts me off."

He nodded, understanding her.

"Norm," she continued, "that other thing—I wish you'd not refer to it. I don't know where you get that idea. Not from Mr. Morgan—I won't believe that."

Norman shrugged. "A lot of things get said, you know, man to man."

"But not that."

He looked at her analytically, then nodded. "No, not that, Nora." He tried to grin at her again but it didn't come off so well. "Are you gonna tell Morgan? How are you gonna go about telling him without shocking the living . . . without shocking him badly?"

Slowly, Nora said, "Well, I wouldn't, under any circumstances, let him know a film is available. The idea is to get Hazel to withdraw, don't you think?"

"Definitely," he said. "To cease and desist without raising some kind of a counterproductive stinkeroo." He looked at her. "And you're ready to move in on him then, is that it, hon?" He didn't sound indifferent about that eventuality.

She had to give him hope, she thought, to be diplomatic about it. "I'm not so sure *now* . . ."

"What'd you mean?"

"The truth is, Norm, I like you."

"No! Hey! Come again?" He winked.

"We're pretty good together, don't you think?"

He nodded. "I like your taste and smell if that's what you mean."

Nora said softly, "And I like the feel of your rough fingers."

"Too rough, probably," he agreed, understanding what she was trying to tell him.

And, she might have added, she liked the squared-off brashness of his face. He was almost a Buck Collins look-alike but that was where the similarities ended. He was real. Buck was a phony. Nora couldn't stop thinking so.

Norman's mind was working wildly. "We do get along, Ellen." Yes, if he could ever remember her name. "That's good, for the time being. Call me, we'll talk. Come down to Washington. I'll come up here. You know, when we're not mutually busy. We're a pick-up team, you and me, hon. You're a blond bombshell and me the detonator."

A blond bombshell? Nora liked that; it gave her weight and substance.

"I always liked the taste of blondes," Norman continued. "Kind of salty, I guess. Brunettes taste more like house dressing."

"And redheads, Norm?" she teased, breathless.

"Yeah." He chuckled. "Well, let's see. Redheads have a very distinctive flavor. Thinking of a redhead, I can't in my mind's eye see anything but some kind of sharp steak sauce."

Nora smiled back at him. "I'm glad I'm not a redhead then, Norm. That'd be kind of like making love to a T-bone steak, wouldn't it?"

Norman winked, extravagantly. "Hey, don't knock it 'less you tried it, hon."

Chapter Twenty-two

It wasn't all bad, not at all, to wake the morning of the New Year to the sound of a man getting washed and dressed.

Norman Vincent was standing quietly in his boxer shorts when she opened her eyes. In his hands, he was holding the reel of film. She watched as he carried it into the next room. He came back and reached for his shirt.

"Hi," Nora said drowsily.

A happy look lit his face. "Hey, good morning, hon! How you doing?"

"Fine."

Physically, she felt like a loose balloon, free and soaring. He had cleared her mind as well as her body of an overload of tension she had never considered that much a burden. Nora knew she had the ability to grant great relief; she had never appreciated the fact that it worked both ways.

Norman's magic tongue, that fibrous wand, had definitely found that exquisite female area which should be called nirvana, and hammered it into submission. She had to acknowledge his skill, and did; the wonder was she felt not a twinge of remorse. She had climaxed, she was sure she had. But throughout, Norman hadn't allowed her to touch him.

And now, she reminded him of it. "I owe you, Norm," she said, her voice choking with emotion. "Do you have to leave so early, today of all days?"

"Hon . . . I got a plane to catch, don't you remember?" He laughed. "Gotta go to Italy! Mission Morgan!" He clucked several times. "Everybody thought I actually left yesterday—get it? That's how come I got to spend some time with you, which I've had in mind since we met at the Jockey Club. Remember?"

"Sure." She got the point. He'd lied to have her.

"While you slept in, Nora," he said, "I took the liberty of using your razor which I assume was *your* razor and for the purpose of shaving unsightly leg hair?"

"Yes, Norm," she smiled. She was uncertain how he would react so she didn't tell him she also used the razor to keep her pubic patch trimmed, for her hair grew fast and thick there. "I'm afraid it wasn't very sharp."

"No problem. I never cut myself unless it's intentional."

She patted the edge of the bed. "Sit down a minute. Tell me, you don't *intentionally* cut yourself. Do you?"

He finished buttoning his shirt and inspected himself in the mirror over the bureau. Nora reached to tug at the bottom of his boxer shorts.

"Norm," she said softly, "I said I owe you."

"Hey!"

"I'm ready. I'll do anything you want me to—so you'll remember where you've been and with whom."

"Hey!" He was flattered and showed it by reddening. "Was I that terrific? You feel you've got to repay me? Me?"

She nodded. "Yes." She could be unequivocal because he didn't mock true statements. With him, there was no need to hide or dissemble. She could do as she'd so often been advised to do—let it all hang out.

The hair was stubbly on his leg, smoother on the thigh. He stared down at her as if evaluating her intentions.

"Norm, I don't want you going away . . . feeling tense."

"Nora," he finally said, "you said you were a virgin and I am too. There's no way I'm going to deflower a virgin, while at the same time deflowering myself."

Quickly, she said, "I don't mean that, Norm. I'll . . .
You know."

He grinned. "Hey, hon! No sweat. I wouldn't let you do
that to me."

"Norm," she mumbled.

But he cut off her protest. "See, I know all the statistics,
all fiddled they are. They try to make out that the young
people of this country spend their whole time going down
on each other more than they spend in out-and-out
procreation. Not so!"

"Then why . . ."

"No why's about it," he decreed.

"But you do," she finally was able to say, rather
desperately.

"No, no." He shook his head. "It's merely something I
was trained to do, hon, that's all."

Feeling she might be delirious, Nora pushed herself
back in the bed and put pillows behind her. She folded her
arms over her bare breasts. "Norm, I have to say I don't
understand your rationale."

"Shoot," he said.

Calmly, she explained, "You claim it's okay for you to
do *that*, because you were trained for it. But not me?
Why?"

"Look, Nora," he said irritably, "I was *taught* to enjoy
it, that's the difference."

"And you do!"

"Yeah. Sure. I told you. I had to. I was taught. I didn't
flunk anything!"

"And it's just not possible that I could."

"That's right," he said heavily, "it's *impossible* that you
could. If you did, well, then you wouldn't be the woman I
think you are. No, no, Nora, you're a *virgin* and your time
will come in holy matrimony in the normal Catholic way.
You *are* a Catholic?"

"Yes," she admitted despondently.

"So there you go!" he exclaimed. "What I do, don't pay
any attention. People like me, we're expendable. We're

garbage on the trash heap of history. We're trained like thoroughbreds—when we can't run anymore, we get a bullet in the base of the skull, like a race horse with a broken leg."

Nora nodded. She felt like crying. She unfolded her arms and revealed her lovely, rounded breasts, still swollen from all the passion, nipples red from the abrasive action of his hairy testicles while he'd been reversed on top of her, though not allowing her one caress of his genital. "Stop talking . . . Norm. Kiss me."

"Yes . . . ma'ammm," he drawled. He leaned over her, barely touching her, lip to lip.

Nora grabbed him by the leg and dragged him down. "Damn it, don't you know what I want!"

"Hey!" He writhed, pulling away. "Hon . . . save it. I'll be back . . ."

Impulsively, Nora plunged her hand into the opening of his shorts. She'd have her way with him, whether he liked it or not. There, she had the genital in her fingers . . .

And then she didn't. She found herself flipped over on her belly, her wrist twisted around behind her back and his hand there to snap the wrist if he wanted to. She cried out.

"Don't play games, Ellen."

"I'm not playing games," she sobbed.

"You are," he stated. "You made an unexpected aggressive move, trying to take me by surprise. That's just not done, Nora. I'm trained to *instant* retaliation. I'll let you go now, but don't ever try that again . . ."

He released her and turned her over. Nora stared up at him angrily. "What's the matter with you anyway? Don't you trust anybody? Don't you see I just want to show a little tenderness?" She let herself go, dissolved in tears. But this had no effect on him.

"Nora, the road to hell is paved with tenderness. I'm sorry, hon, I really am. My reactions are reflexive."

"You're mean," she said bitterly. "Don't make excuses. It's mean to refuse an act of love."

He stared at her. He didn't understand about humanity,

did he? "I said I'm sorry. I better go. You got to learn to play hard ball, hon. When you do, give me a ring."

"Norm!" Her voice rose to a wail. "Not like this!"

He shrugged. He checked the cuffs of his shirt and then the buttons of the button-down collar. He had to undo them to get his tie on; he'd told her the night before it was a club tie, the CIA chess club.

"Listen, hon," he droned, sounding like a recording. "A few years ago, as I told you, when I had my Buddhist training in Thailand, I shouldn't tell you where, I made myself a vow of chastity until I retired from the game. Being a Catholic you can understand that. It's dangerous if you let your physical desires get the better of you. Horniness can spell trouble with a capital *T*, hon. There's not much airspace between horniness and a hard place, if you get my meaning. That's why, with the perfect control over all my physical reflexes, as learned from my friends, the Boods, I can offer you the greatest pleasure known to woman while personally remaining totally unmoved. Get me?"

"Yes, Norm, I get you," Nora sighed. "I get you—but do I need this? I've never met anybody like you."

"Of course you haven't," he crowed.

"You're slightly mad."

"Slightly? Is that all?" Again, he thumped her with his outsized grin. You had to like him when he did that. "No, Ellen, I'm not mad, not in the usual sense anyway. Is it madness to possess such discipline that I can turn down a piece of ass like you? I'll bet you wish you had the same kind of grip on your lusty passions—get you into a lot less trouble with your Church, that's for sure."

Nora tried to detach herself, to cut herself off from him. "I'm not in trouble with my Church."

He was disbelieving. "What! You sitting there, balls-ass naked, wanting to do all kinds of weird things to my body, and *not* in trouble with your Church? Don't tell me your Church approves of all *those things*, Nora," he said.

She said the only thing that came to mind. "The Church approves of love, Norm."

"Yes, love, Nora, but not promiscuous fucking and sucking." He chuckled at her shock. "So don't lecture me, hon."

She was without any hope as he pulled on his sharply pressed pin-striped blue trousers and tucked in his shirt-tail. He thumped himself on the flat stomach.

"There's the tack. I can feel the point of it riding on my middle colon. No problem, not if you think positively, Nora."

She groaned to herself. He was going to start on that now, positive thinking. Did they teach that at Langley?

Nora kicked off the covers, uncovering all of her now to his indifferent eyes. She looked down at her blond body, from bruised breasts to red-painted toenails, and flexed her middle. He paid no attention.

Norman pulled his tie snug and flopped down in the chair by the bed to slip on his shoes. Glancing up, he took note of her sexy pose, and decided that whatever he'd said or done to wound or insult her, he would apologize. He put a hand on each of her bare shoulders. "I gotta catch a plane." He leaned forward to kiss her on the forehead.

Nora could do no more than smile. "Norm, I'm surprised the Boods didn't teach you how to fly."

Was she crazy to consider loving such a crazy man? Norman was so unlike her, his sense of humor so completely wild, and his physical sense of self, his integrity, not like anyone she'd ever known. Norm most definitely was no Kurt Morgan and how different too he was from Buck Collins, not to speak of Paul Jerome, a man she *could* have loved. What was Paul going to think of Norm Vincent?

* * *

Norman had a strange influence on Nora. What he had said about her Church and its response to her desires had its effect. He made her feel she must deal with the question of her conduct as she walked toward St. Pat's to attend New Year's Day Mass. Nora could not help but think the Church would be understanding. Desire was not by definition evil. To lust was not automatically a vote for hell; it depended on how you handled it.

The Lord would be lenient, Nora knew, for He had granted a beautiful, sunny New Year's Day. On a day like this, all could not be bad with the world.

Norman was impressive. Anyone would be impressive who had such superb control over his sexual drive. Nora was sure he had *wanted* her. It would have been unnatural if he hadn't, and she wasn't prepared to believe that Norman was unnatural. He was so boyish, so athletic, so handsome, so honest she felt she could have trusted him with her life.

Mass was in progress when she entered the cathedral and Nora thought she'd donate the time while waiting for the next Mass to the Lord's most special projects. Surely He would be pleased that his servant was starting the new year with a clean slate.

But Nora had this nagging sense of flaw. If her lust had been obvious to Norm Vincent, then all the more so it must be to God above. Nora knelt for guidance, halfway down the main aisle. After a few minutes of prayer, she decided she would go to confession.

She saw to her right an open confessional, a pair of nervous priestly feet beneath the woolen curtain that kept the priest from the public. But how could she begin to phrase what she felt?

Some Mocking Matthew at business school had once told Nora that confession was the cheapest high available in the modern world. You said you were sorry for all kinds of rotten things and then got a blanket reprieve from a mystery voice for acts you hadn't committed.

But purification was the right way and then she'd go to the altar for communion and come away a child of blazing white innocence, innocence reaffirmed and rebuilt.

Nora strolled down the side aisle and dropped to her knees inside the confessional. On the other side of the grate she made out the features of a round face with glittering eyes.

"Yes, my child?"

Nora began the ritual prayer. "Forgive me, Father, for I have sinned . . ."

"Tell all," the priest said; his voice sounded hoarse.

She began mildly enough, admitting a few damns and a dozen or two evil thoughts, five minutes of hate. And, suddenly, she realized she was boring him for in the adjacent compartment the breathing sounded erratic, like snores. Raising her voice, she pressed on.

"I want to confess a bad thing . . ."

"Yes!" His attention returned, it seemed. "What is that, child?"

"I . . ."

"Tell me, your confessor, my child. That's why I'm here, to listen to your innermost thoughts, much like a psychiatrist with an office on the Upper East Side. But *free* here, child! Tell me!"

"It's that I . . ." Nora felt embarrassed. She lowered her head, resting her forehead against her clasped hands. Her voice rose to a mere rustle of words. "With a man _. ." she offered.

"With a man, yes? Yes," he said impatiently. "You allowed a man to do sinful things to your body, is that it? Tell me!"

"Yes . . . no . . . I . . ."

"You made love with a man, child?" The voice was disembodied scorn. The breathing opposite her was more labored. "He touched your body, your most private parts . . ."

"Yes."

"Uh . . . uhhh," the priest lowed softly, as if in pain. "Did he . . . did you allow him to put his . . . *thing* inside your holy body, your receptacle?"

"Well . . ." She felt desperate, sorry now she'd talked herself into this. "Not exactly."

"Not exactly? What does that mean, girl?"

"That means," Nora stuttered, "that I took his thing—I relieved him."

"You . . ." The single word was a very large question mark, uttered then left to hang there, as the voice became even heavier, and then a grunting, almost retching sound.

"I took his . . . his genital and *put it in my mouth,*" Nora blurted, almost too loudly.

"Genital?" Once again, the single word, spoken as if this was all the voice could manage. The nasal grinding heightened. Nora was aware of teeth gnashing. "And you . . . did that . . . in your own mouth . . ."

"Yes, Father, and I'm very sorry. I . . . uh . . . It will never happen again . . ."

She lifted her face, opened her eyes, peering into the other chamber for some hint of forgiveness. Plainly, the priest was deeply distressed by her confession, honestly given—a commentary, Nora felt, on the lying that was done within the sanctum of the confessional.

"Father . . ."

The voice had become even more strained. The priest puffed hoarsely and it seemed all he could do to get out his next words. "How many . . . times . . . did you take such a genital . . ."

"Three or four," she admitted.

"Three *or* four?" The groan was loud. "Long ones and short?"

"Father . . ." That was not a priestly sort of question. The largeness or smallness had no bearing on her case. It was the *fact* of it.

And then she recognized what could not be. He was pointing what looked like a fish head at her through the

262

grating of the confessional. She thought dully of the Miracle of the Fishes, then cried out in horror. No fish, this! The response to her cry was a wild, hysterical giggle, and a mad shuffling of feet. He was gone, and Nora was smothered, choked in shame. She could not move. She was destroyed. His glee was a message, she knew, a message that had been sent from far away.

Chapter Twenty-three

FORTUNATELY FOR HER SANITY, NORA WAS A PRAGMATIC and optimistic person. After a bad evening, in the cold light of January the second, a Friday, she could remember the incident at St. Patrick's as disgusting and revolting, but also, somehow, comical.

In a situation over which one had no control, Nora remembered learning some years before, it was best to smile, grin if you could, and if at all possible to laugh.

Friday, as far as she was concerned, was a normal workday at Diversified, even though the offices were half empty.

Her secretary was not there when Nora arrived, a little after nine. She noted that fact specifically, put down her attaché case, and then strolled down the carpeted corridor to the coffee machine, the place where she had collided with Kurt Morgan not much more than two months ago.

And now she was a vice-president, in fact if not yet in name. Kurt would announce her promotion, she expected, as soon as he got back from Texas. So things were not all bad, were they?

Bad enough, though, she told herself when she saw the backside of the person who was there before her, drawing a cup of coffee and then spooning a non-dairy creamer into it. Nora would have fled if she'd had a chance.

Too late. Helen Marconi turned. She was as surprised as Nora, but recovered swiftly.

"Hello, Nora. How come *you're* working today?"

Nora smiled, remembering she was a vice-president now. She outranked Helen Marconi, her former boss. "I might ask the same question of you."

Helen laughed loudly but without joy. "As if you didn't know, bitch! I've got some things to clean up. It seems I'm being transferred to a . . . *branch* office."

Her rage gave Nora a chance to prepare herself. "I didn't know," she said. It was not quite a lie. She hadn't realized that Kurt would follow through quite so promptly.

"Bitch," Helen snarled at her. "You arranged it, just to get even." She stopped, restraining herself, but the venom surfaced. "Rusty told me. There was nothing he could do to stop it. Morgan was determined."

"I'm sorry."

"You're not!"

Nora ignored Helen's ugly stance. She was standing in front of the coffee machine with her hands on her broad hips, giving off the scent of murder and mayhem. But Nora was not going to be intimidated by this creature, this gnome whose very shadow cast a pall of BO. Helen bounced back and forth to block her from the coffee machine.

"Goin' someplace?"

"I'm going to get myself some coffee, Helen," Nora said with the greatest dignity she could muster.

Marconi reached around to pick up her cup. "You want coffee—you get coffee!" She hauled her arm back. Nora reacted instinctively, dodging out of the way of the rush of hot, black liquid. It dashed against the wall behind her, splattered and trickled down on a stack of table napkins.

Helen was distracted by the move and Nora chose that moment to slap her smartly in the face.

"Get hold of yourself, Helen!" she ordered. "Don't disgrace yourself. It doesn't help to call me names."

But Helen was out of control. She burst into furious tears and sank miserably to her knees. "You cunt! You're an Irish, cocksucking cunt!"

Nora stopped dead. Another time she would have expired on the spot from such a horrible insult. But Norman Vincent's face seemed to appear before her. His words rang. "Hard ball, Nora. The game is hard ball."

Nora was shaking badly but she was able to step around Helen. "I'm getting myself some coffee. I'm definitely *not* impressed by your use of the language."

Helen bawled, "Everybody knows you suck Morgan's cock."

Nora smiled thinly. Would she never hear the end of this vileness? But there would be an end to it, yes, after yesterday.

"You notice I don't mention what everybody knows about you and Mr. Lancer, Helen."

But Helen merely laughed. *"Everybody* knows any girl who ever made it in this place had to go down on her knees for Morgan. Don't think you're the first, or the one and only." Nora calmly poured coffee in a cup. "You're just the most recent, that's all. Morgan likes to put his mark on them. . . . Ask his secretary, you stupid bitch!"

Nora would have liked to pour the whole pot of coffee on Helen's battleship-gray head. But she was steely.

"Vindictiveness doesn't become you, Miss Marconi," she said. "People do not believe such dirty things. You're trying to get even. You hate me for leaving your boring little department."

Groaning, Helen struggled to her feet. "I don't give a damn anyway, Sweeney. Good riddance to this place. Suck anybody's cock you want to."

Nora smiled coldly. "Good-bye. Enjoy yourself, Helen." She couldn't help laughing. Small victories. "Maybe you'll meet up with a handsome Eskimo."

Nora marched out of the room, out of Helen Marconi's life, she trusted. But back in her office, she didn't feel so calm and cool. She began to tremble again. Ugly. Vile. Awful. It was not comforting to know that someone hated you that much.

Norm Vincent called at 10:00 A.M. It was already dusk in

Milan, he reported, and the place was full of Catholics. He had begun his investigation into the enigma of Eurochemie S.A. and the possible espionage program it was conducting against Diversified Technologies. On whose behalf? Yes, *that* was the question.

Paul Jerome rang at eleven. By now, it was cocktail hour in Rome. How was Buck Collins getting along? Fine, as far as she knew, Nora said. She had other things she wanted to tell him, tell somebody, but who would accept her story of confession and retribution?

Kurt Morgan reached her at noon. He had changed his departure plans. He'd be back in the office on the fifth, that was the following Monday.

"Nothing new, is there, Nora?"

"No, sir, nothing at all."

He paused, trying to interpret her mood. "Did you have a nice New Year's, Nora?"

"Oh, yes, it was fine," she said. She was about to blurt that she'd gone to a porno movie but thought better of it. Plenty of time for that. "How was *your* party, Mr. Morgan?"

She knew he didn't like the tone of her voice, her coolness. She could put a meter on his irritation and measure it. His anger always lay there, coiled just below the surface, belying the calm exterior.

"The party?" He concealed his displeasure. "The party was just *super*, Nora."

"I'll bet the stars were out and the eyes of Texas were upon you, Mr. Morgan."

"Hmmm . . . yes," he murmured ominously, "they liked us well enough. I think I did us some good . . . maybe even along the lines that interest you, Nora."

"Politics?" She didn't try to hide her enthusiasm.

"Everybody says to say hello to *old Buck*," he said sarcastically.

Old Buck? What did he mean by that? "I'll pass along the message, Mr. Morgan."

"Yeah, do that," he said angrily, "and tell him for me to

take better care of his ass. I didn't buy BBD so he could run his whirlybird into a cinder heap. Thank God the markets have been closed—there's been nothing in the papers, has there, about the accident?"

God, she thought, horrified, she hadn't remembered to look. Morgan was such a pro; he thought of everything.

"I haven't seen anything. . . . We sure didn't send out a press release, Mr. Morgan."

"Fuckin' well better not," he snapped. "I'll see you Monday, Nora."

"All right."

"Monday," he repeated.

Nora smiled to herself. She knew how difficult it was for him, emotionally, to say anything endearing.

She should have been more careful about checking the papers. It could be a severe blow to both companies if the financial world was informed that anything was wrong with Buck Collins, already being talked of in terms of heir apparent to Kurt Morgan. She sent one of the secretaries downstairs to get all the local papers and copies of the *Washington Post* and *Los Angeles Times*. When she had the papers on her desk, she spent the rest of the morning searching for any articles on Buck's accident.

Nothing. But as she was leafing through the *New York Post*, the headline article on page six did make her sit up straight: FATHER FLASHER NABBED AT ST. PAT'S.

Nora laughed. The article reported the arrest of a dissident friar outside the cathedral. He was charged with indecent exposure before several female penitents in St. Pat's confessionals and then hauled off to Bellevue for observation. The archdiocese had no comment but the alleged priest had been heard to shout obscenities and shriek his disenchantment with the change from Latin to English-language Mass.

The poor man, Nora thought sorrowfully. But in what she assumed was this man's misery, she found a blessing of sorts. She had not, after all, been singled out by the Almighty for this particular act of savage mockery.

Buck seemed better on this second day of January. When Nora was ushered into his room he was sitting up and looked alert. They'd apparently taken him off the painkillers; he seemed as comfortable in his neck brace as he was likely to be for some time.

"Beautiful," he cried, "tell me—how's business?"

"Kurt told me this morning everybody was asking about you in Texas." She frowned. "It *was* quite a party."

"Listen, I can't help what happened, beautiful. I'm sorry I blew it for you, but there'll be other parties."

She shrugged moodily. "I don't care about missing Watson's dumb party. Kurt said he did all right by himself."

"Sure he did," Buck agreed. "Better than if we'd been there, beautiful. Kurt is an accomplished ass kisser. Who knows—I'd probably have gotten bombed and insulted the Defense Department. . . . Give me your hand—why are you looking so depressed, beautiful?"

Nora shook her head. "Does it show?"

He stroked her knuckles soothingly.

"Mr. Morgan told me to tell you to be more careful in that whirlybird from now on because he didn't buy BBD to inherit you in a coffin. He was worried it'd get in the papers and . . . *irritate* the merger."

"Oh shit," Collins exclaimed. "He's still worried about his *consummation*, is he? Christ Almighty, when I think about consummation the only thing comes to mind is climbing into your pants."

Nora sniffed. "You know that will never be, Mr. Collins."

"I know," he muttered, "pure as the driven slush and all that. We ought to erect a statue to the Virgin of the Merger."

"*Not* funny."

"Whataya want? I'm not Bob Hope. I'm Buck Collins, in painful traction." He smiled. "And now that we're alone, beautiful, speaking of erecting a statue . . ."

"I'm not afraid of you," she said primly. "You're tied down on that bed."

"Like hell! I could be on you like a flash!"

Nora withdrew her hand from his. "Why is it you men feel you always have to talk dirty to me?"

"Who else?" He chuckled. "Morgan? That dirty-mouth?"

Nora shrugged and sighed. "I suppose you'd think it was funny if I told you a dissident priest exposed himself to me yesterday in St. Patrick's."

Collins's eyes rounded. He nodded timidly, hoping she'd go on.

"In the confessional," she said, remembering, still not believing it despite the item in the *Post*. "I didn't know what it was at first. Then I did and he ran away giggling like a madman."

Collins's body was shaking. He opened his mouth, gasping, trying not to laugh so hard. Tears came to his eyes.

Nora smiled, or tried to. "Is that *so* funny, Buck?"

"Beautiful, that is funny. Knowing you . . . Jesus!"

But it was not that funny, after all, was it? His laugh became a groan and his grin a wince of pain.

"Hurts," he moaned. "Nora, don't make me laugh . . . please."

"I'm not a funny person," she said. "I'm just a laughing-stock. There's a difference evidently."

Collins gasped. "Nora . . . it's not the most serious thing in the world. . . . Whatever we do to help each other get through the day . . ."

She sat quietly. Slowly his body relaxed so that he could speak normally again.

"Your pal Foster get to Italy okay?" he asked casually.

"Yes . . . they spent New Year's together."

He nodded. "And you? What'd you do, Nora? I know where I was. I was right here—pretty doped up, I guess."

"Some people were wondering if you weren't doped up *before* the accident."

He didn't move his head. "Meaning?"

"Even if you'd been drinking, you would've seen it."

"Maybe, maybe not. Accidents do happen, even to the most experienced guys. It might have been a value judgment, Nora," he said, trying for sarcasm. "Hit the pole here or the power line over there."

"So? Is that what happened?"

He motioned for her to bend closer. "Place could be bugged," he whispered. "I'll tell you, Nora, but don't breath it. Shit! I was high that morning. I had a snort of cocaine just before I took off. I don't know why." He grinned. "Maybe I was excited I was seeing you. Whew! You're right. I could've been creamed."

Nora shook her head sadly. "Buck, you are a fool."

"Nora, you don't have to tell me that," Collins growled. "I learned a good lesson."

"Promise!"

"Okay, okay. So what'd you do New Year's?"

"I managed. I had a date."

"Who with? You're making me jealous."

"Don't be." Or, should he be? "A man I know from Washington."

"Holy Christ! A Fed! Not the IRS, I hope . . . I *trust*."

Nora smiled playfully, thankful the conversation was not sexual and dirty. "Would I, a Harvard MBA, go out with a man from the IRS? Mr. Collins! Really!"

A spasm of pain made him pale. "Blast! This pain goes flying down my spine so sharp it feels like it's going to burn my toes."

"Should I call the nurse?"

"No." He shook his head loosely. "All she'd do is give me a glass of water and a tweak on the balls. No more morphine, such luck!"

"Oh, Buck, stop it."

"It's true, Nora," he maintained. "If you don't think getting your nuts squeezed by a sado-masochistic nurse will take your mind off a back pain, you got another thing coming."

"You are so silly," Nora said, "it is just unbelievable. A man of your rank—"

"I'm just rank, Nora, that's it."

"How long will you have to wear the brace, Buck?" she asked, striving for higher ground.

"Dunno." His eyes closed. "Six months . . . a year. I dunno."

"Hurts again?" she asked sympathetically.

He nodded, mouth twitching. Nora placed her hand on his forehead. He was very warm to the touch.

"You feel like you've got a fever, Buck."

He groaned dramatically. "I'll probably croak of this yet, Nora."

"No, no, Buck. Frogs croak."

"Germans too . . . and the Irish."

He grabbed her hand, gripped it hard, carried it to his dry lips, kissed it, then rubbed her palm across his chest, down his belly . . .

"Buck!"

"Please, just a little gentle squeeze, beautiful. That'll short-circuit this goddamn pain!"

"Buck, the nurse is going to come in!"

"So what? If it works, what can she say?"

Reluctantly, not eager to comply, not after yesterday, but telling herself that he *was* ill and *did* need solace, she slipped her hand down under the crisp sheet and the short hospital nightgown to his hirsute crotch. She bypassed the penis which had instantly stiffened at her approach, and did what he asked, cupped his testicles in her hand.

"Oh, that is gorgeous, beautiful," he sighed. His eyes closed and a smile played at his mouth. He looked better already. "It really helps, believe me."

"That's nice to know," she said. "I'll have it reported in the *New England Journal of Medicine*."

"You could be a lot *nicer* to me, Nora."

"Not here in the hospital," she said tersely.

"Why not? It's not much different than taking blood and they do that all the time."

Men! "Just a minute. I'm going to take your pulse rate."

Releasing the tightly strung scrotum, Nora placed her finger at the place Norman Vincent had called nerve central. Sure enough, under her fingertip there was the distinct pounding of Collins's blood. Nora studied her watch. Eighty to the minute, wasn't it?

"Nora, what the hell are you doing?"

"Taking your pulse, Buck."

His chuckle muffled in ache, Collins said, "Nora, do you know what that spot is called?"

"No."

"That's the *now*." Nora was counting. "As in the old song—'I Wonder Who's Kissing Her Now.'"

"Buck, you are *so incredibly crude.*"

"Please don't hurt me, Nora," he cried, laughing too hard again. He stared at her, appreciatively she thought. "Nora, you're kooky, you know?"

"Sometimes," she said.

"Did I tell you, beautiful, that Connie's coming to see me?"

"Mrs. Broadstairs?"

"Do I know any other Connies?"

"She's still your girlfriend, isn't she?"

She'd left her hand down there, idly stroking him, not seeming to notice what she was doing. Nor did he evidently; at least, he seemed unaware.

"Would I play around with her, behind Pete's back?"

"You might."

"Yeah." He nodded smugly. "I might at that. I'm just a low-down rat, beautiful. What if I did? It wouldn't hurt Pete and it'd keep it all in the family. Get me?"

"That's right," Nora said. "Congratulate yourself. Men!"

"Yeah . . . And women. C'mon, Nora, you play around just as much as any goddamn power-mad male executive."

"I do not, and you know it." She squeezed. "Want to play squash?"

"Hey! I take it back. You hurt, you awful girl." He

winked hopefully. "You know, if you weren't so committed to Morgan, I'd make a serious move on you. You're a funny lady and I'll be goddamned if you're not a *good sport* too."

She knew what he meant, what he wanted her to do. But she couldn't, not anymore. "Thanks so much, mister," she said, playing it straight. "You know there's funny—and there's *funny*."

Why should she seek his approval? Nora knew exactly who she was. She'd known for a long time. And now Buck Collins had opened his eyes at last and seen her? So what? Not knowing exactly what she'd do, Nora folded back the sheet and there he was, sticking straight up like a missile on a launching pad. His eyes bugged and darted at the door. There was no way a hospital door could be locked. Nora stood and stared down at him, at the heaving genital. Buck's accident certainly hadn't interfered with that mechanism.

"What I should do," Nora mused, "is sit on you. Yes?"

He looked anxious. "Hot damn! I wish you could. But I don't think they'd go for that, Nora. I was thinking more in terms of a quick blowjob." He laughed nervously. He didn't think she'd dare anyway.

"I want you to get well." Nora leaned close to the bulging genital. A tear, like a drop of transparent glue, rolled off it. Gently, she blew on it.

"Nora! For Christ's sake—anybody comes in will think you're crazy!"

She tasted the heavy pestil cautiously and, as she expected, there was a bitterness, an acidity as if they'd been sponging him with detergent. She pulled away. "Ugh! Awful!"

"Nora . . ." He sounded like a broken man.

His whine made her throat constrict. If he hadn't been ill and damaged and needy, she wouldn't have continued. As it was, she went quickly, trying to ignore the vile, scorched taste, going so fast she failed to hear another sound until it had passed—the whoosh of a door, an exclamation of disgust, and the slamming of the same door.

Buck yelped hysterically. "She seen it, beautiful—son of a bitch. And she's the one I've been trying to get to do—"

She heard what he was saying but paid no attention. The nurse could never recognize Nora, and even if she did, so what? Nora didn't stop, didn't skip a beat. Soon Buck began making the sounds men make, and finally sighed so long he could be expiring.

"I'm getting better, beautiful. I'm . . . definitely . . . getting well."

Chapter Twenty-four

THERE WERE TIMES, AND IT SEEMED THESE DAYS THEY came more and more frequently, when Nora felt swept away by a relentless tide, as if someone had cast her adrift and she was being carried out to sea. At such times, nothing seemed to help.

Sitting next to Paul Jerome in the cab on the way to the hospital in the week following his return from Italy, the sensation of loss and abandonment hit her again, powerfully.

As unbelievable as it was, according to Paul, Father John was in the process of giving up his priesthood.

"Nora?"

"I heard you." She had lost her breath. His message served as a kick to the stomach, a karate chop to the larynx. "Father John . . . is being released . . . from his vows? It's not possible, Paul. I don't believe you!"

"Believe," he said.

Yes, it was all the same to him. What did he care?

"In Rome," he continued, as if this were something he'd learned that nobody else knew and he was proud of his exclusive knowledge, "in Rome, everything is possible. And at the Vatican, everything is not only possible, but probable. Or so it seems to me—a non-Catholic, really a pagan by your definitions."

"Pagan?" she repeated lifelessly.

"Yeah. Lucia and I, we've decided we're pagans. That's the saving grace."

She paid no attention. *"Why* would he want to be released, Paul?"

"Ah, therein lies the tale. T-A-L-E, that is," he spelled it out. "It's got to do with the Gogarty Foundation, that goddamn mess . . ." Jerome stared at her sympathetically, as if realizing finally that she was in pain. Too bad they couldn't put her in traction to repair a broken idol.

"But surely he doesn't have to leave the priesthood to administer a *Catholic* foundation."

"Well," Jerome said, amused, "there's more to it than that. Lucia's mother's cousin is a big-time cardinal . . ."

Yes, yes, she remembered. Bird. "Cardinal Avia."

"Yes, you knew, of course," he said. "He's a member of the Vatican's financial brain trust."

"So?" Nora demanded, almost angrily.

"Well . . ." Why did he drag it out so joyously? "It seems that Lucia's mother, the princess, fell ass over teakettle in love with Father John."

"God!" Her knuckles hurt, her teeth ached.

"She's the family agnostic, if not atheist, but she's still got lots of pull at the Vatican. Like Gogarty, which I don't understand at all. He was a black atheist, also big man at the Holy See."

"So, so?"

"Well, John Foster reciprocates."

"What! You're telling me Father John Foster fell in love with this princess? I cannot believe it, Paul," Nora cried. She had to struggle to find oxygen in the air, blood for her heart.

Jerome shook his head mildly. "Yes, Nora. He told me in Rome he was sorry he hadn't left the priesthood for your mother. Did you know that, Nora?"

Hadn't he known she'd be devastated? "Paul . . ." Nora's voice broke. "I thought . . ." Should she admit such a shameful thing? Yes. "I assumed if Father John ever wanted or desired a woman, he'd have chosen me."

"You!" Now would he realize how she felt? "Don't give me that, Nora. You never had that kind of a relationship with Foster. Cut it out!" He grew agitated at such an idea. "He's like your father."

"I could take care of him just as well as some Italian princess."

"Yes, sure," he chuckled, "but he's not looking to be *taken care of*, Nora. He's not an invalid, you see. That's just it."

Their voices had risen. The cab driver tried to mind his own business but, naturally, he couldn't. His eyes bobbed up in the rearview mirror. Nora didn't care.

"Damn it," she exclaimed violently, "he's a traitor! He's misused my trust. I'll never, never forgive him, Paul."

"Nora," he said slowly, stiffly, not approving of her, "don't overreact."

But she was fairly launched into a tirade. "He told you to tell me, didn't he? He didn't have the guts to tell me himself, did he? You've got the job of breaking the news."

"He's still in Italy, Nora. He couldn't tell you himself. He wanted you to know. He considers you like his daughter."

"Daughter!" she yelped, laughing scornfully. "Is that what he says? He tried to put his hands on me before he left! That's *true*, Paul!"

The driver's face seemed to shatter in amazement. A disgusted frown lowered his mouth an inch. But she didn't care.

"Nora! Why are you saying such a thing?"

"Because it's true," she snarled. "Now we know about him after all these years, don't we? A dirty old man! Like all men . . . *bastards!*"

She should not have said that word. The driver's eagerness to hear drove her on.

"You too, buster!" she yelled at him.

Jerome took her hand, pulled her back, tried to quiet her. "Nora, I'll tell you what *I think* happened, if you'll hear me out."

"Yes," she said bitterly, "tell me."

"I think Elena, the princess, Lucia's mother, went to

278

her cousin, the cardinal, and between them they figured it out. It was a good argument to release Father John from his vows so he could devote himself to the Gogarty thing and be a free agent in making investments—in other words not under strict Church discipline, more man-to-man with the financial community. See?"

"Yes, I see, of course I see, get on with it, for heaven's sake!"

"Of course, it was understood that Elena wanted to deal with him as a man as well, as woman to man. Avia, naturally, saw it her way. She's a very dominating woman, Nora, very powerful. Avia better agree or she'd create a big ruckus. She writes, you know, she's a poet; she's got something of a following among the moderate left-wing."

"Oh, yes, oh, yes?" Nora mocked ferociously. "I'll tell you what else she is. She's corrupt. She's decadent—"

"Nora, no, she's not," he said gently.

"We know what their aim is," she went on loudly; nothing could stop her. "Their aim is to corrupt, to demoralize the fabric of our democracy."

He scowled. "Where the hell'd you hear that, for Christ's sake?"

"They're everywhere, Paul," she exclaimed. "They're even involved in industrial espionage against us."

"Who is? What the hell are you talking about?"

"I can't tell you."

"Listen, honey," he said, "give Foster a break, will you? He's done his duty for thirty years and more. Why shouldn't he—"

"Because it's not right, or proper!"

Jerome shrugged helplessly. "They're perfect together, Nora, you'll see."

"I won't. I won't ever see anything. I'll never speak to him again. I will never forgive him. He has destroyed my faith, Paul, he has wrecked my faith more completely than a nuclear bomb would." Nora leaned forward. "Stop at the next corner," she told the driver.

"Nora, what are you doing?"

"I'm getting out. I'm going home. I can't bear to talk anymore."

"Come on now," he urged, "let's go see Buck."

"Buck? No thanks."

As soon as the cab stopped, Nora leaped out and slammed the door. The light had changed and she darted across Park Avenue at Sixty-second Street before Paul Jerome could pay and follow her, if he'd had a mind to. He hadn't expected such a violent response.

Nora marched through whistling wind across to Fifth Avenue, and turned downtown.

Son of a bitch, she muttered aloud, son of a bitch. She could drool over the words. Bastards! Men, the bastards! You could absolutely not count on them, ever. They were liars and worse! They were devious, and worse than that! They were corrupters and exploiters of womankind, of the honesty of women! Two-timing rotten sons of bitches, bastards!

The words tumbled around in her brain, all those terrible words she heard so often and never used. Scumbags, turds, pricks.

Nora reached the Hotel Pierre canopy and turned into the lobby. She wheeled to the left and went down the steps into the bar. Loosening the belt of her coat, she slid up on a stool.

"A double!"

"Double what, lady?" the bartender asked patiently.

"Double anything! No. Scotch on the rocks, a little twist."

She might be steaming with rage, but a bartender, a good one, would never be impressed. Nothing like an indifferent bartender to cool one off. Why should he be impressed with her pain and fury? Her run-of-the-mill pain and fury? Nora . . . Foster . . . the memory of her mother. So what? She reflected on the probable ugliness of the Princess Elena.

"There you go, honey," said the bartender, sliding the

drink toward her. Why couldn't they just put them down, why slide them always?

"Don't call me *honey*, please."

He shrugged. "Okay."

"I'm a career woman. I'm *not* somebody's, or anybody's, honey."

"Excuse me," he sneered, "for breathing."

Nora nodded curtly. She didn't need a dialogue with a bartender. There were more serious things to consider, such as Father John Foster, how to get him defrocked, perhaps, not just released from his vows. No, not just allowed to slip gracefully into a Gogarty Foundation so the Church wouldn't risk losing a four-hundred-million-dollar fortune. A mere priest was expendable. An Italian princess, a member of that defunct royalty, *desired* this priest and ergo! presto! he was released to her custody like a prisoner let out of jail. His Church had thrown him to the wolves, that's what it amounted to.

But, however much she debated it, Nora could not understand how such a thing could happen in Rome, of all places, if it hadn't in New York State. Nora had tested Father John at Christmastime and not found him weak. Yet only a few days later, in Rome, he had *fallen,* in that place where his resolution should have been the strongest.

Without guilt, Nora remembered so distinctly how she had shown him her blond body, how she had exhibited her long legs, and, lushly, how she had twirled her silks and let him see her richest treasure, not the ruby itself but the tresses which concealed and protected it from man's penetration.

She remembered the Scotch and tasted it. Good, it helped a little. Fire put out fire.

A moroseness came with the Scotch. Suddenly, everything had changed. What had mattered so much before, things like purity, integrity of body, honesty, didn't matter at all anymore. Virginity? A meaningless state of being, a physical bagatelle, a moral zilch. Nora had tried to maintain the saintly balance but that was over now. She'd be a virgin no longer. She had paid enough lip service to virginity and that had ended too. She would throw in the bloody towel.

Nora thought she'd built a pretty good career on the basis of sheer ability. Think how much further she'd take herself if she used her body, the myrrh'ed ruby of the collection, as well as her brain.

Kurt Morgan hadn't been expecting her until later, after they'd been to see Collins, but that didn't matter. So she'd be early. Nora finished the drink, opened her purse and found a ten-dollar bill. She threw it on the bar.

"Keep the change."

The bartender favored her with a sickly smile. "Thanks ever so . . ."

Morgan was pleased to see her. He stepped to the side and Nora saw him thrust the snub-nosed automatic into the pocket of the paisley robe.

"You look cold, Nora. How's Buck getting along?"

"I didn't get there," she replied irritably. "Paul Jerome shocked me so much in the cab that I got out. I stopped at the Pierre for a minute. And here I am." She tried to smile.

"Jerome *shocked* you?" He'd be curious about that, wouldn't he?

"Beyond belief."

"What did he do to you, Nora?"

"Not do. It was something he said."

"But what?"

"It doesn't matter, Kurt." She paused. "I don't feel like talking about it."

He paused, holding her coat at the shoulders. "Nora, in the last few days, I get the feeling that something's going on around here. People are acting mighty strange."

"Strange . . . how? Kurt?" He himself was not acting so *unstrange*.

"Distant," he said, "uptight . . . childish." He blinked

at her, as if unaccustomed to the volume of heat and light she gave off. "I told you it was not my choice to take Hazel to Texas. I agreed, against my better judgment, that you could come with Buck. It was not my fault Buck cracked up."

"No?" she echoed him weakly. "I'd almost bet you hired somebody to shoot him down."

He smiled thinly. *"Funny,* Nora. I might shoot down a competitor but not a star executive who's on *my* side."

Nora nodded humbly. "I'm sorry. I don't mean to be uptight, Kurt. I'm angry about something. You know me."

"I'm not sure I do know you," he pursued her. "You shouldn't be so jealous of Hazel."

"But I'm not," she cried. "I told you I'd pray. How did you two get on down in Texas?"

"All right." He turned to hang up her coat, conveniently. "We didn't punch each other out. We worked out a kind of *modus vivendi,"* Morgan muttered.

She smiled, despite the pain, always more pain. "A reconciliation, that's good."

"No, a *modus vivendi,"* he repeated. "Do you want a glass of red wine?"

"No. I'd rather have a Scotch on the rocks."

Morgan went from the closet into the kitchen, relieved, it seemed, to put some distance between them.

"Nothing changes for us, Nora," he said uncomfortably.

"Oh, I know," she said daringly. "I'm still *accepted."*

"Now, Nora."

"Don't patronize me. I'm not a child, Kurt."

"What *in hell* is wrong with you?" He came to the kitchen door.

She smiled bitterly. "Why don't we just tell it like it is, Kurt? Why play around?"

"Play around? I've never forced you to do anything . . ." He wasn't quite sure what she was saying.

"I had a talk with Helen Marconi while you were away—not a very nice one."

"Helen Marconi?" Had he forgotten the name already.

"Lancer's girlfriend," Nora reminded him. "The one you're shipping to Alaska."

"Oh, yeah, her."

"She told me it's common knowledge that every girl who joins the corporate office has got to . . . what did she say? Got to get down on her knees for you. True?"

His face flamed in embarrassment. "She said *that*? That's a goddamn lie. Lancer's work, huh?" He scowled murderously. "What's further north than Nome?"

Nora chuckled. "I never believed it." She sat down in front of the fire, running her hand across the cushion next to her. "Come sit down."

"I'll get the drinks," he mumbled, deflated.

"Norm Vincent was here," Nora called. "He's off in Italy now looking into the—"

"Yeah." His voice cracked. "I wanted to ask you. How's that coming along?"

"Fine."

He returned slowly, bringing the drinks, wine for him and the Scotch and water for her. He moved awkwardly, somehow, as if his joints weren't working properly. The robe, loose at the waist, rustled as he walked.

"About Eurochemie," he began, sitting down beside her. "But first . . ." He held up his wine. "Here's to you, Miss Vice-President. I put the appointment through this afternoon before I left, Nora. Congratulations."

"Oh . . ." Gone was all bad feeling, vanished the vindictive thoughts. How could she have doubted him? "Kurt, that's wonderful. Thank you."

"Nothing to thank," he said gruffly. "You deserved it."

"Kurt . . ." She did have to thank him though. She thrust her body at him and kissed his cheek.

"You shouldn't do that, Nora. It's not like you're being paid for something. I said you deserve it, goddamn it."

"All right, Kurt," Nora said. "Thank you. I appreciate that."

"Now about Eurochemie," he muttered. "We talked a

284

little about that down in Texas." Secretively, he added, "You know, Russell was there."

"Abe Russell?"

He almost recoiled, hearing her say the name. People were always impressed. Abe Russell was the current director of the Central Intelligence Agency.

"Russell seems to be shifting ground," Morgan said.

"In what way?" Nora held her breath, afraid to mention Norm's suspicions.

"Eurochemie is playing a funny kind of game," he said cautiously. "I can't really go into it, Nora . . . you understand?"

"*Of course!* Italy is in an awful mess. They're decadent . . . corrupt." The two words again, words just made to describe everything that was wrong with the world.

"Maybe," Morgan admitted, "but they've been around a long time. They're a civilized bunch."

"*Civilized?*"

"Yes, and I'm not so sure about us," he murmured. "Some of those guys down in Texas are enough to scare the living daylights out of you, Nora."

Shades of Buck Collins, she thought to herself. "But they think a lot of Buck, don't they?"

He laughed briefly. "They're all hawks like Buck. I think I've heard about all I want to hear for a while about zapping, first-striking, throw-weight, preemptive this-and-that . . ."

Nora commented dryly, "But it's all part of your business, Kurt. Unfortunate, but there you are."

He cocked an eye at her skeptically. "Tell me something, Nora. Important. Think carefully—*are we sure about Buck?*"

"Sure about Buck? What do you mean?" she said slowly.

"Just what I said."

"Well . . ." What should she say? What *did* he mean? Sure how? Unconvincingly, she said, "We know he's a star, don't we? Like you've always said."

"Yeah." He nodded tiredly. "Yeah."

Nora squeezed more closely to him. They were not talking vice-presidencies now, so she could kiss him again, on the cheek and then on the deep lines that cut his face from nose to mouth, dragging his flesh down, making him look dead tired and defeated.

"You're . . . weary . . . darling," she murmured.

"Yes, I am," he said. "Nora, I missed you an awful lot."

"I know. I'll bet no one comforted you like I know how."

"For sure."

She put her mouth to his, opening her lips delicately and touching with her tongue. He sat slumped, not responding. More boldly, Nora rubbed herself against his silk robe, jostling him gently, yearning for him to put his hands on her. Could she get through to him, or had she waited too long?

"Kurt! Oh, darling!"

Morgan's mouth trembled; it only made the skin on his throat look the more slack.

"Kurt," she said, almost abjectly, "tonight I'm going to give myself to you. I realize I haven't been fair . . . or nice to you."

"You're serious?" He stared at her.

"I want to go to bed with you, Kurt . . . now."

"Good." He sounded so uninterested. "I need bed, Nora. I'm tired."

"I mean more than sleeping."

"Do you?"

She got up, took his hand, pulled him to his feet, and then toward the bedroom—the bedroom of a married man which, she'd always believed, was but a local stop on the express route to perdition. All that had changed now. Her entire attitude toward life had changed dramatically in the last few days, but more particularly in the last few hours, since Paul Jerome had told her about Father John's plans.

Morgan's hands were shaking violently as he undressed

her. He fumbled with the fragile buttons of her cardigan and pulled it off her shoulders. Fiercely, even as he was undoing her blouse, she pressed against him, sure her vitality would give him life.

He clung to her, muttering, "I'm more than tired, Nora. I'm fed up. I feel that I'm slipping away from the system. I've lost my toehold. I saw it in Texas—I'm alienated. I don't believe the bullshit anymore."

"Oh, Kurt . . . no!" This could not be. A man like Kurt Morgan should not even think in those terms. He was strong, an essential component of the system. "You're just . . . tired. You need a vacation. Oh . . . if only we could go somewhere for a month. I'd *heal* you. I could make you well again."

He looked down at her face and for once there was an expression of tenderness. He was so tired he looked like a saint, she thought, his skin drawn, the eyes so loving and understanding.

"Nora, you don't understand—I *don't want it anymore.*" He kissed her forehead. "You're beautiful, you know."

For a second, Nora thought he meant he didn't want *her* anymore. She stripped off her blouse herself and then pulled off her skirt. She shucked her brassiere hurriedly, kicked off her shoes, stepped out of her pantyhose, and slid out of her white panties. Once this much was done, she knew nothing could ever be the same again. Kurt watched her, absently, fingertips arched in front of his face, as if—she hoped—in prayer before her.

Then, Nora simply sank backwards on his bed, arms stretched above her head, the posture she calculated showed her breasts to best advantage. He sat down beside her and ran the soft fingertips across her skin, from her neck, over her breasts, down her flattened belly, to fondle her crotch.

Nora thought she would pass out. "Oh, Kurt . . ." Her voice was a plea. "Darling . . . please don't be rough." She looked up at him, her lips parted, her eyes moist with what she hoped would pass for ecstasy, and placed her hand atop the silk covering his bare thigh and felt for his genital.

His groan was a primitive sound. He shrugged his shoulders out of his paisley robe and it dropped to the floor, making a thump. The gun—God, it might have gone off. But he didn't notice. His next sound was a primeval cry of desire as he pressed his face into her bare belly, thrusting his tongue into her navel. Nora spread her legs. Her pelvis jumped and the next thing she knew he had pushed his entire face between her legs. Now he sounded like a savage eating a cream soup.

Nora cried out. "Oh, Kurt!"

He snorted loudly enough to blister her insides but burrowed still deeper. He was not as accomplished at this particular act as Norm Vincent, Nora thought, but then he hadn't had the advantage of CIA training.

She worked her way around, as his panting seemed almost to inflate her like a balloon, but then to her dismay found herself repelled by his sour smell and the almost stale taste of his testicles. Morgan groaned extravagantly and flung his head back, breathing stertorously. She felt his rough beard on her smooth thigh.

"Nora." His voice was labored. "I've decided. I'm not leaving Hazel."

"What!" Her teeth chomped and he cried out.

"Jesus! She needs me, Nora. I can't leave her now. But that doesn't matter. We'll go on . . . like this . . . oh!"

"On? Like this?" She gave him her mouth again, drawing in her cheeks, pulling hard as if on a siphon, and she knew it was a pleasurable pain, the kind Norman had told her about, for Morgan's lower body jerked.

"Nora, I just *can't* do it."

Nora began to laugh so hard she thought she might choke, on him and on the irony of it all. She removed her mouth.

"Needs *you?* That's the funniest thing I ever heard. She doesn't need you! She's got Joe Mercury!"

"Joe Mercury?" he stuttered.

"Mercury makes love to her two or three times a week. They meet in New York. *You know!* You told me about it."

"That's over, Nora. She told me. It's over." His voice was frightened.

"No!" Nora snarled. "We've got a *film* of them together, Kurt."

"Never. Filthy!"

Desperately, Nora tried to explain. "Norm Vincent did it. Why? National Security, Kurt! Joe Mercury is an industrial spy—*your wife* has been supplying him information about Diversified, about the merger, about *everything,* and it's shipped off to Italy."

His voice was strangled. He cried out, trying to deny it, but knowing it was true. And then he muttered, "Russell warned me, tried to warn me. I didn't understand!"

"Darling, there are *things* people don't want to understand . . ."

A cry of fury and frustration burst from him and he began to sob. It was a horrible sound for her to hear.

"Never mind, darling," Nora whispered.

She bathed him in solace, licked and laved him as his body twisted in torment. He groaned so deeply the sound oppressed her ears.

The heavy slab of genital softened and dropped away from her. He became very still now, as the groan drifted away. She had soothed him. His hand slid away from her hip.

"Kurt . . . darling."

He had fallen asleep, the weary, tortured man. Nora pushed herself up on one elbow to look at him. But his eyes were not closed. He stared back at her, an expression of deep shock in his face.

"Kurt?"

She realized he was dead. She distanced herself from him slowly, and as the horrible fact registered, she leapt off the bed.

"Kurt . . . Oh, my God! Kurt!"

Maybe he was merely unconscious. She'd read long ago you could hold a mirror in front of the nose to see if it fogged up. If not, then he was dead. Nora couldn't stop staring at the inert form. Even now, she told herself, his soul was lofting away from the physical being, twisting along the ceiling toward the window . . . toward heaven.

Finally she forced herself to move, but she couldn't find a mirror. Of course, in her purse!

Keeping as far away from the body as she could, Nora held her makeup mirror under his nose. No. No moisture. She threw herself on her knees beside the nude body and bent her head in prayer, realizing she must call the police.

After a few minutes of silent prayer, Nora returned to the living room and crouched next to the fireplace. She had to pull herself together. The enormity of the problem struck her—her own nakedness, his. He was dead and without a stitch of clothing on him. How would she explain that to smirking police and cynical doctors? It would be obvious to all that Morgan had died in the throes of love.

Oh God, Nora wished fervently that this was a more barbaric time. She could simply have cast the body to the waters, over a cliff, or into a nearby ditch, and marched on. What a horrible thought. She was disgusting, yes, she was merely disgusting.

But he was naked and had to be dressed. She needed help, fast. Her thoughts turned to Paul, her oldest friend in New York City. Paul would know how to handle it. If she was quick, maybe she could catch him at the hospital—was he still there with Buck? Nora got the hospital number from Information.

Collins's room rang. "Hullo." His voice was not as boisterous as usual.

"Please . . . Buck . . . it's Nora. Is Paul there?" She spoke staccato.

There was heavy sarcasm in his reply. "My *financial advisor*? No. He just left." Collins sighed. "Say, beautiful, when you comin' to see old Buck again? Old Buck is *very* restless and lonely."

"Buck! *Where did he go?*"

"To his girl's, for Christ's sake! Stop shouting at me. What the hell's wrong?"

Nora didn't answer. She hung up, thinking, Oh God, how to find Lucia's number? Again, feeling totally desperate, she dialed Information. Yes, there was a Gogarty, on Park Avenue.

"Hello." Lucia's voice was like a bell.

"Lucia . . . Lucia, please help me—is Paul there yet?"

"Yes. Who is this?"

"Nora Ellen Sweeney. Let me talk to him, *please.*"

The body was already cold, freezing cold it seemed to Nora, a lesson of what happens when the furnace goes out in your house. Knowing she had to begin somewhere, she slipped his shorts over the bony, dead toes and dragged them over the knees, as far as the thighs. She had to roll him to the side and then back and onto the other side to get the shorts up under him and then pulled to his waist in front.

Already Nora was perspiring heavily and it wasn't very warm in the apartment. She stopped to pass her hand across her forehead and laughed shakily, almost hysterically. How funny it was—just minutes before *he* had been undressing *her*.

Morgan had never seemed very heavy in life. In death, he was made of pure lead. His shorts looked twisted and funny, but at least he was covered in that strategic place. Now the socks. No, forget the socks. The shirt. She held the button-down white shirt up to her face. It had begun to *smell;* it stunk of sickness and death, like the wind from a plague zone.

Why was she so eager to have him ready by the time *Paul* arrived? Paul would be a fool if he didn't realize what had happened. Did it matter if the deceased was all dressed up to receive him? God . . . Nora began to weep, which made it all the harder to dress him. Blinded by tears, she thought how she had loved Kurt—not crazily or passionately, but with a love born of deep respect. Nora had been at the point of freely offering him her virginity, for the first time eager to give it away, and he had died. It was too much.

Nora knelt on the bed behind the corpse and pulled the right sleeve of the shirt up over his arm. Then she tried to push the inert mass of rotting fat and rigid bones to a sitting position but then, oh God, she realized she couldn't bend the arm into the other sleeve. She could get the trousers on, though, over the feet, as she had the shorts. It was important to put pants on him. The shirt was not so vital; it would be obvious to the coroner that he'd been gathered just as he was taking his shirt off . . . or putting it on. Putting it on? Why would he be putting it on? Why would he have taken it off?

Nora straddled his belly, horribly aware that as she jostled the corpse it began to exude very intimate unpleasant odors.

But she managed to fix her mind coldly on the task. She could not be concerned about the crease in the trousers. Simply pull . . .

Oh God! Nora screamed out in horror. Pulling the pants up his legs, her bare bottom jerked backwards, against his face. Oh, Sweet Mother of God! His heavy nose felt like a dull knife penetrating her anal orifice, and ramming straight to her heart. She went cold with fear and loathing. She hated Kurt Morgan for this final obscene gesture. She would never touch him again.

Nora leaped from the bed, in full retreat. Where were her clothes? That one physical contact, like a gesture from beyond, finally projected her into near-frenzy. *God!* How could he? Even in death he was crude, insidious, and insinuating.

When the intercom rang, she was still naked, still trying to find her clothes and pull herself together.

"Yes?" She barely managed to steady her voice.

"A Mr. Jerome down here, Miss Sweeney."

"Fine. Up, have him come up."

She wasn't able to get dressed. She hadn't the strength now or the resolution.

The doorbell rang. She had to put something on. Morgan's paisley robe lay on the bedroom floor, scattered, it looked, like dead leaves. She grabbed it up and slid her arms into it, feeling the drag of the gun in the right-hand pocket. It was too big and loose but would have to do.

Nora tripped on the carpet in the living room and almost fell, but reached the door, unlocked and pulled it open.

Paul Jerome was standing there, looking anxious. Beside him was Lucia Gogarty.

"Thank God you're here," Nora said.

She sagged toward him, making it clear she'd land on the floor if he didn't catch her. She heard herself panting. Jerome half-dragged her into the living room and lowered her to the couch. Lucia busied herself straightening the robe around Nora's nakedness, thinking it was a good thing she'd come with him.

"Nora, what the hell . . ."

"In . . . the . . . bedroom."

Nora closed her eyes, giving way. She was out of it now. She heard Jerome cross the living room, then his exclamation, grunt of alarm.

"Nora, what the hell happened?" he yelled.

She shook her head.

"She won't speak," Lucia said. Her voice was skeptical, but *she* didn't yet know.

Jerome returned in haste. "I think he's dead," he said softly. "Nora . . ." He reached for her shoulder, shaking her gently. "Did you call a doctor . . . anybody?"

She shook her head, numbly. Finally, Lucia looked shocked, and scared.

"Well, for Christ's sake," Jerome cried. "We've got to call a doctor." His breathing had become erratic too. "The guy downstairs, he'll be able to do it," Jerome said.

All Nora could do was nod, to try to stop her tears, her shaking.

Jerome calmed down when he spoke on the intercom—there was an emergency in the Morgan apartment, medical help was urgently needed.

He hung up and turned. "Nora." His face was puzzled.

Lucia understood everything, instantly. Men were so dense, so dull. "Paolo, Nora must get dressed immediately."

"Yes, she sure as hell must," he growled. Now his stare at her was an unspoken accusation. She had killed Morgan, that's what he was thinking.

"I'm sorry . . . sorry!" Nora exclaimed, but she didn't recognize her own voice.

Jerome was rough. "Nora, get the hell in the bathroom and put your clothes on, for Christ's sake!"

"Yes, come," Lucia said. "I will help you."

Together, Paul and Lucia got her on her feet. Nora shook her head violently to stop the swaying.

Jerome's expression was grim. "They'll be here any minute." He looked around the apartment. "We *must* have a story."

". . . working, discussing the merger," Nora gasped.

He nodded. "Yes, the three of us, sitting here having a drink. Morgan went inside to change. A few minutes went by, we didn't think anything of it. Then . . . too late . . . Nora, get in there and get dressed!"

Voice hushed, Lucia pointed at Kurt's prized Picasso. "We must put that painting somewhere until we can get it out of here."

"Lucia!" Jerome's voice cracked with impatience.

"That Picasso is stolen property," Lucia said harshly. "I recognize it."

Oh, God! Nora's eyes filled with tears again. It was the picture Kurt had always hidden in the closet if a stranger was expected.

Jerome nodded. "Yes, okay, Lucia. You're a genius. *Get her dressed!*"

Chapter Twenty-five

INDUSTRIALISTS, FINANCIERS, AND ALL MEMBERS OF THE business community were shocked and dismayed when the announcement was made the next afternoon, after the stock market had closed, that Kurt Morgan had suddenly died of a massive heart attack while in a business meeting in New York City. Government leaders expressed condolences and the president himself hailed Morgan as having been a pillar of democracy and capitalism, a champion of equal opportunity, the creator of jobs, the inspiration of youth. Detractors said the flag at the Pentagon was even lowered to half-mast for a half hour.

It seemed ironic that Morgan had been worried that news of Buck Collins's near-fatal chopper accident might shake the structure of the merger they had built for Diversified Technologies and Brown, Broadstairs and Dunn. It might have been worse if Morgan, the lawyers, bankers, and financial planners hadn't laid out the plan so perfectly. Deliberately, and with everyone in full agreement, they held the news as long as they could. Ideally, Morgan should have died on Thursday instead of Wednesday, or even better on Friday afternoon, so that the market would have a weekend to get everything back into perspective before buying-and-selling opened again Monday morning.

But some things were not possible. The *New York Times* ran a long obituary Friday morning, tracking Morgan's career from the Pacific Northwest to World War II flight school, college, and the long, tedious, tenacious climb to the top. Even the stories in the *News* and *Post* were fairly innocuous: BUSINESS MOGUL SUFFERS SEIZURE DURING BUSINESS MEETING.

The truth would *not* out.

Nora had pulled herself together rapidly. Even Lucia had been impressed by the way she quieted down before the paramedics arrived. And she didn't crack again until the ambulance team was gone and the coroner's men came to collect the body.

Morgue! Jerome called Buck Collins at the hospital and told him; Morgan had apparently died while they'd been in the other room sipping red wine. And then it had been up to Jerome to notify Hazel Morgan.

It was tiring, a depressing procedure, all of it. Nora thanked God she wasn't asked to do anything until the next day. Then, it was decided by the officers of the company—principally Gerald Ball, number two in the pecking order after Morgan—that it was only proper a brief memorial service be held for Kurt Morgan in the city, after the funeral which was to be in Scarsdale. The task of arranging the memorial for the following Friday morning at ten was given to Nora. A short board of directors meeting would be called for 11:30 A.M. for those directors who'd be in town, and then a luncheon at the Plaza Hotel.

It was going to be a very important, even crucial week, Nora understood. How lucky she was, she realized, that the promotion had gone in just under the wire. She was a vice-president now, one of a squadron of them, she told Paul Jerome modestly, but nonetheless a vice-president.

Paul said they had their work cut out for them. The formal terms of the merger had been set; everything was on paper, public knowledge. What had not been written down was Kurt Morgan's plan for Buck Collins. Morgan had promised, but only orally, that in due course Buck was to move into Jack Frazer's spot as head of Diversified's aerospace activities, and that when Morgan stepped down

Buck would automatically replace him as chief executive officer of Diversified Industries.

But what was going to happen now? How could Collins be sure about his future in the newly formed Diversified Industries, Jerome insisted on asking. And why, Nora retorted, did Paul Jerome always have to be so concerned about Buck Collins's well-being? What about Paul Jerome? His answer was obvious—Jerome's own future depended on how strong Buck's position became in DI, as they were already calling the merged companies.

Moreover, Jerome told her, he'd heard from various sources that Rustford Lancer, Helen Marconi's protector, had suddenly begun promoting his own candidacy to succeed Morgan. He had even been on the phone to several financial writers offering on-the-record interviews along the lines of "Whither Diversified Post-Morgan?"

Shock ripped down Nora's spine upon hearing that, surely a significant indicator of what was coming. "How dare he? When Kurt was alive, Lancer would have been read out."

"Nobody to stop him now. He's one of your ranking executives. Him and Frazer."

"And Gerald Ball. Don't forget about Gerald Ball."

"Nora, Gerald Ball is *very* forgettable," Jerome said spitefully. "My point is, if we expect to carry this thing through, then the details have got to be cleared up . . . *again . . . post-Morgan.*"

"I thought you said postmortem," she muttered. "Appropriate, isn't it?"

"Yeah." He sounded cruel, unfriendly.

"Paul . . . please. Be kind. I need kindness now."

"Yeah, all right." His voice said he was reconsidering. "Nora, there's a place over on Forty-fifth, just off Third. Pietro's. I don't think any of your Diversified high-fliers eat there. Can you meet me at one o'clock? Today?"

Nora spent the rest of the morning analyzing the situation and planning her strategy. She sat staring at the list of Diversified directors, trying to sort them out, to remember what Kurt had said about them. How were they going to respond to the new situation? It was essential to hold them to the merger, but if anybody had had doubts about it, then Morgan's departure was a perfect excuse to renege. Gerald Ball would have to lead the way. He *would*—he was Morgan's man—maybe not forcefully, but he would understand the alternative was damaging, destructive.

There was no reason to doubt that Lancer would kill for Morgan's job, but fortunately Lancer had weak points. One of them was obvious: his liaison with Helen Marconi. Their sordid story was so widely known it was a wonder it had never gotten back to Mrs. Lancer. The liaison indicated not only weak corporate morals, as far as Nora was concerned, but also bad taste because Helen was such a bag. Lancer's other great weakness was the fact that he had nothing in the way of contacts at the Pentagon. In this particular respect, there was no question Buck Collins was superior. Consumer goods were important, of course, and Nora realized that Kurt had favored a better balance between military and consumer products. But the hard fact was that Diversified was still heavily tilted toward missiles, aircraft, and military electronics. No intelligent member of the board could ignore that.

Obviously, Buck Collins had to get the Morgan spot. Nora hadn't worked so hard at this just to be liquidated by Rusty Lancer's clique.

The trickiness of the situation was brought home so forcefully in the next few minutes that Nora decided then and there she should be keeping a diary; this was a textbook case.

"Sweeney!" she said into the phone.

The voice that answered slammed her with *déjà vu*. Nora's heart wilted like an orchid.

"Hello, cocksucker!"

"Oh . . . Helen," she said sweetly. "I thought you'd gone to Alaska."

Helen Marconi laughed harshly enough to melt the phone line. "Not just yet. Since your boyfriend went to the big boardroom in the sky, I decided to delay my departure. Who knows what's going to happen next, *right?*" Nora didn't say anything; all she could think of was how crude and disrespectful Helen was of the dead. "What's-a-matter, cocksucker?" Helen jeered. "Looks bad, does it? Bet you're wondering who's gonna take over, huh?"

Nora shuddered. "I'm not worried," she mumbled.

Helen Marconi's throat rattled with merriment. "I see in the paper you and this guy Jerome were with Morgan. I don't believe that, Sweeney. I think you were there alone and you . . . blew him away."

Nora could not stop herself from shaking with anger. "You'd better believe what you read in the *New York Times,* Helen. It's the newspaper of record. Another thing, Helen—who cares what *you* think?"

"There's one person who does, Sweeney, and right now he's the man who counts. Maybe you ought to consider the Alaska job . . . cocksucker."

In the cab, on the way to the restaurant, Nora reconsidered the events with anger. Lancer would have to be dealt with. They would have to use Gerald Ball. He was the man who would make the difference. Ball and Paul Jerome had gotten on well enough during the negotiations. She could point out to Paul that Kurt Morgan had always thought very highly of Ball, had listened to his advice and never failed to call him when a problem was of importance and urgency.

And, she remembered one other thing—Ball's unassailable position within Diversified. There was that block of support which Morgan had referred to but never discussed, powerful enough to protect Gerald Ball over the years from any number of corporate threats.

Pietro's was off the beaten track, up a narrow staircase which led to a tiny bar filled with red-faced Irishmen. They stared at her, but not for long. She told a waiter she was meeting Paul Jerome.

No, Mr. Jerome wasn't there yet. The waiter showed her the table, next to a window overlooking Third Avenue, and Nora asked for a Scotch and water while she waited. Jerome arrived soon after her drink, complaining he hadn't been able to get a cab, and immediately ordered a Beefeater martini on the rocks.

He inspected her quietly. "Well, you've recovered. You look all right. Not too broken up."

She stiffened and her eyes began to ache. "Cruel to say that to me."

"Sorry." He shrugged. No, Nora thought dismally, he didn't really like her very much. "I had a talk with Buck this morning. He thinks he should definitely attend the memorial."

She nodded indifferently. How could she care when he looked at her so coldly? How could she care about anything?

"I'll get a limo with a big soft backseat," he went on. "Buck thinks he can walk it into the church, on a crutch, like he hurt himself skiing."

Nora agreed pensively. "Shouldn't he be getting out of the hospital soon anyway?"

"Yes. But not by next Friday."

"The fool," she said bitterly. "And now we've got to pull the fat out of the fire for him."

Jerome stared at her wearily. "Is there any other way to go, Madame Vice-President?"

"No."

"But you're *not* enthusiastic."

"How can I be? You think I'm some sort of . . . pariah," she murmured, feeling miserable. "You'd think I murdered Kurt, or something. Do you want to know what happened, exactly?"

"I think I know enough already. Maybe it's better I don't know any more."

She glared at him. "We were making love . . . and he died. There! That's all there is to it. Nothing more, nothing less. I didn't do anything criminal, at least as far as I know."

A smile flitted across his face. "Lucia told me to be kind to you in your bereavement."

"How nice," Nora said dully. "What'd she do with the Picasso?"

He smiled more broadly. "Good question. Lucia will . . . handle it."

"If it was stolen, then she has to return it." Nora frowned. "I'm sure . . . Kurt . . . didn't know it was stolen, if that's what you've been thinking. Whatever he was . . ." Her voice dropped. "He wasn't dishonest."

"Now, look, darling," Jerome said, "I know you don't think Buck is the man Morgan was—and he isn't. He's his own man." He looked vaguely uneasy. "Personally, he's a little impulsive and I'd . . . never say he's not just a little bit irresponsible when it comes to money. But he's all right. He's a good man to work for."

"He's younger than Kurt," Nora acknowledged.

"And more ambitious."

"I admit he's got a good amount of charisma."

"Charisma?" Jerome looked ill. "I don't know what that is. It's a buzz word. If a politician recognizes you and shakes your hand, right away he's got charisma. To me, that's so much bullshit, Nora."

Darkly, she said, "How sweetly you put it. I would have thought he had it. That's just my opinion, of course. More than a Gerald Ball, I mean." She tried at last to smile. "Paul, I was thinking in the cab that we need Gerald Ball on our side."

"We'll need everybody we can get if Lancer is going to be a pain in the ass," he agreed sourly. "The whole thing may start *not* to make sense, Nora. I mean from our point of view."

Nora felt like somebody was digging a spoon into her, hollowing her out. "No, no, we need you—there's more to it than you think—things nobody knows."

"What *things?*"

"Kurt was looking into making an investment in Europe. A big thing. A company called Eurochemie . . . Eurochemie S.A.," she said precisely. "S.A. stands for *société anonyme.*"

"I know that, for Christ's sake. *Why*, Nora?"

She shook her head, looking around cautiously. "He told me he'd been encouraged by Washington." She leaned back, letting herself smile proudly. "I've been researching Eurochemie."

"That's the big international job he gave you?" Jerome didn't sound very interested.

Nora nodded. "Yes, but when he was down in Texas at New Year's, Abe Russell . . . you know . . ." Jerome nodded quickly and seemed more interested in her story. "Seems like Russell advised Kurt to cool it. I don't know why."

"Nora," Jerome said quietly, "Eurochemie is a goddamn *international* octopus. Does Gerry Ball know about this?" She shook her head. "Then you've definitely got to bring him in."

"I know, but how? If I tell him, he'll think there's lots of other information I know from Kurt. And I don't!"

He nodded. "All right, I'll call him," Jerome said swiftly. "I'll tell him that when *we* were all with Kurt that last night, he mentioned Eurochemie. First I heard of it. First *you* heard of it. And what's going on—is this going to screw up the merger agreement in any way, Gerry old boy?" Jerome smiled cleverly. "As a matter of fact, Eurochemie made something of a pass at BBD a couple of years ago."

"You didn't report that in our negotiations," she charged irritably. He was so shrewd he made her feel uneasy.

"No reason we should," Jerome answered smoothly. "It didn't ever come to anything—*we* weren't interested. I suppose it's possible Morgan was concerned Eurochemie was making another try, this time for Diversified."

"They couldn't! They're not rich enough!" she protested.

"The hell they're not. They do twice as much as you guys."

That was what Kurt had said, Nora remembered. Eurochemie was very very big. "Please call Gerry then, Paul," she said shyly.

"Cheers." He lifted his glass.

"Cheers," she said. "I . . . uh . . . I want to thank you, Paul, you and Lucia." She felt better about everything now. "I feel quite guilty about all that, Paul, as you can imagine. But there's something I wanted to tell you, so you'll at least understand if anything were ever to happen to me." She was whispering. "Strangely enough, when Kurt died, just at the very moment when he lost consciousness, just then I'd made up my mind I was going to give myself to him . . . and he died." She smiled. "I know now, Paul, that I'll probably die a virgin." She waited a second, significantly. "You think I'm an awful fool and you don't like me a lot of the time because you think I'm such a hypocrite. I know you suspect my relationship with Kurt, that I took advantage of him. But I did love him, as deeply as I'm capable. I don't know if I *am* capable of loving deeply, Paul. But I did like him and I respected him—and whatever I did, it *wasn't* just to further my career. Do you believe me?"

Embarrassed, he shrugged. "I've always thought you were a good person, Nora." He frowned. "Just let me warn you again—I tried before, remember? Well, don't put all your eggs in the Buck Collins basket either—if you know what I mean."

Nora laughed, almost gaily. "My eggs! Good heavens, Paul, I'm not some kind of a chicken."

He ignored her brittle humor. "You tend to commit yourself too heavily to one person and people are always letting you down."

"I have to do it that way," she said stubbornly. "I *have* to trust people. You're cynical, Paul. I wish I was too, but I'm not. I'm surprised, in a way," she said frankly, "that you could fall in love with Lucia, as cynical as you are."

He didn't like that. His face reddened. "Let's order. What do you want to eat, Nora?"

Chapter Twenty-six

IT HAD BECOME ESSENTIAL FOR GERALD BALL TO HAVE a private meeting with Paul Jerome and Nora Ellen Sweeney, and on Sunday morning at eleven Nora was sitting with Ball in the back of his chauffeured black Daimler, his second car. The first was a convertible baby-blue Rolls Royce Corniche used only during the summer.

At Paul's insistence they were headed for lunch at the Gogarty Castle. The only uncomfortable thing about the invitation was that Father John and the Princess would be there too.

Nora had decided immediately that Gerald Ball was a man of impeccable manners. More importantly, he remained Morgan's man. He made it clear right away that he hadn't had any second thoughts about the merger and in fact was fearful that Morgan's death might raise obstacles.

No one ever saw much of Ball in the corporate corridors. He was a quiet, unobtrusive man, and much of his work was, in fact, done outside the office in conferences with bankers, luncheon meetings with the financial community, and on the telephone. Ball, like Morgan, often worked at home. He was old enough, he explained gently to Nora, to have his way about that and Kurt Morgan had never objected.

Nora understood immediately why Gerald Ball was the man Kurt had called in *after* the crucial meeting, *after* all the arguments had been voiced; between them, they'd decided then what was the smartest course for Diversified to take.

Silver-haired Gerald Ball, she mused, watching him twist the heavy foil off the neck of a bottle of Dom Perignon. Nora was ready with the glasses and a heavy napkin to catch the foam. Ball was a very fastidious man.

He looked younger than Kurt Morgan had, though she would have bet he was a good ten years older. Alongside Gerald Ball, whose face was tanned, firm, and hardly lined at all, Morgan had been an old man. Ball's eyes were gentle, the eyelids drooping sadly at the corners. Nevertheless, there was no question about it, he was a *very* attractive older man who could easily inspire kisses every morning and embraces every night.

"Be prepared now, Nora." His voice was like silk. "If I do it right, it's not supposed to pop and foam all over you. But I'm not an expert." He lifted his voice toward the driver. "Perhaps Freddie will slow down just a mite." It was a suggestion, not a command.

"Yes, sir." Freddie was watching the operation through his rearview mirror, smiling with delight to see Gerald Ball having such a good time.

Ball did seem lonely. She and Jerome had made it their purpose in the last twenty-four hours to learn that his wife had died some three years before and that since then he'd been living a solitary life in a luxury apartment off Fifth Avenue in the Seventies. Ball evidently did not take out any of the local widows.

The bottle opened with a polite hiss, as Ball himself would have opened if he'd been a bottle of champagne. "Ah, Nora, perfect."

"Beautiful," Nora said, very quietly. She held the glasses for him.

He poured, then pushed the depleted bottle into an ice-lined silver bucket in the mini-bar which faced them, part of the executive console with telephone and miniature TV. There was caviar in a tiny refrigerator if she'd like some, Ball had said.

"So," he said, leaning back in the soft cushions which matched the gray glove leather of the interior. He held up his glass. "To Kurt," he said, his voice bright with significance. Again, he looked apologetically up toward Freddie. "Freddie, would you please close the glass? There's something very private I have to say to Miss Sweeney. *You understand.*"

"Yes, sir." Freddie understood.

When they were in private, Ball smiled almost imperceptibly. "He really doesn't mind, you know. He understands there are things—for his own protection."

"Of course." Nora was very impressed by the artless way Ball had put Freddie in quarantine.

"Well, really . . . to Kurt." Ball sipped again. "Excellent, isn't it?" He looked from the bubbly to her. "You loved him, didn't you, Nora?"

A trick question? Maybe. She couldn't know. Why not admit it? Ball would appreciate an affirmative, she judged. "Yes," she said simply.

"I admire your frankness, Nora, and also the obvious fact that you're a very brave girl." His voice was warm. "Despite the talk—there *was* talk, you know—you made Kurt's last days happy ones." He shook his head sorrowfully. "Not that any of us expected these were to be his last days. Life is strange. Kurt took care of himself physically and I always thought he'd be a geriatric survivor."

To this she could agree enthusiastically. "He was in *wonderful* shape." Nora continued with precision, "He never seemed to suffer from tension or stress. He seemed to have everything *under control.*"

"Yes, he was a man who anticipated. And if you anticipate, nothing is going to go far wrong."

"He was *never* surprised, not by anything," she seconded him.

"Well, then," Ball asked, twirling his champagne glass in his perfectly manicured fingers, "what in the world happened?"

Nora had to be careful. Should she divulge to him that

Kurt had, at the moment of death, been a very worried man? Worried about Nora, worried about Hazel and Joe Mercury? Worried that he had been so deeply, so tragically betrayed?

Ball didn't wait for her answer. "I know," he said, "Hazel was always a problem . . ." Nora didn't agree or disagree. "I, of course, am the executor of Kurt's will. Hazel is well-provided for and also the children. He had some other bequests which will come as a . . . surprise to some people."

Oh, no! Her heart thumped. Surely not to Nora Ellen Sweeney!

Ball chuckled fondly. "Dear Kurt. For example, he directed that an athletic award in his name be set up at his high school in Oregon. His college is, as well, to get a scholarship fund." He smiled benignly. "*You* were not left anything, Nora."

"Well . . . I should hope not!" Nora cried softly, actually relieved to hear it. "Why on earth would I be?"

He lowered his voice even more. "You were his companion, Nora. His *mistress.*"

Nora had never heard it put like that before. Helen Marconi had said it, yes, but in another way. She stammered, "I have an aversion to that word, I guess. Besides . . ."

"Yes? Besides what?"

Nora felt Freddie must see her furious blush. She didn't dare look into his rearview mirror for fear he could tell from her face that she was in the hot seat.

"Well . . . I never really became Kurt's . . . mistress."

Ball's neatly clipped eyebrows escalated. "You are saying to me, Nora, that you and Kurt never . . ."

"True, Mr. Ball."

"Well." He sipped his champagne more agitatedly, hardly bothered to run it on his tongue as he had before. "I am surprised. I just assumed . . ."

"So many people did, Mr. Ball," Nora said. "It's hard for people to accept that a man and a woman can have a close business relationship that goes no further than that. In a way, Kurt Morgan was like the father I never knew."

"I see." Ball nodded remotely.

She smiled timidly at him. "Are you disappointed to hear this, Mr. Ball?"

"No, no," he said hastily, "and Nora, you're to call me Gerry . . . please. I *am* surprised, but not disappointed. It just never occurred to me that you two hadn't been lovers in every sense."

The way he formed the words; they slipped like nooses from his thin-lipped mouth. "I am *slightly* disappointed. Although Kurt didn't name you in his will, I was prepared to tell you that because you had loved him *and* been his lover you would be taken care of. I would see to that, Nora."

She nodded rigidly, not knowing how to respond.

He went on cheerfully, "You were just made a vice-president. You deserve it, Nora, and I'll see to it that nobody, and I mean *nobody* tries to reverse that. You are under my personal protection."

"I appreciate that . . . *Gerry*. But why would anybody try to reverse my appointment? I earned it."

"Nora, let's be frank. What they'd say is you did earn it—that's just it." He looked out the window, evidently embarrassed to discuss such matters. "I've admired you for a long time. I've watched you. Kurt always praised your abilities to the heavens. Abilities, yes." He turned his head toward her for a second.

"I don't think I need any protection," Nora said stiffly.

"In other words, you're not looking for any handouts along the highway of life."

"Exactly."

"Admirable," he exclaimed. "It warms me when I hear people trust in their own ability and the virtue of hard work." He pushed himself forward for the champagne bottle. "Now, we'll drink to you," he murmured. "Hold my glass, will you? Steady there." Ball beamed at her. He hit his refilled glass against hers softly. "To you, Nora. By

God, you are a beautiful woman. I don't care what you say!" he cried warmly. "You are under my protection. You're a golden girl, Nora," he beamed. "And now, what is this business about Italy?"

Nora had rehearsed and she quickly recited to him the story of their investigations into Eurochemie S.A., what Kurt had told her about Washington's encouragement, and then Abe Russell's signal that the project should be shelved.

Gerry Ball's first reaction was quite like Paul's—that it would have required far too much capital and clever maneuvering to create a power base inside a conglomerate such as Eurochemie.

"I don't understand Kurt," Ball mourned. "Here we have a merger looming with BBD—one would have thought that was enough for the moment." He shook his head despairingly. "Here's one for you, Nora—Paul Jerome thinks the very company Kurt was thinking of attacking has already opened an attack on us."

"I know," Nora said slowly. "And that makes it a different kettle of fish."

"Precisely," Ball said, as if instant death had been diagnosed. "And from my own brief investigation, I learned that Eurochemie is, in fact, sending a representative over here. It appears Eurochemie has allotted a sizable amount of money to destabilize us."

This was truly shocking. Had all this happened since Morgan's death, or had it been going on all along? "What do we do, Gerry?"

He shrugged, his mouth set in a thin line. "Nothing yet. I certainly do *not* think we should begin acquiring Eurochemie shares. You could begin buying and buy until Doomsday and never know how much you controlled, indeed if you were *in* control, for the simple reason that the management would never inform you. It is all highly secret."

"Is it possible?" she said.

Ball chuckled dryly. "Of course, but I can't imagine the

Pentagon is going to sit idly by and watch a foreign cartel buy its way into a position to have a yea- or nay-say over our missile and bomber programs."

"God, no, never!"

"So, then, what *was* in Kurt's mind? Had he been advised to buy control of Eurochemie before Eurochemie bought control of us? Or even—more insidious," Ball clucked, "to buy them as they're in the act of buying us so that when we're bought we have, in fact, bought ourselves. Does that make any sense?" he asked with amusement.

"It could make sense," Nora ventured.

"Or nonsense? Absolutely right, golden girl," he said, lecturing. "But you'll come to realize as you pass along life's highway, Nora, that *anything* is possible."

Nora knew there were people like this, people who believed that nothing happened innocently or in the due course of human events. No, behind every seemingly innocuous event there lay a capricious will directing desperate men in defense of desperate schemes.

"It's possible," Ball summed up, "that Kurt was spared some unpleasant moments, but you need have no fear, Nora—*you* are under my protection."

"I'm happy to know that . . . Gerry." She did her best to sound nonchalant but all she could think was how completely she and Paul Jerome had misjudged Ball. Behind the silvered exterior, she began to see a barracuda.

Ball touched his glass against hers. "Here's to us . . . golden girl," he said. "To be perfectly honest, I am disappointed to learn you were not Kurt's mistress, because I was prepared to ask you to be mine. I would still ask, you see, even if you were never that to Kurt."

Nora tasted acidity in the champagne. She felt herself wilt. "Me? No, Gerry, there are so many sophisticated women around . . ."

He didn't want to hear her. "I know an island in the Caribbean where I'd like to take you, Nora. Quite isolated and away from the New York City winter doldrums. I hate it here in February and March." He stared out the window of the Daimler. Yes, she could see it too; the patches of snow along the expressway were dirty. "It seems like winter is never going to end and everybody's got the flu. They're coughing and sneezing and the whole city smells of nasal congestion." He turned quickly. "Will you come with me?"

"Me?" She knew she sounded like an idiot.

"Of course, you, golden girl! I told you I found you fatally attractive and I haven't felt that way about a girl since my wife died."

The way he said it made her shudder. "Oh, Gerry . . ."

"I'm sorry." His eyes drifted back to the landscape. "Molly was an earthy woman," Ball recalled, his eyes misting. "She liked her food and drink. All her appetites were big."

Nora nodded nervously, not knowing what to say.

"You, Nora, on the other hand, you're a golden girl. You'll come with me then?" he asked her again.

Nora smiled cautiously, not agreeing or disagreeing.

When Freddie stopped the car at Gogarty Castle, Nora remembered that the last time she'd arrived was by helicopter with Buck Collins. Which was more impressive —a chopper or a Daimler?

Mr. Oswald obviously thought it was a tossup. He'd been extremely impressed by the helicopter but when he swung open the front door of the castle and spotted the Daimler he seemed to stagger.

"A beautiful vehicle," Nora heard him cry. "I myself drive a Studebaker."

Ball peered out the window at Oswald as he came down the stone steps, all legs, like a stalky bird. Paul Jerome appeared behind him, dressed in Shetland sweater, open shirt, and slacks. Everyone had been advised it was a casual lunch; Gerry Ball was dressed for a meeting with conservative bankers.

How much water had passed under the bridge since last

time, Nora thought. Morgan was dead and she was under the protection of Gerald Ball. The thought frightened her.

Oswald had not changed. "Welcome to Gogarty Castle!" he yelled.

Ball sprang out of the car. "Paul. What a pleasure to see you! And here, in the wilderness," he exclaimed heartily. "I haven't been upstate since I visited a friend of mine in Sing Sing."

Jerome laughed and introduced Oswald. "Oswald is in charge of Gogarty Castle."

"In name only," Oswald said, "and not for long for I shall soon be leaving. I was appointed *major domo* of this place by J.J. Gogarty, the late papal knight, but he is deceased now."

Jerome put a hand lightly on Ball's arm to draw him away. Nora noticed how Ball pulled free. He didn't like to be touched. She followed them up the steps, feeling queasy about seeing Father John again, the traitor and apostate. What was she going to say? She'd been so busy with Ball she hadn't had time to consider her speech to Father John.

"We're all in the library," Jerome said.

He led the way through the foyer and down the hallway to the oversized wood-paneled room.

Nora stopped in the doorway. She saw that Lucia and Elena were arranged at the mantel of the fireplace which blazed behind them. At a decent distance from Elena stood Father John. How he had changed! He was getting fat! His face had filled out; he looked less lean and hungry, thus losing that maniacal look in his eyes. His whole appearance was mellow. Was this the result of being in love?

Nevertheless, Nora appreciated how right Paul had been when he'd remarked on the physical resemblance of Elena and Father John Foster. Elena was nearly as tall as Foster and their faces matched in shape, skin tone, and the ironic slant of smoky blue eyes situated beneath the same

313

bony foreheads. Of course, Elena was the female of the twins, finely built, elegantly poised, her legs slimmer than Lucia's.

Lucia, Nora thought enviously, looked more schoolgirl-ish than ever, younger, happier. Her face grew serious when she saw Nora; obviously, she remembered the horrid night of Morgan's death, how distraught Nora had been, how naked and desolate. But Lucia could not be jealous of her now, Nora thought, having seen her that night and the way Paul had handled her.

"Well, everybody here," Jerome said coolly. He went on to introduce Gerald Ball to the assembly.

Responding to Lucia and Elena, Ball cried in courtly fashion, "No, I don't believe it. Not mother and daughter. Surely . . . sisters!"

"No," Elena corrected him, obviously tired of the comment, "this one is my daughter, I must admit it."

"How do you do?" Lucia's eyelashes fluttered coquettishly.

"Gerry," he said, "Gerry Ball. A great pleasure, a great pleasure," he stuttered.

"Welcome . . . *Cherry*." Did Elena deliberately mispronounce the name?

Foster shuffled a step or two. "My name is John Foster," said the about-to-be ex-priest. He held out his hand to Gerry Ball.

"Father Foster, isn't it?"

His eyes went to the round collar. At least, Nora told herself spitefully, Father John hadn't yet taken to wearing a Hawaiian sport shirt.

Nora purposefully crossed the room, keeping far from Foster, and kissed Lucia on the cheek, lips hardly touching skin. "Hello, Lucia," she whispered, then added wistfully, "you're wonderful, Lucia. You look wonderful too."

Lucia turned quickly to her mother. "Nora, this is my mother, Elena . . . Princess Saltimbocca . . . whatever it pleases you to call her."

"How do you do, Princess?" Nora said politely. She'd made an inquiry. This was proper.

Elena sneered royally. "Not so well in this curs'ed weather . . . Nora. It is Nora, yes? You grew up very near here, John told me."

"Yes." Nora nodded worriedly. So the priest *had* discussed her with his beloved. It made Nora almost sick to her stomach to think so. She could have thrown up on the thick and immense Oriental carpet. "The weather is better in the summer, Princess," she said weakly. They were not going to be able to accuse her of bad manners, on top of everything else they knew of her. "It's very nice along the Hudson River."

"So Paolo tells me," Elena grunted, her eyes snapping. "But no place for a poetess. It is *too big* here, the imagination cannot be enclosed, as in a tiny rose garden or small city. So, my friend, Nora," Elena announced majestically, "with the God-of-the-atheist's help, I will not be here to see summer. I do not understand it," she continued, as if somebody had cranked her up, "so many Italians yearn to emigrate to this country. *I am not one of them.* So many Italians *adore* New York City. I am not one of them either."

"You will learn to love it," John Foster said. His voice came from behind Nora and it sounded very melancholy. Nora did not turn.

It seemed the princess expected everybody else to stop everything when she was expounding. All heads were supposed to turn, ears to prick up. Elena took for herself the role of spokeswoman for everyone in the world with a pinch of common sense.

"When John is not occupied with his *tiresome* foundation which *this one*—" She gestured at Lucia with her thumb. "This one has had the bad sense to conceive as a way of saving the late Gogarty's money, and a good deal of mine, then when *belov'ed* John is not so occupied we will not be in this too-big land at all but somewhere in the vicinity of Palermo."

"Sicily?" Ball exclaimed. "Princess Elena, have you thought of Connecticut?"

Elena shrugged contemptuously. "As bad or worse. I have heard that place is populated by savages. There is an Indian tribe . . . where is Oswald?"

Oswald was there, naturally. "That'd be the Rappa-rum-bums, madame."

"Exactly," she exclaimed.

"It was from the Rappa-rum-bums," Oswald stated gravely, as if he were speaking in Congress, "that J.J. Gogarty first acquired the wild dogs."

"Yes, and cheated them, I have no doubt," Elena sneered.

Foster tried to intercede, this time on behalf of Gogarty. Still, Nora did not turn or acknowledge him at all.

"Elena, it's just an elaborate joke Oswald has made up about a mythical Indian tribe. He's having us on." Foster laughed clumsily.

"I certainly never heard of such a tribe," Gerald Ball said heartily. "I think you are pulling our joint legs, Mr. Oswald."

"No, sir," Oswald squalled, "I'm pulling neither your legs or your joints. But never mind. I've come to offer before-lunch libations."

"I thought you'd never ask," Ball said. "I'd like a gin martini straight up, Mr. Oswald."

"A gin martini it is!"

"A little sweet vermouth, Oswald," Elena said, "and *limon.*"

"I'll see if I can't scratch up some vermouth, Mrs. Saltimbocca," Oswald said cheekily.

Jerome said, "Father John will have his usual Scotch and water . . . and so shall I. Nora? Lucia?"

"White wine, please," Nora said.

"And the same," Lucia muttered.

Oswald was soon back, wheeling before him a mobile drinks table. Carelessly, he put on the brake and began preparing the drinks.

Then, finally, it had to come. Father John put his hand on Nora's shoulder and pulled her away from the others. "Hello, Nora," he said, "are you all right? I was very sad to hear about Mr. Morgan."

Nora fairly hissed. *"Is* it true? How *could* you?"

He squirmed, cornered in the very middle of the room. "I knew you'd be upset . . . I'm sorry."

"Don't give me *that,"* Nora grated. "Are you *really* such a traitor?"

"I don't consider—"

She wouldn't let him go on. "An *apostate* . . . The fall of the mighty. The sin of pride. Unbelievable!" Nora stopped in confusion, realizing she had nothing more to say. "I'm shattered . . . disillusioned. You've *wrecked* my faith."

"Nora . . ." Stricken, he whispered, "My little girl . . ."

"Don't call me your little girl." She had to control herself. They couldn't be allowed to see her break down, especially Gerald Ball.

Incredibly, Foster went rigid with anger. "All right, I didn't expect you to understand, Nora. You're too *cold* to understand. Too calculating. *You'll* never find love, acting as you do."

She gasped. How cruel he had become. "I will. Don't say that. I will!"

"I hope so," he said more gently. "I'll pray for you."

"No." Nora shook her head. "You're going to lose your license to pray for anybody."

Saying it and seeing his face drop, she knew it wasn't true. But she hurt him anyway.

As Oswald had always said, a good joint could save many an awkward situation. His pot roast of the evening was laced as tightly as a lady in corsets, it was juicier and more succulent than many things of evil. The fragrance, Jerome told himself, must be exploding into every nook and cranny of Castle Gogarty, even into the creaky papal armor stored in the basement. If a Gogarty ghost was hiding there, this was enough to smoke him out. And moreover they were drinking an excellent Bordeaux. Even Nora eventually ceased burning holes in the tablecloth when she glanced in Father John's direction. She was so obviously livid about Foster it was embarrassing. Nora needed to grow up, Jerome decided; she was angry with everybody, but for no good reason.

Oswald was embarked on some sort of a tear. Even Foster could not keep him in line. Jerome didn't mind; Oswald was harmless. Wasn't he?

Ball held up his glass to be filled and then to the table at large. "May we all have a splendid New Year—although, I must say, it is not begun to the best advantage. Kurt Morgan dead . . ." He shook his head as if in the deepest grief, glancing significantly at Nora. Ah, Jerome thought, Ball knew everything. How would he use what he knew? That was the question. "Not all of you were acquainted with Kurt Morgan," Ball went on in dark tones, "but there was a man! I raise my glass in his memory." He bowed his head at Nora.

"To Kurt," Jerome said cheerily. No sense in being morbid, he thought. After all, the man was simply dead, not destroyed in some other foul manner.

Ball smiled tensely, rolling the wine around his mouth approvingly. "You're right, Paul. This is an exquisite Bordeaux." He made swirls in the linen tablecloth with the bottom of the glass for a second or two and then portentously declared, "What we few say here this afternoon can have the greatest effect on the many."

Ball seemed outwardly to be in such control that it was startling to note an awkward and uncouth trickle of perspiration run down the bridge of his nose and collect in a large globule before dripping on his tie.

Perhaps he had anticipated Elena's deafening indifference. "So?" she growled. Her teeth crunched on the red wine. She was tasting as one should, by chewing the liquid red stuff. "What is so fantastically vital that *we few* are going to talk about?"

Ball stared at her. "Princess," he said softly, "you're unique . . ."

Foster's face was impassive but his penetrating eyes had taken a fix on Gerald Ball.

Jerome decided it was the time to open the next bottle of the Bordeaux.

"Be careful, *Cherry,*" Elena grunted playfully, "I do not take easily to flattery. I see right through you, *Cherry.*"

Ball chuckled moistly. "If you do, Princess, you're the first person in creation who has."

"Well? Well?" Elena demanded. "What *is* it we are to talk about?"

Ball glanced at Jerome, then at Nora, then at his watch. He was wondering if they had time to get into it. Could they talk about Diversified in front of these people? Ball might have expected Elena would be some kind of push-over, somebody's *mother,* after all. But he was baffled by her, and intimidated.

Ball smiled secretively. "I was about to propose another toast—to our ailing friend Buck Collins. May he be well soon, in good time to be with us when Diversified joins forces with BBD! We are agreed on that, aren't we?"

Jerome nodded. "Fully, Gerry."

Looking much happier, and relieved, Nora said, "I'll second your toast, Gerry."

Foster chuckled. "To *our pal,* Buck Collins," he exclaimed. He thrust his glass toward Jerome. "To his very good health."

Father John should think kindly of Collins—after all, he was sitting on eight hundred thousand dollars worth of Collins's bonds. This had seemed to Jerome the safest, and most convenient, way of getting rid of them—to give them back into Father John Foster's custody. When he'd let Buck know about it, Buck hadn't been deliriously happy. But wasn't this better than having them stolen by somebody like Morel, or possibly confiscated by the U.S. Customs? Yes, Buck said, okay, goddamn it.

Ball looked very satisfied with himself. In fact, Jerome realized, he had promised nothing. He had simply wished Buck a speedy and complete recovery. Nothing had been said about Lancer.

"I'll tell Buck you sent him regards, Gerry," Jerome said slowly.

"Do that, Paul. Tell him, tell him for me that everything is looking very good."

"I will."

And what did that mean? Not a blasted thing.

Ball held out his glass again and Jerome poured him wine out of the third bottle, or was it the fourth? Ball turned to Elena.

"Princess, I've heard that you're a superb poetess."

"Quite so! My cousin and his Holy Father are always fearful that I will rupture the Church as surely as Martin Luther. Were I to nail up one of my poems of the sensualist school which I favor on the door of the Milan *duomo,* half of the Church would flock to *my* cathedral, that is the church of the *amour propre* . . ."

Jerome looked to Foster. The heavy eyes were closing. He was enamored of the sound of her voice, so soothing . . .

Chapter Twenty-seven

THINGS SEEMED ALL SETTLED, BUT IN REALITY, NORA knew, nothing was solved, or settled. How the next few weeks would drag! How they would test men's—and women's—souls, their spirits, their strength. She decided, when at last they were in the Daimler and headed back to New York City, that she would dedicate this trying time to Kurt Morgan. What better way to honor him and promote herself?

It was not easy to say good night to Gerald Ball. Though Mr. Fiorello, her doorman, was at his usual station and Nora could thus assure Ball she was perfectly fine and able to get from car to apartment-house door and then safely upstairs, he insisted upon escorting her.

After Gerry had practically pushed his way into the apartment, he peered around curiously, as if he'd stumbled somehow into King Tut's tomb. Nora hoped it wasn't as dusty, or musty smelling, as that.

"Very . . . pleasant, Nora," he finally decided. "Very *nice* not to have miles of carpeting and tons of antiques. Too much of a responsibility—" He stopped, remembering something important. "If I had my way, I'd live in a little grass shack down in the Caribbean—where we're going, don't forget, *golden girl!*"

Nora told him she wouldn't and still he pursued her. He took her hand and held it, looking into her eyes, and then kissing the hand and trying to kiss his way up her arm, even though she was wearing a Chanel-style jacket.

"Ah, beautiful golden girl," he sighed. "Should I call you G.G. for short—like the French—Gigi."

Nora knew better than to laugh. Ball was not the type to enjoy a laugh at his own expense.

"Gerry . . . It's late. And I must get to the office early."

"Oh? Why?"

She wanted to tell him she wasn't rich or retired and had to work for a living. "Well, for one thing . . ." She thought fast and the inspiration came. "I have a date to see *Helen Marconi.*" She put stress on the name; how he reacted would tell whether he knew the stories about Helen and the great Rustford Lancer.

"Do I know her?" He looked blank.

"She's in charge of the research staff."

"Oh, yes. I think I do know her."

Nora went on, "She's been transferred to Alaska."

Obviously, he was not interested. He clutched her hand. "I think if the dumb bitch wants to go to Alaska, then she should—*Hi,* Gigi!" He beamed.

"Hi," Nora answered doubtfully.

"Say, Gigi," his silver voice lowed, "I just noticed something—don't you *ever* have to go to the bathroom?"

"What?" Nora dissolved in confusion. What sort of question was that? "Do you mean . . . should I wash my hands?" Had he caught some terrible odor on her fingers when he kissed them?

"If you do, I'll wait."

"It was a long trip," she admitted. "That's why I purposely didn't have any coffee at the Gogarty place." She laughed with a proper shyness.

"Ah . . ." Ball grimaced eagerly. "Golden girl, I want you to understand me—I'm a completely honest man." His look was positively open. "I mean, I could be a crook, a total *crook* in business which I am sometimes, why not admit it, but never in personal relationships. In the latter, I am always totally honest. Do you understand me?"

"Sure." How could she not? She hoped he was not

322

going to confess something to her he wouldn't want in the *New York Post.*

"You do appreciate I'm very up-front, Nora . . . *Gigi?*"

"Yes, I do. I . . . uh . . . love it for people to be honest with me."

"Okay." He collected a long breath. "When you go into the bathroom, can I watch?"

She stared at him, astonished, openly astonished, so much so he looked down.

"Gerry, do I understand you?"

"Yes!" he exclaimed angrily. "I want to watch you *go potty!* Isn't that clear enough?"

"But . . ." What could she say? How could she elude him? Nora tried not to reveal still more shock. "I don't think I could *go* with somebody watching me. I'd really have to go an awful lot in order to be able to go with you watching."

"Then drink some water," he said impatiently. "I can wait. I'll have a brandy. What kind of brandy have you got?"

"Courvoisier," she said.

"I like Remy Martin."

"Gerry, *I'm sorry.*" Nora was close to tears. It had been a long day. "Gerry, can't you see that this is a very embarrassing thing you're asking me to do?"

"Look," he said efficiently, "it's embarrassing for me too . . . golden girl," he smirked. "But I can handle it." He turned away. "I'll get the drink. Give me a shout when you're ready and I'll come in."

Apparently he was not going to accept any kind of excuse. Nora hesitated, wondering what he'd say if she told him she was having her period. No, better not; that might make it worse.

Finally, she muttered, "I *am* thirsty."

"Good! Why don't you drink some water. A quart of soda or something."

"I've got some Perrier in the refrigerator," she said weakly.

"That's just fine."

How could he sound so acquiescent to the situation—a predicament for her, an aberration for him? Was this what the whole day had been leading to, the ride in the elegant Daimler, the lunch at the castle, the foreshortened shop-talk? Nora stumbled into the kitchen and ran water in the sink for inspiration, then swallowed Perrier as fast as she could.

Ball was calling to her. Nora went to the kitchen door. "Yes, Gerry?" She was so tired, so depressed. What about Harvard Business School? Why hadn't they ever offered a survey course on unusual hang-ups observed in the American corporate male, these giants of capitalism, each more peculiar than the last? It seemed so long ago that she'd been in Palm Springs with Kurt and he'd taken such delight in spending his fluids in the bun at the back of her head. Now this?

Diversified Towers? Tower of Babel . . .

"Nora," Ball was saying, "that's all I want from you really, I promise. It's all I've ever wanted."

"Gerry," she said, not thinking, "can I ask? When Molly . . . Mrs. Ball . . ."

She got no further with the question, a natural one she would have thought. Ball bounded across the tiny living room like a man possessed, his face darkened with anger. His hand whipped back and she thought surely he was going to strike her. But he stopped, just in time, shaking.

"She's dead, Nora. You shouldn't even suggest anything about the dead. If she were alive, I wouldn't mind. But she's dead." His eyes fluttered for a moment and he shook his head as if he'd bumped something.

"I'm sorry," Nora mumbled.

His voice was strong again. "If you're wondering wheth-er this strange desire is something that's just come over me . . . no! My Molly knew about it. She always said she'd heard of odder things."

"I am sorry, Gerry," she repeated.

"No, it's all right." Gerald put his smooth face next to her cheek and she smelled the reticent cologne he wore; it didn't say New York, or even Paris, but somewhere more exclusive, a small country, Monaco or Lichtenstein. His skin was particularly soft, like some sort of plush material. Somehow it didn't even feel genuine, more like a synthetic substitute. Nora wondered if it would ever, in fact, come to that: epidermis transplants.

"*Gerry!*"

It was not her imagination, was it, that having caught her at the kitchen door, Ball was edging her toward the bathroom. She prepared to scream. Most men dragged women to the bedroom, but not this captain of industry. Was it never to be her good fortune to meet a man she could respect *and* work for *and* love? Oh, Norman, she could really have screamed, Norman, save me!

"Nora . . . Gigi," Ball grunted, "I don't want much."

She resisted, but not because she didn't want to go to the bathroom; she did now, more than she ever had in her life, so frightened that fear was poking her bladder and kidneys and in turn those two were pushing her heart and making it hard for her to breathe.

"Oh, Gerry, please!"

"Golden girl," he hissed soothingly, trying to reassure her, but his suavity was dissipating, so frantic was he that she do his bidding, "let me tell you. . . . Let me tell you, please. Molly and me, we had a bathroom made entirely of crystal. It was completely transparent, everything, the bathtub, the john, the sink, the bidet . . ." Nora couldn't believe it. "Gigi! I suppose you think that's disgusting but I could lie there on the bathmat to my heart's content watching Molly do all the wonderful things that she did . . . Gigi!" he cried rapturously, "it was a marriage made in heaven . . ." Ball pulled himself erect, back to business. "Look, Nora, we'll give it a try, shall we? If you find it's within your concept of acceptability, then I'll have a Baccarat-crystal john sent over. It *is* wonderful, you know," he said dreamily.

"I can imagine," she responded listlessly.

It was a tenuous time, a draggy, tiring, and stressful week ahead, and Nora had Gerald Ball, Diversified's chief financial advisor, to thank for being worn out physically and spiritually on the first day of this most crucial week. She hadn't been able to persuade him to leave until almost one-thirty in the morning and by then her innards had turned to sorbet. To please him, she'd made herself go three or four times and even that wasn't enough for him. So, finally, cajoling him, trying to make light of the humiliation, anything to get him to leave, she promised that next time she'd fast all day and drink gallons of tea, even take a mild emetic just before his arrival. So finally, Ball had left his Gigi, as he called her unceasingly, but not before he promised he'd move her to the Baccarat bathroom as that would be a simpler matter than moving all the Baccarat to her.

"Golden girl . . ." He kissed the inside of her wrist good-bye.

"Gerald," she murmured. "I think I *will* call you Gerald. It's so dignified a name."

The morning after was uncomfortable. All in the cause of Buck Collins, was it? What wouldn't they do for Buck Collins? For Buck Collins her insides were all torn up.

Nora's feet were like lead; like dead bodies she dragged them through the corporate carpeting. She herself was so forlorn and abandoned. Why this depressing sense of aloneness when she was a major part of a team? But it was more than simple loneliness, it was as if she'd been forsaken by everyone, from God on down to dear Father John. Nora's eyes filled with tears. Think of him—soon to be Mister. Impossible! Henceforth an emasculated shell of a man—no, already ruined, a being whose life was past, a slave to the senses, a mere creature at the beck and call of Princess Elena.

Solitude, fear, worry drove Nora to call Paul. *He* should be calling *her* but she could not wait.

His secretary knew Nora's name by now as well as she knew her own. "Can he get back to you, Miss Sweeney? He's on an important call."

"All right." She found only a small voice with which to reply. Why couldn't he talk to her *now?*

She hit her desk lightly with her fist, even though there was no one there to see her do it. Influence would have to be brought to bear! Gerald had sounded so sure, as if everything were settled. But he'd left Nora sure of nothing. It was amazing how easily things could become so confused; how shattering to remember how quick and decisive Kurt had been. And Gerald Ball had the nerve to consider *himself* indispensable!

But perhaps she was being unduly pessimistic. Perhaps she worried too much. Maybe it *was* all settled, as Gerald believed. But what about Lancer? In fact, what about his bad-smelling mistress who called Nora a bad name every time she had a chance? Gerald had mouthed vague words about putting Lancer in as interim president, then kicking him upstairs to the chairmanship when Buck came forward as chief executive officer. But what did that mean?

Finally, her phone rang. "Sweeney!"

Paul's voice was low, anxious. "Sorry, Nora, I was talking to Buck. We've got trouble."

"Trouble! I know we've got trouble!"

"I'm not talking about Ball and Buck and the succession, Nora," Paul said angrily. "Buck is in a jam."

"Oh, God . . ." The vitality seemed to drain from her.

"Yeah." Paul didn't sound so good himself. "What they call a *controlled substance* showed up in his blood test after the accident. The hospital tried to sit on it but some . . . *ethical* person has reported it. In other words, *beautiful,*" he said sarcastically, "a trace of coke was found in the blood. It seems he was flying his chopper under the influence."

"The fool!"

"Yes, I agree. Did *you* know?"

"No, of course not," Nora lied, "how would I know?"

"But all is not lost," Paul continued, no less impatiently, "if Buck can prove he was taking a drug-based medicine for another, old back injury. Out of total *ignorance* and *stupidity,* of course. His personal doctor is checking prescriptions right now. Do you see, Nora?"

"Yes, I see. I'm sure that would be a logical explanation. Buck wouldn't deliberately do anything that dumb."

"No, naturally not," Paul said flatly.

"Paul . . ." Nora felt like a water-logged piece of lettuce. "You sound . . ." What did he sound? Disillusioned? As if he were thoroughly fed up with everything and everybody, including, for once, Buck Collins?

He chuckled ruefully. "I sound faintly cynical and ironic of tone? Yes. And you, Nora, are no doubt concerned today about what exactly Gerry Ball means when he says everything is in good shape."

"Yes, that's it," she said. "We don't know where we're at *vis-à-vis* Rusty Lancer. We don't know any more now than we did before the weekend."

"That is very true, Nora," Paul said. His voice hardened. "However, let me tell you something. We at BBD are proceeding under the terms of our understanding with Kurt Morgan—that Buck will move into position as head of the Broadstairs Aerospace Division of Diversified Industries and then, *at a propitious time,* he'll take over as boss of the whole company. This game plan doesn't, in our opinion, change simply because Kurt Morgan dropped dead . . ."

"Paul." Nora stopped. He might have been reading from a contract. "Don't you think this is what *I* want?"

"Nora, what *you* want is immaterial," he replied callously. "The important thing is Gerry Ball cannot be allowed to play games. He has got to be told—"

"Told what?" she cried angrily.

"Told that BBD can walk away. Kurt's death is a perfect excuse to call the whole thing off, *right now.* All we'll have

328

lost is legal fees, printing charges . . . and time. But that might be cheap in the long run."

"Where does that leave me?" Nora demanded.

"It leaves you the obvious person to tell Ball to stop fucking around."

Nora stewed angrily, not replying at once. Then she said, "If Buck gets indicted for a cocaine abuse, it's not going to help matters, is it?"

"No, it's not," Paul said quietly, "and that's why I'm telling you about it. I hope we can slide out of it. I believe we will. If we don't," he added soberly, "then Buck is a goner and we can forget about the whole thing. You and I will be screwed, good and proper. Not so proper, actually." He managed a tight laugh.

"Down in flames, is that it?" Nora echoed.

Jerome laughed more freely. "Backs against the wall, *beautiful*," he said mockingly. "Can you take it?"

Nora felt her pulse leap. At least things were a little more clear. Paul had a certain talent for defining the problem. She laughed harshly.

"I think so, yes," she said.

They agreed, however, that no move could, or should, be made until they were sure Buck was in the clear. Thus, Nora faced more hours of the waiting game and then, she acknowledged, she would have to put the problem to Gerald Ball. Steeling herself, Nora forced the matter almost out of her head for the rest of the day by devoting her attention to another review of the Eurochemie material. It was, she was sure, the Eurochemie business that had gummed up everything. Eurochemie was that which smelled rotten in the State of Denmark. Rustford Lancer was a mere pawn, a nothing. Or at least, Nora assured herself this was so, until the phone rang about four-thirty and a voice said Mr. Lancer would like to see her right away, that Nora would find him in Mr. Morgan's office.

"I understand," Nora said, her voice tight. "I'll be right over."

What? She began to tremble. Had things already climaxed? Nora repressed the urge to run down the executive corridor to Morgan's office. By what right did this upstart *dare* to go there, want to meet her there? He hadn't been elected to *anything* . . . yet? Nora forced herself to relax; she stood very still for a few minutes and then, breathing deeply, sat down at her desk and took makeup from her purse. She inspected herself in the mirror—God, yes, the same she'd used to test Morgan's nose for a telltale breath. Even after a full day's work, following a hard night, given the residue of grief, hope, sadness, anxiety, she looked just fine. Not a hair was out of place in her swept-back coiffure. Nora added a touch of lipstick, unbuttoned her blouse a notch, then up again, rubbed up the nubby tweed of her sleeves, smoothed her skirt at the hip fold. And walked . . . the long mile.

Nevertheless, as prepared as she could make herself, Nora was nearly devastated to confront Lancer, sitting comfortably behind Morgan's oak desk. Had he moved in already? She couldn't believe it—even he, with his history of Helen Marconi, could not be so tasteless. Kurt's paintings were still on the walls, the antiques with which he'd supplemented company office furniture still in place.

Lancer was in his shirtsleeves, thoroughly at home.

"Hiya Nora," he said nonchalantly, "howyadoin'?"

"I am doing fine, Mr. Lancer."

He gestured expansively. "I thought I might as well try it out, Nora. How do I look?" He grinned probingly. "It's not like I'm offending Kurt, my old buddy, and I don't think anybody else would mind."

"Why should they?"

He smiled at her so innocently, the viper, that she could have vomited. "It's just that I want everybody on my side, Nora. I know nothing is final until it's final," he said, "but I'm looking good . . . so I want folks with me, Nora. Understand? You know as well as I do that I've got a lot to learn. I'll need help."

She returned his smile. It was difficult for her to dissemble like this, but, as they'd learned at Harvard, from time to time it had to be done. "Mr. Lancer, *whomsoever* runs Diversified can be sure of having everybody on his side."

"Whomsoever?" he echoed incredulously. "I hope *you'll* be on my side, Nora. That's what I wanted to talk to you about."

She was seized by a violent trembling. If her thighs had been teeth, their chattering would have been heard in the next room. Lancer hadn't asked her to sit down; she did anyway. He scowled at her, then smiled, leaning back in Morgan's swivel chair, fingertips stiff under his chin. He was trying for a posture of utter calm and cool.

"I know you were very close to Kurt. *Very close*, Nora. I know you were his personal confidante, that he discussed things with you that he discussed with nobody else. You knew everything he was carrying around in his head, right up to the *moment* of his death." An insinuating smile strutted across his face.

Nora shook her head. *"No, not so.* Mr. Morgan didn't confide in anybody . . . including me."

"Nora," Lancer said pleasantly, "I know better."

"No," she repeated, "you can't know because you weren't there."

"Nora, I didn't need to be there in order to know," he disagreed irritably. Nora told herself not to be embarrassed. "There's one thing I'll want *you* to do, Nora," Lancer muttered. "I want his things packed and shipped out of that apartment."

Her jawbone ached because she wanted so much to scream at him, tell him to get out of this office, *impostor!* But he went on, sneering. All the hate was there, all the vindictiveness, his and Helen Marconi's.

"Sort all that *shit* out and have it sent to his wife . . . widow." For a moment, Nora felt sorry for Hazel Morgan, much as they had competed by long distance while Kurt was alive. Stiffly, she said, "I'm sure Mr. Morgan would love to hear his things referred to as . . . *like that*, Mr. Lancer."

"Never mind," he muttered. She realized it was a mistake to call this man handsome. Despite the neat hair, the clear skin and eyes, the athletic posture, Lancer was ugly, a misbegotten monster. "Diversified paid for that goddamn apartment, Nora, the whole time."

"A business expense," she murmured. "Mr. Morgan worked hard. He couldn't commute every day, physically he couldn't do it."

"Bullshit," Lancer snarled. "I'm having it redecorated. It's too dark and . . . traditional. I'm going to fit it out with all our consumer products," he told her vindictively, "the toasters, microwaves and juicers, the upholstered furniture—all the pieces that *he* should have had in there. It'll be a showplace, Nora, for Diversified products." He challenged her, eyes blazing.

"Fly one of the missiles in, why don't you?" she couldn't help saying.

"Hah, hah!" he sputtered bitterly. Oh, yes, he'd talked this over with Helen Marconi, how he would incite her, make her quit. He wanted her head on a platter. Lancer studied her, wishing for her to break and run.

But she wouldn't give him that satisfaction. "I'll take care of it, certainly, if that's what you wish," she said icily.

"I hope it won't be painful."

"Why should it be?"

Lancer leered. "I thought you were so *close*."

Nora smiled to herself. A very comforting feeling came to her. However close she and Morgan had been, no one could ever prove it by grilling Kurt Morgan. On the other hand, in the sordid affair of Rusty Lancer and Helen Marconi, *both* were still alive and very vulnerable. Didn't he see that?

Evenly, Nora told him, "I was Mr. Morgan's personal assistant, Mr. Lancer. I studied acquisition details. That was my job."

There was nothing much he could say to that because he didn't know anything about it. Nonetheless, he chose to be nasty. "In a way you were a futurist, Nora, Kurt's *crystal ball*—I always thought that was a lousy way to do business."

"*Not* to plan, you mean?" Her tone made it clear she thought his remark idiotic.

He glared. "I do *not* mean not to plan, Nora. I mean I believe in focusing on today more than tomorrow."

"Well . . ." She shrugged. "Every businessman has his own preferred way of doing business."

"Of course." Lancer twisted his shoulders and hunched forward, trying to get the upper hand. "Don't get me wrong. I always admired Kurt. He let me *get on with it*. So long as we operated efficiently and showed profit, he didn't interfere."

"He *was* brilliant, wasn't he?"

"Yes, I guess he was." Lancer didn't blink. "When the *stuff* is ready to go up to Scarsdale, you can arrange for his things in here to be packed too."

Nora chuckled. "I see my new job at Diversified is in charge of freight."

"I'm asking for your help!" he said.

Nora realized then that Lancer was afraid of her. He knew she was strong and resourceful, and had support— how much he didn't know. She took advantage of his hesitancy to look him over, to reach an objective assessment, exclusive of Helen Marconi. Was there anything there worth saving? Suppose she were to tell him about the spying, about Hazel Morgan and Mercury? Was he ready for it? How would he deal with it? But . . . did it matter now anyway? With Morgan dead, Mercury's pipeline into Diversified was cut. The film? An exercise in futility.

"All the paintings in here are his, Mr. Lancer," she said. "As far as the furniture goes—the conference table is an Irish hunt table, actually, which Mr. Morgan picked up at Sotheby's. Circa eighteen hundred . . ."

Lancer's fist came down emphatically on the solid oak

desk. "Nora," he exclaimed hotly, "understand I'm *not interested* in *circa* eighteen hundred. I'm interested in circa right now, *this year.*"

"To each his own," she murmured.

Finally finding a hook to hang his spite on, he fumed, "That was Kurt's trouble. His one weak spot—maybe his *second* weak spot. He was too soft, too concerned with history and tradition. I know what they think of him down in Washington—possibly *you* believe I have no contacts down there. Not so! They say the world changes and you'd better change with it because it's very easy to get left in the wake, to get caught in the sausage grinder."

"Is *that* the message from Washington?"

"Yes," he said curtly, "that's the message from Washington—one of them at least."

So there it was again, in a nutshell, the charge that Kurt Morgan had been too dovish.

Carefully, Nora retorted, "If Mr. Morgan had a regard for beauty and tradition, Mr. Lancer, that wouldn't by definition make him some sort of a sissy. At least, *I* wouldn't think so, nor would any logically thinking person." His face colored. "I know exactly where that line of thinking comes from. Once, Mr. Morgan said he didn't see the sense of *zapping* the Russians with a first strike. *Ergo,*" she finished, "Mr. Morgan was soft on the commies. Now . . . is that what *you're* saying, Mr. Lancer?"

His malevolent stare jolted her shoulder blades, but she didn't flinch; she gave herself credit for that. She was a woman but she could play hard ball with the best of them. *Let him do his worst!* Whatever apprehension she'd felt before was suddenly replaced by a daredevil exhilaration. Yes, she *could* take it!

"Listen," he exclaimed, "let's quit fucking around. I know all about you and Morgan. I know the whole idea for this half-baked merger with Brown, Broadstairs and Dunn was yours, that you talked that asshole into it! I won't say how. But I do know how!"

"How then?" Her voice was cold enough to freeze the ears off a brass monkey.

"You blew him," Lancer said. "You went down on him whenever he slowed to a walk. You sucked him into it, *Miss Sweeney*." His smile became positively sadistic. "Is that where the expression comes from? Anyway, you sucked the whole company into it, along with Morgan."

She did not have to admit anything, that was obvious, and particularly to this ruffian. "That is a lie which has been put around by my enemies, and I know who—I don't need to say her name, do I? But *that* relationship is common knowledge, Mr. Lancer." She watched as his face slowly began its change from red to gray. "No secrets, are there, Mr. Lancer?" she mocked. "And there's proof. Let me tell you something . . ."

She paused, giving him a moment to react. He did, doggedly. "Yes, tell me something . . . I'm very fond of fiction, Nora."

"All right. But before I go on, let me also say that I know the legal definition of *sexual harassment* and you're verging mighty close to it . . . right now!"

Thinking this was the main burden of her counterattack, he thought he could bluster through. His fingers made fists and again he banged Kurt Morgan's desk, this time harder.

"Bullshit! What sexual harassment? Are you joking? If I find fault with your behavior—which I do—*that* is defined as sexual harassment? Hah! You know that's bullshit, Miss Sweeney. And I can go on about your behavior—very unprofessional and in fact disloyal to Diversified. You got palsy-walsy with those guys at Brown, Broadstairs, starting with Buck Collins, the *daring . . .*" His sneer rolled like a belch across his lips. "The daring young asshole. And Jerome, that sneaky Jew who does their books. *Cooks their books* is more like it. And we bought it, Miss Sweeney, *because of you*."

She didn't have to struggle at all to maintain her poise.

"There's nobody in the financial world or the aerospace industry that doesn't think the merger makes sense, Mr. Lancer."

"*I* don't think so, Miss Sweeney," he barked. "It's going to dilute our stock, knock us down, and the shareholders are going to be very pissed off when they realize what's happened."

"You're wrong," she said calmly. "Let me explain."

His eyes seemed to come unplugged. "Explain? You're an arrogant bitch. Who are *you* to explain to me?"

Quickly she remembered Norman Vincent and gained strength. Hard ball, Nora. "I'll tell you *who*, Mr. Lancer," she said, grinding him up with her voice. "*Me!* I'm smarter than you are and you're scared. You don't know where you're at—you are *out of your depth.*"

His face collapsed with fury and she knew she was right about him then. He couldn't take it. Perspiration popped up like blisters on his forehead and his patronizing expression of male superiority had vanished.

"Mr. Morgan wanted BBD," she said with slicing precision, "because Diversified's aerospace, the whole high-tech division, is stalled. It's moribund . . ."

"Yeah?" He tried to mock, to taunt. "Tell Jack Frazer. He'll be happy to hear it."

"He knows, Mr. Lancer," she said, unloading the truth on him. It was like a ton of bricks. He blinked, as if she'd slapped him. "He and Mr. Morgan talked it over before Mr. Morgan ever went ahead with BBD. Don't you understand *even* that much?" Her voice altered emphasis, became pitying. "No, you were wrapped up in your *boring* little industries . . . *toasters* and *electric knives* and *can openers,* how wonderful for you. The fact is, Mr. Lancer, *Buck Collins* is coming into Diversified . . ." Perhaps she went too far. It was possible she did. She waved her hand, taking in the whole office, formerly Kurt Morgan's. "Collins is going to be sitting in here, Mr. Lancer—*not you!*"

Fear stopped his face from buckling any further. Sheer horror burst into his eyes. He gasped loudly. "Over my dead body, goddamn it! I'm in line and I'm next, you bitch!"

Stolidly, she shook her head. "I don't think so. Everybody who counts wants the merger. You don't. Collins knows the aerospace business. You don't—you know about *toasters*," she said contemptuously.

"Oh, yeah?" He was frantic now. "Oh, yeah? Listen, people were buying toasters before the government was buying those goddamn missiles and airplanes and they'll be buying toasters long after we don't make any more missiles."

"If you'd like to believe that," she said, smiling her total disbelief, "be my guest. Believe *that,* and you're in plenty of trouble."

"Bullshit!" Lancer howled.

Nora estimated to herself that this was just about it. A few more minutes and he'd be on his belly, groveling. His hands, so calm ordinarily, his whole body, so smugly serene in his conceited opinion of himself, had come apart. He shook loosely, his lower lip wobbled as if he'd cry.

"Look," she said, as if preparing to leave, "believe me or don't. Try to fire me—I don't think you have the power to fire me. You wouldn't want me around here, telling you the truth, would you? That's why Mr. Morgan had me just down the hall—to tell him the truth about things. You can't handle the truth, Mr. Lancer."

"Fuck you," he bellowed. He jumped out of Morgan's swivel chair, pointing at her. "Get the hell out of here before I forget you're a woman!"

Nora stood up, facing him. "I'm going."

His voice broke. "I wouldn't give you the satisfaction of firing you—so you'd go running with some goddamn story about sexual harassment. Sexual harassment, my ass, *Miss* Sweeney! If there's any sexual harassment around here, it's the reverse kind, you blowing all our executives, undermining their judgment. Well, I'm warning you—you're not going to do it to me."

Nora's own fury returned. "Mr. Lancer," she said, "there's no way I'd come close to a person like you. Your personal life is *disgusting* and that is common knowledge."

"You're crazy," he mumbled.

"Helen Marconi?"

It was sufficient to pronounce the dread name. Lancer fell back in the chair because he knew the mistake was his—that one, glorious mistake in an unblemished career, when he'd first allowed Helen Marconi to talk him downtown to the Hotel d'Aphrodite for a discussion of double-entry bookkeeping.

"What about her?" he muttered. "That's history—something that happened a long time ago. I broke it off . . . one mistake. So what? Everybody's human."

"She doesn't seem to think it's broken off."

"She's full of shit," he said hoarsely. "Why don't you get out? I don't want to see you anymore."

"As easy as that, you think?" Nora stared down at him. "I've never been talked to like you've talked to me, Mr. Lancer, and I resent it." Her voice was not just cold; it could have air-conditioned the whole executive floor. "Accuse me, yes? But let's not mention Mr. Lancer and Miss Marconi, shall we? A mistake. All over. Does *your wife* know about it?" she inquired. "Did you confess to her?"

He looked up at her. "What are you saying?"

"You know exactly what I'm saying—that it's very surprising that everybody on the island of Manhattan knows about you and Helen Marconi and your wife doesn't."

"So . . ."

Nora shook her head. "So—*nothing*," she said. "I wouldn't tell her." She waited for him to catch up. He looked a little more hopeful. And that was when the awful idea came to Nora; the idea went hand-in-hand with the game of hard ball. "We . . . have a . . . film, you see."

"A what!"

It was a lie, of course, a bald-faced lie. But it *could* have been true. Norm Vincent could just as easily have taped Lancer and Helen Marconi; actually, it'd have been easier because they'd be more conveniently tracked to their rendezvous. In fact, as Norman would have put it, Helen was physically like Hazel Morgan. Lancer, well, he was much bigger than Mercury and not as young of course, and he'd have had to be wearing a wig. But she knew she'd never have to show the film.

Lancer put his head in his hands and his elbows in front of him, in despair, on the desk. "Please leave now. Don't you think you've done enough damage for one day, Miss Sweeney?"

Nora shrugged. She could be heartless, couldn't she? But hadn't Lancer had it coming? In spades?

"I hope so, Mr. Lancer," she said simply.

Once more, he turned his eyes up at her, but now she discerned a defeated man, not a man with any spunk or fight in him. "You would destroy me, wouldn't you?"

"Is it a one-sided game, Mr. Lancer? You would have destroyed me, wouldn't you?"

He didn't even try to answer that one. He couldn't, could he? She was right, she was *so* right. She had never been so right in her life. It was like a religious revelation, a flashing of heavenly light, neon and colored.

"I have an idea for you, Miss Sweeney," Lancer snarled, like a cornered rat. *"Why Buck Collins?* Why don't *you* take over? You've got the balls for it."

Chapter Twenty-eight

FRIDAY AT 10:00 A.M. WAS PERHAPS NOT THE MOST BRILLIANT time for a memorial service, but they hadn't much choice. There would never be such a thing as a *right time* so far as the market or the business and banking communities were concerned, and, of course, there was no way Kurt Morgan's peers could *all* be at the same time in the same place. Friday was simply the best they could do.

By then, Nora was feeling better about things. She'd rested up from the Sunday-night ordeal with Gerald Ball. They'd had dinner together on Wednesday and Nora had laid the heat on him about Rusty Lancer. She'd heard nothing more from Lancer directly, and it occurred to her, as she walked crosstown to the Little Church on Madison, that she hadn't laid eyes on Helen Marconi all week.

They had timed the service for exactly thirty-five minutes. The feeling was, and Nora agreed with Gerald, that less than a half-hour was too short, and much more than a half-hour was too long. Afterwards, the board of directors, or as many of them as could make it, would be chauffeured back to Diversified Towers for a short meeting, this to be followed by luncheon at The Plaza.

But Nora had not been able to plumb Gerald Ball for a reaction to what she'd said about Lancer—that he had attempted to browbeat her, that he considered the presidency of Diversified his, and rightfully his. In this respect, Ball was as uncommunicative as a mummy. He merely nodded angrily. Nora could only hope, and assume, the

Morgan plan would go forward, that Ball would hold the fort.

She was to meet Paul Jerome and Buck Collins outside the church and she arrived with fifteen minutes to spare. She waited, watching for the stretch limo in the uptown traffic, unprepared for the figure that sidled up to her.

"Hiya, Ellen."

"Oh!" Startled, Nora whirled around. She was so relieved to see Norman Vincent, deep in a trench coat that didn't by any means look as brand, spanking new as it had New Year's Day. A smart snap-brim Borsalino was pulled down on his forehead, hiding his eyes.

"Norm Vincent," he muttered, introducing himself unnecessarily.

"I know you!"

"Nora, I was sorry to hear about Morgan. What a shock! But, honey, bear up. Remember—"

"I know, Norm . . . hard ball. I remember."

"Right. Life goes on, Ellen." He looked around furtively. "I'm on a guy, trailed him all the way from Milan, Italy."

"From Eurochemie?"

His dark eyes snapped. "How'd you know?"

"We're informed, Norm. Does he spell trouble?"

Norman shrugged morosely. "I dunno—how *do* you spell trouble, Ellen? If there's any trouble, it'll be trouble for him. Is he perceived as a threat by you guys?"

"We're worried about a financial attack on Diversified," she admitted.

"The son of a bitch, goddamn aggressors—"

"Norm, go on inside," Nora said. "I'm waiting for Buck and Paul."

"How's Collins's tailbone?"

"It better be good enough to get him here," she replied tersely. "Call me later, Norm."

"Yeah—I will. I missed you, hon."

His voice made her weak, but not for long. At five minutes before ten, just as Paul and Buck *must* be arriving, a couple hurried down Madison. The man was tall, tanned, and brawny, towering in comparison over the tubby woman on his arm. With a start, Nora recognized Hazel Morgan and Joe Mercury, and saw that Morgan's death hadn't disturbed the sated look on either of their faces.

Hazel, to give her credit, was in widow's black—a black mink over a black tailored suit. A veiled cloche hat obscured her face. Mercury, on the other hand, was dressed exactly for what he was—an Italian gigolo. A dark blue cashmere coat was draped over his shoulders like a cape and underneath he was wearing a snug double-breasted pinstriped blue suit. Big gold cufflinks hung like handcuffs at his sleeves and a heavy silk foularde was knotted to a cream-silk shirt. All Nora could think was: Morgan's money!

Mercury's face was so smooth, like Gerald Ball's except he was so much younger and, if the truth be known, Ball had never been so good looking.

He knew he was handsome. He caught Nora staring at him. There was no way he could imagine she had seen his naked body on film doing all sorts of repulsive things. Nora frowned when his sneery mouth formed a heavy-lipped pout. Turning petulantly, he helped Hazel up the steps; Nora caught herself in the act of watching the lithe buttocks, sure he bulged beneath the coat.

God, no! She wasn't to think about it. Her legs trembled nonetheless. He was like a cat; he moved like a panther, so smoothly. She could understand the charm of silky muscles. But no—Mercury deserved to be deported, the arrogant pig. Spy! Wanton! Degenerate!

Where were Buck and Paul? Where *were* they?

Finally, just as the organ was beginning, the limo stopped in front of the church. The driver bolted from the front seat in a panic. Obviously they'd been chewing him out.

Jerome emerged. "Well, we made it."

"Not a moment too soon," she said. "It's just starting."

Buck's feet came out of the back seat. He yelped with pain. "Jesus Christ! I'm not sure this was such a great idea after all."

The driver took one of Buck's hands, Jerome the other, and together they yanked him out of the seat and up on stiff legs. He swayed unsteadily, smiling weakly at Nora. "Hi, beautiful. Hey! Gimme the goddamn crutch," he told the driver. "And you make sure you're here when we come out."

"Yessir!"

"Awright," Collins decreed, "Paulie, on the crutch side and catch me if I topple. Nora, let me lean on your right arm. Up the steps we go."

Collins walked stiffly but managed to negotiate the steps. He paused at the top to get his breath.

"Morel's inside, the man from Milan," Nora said tersely.

Buck snarled, out of pain, "Those bastards have started buying BBD now! We'll make them eat it, beautiful. They buy five percent, we'll buy ten percent of them. We'll find out who's got the guts, if they want a fight."

Jerome murmured, "We'll talk about it later." He glanced across Buck at Nora. "What's Gerry saying?"

"Nothing," she said.

"Ball," Buck scoffed, "what the hell does he know? Not worth a shit, is he, Paulie?"

"Buck," Nora said, "just for now, stay on Ball's good side, okay?"

Collins chuckled unpleasantly. "Ball'll be lucky if he stays out of jail."

Inside the church door, Collins straightened as best he could, squared his shoulders, and the three of them made their way slowly down the center aisle, in cadence with the organ dirge, toward seats reserved in the pew right behind Hazel Morgan. Buck moaned painfully as he sat, but once down he was all right.

Nora stared at the back of Hazel's permanent; there was enough gray in her hair. She had a nerve, didn't she, bringing this lout to services for her dead husband? But no one here knew the truth of it, except Nora and, somewhere behind her, Norm Vincent. Mercury was young enough to be her son.

On the other side of the center aisle, Gerald Ball leaned forward to catch her attention. Ball nodded, smiled mournfully, then rose and walked to the podium on the left hand of the nondenominational altar. The organ music trailed away. Ball was to deliver the eulogy to Kurt Morgan, friend, associate and business magnate. Nora didn't want to hear anything more about Morgan but there was obviously no escape from it. Grin and bear it. Not grin certainly. No, that would be out of place, particularly when she looked up at Gerry Ball.

Ball droned and Nora ignored most of it.

Nora hardly noticed the change of tone as Ball's voice faded sadly and a distinct cry—of pain?—burst from the rear of the assembly. People turned, then unbelievably the squat figure of Helen Marconi scurried down the center aisle. She wheeled and pointed at Nora, her eyes crazy, and screeched mad words, almost but not quite incomprehensible.

"Morgan! Morgan! Nora Sweeney sucked his organ!"

And she was gone, like a stubby phantom.

But no, no! No one could have understood. But some of them had seen where she pointed.

"What the fuck!" Buck muttered. *"Who was that?"*

Nora wanted to scream, as loudly as Helen: *It is not true!*

"Her name is Helen Marconi," she stuttered. "She's crazy."

She didn't need to say that. Anybody could see that Helen was crazy. But it didn't matter—the awful words had been said, not privately, in a corner at Diversified, but in public for the world to hear.

"What the hell did she say?" Buck growled disgustedly. "I couldn't understand her."

Nora tried it out. "She's jealous . . . of me. She's

worried about her boyfriend—Rusty Lancer." Cook *his* goose!

Gerald Ball shook his head a little groggily and resumed speaking.

"Kurt Morgan," he said pointedly, "should be remembered as a man who performed calmly in times of the greatest stress. He was a man unmoved by tension. One of his finest hours came during President Kennedy's handling of the Cuban missile crisis . . ."

Ignore, ignore! It never happened! Nothing else could possibly go wrong now. Nobody had made the connection between Helen Marconi's little piece of doggerel and the stately blonde sitting directly behind Kurt Morgan's widow. Nora would put it out of her mind!

Eventually Gerry Ball finished his remarks. Nora tried to be more attentive to a ranking member of the Securities and Exchange Commission, who fondly recalled Kurt Morgan's strict adherence to the financial laws of the land. He was followed by a partner from Diversified's merchant bankers.

It was then that Buck put his hand on Nora's knee, then twining fingers through hers and down on the seat between them. He was trying to comfort her. Oh, Buck. Oh, Buck!

And then it was all over. The organ found a slightly more hopeful finale, but everyone was subdued, reminded briefly of their mortality, of how they were all susceptible to a sudden visit from the stranger. Slowly people stood and began the slow shuffle toward the rear of the church.

Buck muttered, "Sit still till they clear out so he can bring the wheelchair out of the trunk."

As they waited, several men came purposefully to Buck and shook his hand.

Nora got to her feet and drew a deep breath. "You're going back to the hospital?"

"I have to, beautiful."

Hazel Morgan edged into the aisle; she was at Nora's elbow.

"You're Nora Sweeney," she whispered. "I heard what

that woman shouted. But I already knew—*he* told me about you." Hazel's chubby lips pinched spitefully. Malice bubbled in her eyes. "He said that about you, that you were the best *fellatiste* on the island of Manhattan. *He told me.*"

Was there anything worse, more hateful, that Hazel Morgan could have said? Morgan *had* told her then, Nora accepted that now, as he had Norm Vincent and Buck. It was true—he had talked about her, he'd told everybody who would listen. The *bastard*. The *son of a bitch*. Nora's sorrow slid easily into hate. She hated Morgan now, suddenly, violently.

But Hazel Morgan was no better and Nora gave it back to her, just as viciously. "Very well," she hissed, "since you bring it up, take your satisfaction in knowing that *as he lay dying* I told him there was a film of you . . . and *this* . . . animal . . . in your love nest. Him—" She gestured contemptuously at Mercury. "Him sticking his—"

Hazel Morgan's body slumped. Mercury caught her arms. Hazel clutched at the end of the pew.

"Hey, baby! Okay?" Mercury exclaimed. His voice was a liquid grovel. He scowled at Nora. "What'd you say to her, you cow?"

"Let's go . . . Joe," Hazel muttered. She turned away, not able to look at Nora.

Buck Collins looked up, evidently deciding Mercury was annoying Nora. "Get lost, greaseball!"

Mercury's face worked itself into an even more perfect sneer. "Hey. Fuck you, asshole motherfucker!"

Collins squirmed to get up. Mercury leapt back, ready to run.

Jerome put his hand on Collins's arm. "Save it, Buck. This is a punk."

"Joe," Hazel Morgan exclaimed, "I said come on!"

His heavy lips baring teeth like fangs, Mercury allowed her to pull him away. As he went, he mimed spitting at them.

"*Who* is that bastard?" Buck snarled.

"Hazel Morgan's boyfriend," Nora said.

"You mean *Morgan's wife's . . . lover?*"

"Exactly."

Buck grinned. "That's reassuring."

As Hazel and Mercury reached the rear of the church, a man Nora had never seen before slid out of the shadows. Swiftly, he extended his hand to Mercury, clasped him lightly by the shoulders, and kissed both his cheeks.

"That's Morel," Paul Jerome said, surprised. "From Milan."

Nora smiled. For she was pleased and reassured to see another figure at the back of the church. Norm Vincent, the ever-vigilant, crouched on his knees, playing Catholic, in the last pew. As Morel, Mercury, and Hazel Morgan left the church, Norm slid out of the pew and into his trench coat to follow them.

Gerald Ball was still boiling mad when Nora got back to Diversified Towers and joined the group in the penthouse conference room.

"Who was that woman?"

Before replying, Nora looked around the room for Lancer. He was not far away, hovering by the double doors, watching them anxiously.

"Helen Marconi, Gerald," Nora said quietly. Her face was turned so Lancer could read her lips. He turned white and looked like he might be sick.

"Ah . . ." Gerald, for some reason, didn't seem surprised.

Only an informal meeting was intended before lunch, because a majority of the board of directors could not be present on such short notice. Gerald Ball, now the ranking officer of the company, presented the agenda, smoothly, like an accomplished croupier managed a roulette table. Point one, two, three, bang, bang, bang. Then, painlessly, he got what he most wanted—an informal vote of approval for the merger with BBD to go forward as planned by Kurt Morgan.

While this was happening, Nora wondered why Ball wouldn't himself go for Morgan's job? His mind was like the proverbial steel trap. There was no hesitation, not a hint of nerves or uncertainty in his conduct. Not once did he refer to the notes he'd written for himself on a yellow legal pad.

When the unanimously favorable vote had been taken, Ball turned and stared for an instant at Rustford Lancer. The look seemed to mean something, for again Lancer looked ill. Next, Ball smiled slowly, as he often did, at Jack Frazer. But there was no hidden message this time. The brief meeting ended with Gerald Ball's reminder that all were invited to walk over to The Plaza for lunch.

Ball stood up, smiling. His expression did not change when he turned to Nora and whispered confidentially, "The Italian is here."

She nodded. "Is it . . . the man named Morel? The Eurochemie representative you heard was coming to New York?"

"Yes." Ball continued to smile at her. "He's announced himself. He'll be at lunch."

"What does it mean?"

"I don't know yet," Ball murmured softly. "He tells me he's carrying a lot of proxies with him, from European shareholders in Diversified."

"God!" she exclaimed. "Buck said this morning they'd started buying into Brown, Broadstairs . . ."

"Yes. BBD opened this morning up five dollars. Fifty-two."

This was the most alarming news yet. "My God, Gerald, that puts it two dollars above our tender offer." Diversified had offered fifty dollars cash to holders not opting for a share exchange. "Gerald, if they keep buying, it'll wreck the merger."

"They're playing with fire," Ball said gently.

"You said Eurochemie had a war chest available to fight us," Nora reminded him. "Now they're going to fight us for BBD? It seems incredible."

"They will *regret* it," Ball grunted. "This man Morel will regret it more than anybody. What is his authority? We know he's from a bank that's close to the Vatican . . ."

"We have a man following him," Nora told him. She explained about Norm Vincent.

"Ah, good," Gerald said. "Very good."

"Paul told me that Eurochemie made a move on BBD once before. BBD turned them down."

Ball's smile became lethal. "Quite right too. Nora, there is no way an Italian cartel is going to be allowed to buy into the American defense industry." They were still standing next to the conference table, as the guests slowly left the room. Ball put a contemplative finger to his chin. "Does it mean we're going to have to start actually buying BBD shares on the market? *Damn it,* Nora, the one thing we didn't want was to go to our treasury to pull this off."

Nora nodded. It seemed everything was a textbook case. "Gerald, we'll have to test them—buy in at fifty-two. If they go ahead, we follow them up, then at sixty-five or seventy, dump it, everything we can find—the price would collapse, they'd lose their shirt."

Ball nodded, a gleam in his eye. "Yes, you're right, Nora. Good thinking. But remember the *ifs*—that's *if* we sell off before they do, and *if* they don't gobble up everything we unload. It depends how much they've got in their war chest, Nora."

"Yes, I know." Her mind was working fast. "But why would they try it, Gerald? As you say, Washington would never let them take control of a company like BBD. If we resist, they've got to fold."

He shrugged elaborately. "Well, there's another way of looking at it, Nora. We could take the profit and . . . you know, let 'em eat it. Give 'em BBD."

"Cancel the merger?" she cried.

"Sure." He scowled at her. "What's at stake? What do you care? It's not going to effect *your* appetite either way—or is it?"

Nora shook her head. He was right. Whatever she was

going to get out of a merger with BBD, she'd already gotten—a vice-presidency, a few bouquets. With Morgan gone, she was not likely to get much more. In fact, she thought dismally, it might even be time to start thinking about moving on.

Gerald looked over her shoulder. "Hello, Jack . . ."

"Went well, Gerry," Frazer said quietly. He was a quiet man, thin, white-haired. He wore rimless glasses.

"Like silk," Ball said in self-congratulation. The word suited him. It seemed to fit his mouth. "Well, we have a treat. Come on, Nora, Jack. I have a treat for you, Nora. I took it upon myself to invite our *unknown Italian quantity* to lunch. Why not? After all, he's investing millions in our company. Least we can do is buy him lunch."

Frazer seemed to know all about it. He laughed mockingly. "Let them send their money, Gerry. We'll know how to spend it."

These two were such old hands, Nora was almost embarrassed to be seen in their company. Nothing impressed them. As they were crossing Fifth Avenue, Gerry amusedly told Jack Frazer, "Nora here thinks all the romance of big business is in the front office— She's learning now what happens in the back room."

For a second, Frazer stared at her. His expression was kindly, but she would have bet there wasn't much he didn't know, or hadn't experienced. She suffered a pang. Had Morgan told *him* too?

Chapter Twenty-nine

"MEN!" THERE WAS SOMETHING RARE ABOUT LUCIA'S voice. In one hand she was waving a late edition of the *Post*.

"Lucia," Jerome said, smiling at her, "you seem excited."

That she was. It was not an unusual state for her, but tonight she seemed more so. She was hopping up and down, fuming in the brightly lit foyer of her apartment where nothing of bare wall showed these days.

"I know," he said, "you got in a new shipment."

"Quiet, you."

The living room was as crowded. Father John perched on one of several long wooden crates which Jerome by now knew would contain carefully packed paintings. It seemed to him sometimes that both mother and daughter must have stripped Italy of *objets* to bring to this place which the whole Italian nation had decided was the last and safest in the world. And that was in spite of the disparaging remarks Elena never stopped making about the city, the state, the country.

It was usual these days to find Elena and Father John sipping a cocktail at about this time. Elena lay sprawled across a velvet-covered chaise lounge while Foster gazed at her with undisguised delight. She was dressed in a pair of silk lounging pajamas, the top cut deeply enough to reveal the swell of very substantial breasts, Jerome judged, slightly overlapped at point of cleavage and freckled. She

351

was not wearing a bra, he realized, for the pointed nipple of her right breast poked like a thumbtack at the light fabric. Foster focused on that.

"Cheers, lad," Father John said, raising a martini glass.

Jerome stopped, considering for a second the matter of what seemed to be the ruination of a perfectly good priest. Then he glanced at Lucia who had flung herself down on the couch facing Elena and lay with one hand draped dramatically over her face.

"This one," Elena explained sourly, "has been hysterical all day."

"Totally," Foster agreed. Clearly, he was very amused about something.

"And why not?" Lucia cried. "Men!" She waved the newspaper at him.

Obviously, he was supposed to take it from her and he did so. "What's this about?"

"Open it," Lucia told him, "to page three. There is a picture from the Morgan festivity."

"Festivity? It was a wake more than it was a festivity, Lucia." Staring at him from the paper was a picture of Hazel Morgan and the nasty piece of goods she'd been with. "So?"

"That man, *caro,* is none other than Mercutio, *the youth.* Do you remember what I told you?"

Jerome frowned at her. "Of course I remember. Your old boyfriend. I should forget *that?* He was with Hazel Morgan. Nora says he's Hazel Morgan's boyfriend now."

"Poor Hazel Morgan," Lucia sighed. "He is a terrible man."

"So you said," he snapped. He turned to Elena. "That was your daughter's lover, did you know?"

"Hush," Elena bawled. "Never! That man was a peasant from Calabria. He came to Rome to work as a male whore and ended in Gogarty's disgusting movie." Foster slumped awkwardly and Elena laughed. "Poor John, he did not know about Gogarty's pornographic movie, did he?" She sat up and beckoned him to sit beside her. He was drawn off the packing crate. Elena put her arms around his shoulders and hugged him. "So naive, this one, so innocent and good."

"Thank you," Foster muttered.

"What you say is not true," Lucia said bitterly. "The youth was never my lover. Gogarty would have killed him, or had him killed."

"You told me," he growled.

"Only a story, Paolo. Not a serious matter."

"My nerves are frayed, Lucia," Jerome said. "Be very careful." He realized then, of course, that he would never know the truth of it. "At the church today, when we were all leaving, he shook hands with that awful Jean-Jacques Morel from Milan."

"I am not surprised," Elena said. "The repulsive person probably catered to Morel's evil desires as well."

Jerome felt a band tighten on his forehead. "But you're *not* surprised to hear he's in New York? You call Morel evil and here he is, in New York, and he represents your financial interests." He glared at Elena, wanting an explanation. But she was unmoved. He turned to Foster. "And you talked to the same man about your foundation, didn't you?"

Foster shook his head. "No," he said sharply. "Morel will have nothing to do with it. The cardinal will see to that." He stared back at Jerome. "Morel is a marked man. I can't imagine what he's doing here."

"For one thing," Jerome said, "he's buying BBD and driving the price out of sight. He is going to screw up the merger and cost everybody a lot of money before he's done."

"Scoundrel!" Foster exclaimed angrily. "Whose money is he using?"

"*Somebody's,* that's for sure. The Vatican's, most likely. Or that bank, of the Sacred Heart of Jesus."

"No," Foster cried, "that's impossible. The cardinal told me . . ."

"I think your cardinal is playing games," Jerome said.

353

"Morel told Gerry Ball he represents something like twenty-two percent of Diversified's equity."

"*Stupido!*" Elena shouted. "I will call my cousin immediately."

Foster grabbed her hand. "No, it's too late. It's after midnight in Rome. You cannot call him now."

"*Stupido!*" she raved. "This Morel has gone mad!"

"*Mama, prego,*" Lucia said faintly.

"Yes," Foster said, "possibly he has gone mad." He glanced inquiringly at Jerome. "What are you going to do about it?"

"Spend money," Jerome said. "We have to match them. I've talked to Ball. Nora's idea is to go out on the limb with them and see who drops off first."

"Buck could cash his bonds," Foster suggested.

"Bonds! Jesus Christ! Don't mention those things," Jerome exclaimed. "Where are they? No, I don't want to know. You left them in Italy—not with Morel, I hope."

"No, no." Foster smiled. "I brought them back. I . . . left them up at Gogarty Castle. I don't want them around."

"You *hid* them up there? Are they safe?" Jerome felt weak. The bonds, nobody wanted them. Buck should have kept them in Connecticut, hid them away himself, or sold them.

"Safe enough, I should think." Foster's long face was impassive, eyes calm. He held both Elena's hands on her thigh. His voice was its old hollow baritone when he spoke again. He sounded as though he were saying a funeral Mass. The chill swept up, then down Jerome's spine. There was something there that was not soothing. "I *think* we will invite Signore Morel to the castle—if you agree, my dear—on the weekend after this. We will talk to him." He smiled thinly. "We will reason together before he goes too far."

Jerome didn't get the point.

Lucia broke in. "What about me? Everything is arranged and what about me? Is no one to pay me any attention?"

Jerome looked at her, then at Elena and Foster. "What's eating *this* one?"

"Men!"

Jerome turned curiously. "That's the second time you've said that tonight. What's the sudden problem with men?"

She was on the edge of tears, yet smiling, like the sun through a rain squall. "You! Terrible scoundrel! I am *pregnanto!*"

Jerome turned to Foster. His legs were not very strong. "Could I have a little gin?"

"Of course."

Then Elena. "You must marry this one now, Paolo!"

"I must? Why?" he said, gratefully taking the drink and swallowing it. "This one is twenty-one years old. She knew what she was doing."

Lucia commenced an exaggerated wail. "You see, I knew he would not admit to being the father to this child." She punched herself in the stomach.

"Hey! Watch it!"

"You do not care."

Grimly, Jerome stared at Foster. "This is a plot. I'm being shot-gunned."

"Yes." Foster grinned. "And you love it, nasty boy."

Chapter Thirty

THANK GOD, NORA TOLD HERSELF, FOR NORMAN VINCENT and his ability to see instantly into the very heart of the matter. His logic might have been taught him by the Jesuits; it was like acid cutting through subterfuge; he was without hypocrisy or phoniness.

Norman Vincent was probably the most honest man she had ever met, now that Father John had disqualified himself. The clarity of his thinking was such that his thoughts could have been flashed across his forehead like the latest news on the *Newsweek* ticker tape in Grand Central. Yes, he was brave, honest, and dedicated.

Norm had tailed Morel all the way from Milan and now the latter's presence in New York was documented. As of Sunday night, Morel was staying at the elegant and exclusive Hotel Napoli, a place frequented by Italian visitors. It was Norm's theory that, so far from Morel being a threat to them, he was actually on the run.

Moreover, Norm had the Diversified situation pretty well sized up, beginning with Lancer whom Norm concluded had had his lights shot out, that he was around the bend. "Accusing you of sucking off Morgan is one thing, Nora," Norm speculated, "but inciting his girlfriend to put it on the seven o'clock news, now that's something else and not good for his cause."

"He's finished," Nora agreed.

"What was the name of that broad again?"

"Helen Marconi."

"Holy shit, that's as Italian as spermoni ice cream!"

"Spumoni, Norm," Nora corrected him.

"Yeah, I knew I was close. Nora, let 'em swing in the wind, that's what we always used to say."

She'd told him about her confrontation with Rusty Lancer and his final bitter shot—why don't *you* take over the company, Nora Sweeney?

Norm said he'd think on that. They were to meet later—at midnight, in fact, at Elaine's. Norm was surveilling a man who went there often and he told Nora she'd make a good decoy, throw the guy off guard.

And why shouldn't she try for it, Nora asked herself? Was it within the realm of possibility? She was equipped for the job, if she did say so herself. Her study of BBD prior to the merger move had acquainted her better than most men with the inner workings of the nation's aerospace industry; her close association with Kurt Morgan had taught her the inside of Diversified Technologies. Moreover, Nora told herself excitedly, as she paced her apartment, whose strategy had they adopted for this struggle with Eurochemie? *Hers!*

It was war. If Eurochemie wanted to play chicken on the New York Stock Exchange, it was all right with Diversified. That very day they'd accepted the challenge, had done what Kurt Morgan most emphatically hadn't wanted to have to do. They'd gone into the market Friday afternoon for the first 100,000 BBD shares at fifty-three— an outlay from the Diversified war chest of $5.3 million. That was just for openers.

It was Nora's hunch that Morel would drop out almost immediately.

The intercom rang. It was Mr. Fiorello in the lobby.

"Miss Sweeney, guy down here from a florist. He's got some roses for you."

"Oh . . . all right. Send him up."

Flowers? From whom? No matter. She deserved them. Possibly from Gerald Ball to say thank you for *any number* of things. Nora's nose twitched with distaste. At least

Norm didn't have those kind of hangups. His sexual tendencies were slightly puzzling to her, in fact she wouldn't have been able to describe them at all, but he was dear to her as much for what he didn't want as for what he did.

His encouragement was precious. Nora didn't require much more of him than that. Go for it, Nora, hon! The elation made her quiver. She hugged herself with both arms.

The door buzzed. She'd forgotten. Oh, yes, flowers. Deservedly, for her. She hoped for a dozen long-stemmed red roses.

The delivery boy's face was hidden behind a cut-glass vase stuffed with a forest of long green stems topped . . . oh, yes . . . with juicy budding roses. Red.

"Put them down, please. Just a moment." She would tip him, she decided, a dollar or two. Nora turned to get her pocketbook on the table under the wood-framed mirror.

The door closed behind her. "But wait . . ." She turned swiftly.

He had waited. She was staring into the handsome but menacing face of Joe Mercury.

"Hey!" His voice was low and ugly, given over entirely to a sneer of unsurpassed scorn and arrogance.

"Get out!"

"I bring you flowers." He didn't cancel the loathsome smirk. His eyes ate at her, like vultures tearing meat. "I see you in the church." He thumbed his chest. "Joe Mercury."

Nora pointed at the roses which he'd set down on the floor. "Take your flowers, buster, and hit the road."

He looked aggrieved. How could she be so cruel? "Hey . . . I hear you like to suck it!"

Nora's eyes began to ache from the force of the scream she contained in her throat. She would never be able to speak again.

But she did. Gulping furiously, hurting herself, straining

her larynx, she cried out. "Get out of here! I'm going to call the police!"

"Nah, nah!" He grinned at her obscenely, his eyes buckling to the weight of the heavy lids, and moved toward her invitingly, pelvis front and center.

Nora backed toward the kitchen, trying feverishly to decide whether the provocation warranted violence. What could she hit him with that would not kill him? If she could get through the door, she'd slam it in his face, bust up his nose, long and pointed like a woodpecker's, and grab for the intercom. But she couldn't get space between them. He followed her, step for step, until she was backed against the dining room table.

"Hey, c'mon!"

Nora remembered the film, most of which she hadn't been able to watch.

"Get out! You're not touching me, you bastard!"

But he was touching her already. He put a hand on each of her shoulders, thumbs pointing inward toward her throat, stroking the underside of her chin. The feel of him made her shake violently. Was he here to kill her?

He was shocked at her reaction to him. "Hey . . . I'm a nice guy . . . *Nora*. Your name. Nora. Beautiful name."

"No. It's not." She was sure if she closed her eyes he'd kill her. Or rape her and then kill her. Or rape her and not kill her. Or not kill her if she gave in! Ah, that was it. She understood. She had to give in now, or die! Give that which had never been given. Oh, God, Nora thought hopelessly, why not to Norman Vincent then, if it had to be somebody, finally?

"I ain't some monster," Mercury pouted.

"What is it you want?" she asked. Terror, a warm fear, drained her of energy. "Is it the film? Did she tell you to get it from me?" He seemed not to know what she was talking about. "It's not here—I won't tell you where."

"Hey . . . I come to give you a little piece of ass," he protested, not understanding.

"No!" Her voice reached for the heights, faltered, cracked, collapsed. "You can't! I'm a virgin, Mr. Mercury!"

His response was a thunderous negative. "You crazy woman! *No way!*"

"I am," she screamed softly, "I'm a nun, a woman of the church, a bride of Jesus Christ!"

He was Italian, she reasoned, and such an argument was bound to impress him. But it didn't.

"No," he hollered, *"no way!"* He laughed menacingly. "I'm gonna fuck you, Nora Sweeney, and you gonna like it very much."

"No, no!"

Where was Mr. Fiorello? Mercury's hand hit her cheek, not hard, but with definition—a warning? Fiorello was downstairs watching TV. Nora steeled herself. So it was going to be like that, do or die. She closed her eyes and waited for the next blow.

It didn't come. Instead, she was confounded by his lips, heavy, blubbery, pressed without warning against hers, then all over her face, his tongue that slavered like some awful hound's.

She wrenched away, long enough to gasp, "I'm expecting a gentleman caller. He's due here any moment and you'll find yourself in a great deal of trouble, I can assure you of that—"

He cut her off contemptuously. "Not me. You! You're gonna be screaming for it, Miss Sweeney. It's good, I'm not jokin'. It's real good." He laughed, trying to transfer desire, his low-down dirty lust, to her. "Good, good . . . I'm promisin', Miss Sweeney, right up to your tonsils, you'll be chewin' on it."

"No . . . Mr. Mercury," she gasped. "Your tongue is filthy!"

He slobbered on her blouse. His hands dropped to the zipper of her skirt. He groped her buttocks, pulling her forward into his loins. God! She felt the long slab of his manhood, like a body on a stretcher it was so long and dead feeling.

"You can't! You must not! It's a sin! What did they teach you in the Church?"

Mercury growled, "To fuck all the girls. You never was a nun. You're a lying bitch for saying that."

Of course, she knew immediately, she'd made a mistake. He probably had a sister who was a nun. A bad idea to represent herself as one.

"I'm like your sister," Nora hissed. "Would you do such a thing to your sister?"

A cry burst from him. "Liar!"

"I am, I tell you." She began to sob.

Mercury was ruining her clothes, trying to pull everything off at once. Nora flexed her forearms, resisting, but she'd accepted she was going to be raped.

"You're a pig!"

Mercury nodded, his forehead nudging her breasts. "You got it, baby."

Oh God, and her blouse. She had never been so frightened when Morgan had tried to have his way with her, or even when she'd been alone with Buck Collins. And Norm Vincent—he had never frightened her at all. There was such a thing as innate trust. She had no trust in the likes of Joe Mercury.

"Nice tits." He grunted his approval. "Good ones. Straight up." He hit them playfully, batting them from side to side. "Let's see what else you got."

Nora was ready to faint. She didn't want to be a party to any of this. If he took her by force when she was in fact unconscious, it was all the worse for him, the better for her not to be aware when her honor was shredded. She was stripped naked.

With great agility, Mercury dropped to his knees to yank down her white panties and indelicately roll her pantyhose down her legs.

"Good legs!"

His heavy tongue rolled like sandpaper up her thigh.

"Oh, please . . . no!"

He chuckled excitedly. No, the giggle was that of a half-crazed man. Suppose Mercury was infected with some dread disease? Then she would get it and that would end her life. But that was irrelevant now, for he was so determined to take her she knew she was lost. She might scream but who was going to hear her? Certainly not that idiot Fiorello. She could try a karate chop at Mercury where it would hurt most, but then he'd no doubt mar her face in revenge. No, she was defeated.

His fingers clutched roughly at the entrance to her vagina, as if he wanted to part it so he could crawl inside. He steadied her with one hand.

"Nice hole," he muttered. "Looks tight."

"Didn't I tell you I'm a virgin?" she almost screamed.

He frowned, deep in thought. "It ain't gonna hurt," he finally decided.

Mercury had her propped against the dining room table. The edge of wood was cold on her buttocks. Quickly, he began to undress. She might have run but she'd never make the door. She knew it. Mercury was careful with his clothes. He hung his white shirt over the back of a dining room chair. His shoes were next. He lined them up side by side next to the chair. Then, only then, did he unzip his trousers. She was not ready for the reality. Her heart jogged in her throat.

Mercury wore jockey shorts and his penis was already pushing them out dangerously. He was careful when he unstrung himself. She was even more shocked when he smiled down at it, so smugly, so happy about himself. He looked up, inspecting her face for a reaction.

"Watcha think of that, baby?"

Nora opened her eyes ingenuously, let her gaze drift deliberately from his greasy face to the focal point of his being.

"What?" she asked.

"What!" He was insulted and that would cost her, she knew. *"That,* baby!" He shoved it out, like an exclamation point.

Nora tried to remain calm; she knew that panic would get her nowhere. But her insides were shaking, quaking. A terrible sickness was building within her.

"Listen," she said, "I think you'd better put on your pants and leave, before you get yourself in a lot of trouble. I feel ill."

"Trouble?" His voice was threatening. But he held back. He was impressed with her, perhaps not frightened of her but she did make him stop and think.

Nora stared at him, like a trainer facing down a ferocious and unpredictable animal. She dared not look away because she knew that if she did he would pounce. He surely could see her legs trembling. But he faltered and that familiar pouting smirk twisted his lips.

Suddenly, she was struggling against his bare body, slimy now with his perspiration. Gummy discharge from his engorgement wet her belly. His hands squeezed her breasts, then around behind her, her back, his nails sharp and scratching, fingers pinching behind and under her. Mercury made strange, grunting noises, strong enough to drown out her own piteous cries. Nora felt herself sagging, a web of sickness rising in her throat.

"C'mon, c'mon!" He began pulling her into the living room. On the rug!

God, Nora thought to herself desperately, they would positively hang him. "You're going to hurt me!"

"Shut up. No, I ain't." His voice was hardly recognizable as human.

He forced her down on her hands and knees but she braced her joints to prevent him from pushing her to the floor. He was laughing now, the personification of evil. He yanked on her buttocks, trying to tip her, but she fought back. His hand then, what! She felt it behind her, a finger pressed against her anus, wiggling, pushing in. He chuckled coarsely.

363

"Here's where I'm going to stick it in, baby, so I ain't gonna take your virginity!"

And then it happened. The shock of that finger, the fingernail cutting, burst her emotional dam. She turned to him as vomit flooded from her throat, gushed out of her mouth toward his smirking face. She saw with satisfaction the horror in his eyes. He would kill her now for sure but first he would be very dirty. His face turned color, from bloaty tan to red, and then dead white. *He hated it!* Nora flung herself down on him, bare breasts knocking the wind out of his chest, and she kept vomiting on his chest, his face, his hair, and ears. He tried to push her up, slapping at her, but she became a dead weight. He couldn't move and she continued being sick. Mercury weakened and then began to gag. He bellowed and finally tore himself away from her, jumping up, looking around wildly. He wanted the bathroom. Nora pointed. Mercury stumbled across the living room, through the bedroom, into the bathroom, and she could hear him coughing and vomiting, making sounds like a wounded animal.

Finally, he stopped. The sound of the shower started. He was now yelling threats and swearing in bad English. Nora did not move. She sat there on the rug where he'd left her, filthy, malodorous. Let him see her again, like this, and appreciate what he'd done.

It seemed that he stayed under the water for at least a half hour. Finally he reappeared, hair wet, body gleaming, clean. When he saw her, he looked away and headed for his clothes.

"That was a dirty thing," he muttered.

"You were raping me. What did you expect? You made me get sick. It wasn't my fault!"

He looked at her over his shoulder, very briefly. "Shut up."

"You'll pay for this," Nora whispered.

"Fuck you!" he cried. "One word and I break your ass."

He had his pants on and the shirt. He tucked in the

shirttails, then sat down to put his socks on and slip into his shoes. He looked at her again and tried to laugh.

"You pig—you look like a pig," he snarled.

Nora stared back. "It takes one to know one, Mr. Mercury."

He was putting the dark blue topcoat over his shoulders. "I'm goin' now." He sneered. "Someday, I come back. You're gonna love it." He closed his hand over that place in his pants and pushed it toward her suggestively.

Nora put her hand to her mouth. That was enough for him.

"So long, baby," he growled.

Mercury opened the door and slipped out. He didn't bother to close it. Nora got up quickly, slammed it, and dropped all the bolts into place. She leaned back against the door, sighing, sobbing softly in relief. The cold metal of the dead bolt bit into her kidney, waking her up.

She was still in one piece. He had taken nothing from her, except a memory of nausea which he would not soon forget and hopefully would always remember when he was climbing on his women. Nora went into the bathroom, turned on the shower to cleanse and make herself pure as the driven snow once more.

She was toweling and putting on her terry robe when the intercom rang for the second time that night.

"Fiorello speaking, Miss Sweeney."

Oh, yes, she thought, Mr. Fiorello, the dumb fool. "Yes?"

"Another gent down here to see you. Busy tonight, ain't you, Miss Sweeney?" he joked stupidly.

"Who is it?" she asked coldly.

"It's Mr. Ball, your friend Mr. Ball."

"He can come up, Mr. Fiorello." She stopped and then said, "You'd better be more careful about the people you let into that elevator."

"What?" She had him. He was frightened already. His job . . .

"That delivery boy was not a delivery boy, Mr. Fiorello. He was a *rapist.*" She said the dread word carefully.

Horror thumped in Fiorello's voice. "A rapist? Jesus, Miss Sweeney, that kid was Italian . . ."

"An *Italian rapist,* Mr. Fiorello."

His voice was shaking. "I'll call the cops, Miss Sweeney."

"Too late, Mr. Fiorello," Nora said calmly, feeling good with the power she had over him. "The deed is done."

"Are you . . . all right . . . Miss Sweeney? Do you need a doctor?"

"I'm all right."

She heard Gerald Ball's voice in the background and then suddenly he was on the phone.

"Nora, what the hell happened?"

"Oh, Gerald . . ." Nora struggled not to cry, but his compassion was too much for her. She sobbed, "Please come up . . ."

"Yes, yes," he said hurriedly. "Were you raped, Nora? Good God! Were you? Get it out, Nora . . ."

"Come up—quickly!"

All she had to do, really, was to mop up the rug where she'd been sick, then put a throw rug over the spot. She was ready for Gerald Ball when he buzzed.

"Oh, Gerald!" She threw herself in his arms.

His smooth face was a mass of worry wrinkles. "Are you all right?"

Wordlessly, she nodded.

"I saw a man hustle out of the elevator. Was that him? Wearing a blue coat?"

"Yes. I know who he is . . . Gerald," she murmured, smiling bravely, "so not to worry. It didn't actually happen. I . . . fought him off. I just wanted to scare Fiorello—he never should have let that man in the elevator. And he knows it!"

"*Quite right,* golden girl," Ball exclaimed. "Good for you, Gigi. How did you do it? You're a brave girl, I can tell

366

you, that son of a bitch will pay for it, Nora. Tell me his name."

"Not now, Gerald. I want to forget. Come in. Sit down."

"Are you sure, golden girl? You're not just saying that so I won't be worried?"

"No, no, Gerald, I promise you. Nothing happened, really. It's sweet of you to be concerned."

His face was flushed. He shifted his tailored black overcoat from one arm to the other and then put it down on a chair.

Nora laughed loudly then, pointing. The vase and the bundle of long-stemmed roses still sat on the carpet where Mercury had put them.

"That's how he got in," she said. "He pretended he was a delivery boy."

"The son of a bitch," Ball repeated hatefully. "You're sure he didn't . . . touch you. If he touched you, it'd ruin everything for me, golden girl."

"No." Nora shook her head. "He didn't. I touched him though—you know where." Such false bravado. But it was the only thing a man would understand. Yes, hadn't she fought him off with a good knee to the testicles?

"Why don't I build us a drink," Ball murmured soberly.

"Yes, that'd help. I think I'd like a vodka on the rocks." Nora remembered she'd just been so sick—was a drink going to bring back her nausea? "Gerald, please excuse me." Oh, God, she remembered, she had to go to the bathroom again. "I must wash my hands." She chuckled aimlessly.

His smile flexed. "Well, go on. Leave the door open . . . so I can talk to you."

She really didn't like this, did she? But, what the heck? He was easier to handle than Joe Mercury.

She went into the bathroom and lifted the toilet seat. "Gerald," she called, "I thought you were sending me some Baccarat . . ."

367

He sighed loudly. "Whenever you say the word, golden girl."

Sitting down, tented by her robe, Nora asked idly, "So what's the big news, Gerald?"

Slyly, he stuck his head in the door and stared down at her, a strange yearning disturbing the peace and quiet of his eyeballs.

"Oh . . . damn it, golden girl, can I sit down?"

He didn't wait for permission but collapsed on the bathroom rug, woolly and soft. He put his hand on her bare ankle to stroke it gently. His eyes swamped with ecstasy.

"You see, golden girl . . . oh gosh!" He hadn't missed the sound.

Nora finished. Before he'd summoned the energy to boost himself off the carpet, she'd swept her robe about her and lunged back into the living room.

"I am ready for my drink now!"

"Right away, Gigi, right away," he mumbled.

Now, Gerald was very embarrassed, averting his eyes as he busied himself with the glasses and the vodka. Nora helped by disappearing into the kitchen for ice and a lemon.

"Here you are," Gerald said, handing her the drink. He stared at her almost angrily. "Don't think me some sort of perverted man, please, Nora."

"Never!"

"Hell," he cried, "sometimes I hate myself but I'm going to say something right out—I want to lick the last drop off you, that's what. *There!*"

She drew a breath which was deep and somehow painful. This wasn't her way; she was sure this was not her sort of thing. Best to ignore what he'd said and move right along.

"So, Gerald, how goes the good fight? Anything new?" Nora asked brightly.

"Not just yet. We'll probably have to repeat the exercise tomorrow. In the meantime, I'm trying to get a line on what's behind this Morel—or who's behind him. Did you ever in your life see a more gruesome and unwholesome looking man?"

"Jet lag, most likely, Gerald."

He looked at her as if he were wondering whose side she was on. Gerald was somehow, for some reason, quite disgruntled, dissatisfied with her. "Nora, *everything* is wrong with him, from bloodshot eyes to oily skin and dandruff."

She shuddered. "He sounds like . . . that man who was here."

"Nora." His voice was sharp. Then he shrugged. "What I really came here for was to tell you that *you've* got a problem."

"Another one! Good heavens! What else could there be?"

He frowned. Ah, whatever it was, Nora realized, he was making it her fault.

"It seems," Gerald said, "that Miss Marconi, that *woman* who interrupted my talk, has barricaded herself and Rusty Lancer into Kurt's office—they won't come out."

"Oh, no!" Nora groaned. "Impossible, Gerald—how ludicrous! She's obviously gone crazy. My God, how long have they been in there."

"It seems since Friday night," he said. "The security people didn't realize it until early this morning when the cleaning staff went in to do the carpets. The security people reached me this afternoon. I tried to get you," he said reproachfully, "but there hasn't been an answer all day."

"I was . . . out to church," Nora said, hopeful he would accept that. Actually, she and Norm had been walking and jogging in the park all day, Norm giving her an introductory course in guerrilla infiltration.

"This *creature* has taken Lancer hostage—or maybe the other way around."

Nora could not stop herself from laughing.

Ball shook his head. "I guess you can laugh about it—what else *can* we do?"

"Tear gas?"

"And hope it doesn't get into the papers. You understand, don't you, Nora?"

"Yes. We'll talk them out in the morning. Let them stew another night. Nothing to eat, I presume."

"She's got sandwiches and there's water available in Kurt's private bathroom, of course."

Nora pursed her mouth philosophically. "Stress, Gerald. Stress is the curse of the latter twentieth century."

"I suppose," he said morbidly. "I'm afraid Rusty is just not presidential material, is he, Nora?"

"I fear not, Gerald."

"Of course, we don't really know, do we? This woman seems to have some sort of strange hold over him."

Vodka improved Nora's spirits. "Gerald, be realistic. They've both popped their buttons."

He smiled. "Lost their oars, you mean."

"Blown their fuses," she suggested cheerfully.

"*Oh*, golden girl," Ball smiled gratefully. "You've got a wonderful sense of humor." Then his mood lowered again. "You know, my hunch is that this man Morel came over here with some idea he could promote Rusty Lancer for Kurt Morgan's job."

"*Really?* I wonder why?"

"God knows," Ball shrugged. "But *they* should know better than to think they can influence our affairs. Why, good heavens, they're *Europeans*." His eyes twinkled. "You know, Gigi, I've got half a mind to promote *you* for that job. What would you say to that?"

"Me!" She was genuinely surprised, despite her wild dream. "Gerald, you're not serious—there's not a snowball's chance . . . is there?"

"Why not?"

Nora moved to kneel beside his chair, to kiss his satiny cheek. "Gerald, you're a dear, but you shouldn't make fun of me."

"Golden girl . . ." Ball got to his feet and pulled her with him, throwing his arms around her waist, pressing his chubby little belly against hers. "If I had my way, Gigi, come *consummation* day I'd put you in charge of the whole blasted company, Diversified Industries. I happen to think you're smarter than any of the men in the running."

"No, Gerald! Why not *you?*" Nora cried forcefully. "You're playing some clever kind of game."

He shook his head, staring down into her robe, placing his dry nose at the point of her cleavage. "No, *not me,* Nora. I've told you, I'm the man *behind* the scenes."

"Why not, Gerald?"

A sad smile played on his mouth. "They'd never let me."

"Who?"

He smiled again. "My backers. I say no more." He was not going to answer, was he? "But I *can* tell you this stupid Milanese is making a big mistake. He should've kept his head down. No," he said determinedly, "as I say, I do really have half a mind to push you, Nora."

"That's just unbelievable. Do you think I could do it?"

"Of course."

"You'd be at my side," she pointed out.

"Golden girl . . . oh, golden girl," he sighed, "always at your side, watching, guarding." He laughed merrily. "I'm your lap dog, golden girl. Do you understand?" he asked keenly. "Must go. Can't stay. Busy day tomorrow, ruining Eurochemie S.A." He didn't seem worried about it, did he? He moved toward his coat on the chair by the mirror.

"Gerald," Nora said affectionately, "dear man . . . good night."

She took his coat and held it for him, but as her hands were in the air he dropped all pretense. Going swiftly to his knees, Ball ducked his head under her terry robe and before she could dodge away, he had pushed his face into her bare crotch and kissed her with such a loud smack that

371

it echoed into her like a sonic boom. His eyes were blinking wildly when he surfaced.

"Still damp there, just as I expected."

"Gerald . . . I . . ."

On his feet again, Nora numbly helped him slide into his overcoat.

"Say no more, my golden girl," he sang, "the deal is struck and cast in stone. Am I right?"

Nora took him to the door. She smiled back at him and nodded. But there were other ideas in her head. Gerald Ball might think he was buying the right to take these liberties with her; but he would learn soon that he couldn't just barge in any old time and shove his face into her privacy.

Chapter Thirty-one

AMONG OTHER THINGS, NORA REALIZED DURING THE
night, Gerald Ball had come to see her because he didn't
want to soil his hands with the sordid matter of Helen
Marconi and Rustford Lancer. Without saying so, he had
made it obvious she was to handle it.

When Nora arrived at the corporate reception area on
the Forty-fourth floor it was 8:00 A.M. A small, concerned
crowd had already collected. Diversified's chief of security, Crawford Longboat, thumbs caught in his red suspend-
ers was the center of attention. Longboat was fat, too fat
to qualify for the New York police department. But it was
said he was good at his job.

As he'd promised, Norm Vincent was there ahead of
her. Norm was standing next to Longboat. His smile was
cheerful enough, but Norm was exhausted, Nora could see
that.

"Hi," Nora said casually. "Good morning, Mr. Longboat."

Longboat hadn't the faintest idea who she was. But how
could he? Until this morning, Nora would have been just
one of the faceless thousands of security risks roaming
Diversified's corridors.

"I'm Nora Ellen Sweeney," she said, making it easy for
him.

But that didn't help either. Possibly Longboat didn't
read internal memoranda. "Hello," he said cautiously.

Norman laughed heartily. "Typical of Craw," he said.

"Don't know which end is up. Craw, Nora Sweeney here is one of your own vice-presidents." He put his hand on Nora's shoulder, not seeming to mind when she sidled away. Such familiarity wouldn't do, not in public. "Craw and I used to do . . . a little *business* together." He studied her a moment coolly. "Are you *all right* today, Nora? No more sign of your *little friend.*"

She shook her head, almost impatiently. *That* was past history. Nora had called Norm at Elaine's to tell him she couldn't make it. Attempted rape. Then, she'd told him about Helen Marconi holding poor stupid Lancer hostage. Norm had insisted on knowing who tried to rape her. Mercury would pay, he promised.

"Hullo, Miss Sweeney," Longboat said finally.

Nora straightened her shoulders. "What's the situation?"

"Still in there," Longboat grunted. "Goddamn pair of loonies. Got the door locked, shit piled up against it."

"What," Nora asked sternly, "are our options?"

Longboat shrugged disgustedly. "Gas . . . bust the door down . . . riot guns. We don't know what she's got in there, that's the trouble. We got to assume she's got a weapon."

"Aren't they hungry yet?"

"Crazies can live off their fat for a long time."

Nora smiled grimly at Norman.

"Craw, we could lower a guy from the roof to pot 'em from the window."

"No!" Nora said vigorously, "no violence." They looked at her, surprised by her vehemence. "We've decided—no violence." She looked around, lowering her voice discreetly. "And no publicity. I assume no press people are getting up here." Nora directed herself to Longboat. "Tell your people not to let *anybody* else onto this floor until we've cleared up the situation."

"Yes," he mumbled, not liking to take orders from a woman, "all right." It didn't occur to him to ask to see her authority.

"Can she phone out?"

"We rerouted all the phones," Longboat said. "Everything goes through the switchboard so we'll be able to monitor—"

"That's good," Nora cut in. "I have to go to my office. I'm waiting to hear from *Mr. Ball*. You'd better come with me, Norman."

Norman Vincent looked puzzled. But he followed her down the hallway. She offered him coffee and told her secretary to get two cups. She and Norm both drank black coffee; that made it cozy.

He gazed around the room, not impressed, but then she wasn't sure he was really looking at her furnishings.

"Thanks for getting here so early, Norm," she said. "Sit down, why don't you?"

He glanced at her. "You know, hon, I hate to tell you this but you've got a real problem out there. You're just playing it cool, I guess."

"How else?" she responded. "Ball wants me to manage this. He can't face it."

"I know. He's not your front line kind of *soldat*, Ellen." The thought seemed to make him gloomy. "Looks like Lancer's lance is busted, doesn't it?" He shook his head disbelievingly. "This is a guy who doesn't need any enemies if he's got friends like that fruitcake. I guess this blasts *your European friend* out of the water too."

Slowly, Nora said, *"My* European friend?"

"Morel," Norman said. "My suspicion is that Lancer was working hand-and-foot with the Italians—i.e. Morel, Eurochemie, and that Bank of the Sacred Heart of Jesus . . . Jesus Christ, what kind of a name for a goddamn bank? Can you believe it?"

"I don't understand the connection," Nora said slowly.

"Ah, ha! There's where I've got you! You are not aware that one of the subsidiaries in Lancer's division makes *laundry equipment.*"

"So?" Nora was not reading him too well. For a second,

she had the impression that his mind was uncoiling like an overwound watch spring.

"So, the *vying*, hon, is between Morel—*i.e.*," he stressed, "Eurochemie and the Sacred Heart bank—and our home-grown interests, most probably those backing Gerald Ball to the hilt, over the laundry-equipment subsidiary which is under the aegis of none other than Rustford Lancer!"

"You've been talking to Gerald Ball?"

"Absolutely not to Gerald Ball. No! No! No!"

Nora was preparing to ask Norm to go over it again, very slowly, when her phone sounded.

"Sweeney."

It was, ironically enough, Gerald. "Nora," he said hurriedly, "the affair of these two . . . cretins . . . is definitely something I do not want to be mixed up in. Nora, the ball has been tipped into your court," he said, in more measured tones. "You know this Marconi woman—*you* talk her out of there."

"All right, Gerald," Nora said.

"Look," Ball's voice dropped, "I have full confidence in you, Nora. You know what that means."

"Gerald," she said firmly, "no problem. Don't give it another thought. Thanks for calling . . . good-bye."

The same surge of excitement and energy she'd felt the night before gripped her.

"Well?" she asked Norm. "What do we do? It's up to us, Norm."

Promptly he said, "Starve 'em out. Nonviolent."

Decisively then, Nora reached for her phone and punched for the operator. "This is Nora Ellen Sweeney. Put me through to Miss Marconi, please, in Mr. Morgan's office."

They knew about her. No questions asked. The phone rang through.

"Hullo . . . yeah." Helen's voice was dull, hoarse, without hope.

"Helen, it's Nora."

"Speaking." Helen sounded totally dazed. How was Nora to negotiate with a woman in a trance?

"Helen, listen to me. You've got to get out of that office."

Silence. Heavy breathing. "It's *his* office . . . Rightfully his, and nobody else's," Helen said harshly. She was waking up, finally. "Who is this?"

"Helen, it's me, Nora Ellen Sweeney."

A touch of the old Helen returned and despite that word again, Nora was relieved.

"Cocksucker!"

"I'm not going to argue with you, Helen. Nobody will hold it against you if you come out of there . . . *now*, without making any more trouble."

"You rotten bitch."

"Helen," Nora said coldly, "listen carefully. You are coming out of there, one way or the other. Think it over now. How is Mr. Lancer?"

"Sleeping," Helen mumbled. "He drank all Morgan's booze."

"The whole cabinet?"

"Yeah." Helen didn't sound very happy about Rusty Lancer.

"How about a couple of pizzas, Helen? Help you think." Cheerfully, Nora added, "Pizzas with all the trimmings—anchovies, black olives, tomato, double cheese, thick crust . . ."

She looked at Norm. He was licking his lips and swallowing.

"Yeah," Helen said, her appetite piqued, "put some pizzas by the door. Tell 'em to knock twice. No tricks!"

As Nora put the phone down, Norm muttered, "Christ, hon, I'm ready for lunch."

"In due course. Look, she wants the pizzas. Arrange it, will you, Norm. With everything on them, I mean everything. What you've got to decide, Norm, is what to put *in them*. Those two have got to be knocked out cold as cucumbers."

Norman looked at his watch. "What've we got? Ten-thirty? Hon, leave it to me." He leaned back on her couch, clasping his hands behind his head. "I'm sure old Craw has got some knock-out drops stashed away in his dirty-tricks cupboard. You know, hon," he mused, "we got stuff that tastes like steak sauce knocks you on your ass like a hit from a two-by-four."

"Not dead," Nora repeated, "just out."

"You got it," he said. "Let 'em drool a while. Get the pizzas in about five P.M. tonight and Whap! We go in about eighteen-thirty hours, maybe nineteen hundred when everybody's out of the building, take 'em out on stretchers, straight to Bellevue and nobody's the wiser. How's that sound? Hey, *what about lunch,* hon?"

It was about time, Nora had decided, that Norman Vincent meet Paul Jerome. These two were the most important men in her life, discounting Buck Collins. Jerome reported that Connie Broadstairs was in the city and spending every hour with Buck. He was due to be discharged from the hospital before the weekend—not bad, Paul speculated, to have Buck with them at the castle for the meeting with Mr. Jean-Jacques Morel.

Norm went out to arrange the banquet he and Crawford Longboat would cook up for Helen Marconi and Rustford Lancer, and Nora called Gerald Ball back to reassure him everything was under control. "With a little luck," she said, "we'll have them bundled out of here by eight o'clock tonight. The operation will be conducted after closing hours."

"Nora . . . golden girl," he breathed softly into the phone, "you're so level-headed."

"Gerald, you're too kind."

"Dinner?"

Oh, no, she'd be with Norm Vincent. "No, Gerald, I can't promise," she said firmly. "I won't leave here until this is done . . . and then, I've . . ." Yes, it was so. She had to talk to yet another of Diversified's family of wives, Mrs. Rustford Lancer. "I'll have to get Mrs. Lancer's agreement to have him committed briefly for observation —I hadn't thought about it, but why do you suppose we haven't heard from her? Wouldn't she worry when he didn't come home Friday night, or Saturday, or yesterday?"

Ball brooded on that. "Maybe she thinks he's out of town on business, Nora. Maybe Mrs. Rustford Lancer doesn't give a damn if he doesn't come home on the weekend. Could we have him committed?"

"Gerald," she said reasonably, "she couldn't object to him being put under observation." She chuckled. "After all, for all we know Helen may have abused him somehow. . . she's had him in there alone all weekend."

"My God," he cried, "what a horrible thought."

Nora waited until they were sitting at a corner table upstairs at Pietro's before saying what was in her heart.

"You two are the men I trust most. I say that because it's the truth." She laid a hand on them for a moment. "Let's order a belt."

Norm spoke emotionally. "Ellen, hon, you know I'd put my ass right on the line for you."

Nora smiled faintly. He had a way of putting things. "Did you arrange . . . the *pizzas?*" she asked, for Jerome's benefit. "We're feeding Rusty and Helen *pizzas* for dinner."

Jerome nodded, grinning. "Hearing about that, I begin to wonder about merging with a bunch of goddamn lunatics like Diversified."

Norm didn't appreciate the remark. "Those two fuckheads are not the norm, Jerome. Besides, Lancer's goose is cooked. He's definitely a dead duck."

Jerome smiled. "That's what happens when the chickens come home to roost."

"Hey!" Norm chuckled. "Fowl weather . . ."

But Paul's face turned somber. "Speaking of lunatics," he said, "it seems we've got another small problem with Buck."

"*Hell!* What now?" Nora said.

"I told you Connie Broadstairs is in town. I heard from *Pete* Broadstairs this morning, after you and I talked." Jerome folded his hands around his Beefeater martini. "It seems little Connie lifted something that didn't really belong to her out of Pete's desk."

"Such as?" Nora demanded sharply.

"*Such as,*" he responded bitterly, "property of Pete's that Buck, through *your* good offices, forwarded to *me* in Italy via Father John Foster."

"I . . . hate . . . to ask what."

Jerome studied Norman Vincent for a moment. "Go ahead," Norman barked softly. "Anything you tell me, you can tell her."

"Is that so?"

"Yes. Go on."

"All right. That package was eight hundred thousand dollars worth of BBD bonds, the kind of bonds with nobody's name on them. You carry them into a financial institution and barter them—for cash." His voice was even more heavily laden with sarcasm.

"The broad took her own husband's bonds and sent them to *you?*" Norman demanded incredulously.

"To Buck." Jerome looked disgusted.

Norm Vincent stared across the table at Jerome as if he were defective. "And he sent them to you."

Wearily, Jerome said, "I didn't know they'd been stolen. Now, Pete says he's coming to New York, and if Connie doesn't come up with the bonds he's going to have her arrested."

Norm grinned, a not very appropriate reaction, given the situation. "He who steals my good name steals shit, but he who takes my bearer bonds is in a mess of trouble."

"Yes," Jerome said glumly, "more or less. But Pete is

also talking about withdrawing his approval—it was never very strong—for the merger."

"Damn!"

"Well, obviously he's not going to have anything to do with any enterprise Buck is running. He wants Buck's hide."

"And if he gets the bonds back?" Nora asked.

Paul shrugged. "Then, I assume—I hope—Pete would withdraw. At least, he wouldn't get a warrant out on Connie. About the merger, I just don't know. You can imagine how he feels about Buck."

She stated the obvious. "He knows about Buck and Connie."

"He always did. It's just a matter of getting your nose rubbed in it."

"I see." Nora leaned back, pulled on her Scotch. "What do we do? Where *are* the bonds now? I know, don't tell me—sold. The money's in a Swiss account, I suppose," she deduced gloomily.

"No," Jerome said. "The one smart thing I did. I *was* going to hand them over to that man Morel." He shook his head. "He *happens* to be Lucia's banker, or his bank is hers. Don't ask me why."

Norm growled, "That's the smartest thing you ever did in your life, buddy."

"Thanks. I just . . . returned the package to dear Father John and he brought them back home."

"Father John has them?" Nora's heart sang. "That's easy then. Father John just gives them back to Buck."

"I know. And Buck gives them to Connie and Connie gives them to Pete." Jerome smiled awkwardly. "Can anything *these days* be that easy?"

Suspiciously, Norm asked Jerome, "Did Collins tell you to give them to Morel?"

"No. He doesn't know Morel."

"Are you sure?"

"Yes. Why?"

"Because I could suspect this was all part of some goddamn kind of payoff arrangement, that Collins was maybe buying something from Morel . . ."

"Norm," Nora reminded him, "you already suspect that Rusty Lancer was in alliance with Morel." She shook her head. "It's not likely that Buck would be in alliance with *them.*"

"Suppose Collins don't know Lancer is already bought?" Norm insisted. "Or, suppose, it *is* an unholy trio? Nora, you just *don't know.*"

Jerome nodded idly. "Who knows anything?"

"Exactly," Norm said.

Nora wanted to tell them not to give her a headache. "Listen, the question now is, can we save Buck? Buck is a *damn* idiot! I told him that after the accident. First the business with the cocaine, and now this. Paul?"

He sounded beat. "The only question I've got, Nora, is whether he's *worth* saving."

Norm, ever realistic, supplied the obvious answer. "You don't even try to save him. You toss him overboard. You jettison him, throw him to the wolves, kick him off the back of the truck."

"Try that plot on the *Wall Street Journal,*" Jerome muttered.

Norman slapped the table, almost knocking over his drink, a Virgin Mary. "Hey, you guys, don't talk so defeatist. It's always darkest before dawn."

Jerome looked at him wanly. "Are you talking silver lining?"

Nora frowned at him. Paul absolutely must not make fun of Norman.

Norm didn't appear to notice. "Promise Broadstairs anything, everything. Deliver nothing. First, you got to talk turkey to this Connie. You've got to tell her if she doesn't get her keester in line, then her tit is going to get caught in the wringer. In due course, this Pete Broadstairs forgives her. These things always blow over, take it from me."

"No," Paul said. "Pete will never forgive Buck."

"Well, then the only other thing you can do is to have an accident."

Nora pounced. "Don't . . . ever . . . say things like that, Norm."

"Hon," Norman said, pained, "we are talking hard ball of the hardest sort."

"I know . . ." It was, Nora thought, not an unattractive idea to have Buck Collins bumped off. He'd twisted them all around his little finger, starting with Connie, then Jerome, old Pete. But *not* her.

"Damn him," she said fiercely. "Buck Collins, I mean. I *used* to think Buck could do well in politics. I still think he's got charisma and the background in the industrial-military complex to make a run for it. So I don't want to see him thrown to any wolves. Not yet. Understand?"

She could feel resistance rising in Paul Jerome. It was as if she'd prodded him with something unpleasant. His face went taut. "Nora, I'm sorry, but as far as I'm concerned he's thrown Morgan's job out the window. He used me and I don't like it. If you tried to force the issue, I'd quit." He picked up the menu and began to scan it angrily.

"I know," Nora cried, with a sudden flash of understanding. *"You* want the job."

Paul didn't even look up. "You would think that, wouldn't you?"

"What am I supposed to think?"

"Think whatever you want," he said harshly. "Buck can hang by his thumbs for all I care. Drag him into politics if you want to—he'd be with his own kind."

Norman sputtered, "Jesus, you've got some great opinion of our nation's leaders, don't you?"

"Well?"

"They're not all crooks, buddy."

It began to appear that these two, her favorite men, might not hit it off very well. On the other hand, there was that phenomenon called creative tension to be considered.

Between them, agitating and annoying each other, they might just get to the bottom of things.

"You know what's going to happen, buddy," Norman muttered speculatively, making it sound like a dire threat, "is that Nora Ellen is going to wind up being the next boss of Diversified Technologies."

Jerome's face underwent a marvelous transition. Norm's words registered and made Paul frown. He began to smile, abruptly cut off a laugh. His eyes changed color reflectively, as if someone were making waves in a think tank.

Before he could speak, Nora said impatiently, "You mean I get the job by default, Norm? Because everybody has disqualified himself?"

Jerome shook his head. "Not necessarily . . ."

As desultory as the remarks had been, Nora was conscious of her blood rushing to, of all places, her groin, as if Norm had stroked her there. Warmth, a definitely erotic flush, coursed across her belly and made her breasts ache. She contained the final expression of passion, a gasp of pure joy.

"It's a concept," Norm said knowingly, "the concept of a woman doing a man's job. Are we ready for it, *buddy?*"

"Sure," Paul said. "I am. How'd you like that, Nora, being the first woman to run a multibillion-dollar conglomerate?"

"Megabucks," she sighed, smiling at them as though they were utterly mad. "Megacrazy idea . . ."

Chapter Thirty-two

NORA'S BLOOD WAS STILL SINGING WHEN SHE FINALLY GOT home that night. The seige at Diversified Towers had been lifted. The pizza scheme had worked perfectly. Within minutes of delivering the pies, the door of the Morgan suite had opened a crack and Helen's grubby hand eagerly grabbed the food. Twenty minutes later, they heard a commotion inside. Crawford Longboat nodded his head wisely. Next came a scream of groggy rage; the door opened again, for Helen Marconi's last message.

"Drugged us! Motherfuckers!"

After that, it was merely a matter of cleanup. Norman told Nora to peel off for home; he'd take care of the aftermath. Nora waited long enough to see Lancer go by on a stretcher; his face looked as if he'd already left for another planet.

Nora peered into Morgan's vacated office. She wondered how everything would work out. She was torn by an intense desire to move her confidential files in there right now. But no—unwise to act impulsively or prematurely. Look what had happened to Rusty.

"Nora," Norman repeated, "I told you—hit the trail. I'll be along after we deliver these two to Bellevue."

"Yes, Norman," she said, "and *thank you*, Norman."

"All in a day's work for guys like me, hon."

"I'll just go call Mr. Ball and tell him it's over."

"Tell him," Norm smiled broadly, "no extra charge."

A man who answered the phone at Ball's apartment, however, said Mr. Ball had gone out for the evening. Nora left her name.

She felt so elated, it was a good thing she was modest and well-modulated. Nora suppressed her wild imagination. No, she wouldn't think yet of moving to a larger apartment. She was fine right where she was; physical possessions didn't mean much. Accomplishment was much more important, fulfilling the potential of the spirit. *Thank God* she hadn't done anything about Rustford Lancer's tasteless order that she get rid of Kurt Morgan's art. And by the way, what had happened to that Picasso?

She would *not* lead a less modest life. Sure, it would mean more time at the hairdresser and out in restaurants, because looking good and living well went with the job. People paid for your meals, they flew you around the country, and when you reciprocated it was off an expense account. But she *would* buy nice gifts for people, something for Norm and something for Paul and something utterly fabulous for Father John when he married the Italian courtesan, just to show she accepted it without hard feelings.

Recklessly, Nora made herself a high-powered Scotch on the rocks. But before getting into the tub, she called Gerald Ball's number again. He was still out. This time, Nora's message was that the problem at the office was solved and that she was going to bed for some much-needed sleep.

Actually, she and Norm were going out to a really luxurious restaurant. A drink here first, and then a gourmet meal, and then . . . well, she'd just see . . .

Nora carried her drink into the bathroom. She looked at herself in the mirror and was suddenly fed up with the efficient bun on the back of her head. She remembered Kurt—Kurt was gone. Just for tonight, Nora thought happily, she would let her hair down, she would look like a jewel in the capitalist crown.

She had to search to find the shoe box full of curlers, not

worn in years, it seemed, and no wonder—they were ancient plastic things, artifacts from some weird civilization. But she didn't know of a better way to put a quick curl in her hair. . . .

Finally pampered and pure, she snuggled on the sofa, drink in hand and curlers in hair, and felt for a moment like a college girl again, waiting for her date to arrive. But the man-sized Scotch made it a bit different, didn't it, and the career imponderables were enough to choke on. She hoped, but hope should be kept under control, Nora warned herself.

It was nearly nine o'clock now and where was Norm? She found herself anticipating him nervously. What was it? Did she really want him? Was it possible? Could they work it out, Norm conducting business as usual in Washington, D.C. and Nora at Diversified in New York?

And would it work emotionally? Sexually? By and large, she had to admit, Norm was something of an enigma to her. He was not a straight-ahead lecher like Buck, nor a man of tender feeling as she assumed Paul was. He was not crude like Morgan either, nor so malleable as Father John. Norm, in a way, was worrying. Behind all his talk of celibacy and abnegation, he might be more frightened of it than she had once been herself—but, she hoped, was no more. No, sex was not everything; actually, it was no more important in the world scheme than whether you took coffee or tea in the morning at the office.

Where was he? *Hell!* She hoped he hadn't had to go off on another surveillance. Nora pushed herself off the couch to pour another drink. Careful, she was thinking, she'd be bombed by the time Norm got here.

At that moment, the hands came down on her shoulders. Nora screamed, very loudly too. The glass fell out of her hand and cracked on the floor, ice and liquid flying everywhere.

There was a dirty chuckle in her ear.

"Norm!" She was so relieved she could not be angry. "How . . ."

He laughed gruffly. "Lesson to you, hon—always put the safety latch on. Picked the lock, hon. Here I am . . ."

Oh, God! Her hands flew to her head. The ugly curlers! She turned and kissed him on the cheek, pulling at the curlers, trying to divert him. A girl absolutely *never* lets her date see her in curlers.

"Is everything taken care of?" she gasped. "Norm, you rascal! Norm, God, you scared the *hell* out of me."

"You'll recover," he said. His lips were stiff. "What're you *doing*, Nora?"

"I'm just . . ." She fumbled nervously with the curlers, her fingers all thumbs.

His eyes blazed. "Those crazy goddamn things—where did you find them, Nora?"

"Well, I had them . . ."

He grabbed her hands, pressed her arms to her sides, held her very close to him. She felt something nudging against her thigh, as if she were being pushed by a lever, the lever attached to a powerful spring. He laughed unsteadily. "Hon . . . I remember . . . those things, from years ago."

"Norm, they're hair curlers. I'll take them out—they're awful," she stammered.

"No, no, no," he stuttered, "they're fine. Leave 'em." Nora tried to work free of his hands. "Don't move an inch!"

"Norm . . ." What now? She couldn't stand it! What had she done? What was happening?

One of his hands released one of her wrists and she feared he was going to strike her. But as suddenly as the hand flew at her head, it stopped and fingers came down, very gently, on her hair. Ah, the hair—the hair, freshly washed, scented, wavy, thick, golden, lustrous, it had the power to drive men mad. She remembered Morgan that night in Palm Springs, Kurt, that terrible man, defiler of her reputation.

"I love the pink ones, Nora," Norm muttered, almost brokenly.

"The pink ones?" She didn't connect.

"The pink curlers, for Christ's sake, Nora! Don't you have some more pink ones?"

"Well, yes, a few," she whispered.

"Take the blue ones off and put on the pink ones then," he told her excitedly.

"All right," she said, not comprehending. Norm followed her into the bathroom and stood behind her watching as she unwound the blue curlers and replaced them with six pink ones.

"Oh, Jesus," he groaned.

To her astonishment, he began to shake. Tears trickled down his pale cheeks.

"Norm, I'd better get dressed if we're going out."

"No, no!" He cupped his hands over her head and pushed against her, her back against the sink. His face dropped into the opening of her robe and she realized with a shock that this was the first time, ever, that Norm had exhibited any sort of interest in her breasts. His mouth, tongue, lips worked to reach her nipples. Words of love, despite the grotesqueness of his position, reached her.

"Norm . . . sweetie . . ." Nora put her arms around him and hugged. Let him do what he wanted. Oh yes. Nora realized he had managed another first—he erected massively against her.

"Hon," he grunted, "please . . . come on."

Good God, he wanted to drag her into the bedroom and get astride her, while he fondled . . . the pink curlers.

No one would believe this, she thought despondently, not a psychiatrist east or west of Manhattan. She lay under him like a corpse, inert and hopeless. What could she do? He moaned and jabbered some baby language she could not understand. Quite obviously, this all had to do with his mother, the hardest hangup of them all. Halfheartedly, Nora twisted herself into position and kissed the end of his erection and sensed, more than actually tasted, baby powder—good God! But this scarcely diverted him. He couldn't let go of the *damn* curlers. He clung to them as if to the lip of a precipice. His body became cramped finally and he stretched it along her smoothness but his eyes remained wide, unseeing, and though she spread her legs wide she could not induce him to enter her. She could not twist it or bend it or double it over—it would not go. Moistness fell on her cheeks; he was weeping. Her concentration was eviscerated by the sound of his teeth on the curlers. She might have screamed. God, why hadn't she merely let Joe Mercury do his worst? Was this any better than *that* would have been? Now, Norm was actually trying to *eat* a curler. But if that's what he wanted, then let him go ahead. Poor Norm wasn't interested in the actual act of love; the swell of his unrequiting manhood made Nora feel sick. It *would not go!* She was conscious of a swell of muscle inside her, like a gate across her chastity.

A crackling, splintering sound disrupted Nora's spirit even more. He bit through one of the curlers with the force of his long-pent bodily fluid. The latter now proceeded to flood across Nora and her bed. Norm uttered a crazy piercing cry, then began hacking out broken bits of plastic.

"For heaven's sake, control yourself," Nora told him tersely.

"Oh, Jesus, Nora . . ." he gasped, so desperately he might be choking. "Oh, hon," he sobbed, "was it good for you too?"

She had won him, but did he really think his genital had been inside her and that he had ejaculated up into her receptive womb? The fool.

"Yes, Norm, it was wonderful," Nora murmured.

"Hon, I'm sorry about the curler. Those goddamn things. I don't understand. It won't happen again. I'm ashamed of myself, I'm so ashamed!"

"Don't give it a thought."

"I feel like having myself hit."

"Don't be silly. I'm not unhappy with you, not at all. I've been thinking I'm in love."

"You?" His discharge caused him to slide off her. "You and me, you mean?"

Nora didn't know what she was saying. She knew she was mad. Though she had satisfied him in this odd way, it didn't mean she was in love with him. "I don't know why not, Norm."

Awestricken, he chuckled. "I'll tell you one thing—the only signal I need is one of those little pink things and I just go bananas."

She put a forefinger to his lips. "But shush about that. I'll do anything to make you happy, Norm."

He kissed her fingertip and was reaching for her head again as she caught his hand, forcing it down to her breast. "Ah, Nora, you know something, I think I've found the answer to my predilection for cunnilingus."

"The medium is the curler, Norm," she mused. "Thank God I'm a good Catholic."

Chapter Thirty-three

THE RED MERCEDES TWO-SEATER WAS PULLED UP NEXT TO THE *porte-cochère* of Gogarty Castle. In a sheepskin coat, leaning nonchalantly on a cane that may or may not have been necessary, Buck Collins was talking avidly to Father John and Mr. Oswald.

"Ahoy!" Collins roared, waving the cane at the black limo Lucia had hired for the wintry weekend. "Ahoy there!" His face was ruddy; with the close-cropped graying hair, Buck stood out.

Nora had to wait for Elena to get out first. Lucia nudged her shoulder with her soft bosom. Dear, *pregnant* Lucia. Nora had been crazy with envy for about fifteen minutes. Oh, to have a child! No, not yet, she advised herself.

Father John waved to them gaily. He'd been up to Albany the day before by train. Business. Bond business, Nora hoped. Oswald had picked him up and driven him to the castle that morning.

Moving carefully, Buck crossed the frozen gravel and opened the door of the car. "How's everybody this fine, brisk day?" He grinned at them broadly, obviously wanting love, adoration.

Jerome's voice was flat. "You're kind of happy to be on the loose again."

"Jesus, am I ever!"

Father John didn't even notice the curse. Solicitously, he helped Elena out of the car. He kissed her on both cheeks and she stood for a moment, an embarrassing moment for Nora, pressed against him.

"Where's Connie?" Jerome asked.

"Inside," Collins grunted. "She's not feeling so great—I'll tell you about it some time."

Jerome nodded, softly telling Collins, "I know about it already, Buck."

Collins looked shocked. "What?"

Jerome stared at him, then at Father John. "I had a call from Pete. He's in New York. He's out for blood."

That substance seemed to drain from Buck Collins's face. "Holy Christ!" He turned slightly to Father John. "Sorry, Father."

"Don't call me Father anymore, Mr. Collins."

Ever-present Oswald came up behind Buck. "That's right. The padre's been telling me he's been released from his priestly functions. And about time too, I'd say. The padre has served long and well and he deserves to be able to sleep in Sundays."

Father John laughed modestly. "Well, something like that, Oswald."

Sternly, Nora corrected them. "A priest is *never* released from his function totally. Once a priest—"

"Always a priest! Right!" Buck chortled. He looked very significantly at Foster. "Dutiful, and *honest* as the day is long."

Lucia came around the car and took Paul's arm. "Could we go inside do you suppose?"

"Oh, Buck, sorry," Jerome broke in. "You've never met Lucia and her mother, Princess Elena."

Collins's eyes darted from one to the other. "My pleasure," he murmured. He spent more time looking at Lucia. Well he might. She glistened in the cold, eyes bright, skin glowing.

"The last time you were here, Mr. Collins," Oswald exclaimed, "you climbed out of a helicopter, just over there."

Collins smiled at him caustically. "That's when Nora and I were here delivering the *package. Remember?*"

"Paekage," Foster repeated. He looked puzzled.

Buck punched Nora's arm lightly. "Hear that? The padre has forgotten about the package."

She must have showed shock for Father John smiled at her. "Surely not!" she gasped.

"Talk to him, beautiful," Buck told her. He had trouble with the stone steps, but managed better than he had that day at the church. "How am I doing, Paulie?"

"You'll make it," Jerome muttered.

To Nora, on his cane side, Buck muttered, "Jack Kennedy got along okay with a bad back, didn't he? Never interfered with *his* humping, did it, Nora?"

She looked him up and down, critically. "I wouldn't know."

"What the hell is wrong with you today?"

"Winter blahs, I guess."

"No." Buck shook his head, for once making sense. "It's just everybody is on tenterhooks, waiting for the merger to get done, waiting for . . . *what*, Paulie?"

"Pete," Jerome said sourly.

"Bullshit," Collins barked. "*I'm* not waiting for Pete."

Jerome shook his head stubbornly. "He knows where we are. I told him we're having a meeting and that everything's going to be settled. With the Italians—and *everything*."

"Shit!" Collins growled. "What the hell'd you tell him for, goddamn it?"

"I told him," Jerome said firmly, daring Collins's glare, "because I thought he had a right to know. Because I've always respected him and still do. Is that good enough reason?"

"Yeah . . ." Collins nodded uncertainly. "I guess so, Paulie." He looked miserable. "We'll have to work it through."

"You're going to do the talking to Morel," Nora said. "Is that right?"

"If he shows up," Collins said.

"Lucia invited him," Jerome said. She was standing in

the doorway, waiting for them, hands on her hips. "Would he have the nerve not to come?"

"I'll find out if his intentions toward BBD are honorable," Collins said. "Sometimes I couldn't care less about . . . any of it. We've had nothing but trouble ever since *you* got this merger going," he complained to Nora. "Morgan croaks . . . we run into all this flak from Pete . . . him and Connie. Jesus!" he muttered.

"Surely you don't think Kurt died of the merger, do you?" Nora demanded.

" 'Course not. He died of stress," Collins said, looking at her. "What a way to go." Then, joining Lucia in the black and white marbled foyer, he smiled sweetly. "Oh, this is just gorgeous. I just wish I could handle stairs better."

Lucia studied him gravely, evidently finding it difficult to make up her mind about him. "Gogarty had an elevator put in, but it is not in working order, Mr. Collins."

"Buck. Call me Buck, please. You see . . . may I call you Lucia? You see, this stupid accident of mine in the chopper, it aggravated an old war wound. A piece of North Korean shrapnel ripped up my back a few years ago. Then . . ." He looked around. Even Elena was listening. "Then to make matters worse, I got nailed on a coke charge and *damn and blast* if that wasn't because some medicine I was taking actually had a mild cocaine ingredient. But I'm in the clear." He looked at Jerome happily. "I am, you know. I'm free to go about my business—which right now is to prevent us being gobbled up by a bunch of Europeans."

Paul didn't say anything.

"*Right,* Paulie?"

"Yeah, right, Buck."

"Everything is supposed to be in the bag, isn't it?" he demanded, almost ferociously. "Nora?"

"Sure," she answered.

"Well, you two don't sound like it's in the bag. Has

something gone wrong? I mean aside from the Europeans trying to buy us—I can't figure that out. They haven't got a Chinaman's chance."

"Tell Morel," Nora said. "In the meantime, it's costing us money."

"And heartache," Collins added. "You look tired, beautiful."

Nora shrugged. What did it matter how she felt? She glanced at Lucia. Lucia didn't look tired at all. "It's been a tough week," Nora said.

Collins nodded. "You've got to brief me, Nora—as much as you can. This has got to be costing Diversified a bundle."

She nodded. "A big bundle." And she was worried about it. If her scheme didn't work out, the name Nora Ellen Sweeney would be pronounced Poison. So far it had cost Diversified eighty million to keep up with Morel's buying spree.

Oswald pushed the heavy front door. It shut with a hollow thud.

"Mr. Oswald, where can I have a quiet word with my . . . advisor here?" Buck smiled ingratiatingly at Nora.

Lucia answered from the staircase. "The library, Mr. Collins! Oswald, turn off all the recording devices. Come, Paolo!"

Jerome reached her on the third step. "Take it easy, Lucia. You know all they think about is business."

"You as well . . . *beast!*"

Paul was whispering to her. Suddenly Lucia smiled at him radiantly, so obviously at an improper suggestion that Nora could have blushed. Lucia twined her arms around his neck and, with a moderate heave, Jerome picked her up in his arms.

"Out of shape, Paulie!" Collins bawled.

Jerome took Lucia's hand and ran her down the hallway to the big corner bedroom suite. "Have a little rest," he said. "You shouldn't tire yourself."

"Paolo, I am only one month pregnant, for heaven's sake!"

"A half hour," he said, "that's all I need with them. I *beg* of you."

She mocked Collins's boisterousness. "Paulie! One half hour and you be back here!"

"Farewell . . . one half hour."

When he went down the hall again, Connie Broadstairs was coming toward him. She looked worried, anxious. "Where did Buck go?"

"He's downstairs with Nora," he said shortly. He was unhappy with Connie.

She walked silently with him to the staircase before asking tensely, "Did Buck tell you about all the trouble with Pete?"

"I already know about all the trouble with Pete."

Her voice trembled. "He's accusing me of stealing some securities out of his desk—how could he accuse me of such a thing? He's gone senile," she said.

"Old but not senile, Connie. You know how I feel about Pete."

"I don't care. He's an old coot," she sniffed.

Jerome opened the library door a crack, then widely. It was always a good idea to be circumspect when opening a door into a room where a man and woman were alone, particularly a man like Buck and a woman like Nora, who, however she might deny it, was very attracted to Buck. But there was too much tension in the air to allow for sensuality. Buck already had a drink in his hand and Nora was seated far enough away from him so that he couldn't reach her on the first pounce.

"Here's Connie," Jerome said.

"Yeah, *Mrs. Stupid,*" Connie muttered.

"C'mon in, Mrs. Stupid," Buck said sourly.

Connie ignored him, crossing instead to Nora. "Hello, Nora, how are you?" She sat down beside her.

With little enthusiasm, Collins managed another quip.

"Here's two good-lookers, Paulie. We make quite a four-some, don't we?"

Jerome didn't take him up on it. "What are you drinking, Buck?"

That most hateful of his expressions twisted Buck's face, something between arrogance and quizzical disappointment.

"You assume I'm drinking, Paulie? Water, if you must know. No, actually . . ." He chuckled stiffly. "A triple vodka martini over which the word vermouth has been lightly pronounced."

"Nerves?" Jerome asked.

Collins shook his head. "Me? Nah! Perturbed, yes. Nerves, no. Nora and I were just talking about our European friends . . . Jesus!"

Nora said, "I've been telling him what I know—Kurt's first mention of Eurochemie, the suggestion from Washington, then Abe Russell hinting he should cool it."

"So we're up to your private eye tracking Hazel Morgan and that slimy Italian who came to the church with her," Collins said.

"An industrial spy, working for Morel, for Euro-chemie."

"I'll be a son of a bitch," Buck sighed. "And Hazel Morgan is feeding him stuff?"

"Was," Nora corrected him.

Collins shook his head. "And Morel's coming *here?* I'm liable to flatten the bastard. We could call the cops and have him arrested."

Okay, Jerome thought, the time had come. Mention of cops and arrest triggered him. Quietly, he said, "The bonds have got to be returned to Pete."

Collins bleated and dropped into a chair. Jerome handed him his fresh drink.

"What bonds?" Connie whined.

"The bonds you took from Pete, for Christ's sake!" Jerome said. "I don't understand either of you. Pete's been like a father to you, Buck. The only reason he agreed to this merger at all was because he thought he could buy you the top spot."

Collins stared down at his shoes. "I didn't know she'd lifted the goddamn things . . ."

Connie didn't disagree. "I took 'em for Buck," she muttered, her face ravaged. "Anybody could have had 'em, a gardener or even one of Buck's sons. I didn't know what to do with them—Buck said he'd know. We thought, in a way, we could surprise Pete, make him take better care of valuable property . . ."

She'd tried but the reasoning didn't hold up.

"Some surprise," Jerome said. "The trouble was he noticed right away that they were gone, didn't he?"

"Yes," she nodded bitterly. "Old buzzard."

"If you don't give them back," Jerome told them, "he's going to lower the boom on you. Fortunately, I didn't unload them in Italy—Foster's got them and I assume *he* hasn't sold them."

Collins looked furious. "The only trouble with that, Paulie, is when I asked him for them, your priest said, 'What bonds?'"

Jerome laughed. "He wouldn't do that." He appealed to Nora. "Would he?"

She shrugged. "I . . . don't think so. Could it be amnesia?"

Jerome decided it was time for a drink. He turned his back on them, going to the bar. He felt like laughing. If Father John Foster pulled this off, he was more of a man than Jerome had given him credit for being. The ironic thing was nobody would ever be able to prove anything—against, or for, anybody.

Collins said it all. "How can you be *sure* he didn't sell them?"

Lucia was sound asleep under a loose blanket when Jerome came back to the room. Making not a sound, he lay down and wrapped his arm around her, under her breast, soft and warm. He pressed against her, feeling so cold, old, and destroyed. It was as if his horizon had been chipped, like the edge of a precious plate. He lay still, studying Lucia's sleeping face. She must have been dreaming, for a slight, secretive smile twitched her lips. He inhaled her special scent, fresh as the outdoors mixed with the residue of an expensive perfume.

Jerome decided they'd marry soon, and, thankfully, his thoughts moved from Collins's predicament to his own sweet problems. It was not essential that he and Lucia marry, he told himself drowsily, and he didn't particularly want to be married again, having had enough of that with Shelley. It seemed such a risky and defiant thing to do when things were going so well. But on balance, it was a chance he thought he should take. It was a risk, but worthy of them.

Lucia came half-awake and turned toward him for a kiss. Her mouth was sticky and sweet, and he wondered if her dream had been sexual. She was warm. Being pregnant seemed to make her sleepy at odd times and in constant need of reassurance. Lucia moaned again, as if in pain. He stroked her bottom comfortingly and she sighed, pressing against him.

Her eyes came open, gleaming. "Paolo, we could get under the covers, no? Did your business go well?"

"Oh, very well," he muttered.

Chapter Thirty-four

OSWALD DELAYED LUNCH BUT JEAN-JACQUES MOREL DID not appear, and finally, when two o'clock came and there was still no sign of him, they sat down at the heavy dining table.

At eight in the evening, there was still no Morel. He hadn't phoned either. In fact, there was no news of Morel at all and in this case no news was not necessarily good news.

Buck Collins and Connie Broadstairs had gone walking after lunch and now his back was stiff and he was in a grouchy mood. Buck wanted Paul Jerome to call the Hotel Napoli in New York but Lucia ruled against it. If Morel had broken the date to drive up to Gogarty Castle, after everything J.J. Gogarty had done for him in the past, it was an act of great disrespect, for which he would pay dearly. Morel was, after all, a mere banker.

Jerome and Lucia went out in heavy coats just toward dusk and walked in the park Gogarty had created along the river, where in the ancient days Jerome and his friends had sometimes beached a motorboat and defied the No Trespassing signs to peek at the monstrous house.

Along here, they found a soft leather wallet, empty of everything, sodden from the lapping waves. Then it began to rain. Lucia pulled herself close to him as she had the first day they'd come up here.

"Lucia, you know what they say about March—in like a

lion and out like a lamb, or vice versa. It think it's going to be a horrible month. In *many* ways."

"Including the *ides* of it," she agreed.

"I'm afraid, Lucia," he confessed.

"Of what, dear love?"

"I don't know . . . Where's Morel?" Jerome mentioned something he could not bring up in front of the others. "He's probably unloading *your* BBD shares," he said. "You've made over ten million by now, Lucia."

"I know." She said no more but Jerome understood. She'd sold them, hadn't she, probably at the high-to-date? Oh, Christ! "We will say no more, Paolo. They were in my mother's name."

"Then Father John sold them! Oh, Christ! And Buck's bonds—he says he never saw the bonds."

She laughed, almost happily. "Father John is a crook— such a relief, *caro*. He made me uncomfortable as a holy man."

Buck claimed at dinner that earlier in the afternoon an airplane had made a pass at the house, veering away down river and then had come back, flying low. Buck said he was sure the plane was a World War II vintage P-38, a fast night-fighter.

"I didn't know those things were still flying," Jerome said. Buck looked at him strangely and Jerome realized what he was thinking—that it was Pete Broadstairs come to have his revenge. Maybe he was challenging Buck to an aerial duel. Such a thing would not be past the old romantic.

Oswald pushed in his rolling hot table, the smoking joint under a silver top, gleaming carving knives beside it and plates piled on a warming ring.

Connie finally said it, fearfully. "It's Pete, I know it is."

"Shut up," Buck muttered.

"Pete?" Oswald was unconcerned, as he carved. "A man called this morning. He said he wanted to catch his bearings—how far south are we of Paradise Point and where's the bridge . . . Now, Miss Sweeney," he murmured warmly, "would you like it rare or well-done?"

"In between if possible, Mr. Oswald."

"In between it is. Moderate in all things. The secret of longevity is moderation, yes, moderation."

Collins was staring at him. "You're saying Pete Broadstairs called here?"

"If that's his name, yes sir, Mr. Collins." Oswald cut deftly.

Connie scowled at Buck. "He knows we're here."

"Paulie told him, sweetheart."

She flared. "Thanks a lot."

Jerome shrugged. "We are going to settle things, aren't we?"

"We're lucky he didn't strafe us, sweetheart." Collins laughed shakily.

Haughtily, Lucia said, "Your *husband,* is that it?"

Connie nodded. "He's mad at me."

Oh, come on, Jerome protested silently, *mad at me?* She'd lifted $800,000 worth of his bonds and he was mad at her!

"Pete's old and tired," Collins said thoughtfully, as if that explained everything.

But it didn't explain their betrayal of the man who'd helped them both so much. The way a judge would see it, unless there had been some terrible misunderstanding, Connie was guilty of grand theft and Buck of receiving stolen goods. Christ, Jerome mourned—by inference he could be considered part of the operation.

Elena had turned her attention to Connie and was in the process of asking a series of very embarrassing questions about her husband. Elena was fascinated by unhappy marriages, the living proof, apparently, that she was not the only one who had been so disastrously married. Finding someone like Connie reinforced her belief in the unfairness of Fate and possibly even the vengeful works of a malicious God.

Foster was far away. He ate so neatly, with such

precision, scooping up mashed potatoes, spearing his lima beans two at a time and feeding the mixture into his mouth. Amazing this sort of food—Nora's mother had also been a meat-and-mashed-potato specialist—had never stuck to his matchstick frame.

No hint of Morel. Finally, when Lucia had Oswald call the Hotel Napoli, the hotel would report only that Mr. Morel was not in; they were no more informative than that.

"Naturally," Lucia said waspishly, "a very confidential Sicilian place."

They had gone back into the huge library. Oswald stumbled around, serving hot coffee.

"Please, Paolo," Lucia murmured, "after-dinner drinks?"

"Make mine a double brandy, Paulie," Collins bid eagerly.

He was restless and irritated, annoyed with Elena for being so nosy, with Connie for putting up with it, and with the rest of them for just being there. Buck kept glancing at Father John out of the corner of his eyes, clearly unable to decide what to do about that situation.

Nora watched Buck closely, confused about him now, as they all were. But obviously she had some hidden design, Jerome decided. Whatever it was, he told himself, it had nothing to do with love or even passing passion. Buck had become an intellectual challenge for Nora, he thought; she must still be fascinated by the war hero and corporate freebooter. Buck was a pirate, a buccaneer.

Buck suddenly got up, coming as close to springing to his feet as he could with his bad back. "Okay, padre," he exclaimed, "let's just get this thing settled right now about the bonds!"

Foster's eyebrows arched. "Bonds?"

Chapter Thirty-five

EVERYONE WAS TIRED. NORA WAS IN BED TRYING TO read herself to sleep in the castle on the Hudson, so few miles from where she'd been reared. They'd all forgotten about those years, hadn't they? Father John didn't remember any of it, even though it hadn't really been that long ago that Nora had spent her youth under his clerical black wing. Twelve years, fifteen? A meager ten seconds on the universal clock.

Paul didn't remember anything either. He'd become so worldly, so sophisticated, he wouldn't remember a soda at the drugstore in Paradise Point. Never was Paul seized and bent double, as she was, by a memory pang. People, all of them, so callous, unsentimental.

Nora shed a tear on her book. She was in a highly inflammable state of mind, worried about herself. Joe Mercury's assault hadn't damaged her physically, but it had scarred her emotions, set loose all sorts of fears, desires, and regrets. Properly, Norm Vincent could have soothed her—but his lovemaking? Nora wept the more forlornly. She must resign herself, there was no hope.

She laid her book aside and closed her eyes for a moment, clasping her hands in prayer. These times *had* been trying, hadn't they?

Nora started, hearing a foreign sound. She flicked open her eyes. Her door was open and a figure was outlined in the light from the hallway.

"Oh!" She sat up.

"Nora . . . It's John. May I come in?"

"Oh, yes. Of course." Her mind reeled. How could he come into her room like this, alone? How did he dare? What would Elena say, if she knew? Stiffly, Nora crossed her arms over her nightgown and blanket which she clutched to herself. He was Elena's lover—how did he have the nerve to defy her? God, the princess would *kill* him.

"I've brought you some of Oswald's hot chocolate, Nora." Father John closed the door and came to the bed on which she was, for some reason, almost cowering. He chuckled embarrassedly. "Here." He put a tray down on her knees. On it was a steaming cup of chocolate; she could smell the fumes. Beside it, on a saucer, there were three cookies that looked like oatmeal. "Should I sit down for just a moment, Nora?"

"Please, yes, Father John." She was going to keep calling him Father John even after he'd been defrocked. No, he wasn't being defrocked; he was being honorably discharged.

"Nora," he said softly, "Paul told me about that man Mercury trying to rape you . . ." He looked extremely pained.

"Paul told you?"

"He knew."

Then Norm must have told him. Paul hadn't said a word to her—why? Didn't he believe her?

"No damage done," she said.

"That I don't accept. There is sure to be damage done, even though . . . nothing happens. How *did* this happen?"

She shrugged. "He got past Fiorello by saying he was making a flower delivery. He had a huge vase of red roses, and I let him in, and when I turned around to get money for a tip he surprised me . . ."

"Oh my . . ." Foster moved his head sympathetically. Oh my, she thought sardonically, how could such a horrid thing happen to Nora Ellen Sweeney? "I hate to even think about anybody actually *defiling* your sweet body, Nora."

"But he didn't, Father John," she stressed.

"Child," he said kindly, "you're going to have to stop calling me Father, you know."

Nora shook her head. "No, I've decided—whatever happens, you'll always be Father John to me."

Foster chuckled. He stared at her intently. "You wouldn't if you were aware of the deep feelings of pure . . ." He paused and a little smile lofted his mouth. "Pure lust, Nora, that I always harbored for you."

"Oh, my God!" Her voice was faint. She had never expected this much of an apostasy of the man. *"Father John*—surely you're trying to shock me into changing my mind about you!"

He nodded. "Well, yes, I am," he admitted, as though that should be clear. "But Nora, surely *you knew*—that night at your apartment, before Christmas . . ."

"Nothing happened!" she cried out, denying whatever he might think had happened.

"But . . ." He looked very puzzled.

She was crushed. He had misinterpreted the whole night. How could he have? She twisted her head to the side, away from his stare. A great tumor of despair seemed to come to life inside her and it was pressing on her heart. Nothing had happened! That was the trouble, just that. Nora turned her head and looked up at him, tearfully, pleading.

"It *could* happen," she said.

"No." He shook his head firmly. "It would be very unjust of me to take advantage of you, Nora."

"Not if I wanted you to take advantage of me."

Again, he shook his head, looking numb. "Nora, you need a lover."

"Not you?"

"No."

"But I love you," she said.

"No, you don't," he disagreed anxiously. "You love

what I was. You were in love with the Church, therefore with me, a priest of the Church, this *person* who represented such authority to you."

"Analysis!" Nora muttered.

"Whatever works, Nora," Foster said quietly.

He gazed down at her, at her face, the neck, the flesh in her forearms, the swelling breasts, yes, oh God, the swelling breasts, aching for him to touch them, to caress them as he had caressed his silk vestments once.

"It's past," she said harshly. "Now look . . ." She eyed him with a new understanding. "Let's talk about those bonds, Father John. You *do* remember us handing you that package, don't you? "

He smiled. "I remember a package, yes, of course. I was just dangling Buck Collins a little. It is not ethical to be asked to carry stolen property, Nora."

"Father John . . ." She smiled at him. "You will return them, now, won't you? At least we can put that much behind us—yes?"

Father John grinned and chuckled. "Yes, my darling Nora . . . Now, may I kiss you good night, wish you sweet dreams and be on my way?"

She agreed and Foster bent and put his dry lips to her forehead. She remembered all the times he had done that. The lips moved to her cheeks, one side, then the other; he kissed her eyelids then and next the tip of her nose. She hadn't expected it but she was ready when he kissed her lips. She fed him a millimeter of her tongue and felt his quick breath; he tasted of red wine. Hastily, he pulled away and stood up.

"Good night, Nora."

After he'd gone, Nora twisted and turned and drifted along the edge of sleep, not the sleep of the angels but not a sleep of self-hate and destruction either. She felt more groggy than sleepy from the chocolate, bumping along lush border country where the brain develops its dreams.

Her eyes must have been open for swimming into range came a new figure, all in black with a white priest's collar at its neck. It was Father John, Nora told herself in the netherland of her consciousness, come back to her and properly dressed at last to take her body. The figure knelt by the bed and she basked in the glimmer of dead white face and clerical raiment, black as night and white.

A hand stole across the covers and brushed her face lightly.

"Oh . . ." She heard the voice. It was her own.

"Sssh."

"Will you . . . now?" she whispered, so faintly he couldn't have heard.

"He-eeey!" It was a hiss she should have recognized. "Back to sleep, hon . . ."

Nora fell out of the land of dreams. "Norm! My God, you gave me a scare." She put her hands on his black shoulders and caressed a rubber suit and the top of a white turtleneck sweater. Gosh, how she'd been fooled. "Norm! My darling," she gasped, almost sobbing, "what are you *doing* here?"

He coughed. "I was in the vicinity and I thought I'd just drop in."

She put her arms around his black shoulders and hugged him to her blue nightie. "But how did you know where to find me?"

"Are you kidding?" he hissed. "I been sitting in a tree out there half the night. I saw you come in this room. The rest is duck soup. Security in this place is as leaky as a sieve—took me three seconds flat. *I missed you,* hon."

"Me too, Norm. Come into bed," she said hopefully. God, yes, there still had to be hope. Somehow she would chase away the ghosts.

"Hon," he acquiesced solemnly, "come the dawn, I must be gone."

"I know," Nora said.

She watched him thrashing his arms as he pulled at the black suit and struggled with the black and white turtleneck. An idea came to her. "Leave it on, Norm. You must be cold."

"Cold? Not on your bottom dollar, hon. I came by river—this is my wet suit."

But he left on the turtleneck which excited her and she realized that he was not wearing underwear. Underwear, he explained, constricted his movements. Shyly then, he lifted a black bag she hadn't seen and clicked it open. "I brought you . . . a little something, hon."

"Come in bed where it's warm, Norm," Nora urged. Under that shirt, his white-skinned body looked as powerful as Samson's.

"Okay, hon."

She squirmed over and he got in beside her, the black bag as warm as human flesh between them, like, dare she think it, a baby. He stuck his fingers in—she expected jewels to roll off them. No, good God, it was a collection of pink hair curlers.

"I know," Nora said, "you want me to put them on."

"Just a couple, hon, *please.*"

"All right." Yes, it was all right. Why not? Nothing so terrible about that. "They're rubber," she discovered.

"They won't break."

Quickly, Nora rolled stands of hair around a few of them. Norm burrowed deeper into the bed, making whimpering noises, and when the curlers were in place he turned to face her and she kissed his lips passionately. Norm cupped curlers with one hand and his other hand touched her body under the blue nightie. He stroked her breasts, which began at once to ache, ran his fingertips down her rib cage, to her solar plexus and into the blondness of her crotch.

"Hon," Norm cried softly. He ceased talking; she realized he was chewing on a curler.

Nora panted helplessly but Norm didn't notice until she drew her fingers down that muscular genital. He responded with a pleasured gasp. "This is it, Nora," he mumbled. "Kiss and tell . . ."

She rolled her head from side to side, hoping.

"I don't want to hurt you."

"I *want* you to," she whispered. He had stopped chewing the curler. "Get on me," she begged.

She spread her legs, and Norm knelt between them. She took him with both her hands and drew him to her, feeling his hairy knees on her thighs, the hardness of his genital. This time, she promised herself, it would go in. She gripped him and he helped by pushing, and she, spreading until he was slowly sliding into her. She realized he had filled her to bursting. Norm pumped easily and pulled back. It was then Nora seized him in her legs in a scissors grip she'd learned as a tomboy. She held him, pushing upward into this close quarter. A shock went through her, down her spine and up and down again into the very living center of her. Nora began to shudder; vaguely, she realized Norm had cried out, a stifled sound. His wiry body seemed to stop, to hang, to tense, to release and then to fall downwards. But he didn't stop. He couldn't. She urged him on and then she seemed somehow to dissolve, to turn to liquid. She tried to contain her cry the same way she'd heard Japanese women did by biting on the corner of a sheet as the sensation of flood swept through her.

Nora understood what had happened; she had climaxed. Her body ached now luxuriously. Her limbs felt soft, languid. She stretched beneath him, stroked his knit-clad back to the white collar, and pulled his head down to kiss him passionately on the lips.

"Are you all right, hon?" he asked, voice subdued.

"All right?"

Nora realized that she could tighten those newly discovered muscles around the waning genital and keep it inside her, setting loose a thousand tickling reverberations, flittering and fluttering and gathering as one to point straight into her heart. She experienced a minor, secondary climax. Good God, heavens above, she could go on like this for hours. Father John was right and she should have arranged it for herself years ago. Now she had *Father Norm* in his black shirt and white collar parked above her on his knees, shifting his head so he could switch his lips

411

from nipple to nipple, suctioning them forward until she felt stretched to the extreme.

"I like these, hon," he whispered.

"Good," she breathed. "I like you a lot too. Has anybody ever told you what they feel?"

"Who would?" Norm asked. "This is the first time, Ellen."

"I know you worry," she assured him, "but you needn't, Norm, because we've found the combination that opens all the locked rooms—like a boat sliding into the water . . ."

"Yeah . . ." He snickered. "The *QE II* or the SS *America.*"

"I'm such a good Catholic, Father Norm . . . crazy when you think about it. Forgive me, Father Norm, for I have sinned . . ."

His face was buried in her neck, lips speaking to her skin. "Yeah, hon, you really have, you know—you plucked my cherry."

She laughed. "I don't believe you. After all these years in sordid faraway places?"

"Sure as shootin' you did, Nora, and there's going to be a lot of penance for you to do."

She shivered. "What?"

His eyes were inches from her nose and at the other end of him she still held what remained of his erection in the muscles of her pouch.

"Hmmm," Norm murmured. For a second, he fingered the rubber hair curler she'd put just above her left ear. God, please not something peculiar with the curler, she prayed.

"Can I ask you to do something, hon?"

She nodded apprehensively.

"Can I take it out now?"

"If you insist," Nora tittered.

"Well, all right." He hesitated and she knew that wasn't all. "Hon, will you kiss my pecker?"

Then she knew. That was what his mother used to do! She would bring him back from infancy, a step at a time.

"Shall I keep on the turtleneck, hon?" he asked, as if divining her thought.

"Please, for now."

"But I get to take it off, Nora, when I go to the shower."

"Of course, silly," she said.

At the crack of dawn, as he had promised, Norm prepared to leave. Nora had slept peacefully, better than she had in her entire life. She was awakened by his getting out of bed. Then, she heard the sound of water. When Norm came back to the bedroom, he plopped down on the edge of the bed and bent to kiss her.

"Like a new man am I, hon."

"You must go?" she asked. She didn't care now whether he got caught here with her. How shocked they'd all be.

"Yes . . . I must."

He squeezed his body back into the wet suit, sat down again, and pulled on what Nora saw were lightweight black sneakers.

"Will you be in the city when I get back this afternoon?" she asked.

"Will I?" He joked boyishly, platinum hair plastered down. "Just leave the window open a crack."

When he was dressed, Norm kissed her once more and went to the window. He cocked one leg over the sill. Good God, Nora thought in alarm, he'd fall. But no. He lifted his hand in salute, said, "See you," and he was gone. By the time Nora could get across the room, Norm was on the ground, running across the frozen lawn to the thicket closest to the Hudson River. When he attained the cover of a big tree, he turned again and flung her an exuberant kiss.

There was a man, Nora told herself. She hugged herself and closed the window.

At seven-thirty she was ready. The rest of the castle was

still deep in slumber, except Oswald, whom she found in the kitchen. He was at the stove, a skinny stovepipe figure dressed only in his long johns.

"Hello," Nora said quietly.

His close-shaven head jerked around. "By God, you scared me, Miss Sweeney. I'm not even dressed."

"Dressed enough," she said.

"Shouldn't want to be immodest."

"But you're not."

"I'm making coffee—would you like some?" She said she'd love it and he poured her a cup which he set on the counter next to a mammoth cast-iron sink. "There you are . . . Nora. I used to know your mother."

"Is that so?" she asked curiously.

"Didn't I just say so? When she was still a high school girl, she used to come here of an afternoon to help Mr. Gogarty with his office work."

"My mother has been in this house?" What did that mean? Her mother? "She never told me that."

"A blond sprite she was, like you, so full of life. Mr. Gogarty loved the girl dearly."

"Oh, no!"

"Don't believe what they say about Black Jack," Oswald cautioned her. "We all loved the girl. Nora, how would *you* like to sail around the world with me?" he suddenly asked, eyes lighting.

Nora didn't know how to draw him out. She wanted to hear more about her mother but she scarcely dared ask. "Oh . . . Mr. Oswald, it's a nice invitation. But I couldn't. I couldn't leave my job just now."

He didn't hear. "I can just picture you laying stark naked across the bow of my *Sea Hawk* in mid-Pacific, brown as a she-devil . . ."

"Oh! Mr. Oswald!"

He stared at her. "You needn't have any fear, since long ago I lost the use of my testicles."

"I . . . I don't understand what you're telling me, Mr. Oswald."

"Surely you know what a testicle is, Nora," he cried. "Each man is given two of them . . . No matter. So you won't be coming with me then on my adventure?" His eyes blinked. "Maybe just as well, for I'm sailing around the world in order to remain close to saltwater, which I'm told can be very rejuvenating."

"Have you tried the waters of Saratoga Springs, Mr. Oswald? That's so much closer."

"I did. I dipped my testicle into the sulphur springs but it served no restorative purpose as far as I could tell, Nora. Merely stunk me up with sulphur so much that I had trouble sleeping at night . . ."

There was a noise behind them. Buck Collins crashed into the kitchen. His surly voice demanded attention.

"*Who* had trouble sleeping. Not me for sure. I slept like a goddamn log."

"Good morning," Nora smiled at him widely, for she was thinking of the earlier hours and how wonderful it was that she had been taken by the one she loved.

"What about some coffee, Mr. Collins?" Oswald asked.

"That'll hit the spot," Buck grunted.

"How's Connie?" Nora asked.

He shrugged. "How do I know? I haven't seen her. You think I'm shacked up with her? No way. I gave her a little yardage last night and then headed for my own room." Oswald craned his neck, not quite understanding. "I like to sleep alone." Buck was making it clear that he didn't really like women; he despised them. "How 'bout some bacon and eggs, Oswald?"

"All right," Oswald said. "And you too, Nora?"

"I'm famished," she said.

Buck winked at her. "You'd be a lot more famished if you'd let me come down the hall and unreel a little of that for you too, beautiful."

Oswald's back jolted. Surely, he understood what Buck was saying and he didn't like it.

"Forget that," Nora said. There was something else they should talk about, now that they had time. "You know, when he died Kurt already had something like sixty speaking engagements scheduled this year, all over the country, in front of the most influential groups of men and women."

"So?" Collins sneered. "No wonder he decided to die. Nothing worse than making goddamn speeches."

"On the contrary, Kurt learned to enjoy it. I wrote most of them. But he never did appreciate what all the exposure was worth."

"Millions," Buck grunted, "billions . . ."

"*You're* going to have to step into the breach."

"Like shit!"

Oswald whirled around. "I don't allow profanity in my kitchen."

"Sorry, Oswald, sorry." Buck retreated. "Hey! Take it easy on me, you guys."

"Why don't you listen to the lady instead of swearing and behaving with such bombast, man?" Oswald demanded.

"Okay . . . okay." Buck stared down at the floor, shaking his gray-blond head. "*Shucks*—my daddy always wanted me to have my own company but he never told me I'd have to make a lot of speeches."

"Really," Nora mocked. He was almost, but not quite, funny.

"Get Paulie for the speeches, beautiful."

"You don't understand anything I'm saying, do you?"

"I understand all right. Trouble is, I don't like it."

"You'd better learn to like it."

"Hey, listen, what the hell is going on anyway?"

Nora shook her head. "You really *don't* understand, do you? You'll be lucky to stay out of jail—we're doing our best to save you."

"Listen," he said angrily, "I've been thinking about this whole thing. Now, I didn't know those goddamn bonds were stolen. How was I supposed to know? I thought Pete gave them to Connie. You know, for mad money, or something . . ." His face twitched to a smile. "Uh, oh . . ."

Connie was standing in the doorway of the kitchen. "It's goddamn cold in this house," she announced. She was wrapped in her fur coat, nervously carrying a cigarette back and forth to her mouth.

Oswald frowned. "I don't allow filthy cigarettes in my kitchen . . . or profanity!"

"Shit," Buck growled. "You give *all* the orders around here?"

"Exactly." Oswald raised his arm, pointing it like a rifle. "Out!"

"What about breakfast?"

Connie was blocking the doorway. "I heard what you said, you bastard! You knew very well that Pete didn't *give* me those bonds."

"I didn't know," he yelled.

"Now, look here," Oswald began, when they heard the high-pitched sound overhead, piercing like a siren, demanding instant quiet.

"The plane!" Buck yelled. He ran to the window.

An instant later, the barn went up in a gigantic ball of flame.

"Nuclear war!" Oswald bellowed, "they've destroyed my Studebaker, the goddamn Russians!"

"It's Pete," Buck whispered as the sound died away. "That was a rocket. The son of a bitch is going to kill us."

From the window, Buck dashed to the kitchen door and flung it open. He ran outside, toward the burning barn, shaking his fists at the sky.

"My Studebaker," Oswald moaned.

The tail end of the car was just visible under a heap of blazing clapboard. Even as he raved, the windshields exploded, back fenders and bumper sagged in the heat.

Oswald stumbled after Buck, but it was too late to save the Studebaker. Another enormous burst of flame blew what was left of the car into the air.

"The gas tank!" Buck screamed. "Careful . . . Don't come out here, Oswald. Get back!"

And then the awful whining sound began to rise again. Pete was coming back, down river from the north. An instant later, Buck knocked Oswald to the ground and the plane missed their heads by inches.

Buck leapt up again. "Pete! Pete! Goddamn it! Stop it, you crazy old cocksucker!"

But Nora knew Pete could not hear Buck. Dazedly, she watched the flight of the antique plane. Now the others were in the kitchen, Paul and Lucia, Father John in an incongruous pair of striped pajamas and Elena in a revealing kimono.

Buck ran back inside. "Paulie . . . goddamn it, I told you! It's Pete and he's trying to kill us! He blew the barn!"

The engine noise faded once again and they stood numbly staring at each other. Oswald staggered through the door, limping, rubbing one arm, his face white and dirty.

"Why can't he wait?" Buck hollered. "He's going to get his goddamn bonds back . . . He's crazy!"

Jerome didn't move. "Your car is gone," he mentioned to the violently trembling Oswald.

"Gone . . . into a thousand million pieces," Oswald said dully. He began to cry.

The plane was coming back.

"Get down!" Buck shouted. "Get under the table!"

Quickly, they ducked, looking stupid, Nora thought, hands over their eyes and ears like monkeys. With the moaning and whining of the engine, this time there came a chatter and thudding noises.

"Machine-gunning us, the bastard!"

Nora saw the shadow of the plane as it passed. It was reaching for the edge of the woods and they were on their feet watching as Pete banked to return for another run. But then something happened. No more than a hundred feet over the forest, the plane coughed, suddenly stood still, hung there suspended in midair for what seemed an eternity, and then began to fall, to lose its grip on the sky. It hit the field and blew up, shooting plumes of flaming fuel in every direction.

Buck screamed again, in terror.

"Pete! Pete?" He turned to glare at them, his eyes mad. "Pete's bought it!" His voice rose to a quavering wail and he bolted again from the kitchen door, running as fast as he could toward the burning wreckage. He continued to shout for Pete to get out, but there was no hope.

Jerome took off down the field after him and grabbed his arm, pulling, cursing and dragging him away from the fire.

Elena sank to her knees and put her hands in front of her face.

"Oh, John . . . John . . ."

Connie staggered out of the kitchen, but then fell against the wall and collapsed on the floor.

Nora could not make herself turn away from the fire. Her eyes smarted and she sobbed silently. There, just a few hundred yards away, Pete Broadstairs was dying. No, he was already dead. He had been dead before the plane hit the ground, that she knew. He had failed with the engine.

"What should I do?" Oswald asked weakly. His voice shook. "Padre, you had some papers in the car . . . nothing important, I hope."

Chapter Thirty-six

IT HAD NOT BEEN AN EASY DAY, AND IT WAS LATE SUNDAY
night by the time they finally left Gogarty Castle. Hours
with officialdom began with the Paradise Point fire department and ended with investigators from the New York
State Police. Try as they might, and everybody did try all
day, there was no explanation for what had happened. As
a matter of fact, legally it was only supposition that the
man in the plane had been Pete at all. Final identification
would be left to that most arcane of departments, the
pathologists, and to this end Buck Collins was delegated to
remain behind to assist them in whatever way he could.

Nora said she *thought* she'd recognized Pete in the
cockpit of the plane as it had zoomed past. But that wasn't
definite enough. Chief Fred Hudson of the Paradise Point
police department, acknowledged as the expert on the
ground, speculated that it could have been anybody. A lot
of local people still had it in for Black Jack Gogarty and
this could even have been the work of a lunatic working in
retrospect. Why else destroy Mr. Oswald's old Studebaker?

Buck offered the best guess. Pete, always the prankster,
was finally a victim of his own daredeviltry. Fly under a
bridge, buzz the Gogarty place. Obviously, Buck speculated sadly, Pete had misjudged, and that wasn't surprising
for a man of his age. He had clipped the rear of the
Studebaker and that by itself was enough to spin the plane
out of control and take poor Pete to his fiery death.

"I don't mind telling you, chief," he told Fred Hudson sadly, "this is the way Pete would have wanted it. No lingering death for him. Down in flames . . . or live in fame . . . that's the U.S. Army Air Corps."

"I remember the song," Fred Hudson muttered. "If he served a long time in the Pacific, one might say then, that Pete Broadstairs was the last of the kamikazes."

"One could say so," Buck agreed.

Privately, however, while Hudson was outside poking around the smoldering ashes of barn and plane, Buck muttered to Jerome, "The crazy old bastard. I think he thought Oswald's car was a submarine. He was making a run at a submarine pen . . . flipped out totally. Christ Almighty."

Jerome decided there was not much point in reminding Buck that all of it was at least partially his fault. "He took the bonds with him, didn't he?"

Collins smiled. "Kind of careless of the padre, wasn't it, to leave them out in that goddamn car?"

"Why? Normally it would've been the safest place in the state."

"Pete homed in on his ESP, I guess," Buck said.

If, Jerome told himself, the bonds had, indeed, been in the Studebaker.

Connie Broadstairs, who had collapsed at first, began to scream at noontime and kept right on. Nobody could figure out whether she suffered this nervous collapse because of the way her husband had met his end or because the bonds had been destroyed.

They couldn't get Connie to stop, and though Buck thought it embarrassing, at two in the afternoon she was taken in an ambulance to a hospital in Albany.

Oswald had been sitting in the library all afternoon, holding his head in his hands. He seemed hardly less distracted by events than Connie Broadstairs. But he was grieving for his Studebaker.

"Tried and true," he said hoarsely, "she served me well."

"Oswald," Buck told him, "the company is going to buy you a new automobile."

"But 'tis old Stude that I want."

"Yes. But think how lucky you weren't in it."

At seven that Sunday night, Chief Hudson told them they could leave. He realized they wanted to get back to the city where life went on.

"It seems a matter of routine misadventure," Hudson told them. "If we need you, we'll be in touch."

Collins came outside to help them into the limo. He tried a joke on Jerome. "If you don't hear from me in a week, call the cops."

In the car, no one had anything to say. They sat, staring at each other. Finally, Lucia put her head on Jerome's shoulder and went to sleep. Nora gazed into space. John Foster sat stiffly next to Elena, an expression of pure misery on his face. Foster didn't understand that there was nothing anybody could have done.

Connie Broadstairs would have to suffer with it, she and Buck, if suffering was within his power. It was frightening, Jerome thought, that Pete had cracked. Pete had always been such a strong man, such a scoundrel in his own right that you did not expect him to collapse emotionally. And then it occurred to Jerome that Pete could not have been in the airplane. Pete, no matter how old he was, could not have made such a mistake.

He was still thinking these optimistic thoughts as the black limo drew up outside Nora's apartment house. She would be first off.

They stirred themselves.

"Well," Nora said hesitantly, "good night." She shrugged. "I hope we see each other again soon."

Lucia simply nodded and touched Nora's arm for good-bye.

John Foster murmured, "Consider yourself part of the family, Nora."

Jerome helped her out of the back of the car. "I'll take

you inside." He managed a broken smile. "Who knows—maybe Joe Mercury lurks within."

"No." Nora shook her head. "Mr. Fiorello is watching now. Paul . . . what's going to happen?"

"Nothing," he replied shortly. "Whatever Pete did, he did himself. *If* it was Pete."

"Surely it was. Who else could it have been?"

"I don't know." He tried not to give up hope. "He might have hired somebody to buzz us . . . and it went wrong."

Nora pressed his arm. "I know you loved him, Paul—but I don't think there's a hope in hell that you're right."

"I know." He pushed the revolving door and when they were inside, he spoke to her again. "This goddamn merger. Pete would've died in bed if it wasn't for that—he couldn't stand the idea of BBD being lost in the Diversified maze."

Nora whispered the word. "Suicide? He meant to do it?"

"*If* he did . . . yes. The bonds and Connie were only the last straw."

There were tears in Nora's eyes and she pressed close to him. "That's *so* sad, Paul . . . Oh, God, everything is so hopeless." She hugged his hands to her bosom, and he noticed a fiery light in her eyes. Then a voice came at them from the shadows and Jerome realized Gerald Ball had been standing on the other side of a potted palm.

"Nora . . . Paul?" His voice was subdued. Had he already heard about Pete? But he had never known Pete. His death would not have been of more than passing sadness to him. "Nora, I've got to see you."

"Gerald . . ." She was puzzled. "You're waiting?"

"No . . . I . . . I called upstate and they told me you'd left. I came a couple of minutes ago."

"Well," she said, "is anything wrong? Gerald, you look . . . you don't look very well."

He grinned at Jerome. "I don't know. The winter is

getting to me." His overcoat was buttoned tightly, a scarf bunched at his throat. "Paul . . . I've got to talk to Nora. Company matters." He chuckled cagily. "We're still separate, you know."

Jerome nodded. "Gerry, be my guest. I'm just dropping Nora off. Good night." He leaned to kiss her cheek but she turned her head and kissed his mouth. For an instant, he felt the cool point of her tongue and was startled.

"Good night, Paul," she murmured. Poor Paul, he had loved Pete Broadstairs. Oh, Paul, and just then she wanted him badly, her childhood idol. She would have taken him upstairs if only she'd been able, and gathered him like a harvest.

"Well, Gerald," she said, as Jerome left, "come on up."

She tried to sound friendly and cordial. In the elevator, he made vague and distressed reference to the weather and finally Nora interrupted his self-pity to inform him of the death of Pete Broadstairs. Had it been on the news yet?

Gerald looked startled and shook his head. No, it had not.

She opened her door and went inside, leaving it for Gerald to close. Turning she said, "Gerald, we'd better have a drink. You look ghastly."

"I know. I'm sorry. I can't help it," he murmured. "Oh, Nora! Oh, golden girl, come away with me."

"Gerald! What is wrong? Tell me."

"A brandy, please," he said. "Golden girl, remember, you promised. We'll leave tomorrow. We can go to the sun. Leave all this, I beg you."

"Gerald," she said quietly, "you know I can't. Especially not now. We're in a serious spot. . . . This week is going to be horrible, you know that. We're in a war!"

"Forget the war," he exclaimed hotly. "You're not part of it. Leave, Nora. Come with me, golden girl!"

"No." She shook her head. "I cannot. My job is *here*."

"Don't be a fool," he said, accepting the brandy glass

from her trembling fingers. "I'm leaving for the Caribbean at nine-thirty tomorrow morning—"

"You *cannot* leave," Nora exploded angrily. "What are you talking about? We're in a war with those Europeans—you *cannot* just walk away."

He smiled archly. "Can't I? Watch me!"

"But . . . who . . ." She stared at him blankly. The question was who would be in charge.

Gerald grinned at her. "I was going to turn everything over to you, golden girl. I was going to name you interim chief operating officer, until . . . But they wouldn't have it . . ."

"What!" Her face must have gone white, then red, then white again. "Why? I could've . . ."

"I know that," he said bluntly. "No. *Not you.* It was too much for you to hope for."

"*You* led me on."

"Jack Frazer," he snapped. "Who did you think it would be? You didn't really believe you had a chance, did you, Nora? That's why I want you to come *with me*, golden girl. Forget all this. Who needs it? We'll have plenty . . . I'm a rich man, golden girl!"

Slowly, Nora nodded, lifting her own brandy snifter to her lips, studying his face, the smooth effete face of Gerald Ball, a quitter.

"I cannot believe you, Gerald," she said softly. "You're asking *me* to run away? What kind of life would that be? I'm not a vacation person. I have to work, to *achieve* . . . and you, you . . ." She found it very difficult to say this to him. He had not been an unfriendly influence in her life. "You just want me to be there . . . so you can watch me . . ."

Uncharacteristically, his laugh was callous. "Piss, yes, that's right, Nora."

"My God!" She sat down with a thump on the sofa and stared at the brandy. *"Oh, my God."*

His next words came in a rush. "You're a woman, Nora,

425

a woman, not a career drudge! How far do you think you'll get?"

"I'm a vice-president, Gerald," she reminded him vainly.

"Yes, because Kurt Morgan made you one. You were his mistress. Frazer knows that, Nora."

"How?" she cried.

"Everybody knows," he said, deflating her. "Frazer is straitlaced. Your days are numbered at Diversified. . . ."

"The merger!" she muttered. "All my idea . . ."

"Costing us, Nora, costing us dearly."

"And that's not my fault," she said bitterly. "The European threat was mismanaged—at *your* level." Her eyes drilled him. "Why? Why did you let that happen, Gerald?" And why hadn't she stumbled on this explanation before? "Gerald, how much have you made on the stock battle?"

The sweat formed on his forehead and a globule of spit nestled in the cleft of his lower lip.

"I . . ." No, he could not face her. He turned away and his hand came up with the brandy. "Not my doing . . . Morel, he's responsible."

"You bastard," she hissed. "That's why you're leaving town, isn't it? Because the S.E.C. is going to be on your tail. *How much,* Gerald?"

He turned on her, spitting like a snake. There was panic in his eyes; he was like a man drowning.

"Golden girl . . ."

Nora laughed. "When you get on that airplane, Gerald, you'd better keep going. Where is it your type goes? Brazil, isn't that it?"

She realized she could push him only so far. His expression turned menacing. "You could be dead, Nora," he whispered, face white. His eyes were small, like bullet holes now. "Just be very careful, Nora. *You could be dead.*"

"Get out," she said. "You're evil. You're the personification of evil."

"Be careful, Nora," he repeated.

"Get out!"

Ball gulped what was left in his glass and put it down without a sound on the coffee table. He drew a deep breath and his old, soft smile returned.

"Pull your scarf up tightly," she advised, "it's very cold out there."

He knew what she meant by that. His face tightened. As he buttoned his coat and picked up his hat, he nodded at her, putting on a great show of indifference. And he was gone.

Nora sat alone, feeling she was abandoned and at the mercy of evil and threatening forces. She understood now she had been used. Gerald Ball had built up the European threat and behind that he had been buying and selling as the BBD price rose at the market. God, how much could he have made? Millions. And the man he had used was Morel. Nora had a second brandy as she sat there, forlorn. She had lost her private war, that was obvious. Ball had said it.

When the doorbell rang, she went to answer it in a trance. She half expected to see Joe Mercury or some mysterious hit man who would blow her brains out. After all, Gerald Ball needed a head start, didn't he?

She quite literally fell into Norm Vincent's arms and suddenly realized her teeth were chattering with fear and anxiety.

"Hey . . . hon . . ."

She slid down the length of his shiny black leather coat before he caught her and lifted her back to her feet. Under the wide lapels of the coat she saw the top of the white turtleneck.

Nora began to laugh almost hysterically. "Oh, Father Norm, thank God you're here."

"I told you I'd be here, didn't I?"

"Yes, oh, yes." Her eyes were radiant. "Did you hear the awful thing that happened at Gogarty Castle after you left?"

"Yep. Plane crashed. I know. Broadstairs, huh? Crazy old fart."

"Insane." She remembered what Paul had said. "If it *was* really him."

"Why wouldn't it be him? Wasn't he all busted up over his wife and Buck?"

She shrugged. "I don't know. I don't understand anything, Norm."

He unstrapped his leather coat, smacking the tails of it with the palms of his hands. "Hon, let me tell you. Last few days have been hard ball Olympics. I can't believe all the action—all seemingly extraneous but somehow there's linkage."

"Oh, God . . . what else? Is there even more? Things I don't know about?"

Importantly, he said, "Morel is missing."

"We know that," she cried impatiently. "He didn't show up at the castle."

"I mean *missing*. *In toto* missing. Gone, disappeared."

"Oh . . . *hell!*" She stared at him lovingly. "You know everything, Father Norm."

He held out his hand, showing her the palm, a section in the center blackened. Her stomach turned. He'd been doing *that* again. But he was not opening his hand to impress her but to make a point. "I got everything, all the facts, right here, hon. The smartest thing Kurt Morgan ever did was to hire me, Nora."

"Yes, I know."

He flung himself backwards on the sofa and threw his feet up on the coffee table with such a clatter she jumped with nerves. He lifted his face and laughed boisterously, happily, and she knew he really did have everything under control.

"What can I get you, lover?" Nora asked.

Again he laughed. "I'll have . . . *you!* You and only you, hon, blessed art thou amongst chief executive officers."

That reminded her, wretchedly. "But I'm not going to be, lover. Ball was here," she said moodily, "the horror! Frazer has got the job."

He nodded. "Well . . . look, hon, don't worry about it, okay?" His eyes were sympathetic; he understood her disappointment. But his words were more, they were logical and comforting. "Hon, the thing is, I believe nothing should come too easily. I think you're lucky— you're going to be privileged to have another few years of struggle before you reach the absolute . . . zenith. Doesn't that make sense to you?"

"If you say it, lover, it makes all kinds of sense to me."

He nodded with satisfaction. "Nora, hon . . . you're beautiful. Utterly and spectacularly beautiful . . . your hair . . ."

Nora's hands flew up. "My hair! Is it a mess?"

"No, no." He chuckled self-effacingly. "Let me tell you. Remember what I said about the Buddhists and my own Bood training? Mind over matter, right? I got it all fixed in my mind now, you see?"

"I'll . . . uh . . . make you a drink."

"Make it a bourbon with a little water. I'll just turn on your TV for the news, if that's all right with you, hon."

"Of course it's all right."

Behind her, she heard the buzz of the set and then the ten o'clock news. And then she felt Norm behind her. He put his arms around her waist, snuggled close, and rammed into her rear she felt the urgent bulge of his genital. She didn't understand. She hadn't *prepared* for him. He answered the question, whispering in her ear, his mouth in the silky hair at the nape of her neck.

"See, hon, just that one time was like a key unlocking all my repressions and turning loose the hound dogs of my desire. Now I just picture one of those . . ."

"Norm, don't say it," she gasped.

She was turning to liquid. Her knees were weak, her thighs rigid with desire, her crotch was moist from the passion coursing through her. Her legs had to be opened, spread wide if she was to have any relief. Norm hiked her skirt—God, she remembered Kurt had done this to her once and she had nearly died of shame. Her skirt was up behind her and she stood like a zombie with one hand wrapped around the bourbon bottle, the other shaking enough to shatter glass. Her panties were down and she was bared to him from behind and then she felt the pulsing warmth of his genital. Nora set the bottle and glass down carefully and stayed where she was, but Norm was turning her to the other side of the drinks cart, so she could lean.

"Wanna watch the news?" he panted.

"Yes, lover," Nora murmured, thinking now she was turning to cream. Feeling the slow intrusion of his genital, she sighed heavily and squirmed backwards against him to complete the fitting. "Just stay still for a minute or two," she murmured, wiggling from side to side, remembering to use her newly discovered muscles.

Half-conscious by now, she heard the item about Pete's crash up the Hudson. The announcer said the identity of the pilot was still not established and police refused to speculate until necessary forensic work had been completed.

Norm grunted when the next item came up.

A body had been discovered in a watertight Gucci steamer trunk floating in the Hudson River ten miles north of the George Washington Bridge. According to the police, there were no identity papers on the body but the conclusion was being drawn that since all the victim's clothing bore Italian labels chances were he was an Italian.

"Brilliant . . . ain't . . . they?" Norm breathed into her neck.

"Yes . . . so very . . . brilliant." Frantically then, Nora reached behind her, trying to pull him closer, further into her lower recess. Holding her, his movements became sharper, faster, rougher, and Nora expected to be ripped to shreds. Then he let out an agonized cry and grunted, pushing and yelping. He had spent his seed, Nora told herself. She crouched, moving her feet further apart so her legs would be more widely spread. He ran his genital around and around inside her, and suddenly all her life came to a head right there. Nora was unable to speak, scarcely to breathe. Everything seemed to come almost to a shuddering stop as she gave herself to the totality of sensation, passion, lust.

"I think the earth moved, hon," Norm said finally.

"What other ways are there for us?"

"Hon, I'm told there are all sorts of ways. We could just experiment."

"Yes, I would like that," Nora said.

Chapter Thirty-seven

THE MYSTERIOUS DEATH OF JEAN-JACQUES MOREL HAD
a dampening effect on the proceedings leading up to the
merger date of Diversified Technologies with Brown,
Broadstairs and Dunn. After Pete's supposed death then
the discovery of Morel in the Hudson, everything else was
anticlimax.

Morel's body was identified by Joe Mercury, who was at
once deported. It seemed he had been living illegally in
this country for some time, working now and then as an
actor. When located in a scruffy downtown hotel, Mercury
had not been a pretty sight, having been beaten. In a half
hearted attempt to have the deportation order rescinded,
he had given the police one name, a person who could
vouch for him, a Mrs. Hazel Morgan in Scarsdale. When
telephoned, Mrs. Morgan said she'd never heard of Joe
Mercury.

On Monday, the run on BBD shares ended and the
price began to decline, not dramatically but a bit each day
for a week, as profit-takers climbed or jumped off the
bandwagon. By week's end, the BBD price was once again
manageable, at just a dollar over Diversified's tender offer
of fifty.

On Friday of that week, an anxious Nora Ellen Sweeney
was called for her first face-to-face meeting with the new
interim chief executive officer of Diversified Technologies.

There was something comforting in seeing Frazer behind Kurt Morgan's desk. Rustford Lancer had not fitted

432

the swivel chair, but she told herself that Jack Frazer did. He watched her closely, devoting his full attention as she came across the expanse of carpeting.

"Sit down, Nora," Frazer said quietly.

He seemed a very quiet man, indeed. His face was almost professorial, with the neat bush of graying black hair, cut evenly, she noted, at the ears. The eyes were like metal behind the frameless glasses, his voice muted, crisp, uninflected. If he wasn't a professor, then he was a minister, she thought. He formed his hand into an upside-down V in front of his face, the elbows braced on the arms of the leather chair.

"Well, Nora," he murmured.

"Yes, sir," she said. What was she to say? Nothing, until he said something.

"We took a bath on that BBD stock, Nora," Frazer told her.

She blushed. She knew it! She was going to be blamed. Not Gerald Ball who had fled. No. Nora Ellen Sweeney would take the rap.

"Yes, I know we did," she admitted. She had determined she'd go down with all flags flying. "I'm sorry. But we were in that spot."

"We couldn't sell off like the other side did," Frazer said relentlessly. "We took a bath. . . . We had to. If we sold off, our name would be mud. They'd put us out of business. Nora, we're not thieves in the night. We aren't in a position to fold our tents and steal away with our ill-gotten gains. *Are we?*"

"No, no, Mr. Frazer, definitely not." What was he saying?

"So we were trapped. Stupidly," he continued evenly, the steel in his voice too, not just his eyes. "Gerry Ball should have known better . . . now he's gone, Nora. What do you make of that, pray tell?"

She cleared her throat, collected her wits about her. "My opinion?" she asked timidly.

"Yes, all right. Let's have it."

433

"I may get burned for saying so—but my opinion is that Gerald Ball manipulated this. He talked us into believing the European threat—it wasn't the man Morel who was driving the price up, it was Ball and his friends, whoever *they* are." She paused, feeling nervous. "Then last Thursday and Friday, they spread the stuff around the corner and sold off, leaving us holding the bag. . . . That's it, Mr. Frazer. Partly, maybe largely, my fault. I felt our strategy had to be to follow them up."

"You didn't know it would be Ball's last stand and also his *farewell* gesture, did you?" he demanded sternly.

"No, I didn't."

"He pulled the wool over your eyes, Nora. He sweet-talked you, didn't he?" Frazer said caustically. "How did he do that, Nora?"

Shamefacedly, she squirmed. "Flattery, that was how."

Frazer laughed mockingly. "He told you that you were a beautiful girl and that you could go far in Diversified, didn't he, Nora? All you had to do was be *nice* to him . . ."

"No!"

"What do you mean, *no?*" he said sarcastically. "Of course you had to be nice to him. What did you have to do for *our* Gerry Ball?"

She felt faint. "Nothing. I didn't do anything. I threw him out."

"Not soon enough, Nora, did you?" He stopped and turned his chair slightly to the side so he wasn't staring at her anymore. His tone of voice became kinder. "All right, never mind. So we took a bath. Not so terrible, is it? Is it, Nora?" He whirled to stare, turned away when she shook her head. He had her completely floored. He was a tough customer, tougher even than Kurt Morgan. "So we've bought some BBD stock—so what? We were going to have to buy a lot of it anyway. So we paid more than we otherwise might have. So? So we blew a hundred million out of our treasury—so what? Right, Nora?"

Uncertainly, she nodded, not having any idea what he would say next.

He thumped the arm of the chair. "You've got a lot to learn, my girl."

"I realize that, Mr. Frazer, only too well."

"Call me Jack," he grunted. "Everybody calls me Jack." Before she could acknowledge the order, he continued, "So Gerry told you what a beautiful kid you were, did he? And Kurt? The same?" he demanded. "What about me, Nora? What is it you expect I'm going to say to you?"

She could not speak effectively. "I don't know . . . Nothing, I hope. I'm a professional, I believe. I don't expect . . ."

Frazer laughed at her gently. "You're very young, Nora, aren't you? Very young and very innocent. That's good. I like that, Nora. Nothing becomes a woman more than innocence, or at least a *seeming* innocence. For nothing is really as it seems, is it? Tell me what you are way down deep, Nora."

She was flustered. "Ambitious, I guess."

"Ah, now that's good, that is very good." Frazer looked around the office; he seemed to study the walls as if he were seeing them for the first time. "I didn't want this job, Nora," he said suddenly, "and I didn't expect I'd get it. According to Kurt's master plan I was supposed to hand over to Buck Collins and then gracefully withdraw. Trouble with that is Buck has cocked everything up. It'll be a while before he's cooled off enough to take over any kind of a job."

Nora nodded soberly. "I'm aware of that . . . Jack."

"Jerome is okay," he said. "He'll be fine. Buck . . . what the hell do we do about Buck?"

"I know," she said firmly. "Buck makes the speeches. He goes to Washington to testify . . ."

"Front man," Frazer nodded, smiling. "Yeah, you're right. Very bright, young lady. Buck will be Diversified's house bullshitter. Every big company needs one. That's wonderful, Nora. Bright *young* lady. I like young people. Young skin. Young brains. Young bodies, *firm.*" He nodded to himself, eyes gleaming at her. Nora knew what he was asking. He was asking what she liked.

She didn't answer. She merely stared back at him.

Chapter Thirty-eight

JOHN FOSTER'S NEW OFFICE WAS BEHIND AN UNMARKED door, a simple door in a red-brick building a few blocks from St. Patrick's Cathedral. The lush and elegantly furnished building had once been the New York townhouse of one of America's most fabled robber barons, who had willed almost everything to the Church.

The longish face was set benignly. It was fuller now, in keeping with Foster's new station in life. He ate more meals these days than he ever had as a man of the Church. Elena looked after him, seeing to his every need. Foster and Elena were in a place of their own and to be married soon.

"Well, do you like it?" Foster asked them.

"It is very nice," Jerome replied.

Indeed, it was a beautiful office, completely paneled in light cherrywood; the desk behind which Foster sat was long, delicately legged, shining under a century of polished veneer.

It was amazing to Jerome that Father John seemed not to have aged at all since the years of Paradise Point. He looked younger now, if that was possible. Elena? Yes, Elena. His suit was elegant too, a crisp pin-striped gray which Father John wore with a starched, plain-collared white shirt and a silk tie that was one of a kind. As Jerome stared at him Father John seemed almost to fade with embarrassment.

"And you two?" he asked.

"We are very well, John," Lucia murmured.

"Well," Jerome said thoughtfully, "we all seem to have come through all right . . . most of us, that is."

"Most of us, yes," Foster said thoughtfully. He did not look comfortable with the insinuation.

"Except for Pete," Jerome added.

Father John smiled. "And Connie? How is Connie?"

"She's recovered," Jerome reported, also smiling. "She is going to try to make an honest man out of Buck."

"Buck is going to marry her, is he?"

"So the story goes, yes."

Foster hummed. "Well . . . I suppose . . . What does it matter, really?"

"What's that, Father John?" Jerome had determined there was nothing else he could call him. Maybe, someday, John. But not yet.

"Well, you know . . . I've never believed really . . . that Pete died that day, Paul, to tell you the truth," Foster murmured uneasily. "You know, I haven't said anything, but those bonds did not burn in Oswald's Studebaker."

"Ah!" Jerome exclaimed. "Now we hear the truth."

"I had already given them back to Pete Broadstairs, you know. In New York. I know you told him I had them."

Jerome nodded smugly. "So I did, Father J. Tell me then—who was in the airplane?"

Foster shook his head. "I don't know, Paul. I have no idea . . . Do *you* think it was Pete?"

Jerome laughed embarrassedly. "No, I don't. I think they hired somebody to fly the plane and then blew it out of the sky—Pete had unloaded lots of BBD stock, you realize, when the price ran up."

Foster shook his head. "In other words . . ."

"In other words," Jerome mused, "he's pulled a fast one on everybody. He's probably, at this very moment, in Bali or Bombay."

"Or dead."

"True," Jerome said sadly. "Anybody's bet."

They left Foster posed in avuncular fashion behind his shining cherrywood desk. Walking through the thick crimson carpeting of the hall, down the curving staircase and then outside, Lucia thought about what Jerome had said.

"You do not believe that," she baited him. "As usual, you were giving the poor padre a gas attack."

"Maybe. Maybe not," Jerome said.

"Terrible man, Paolo."

"Look, why don't we go to your homeland and grow wine?"

"All right. As you please. You do not wish to work for Diversified Industries?"

"No," Jerome said. It was as simple as that. No. "You know what else?"

"What?"

"Ask me what happened to Jean-Jacques Morel and I'll tell you."

"I'm asking," she said, gripping him tightly.

"I think he was killed by Father John and old Oswald. I think they caught him along the river and killed him."

"Surely not. You are insane and a troublemaker," Lucia charged. "Why would they?"

"Because your cousin told Foster to. It was his last job for the Church. Don't you remember Avia's warning? Morel was a dead man—he was caught holding the bags."

"No, I think someone else killed him."

"Who then?"

"How would I know, Paolo? I am not psychic."

Jerome nodded. It was windy outside, close to the end of March.

"Sweetheart," he said, "let's get out of town. I don't like it here anymore. It worries me . . ."

Chapter Thirty-nine

"REMEMBER, BUCK," NORA REMINDED HIM, "YOU'RE A *star.*"

"Big deal." He was surly. "And what are you?"

"The virgin of the merger."

"And virgin no more, right?" he asked.

"Yes, true."

Buck knew about her and Norman, and he could not understand it. He accepted Norman in only the most casual way. But nothing more was necessary since Norman was usually in Washington. Buck made no bones about the fact that he considered Norman nutty as a fruitcake and she nuttier still for planning to marry him.

"Want to have a quickie?" he asked her, evil in his eyes.

But he was talking about a drink. His eyes wandered up and down the stewardess who serviced the Diversified plane. She hadn't much to worry about on this flight—it was only Nora and Buck headed from LaGuardia to Washington National.

"Much too early," Nora said.

"Beautiful, it's *never* too early."

"It's too early and you're speaking tonight. I don't want you drunk, or hungover, as the case may be."

"Goddamn it, beautiful," he grumbled.

But she was boss and he knew it. Buck was to speak that night to the most powerful aerospace group in Washington with a membership of former naval officers who now worked at various spots inside the defense industry. There hadn't been any argument against Buck accepting this invitation; Deke Watson, the majority shareholder of Watson Avionics and now a strong presidential hopeful, had been one of the founders of the association.

Nora had been studying Watson Avionics very closely. If Deke prevailed in his run for the presidency, he might very well be in the market to sell his holdings; if so, Diversified would be waiting. Nora had Jack Frazer's agreement and his go-ahead for the preliminary approaches. While Buck sat sulking, Nora went over all of it again. Frazer was a first-class mind for seeing the possibilities even before, or simultaneously with, Nora. A bid from Diversified would certainly serve to bring Nora to Watson's attention, she hadn't failed to appreciate that. And if there was anything she desired in this life, right now, it was to come to Deke Watson's attention.

He was the dream of American politics, handsome, clean-cut, straight-arrow, with a reputation that was completely unblemished. And he was brilliant.

"How's Connie getting along?" she asked eventually. She could not dream about Watson too much.

"She's all right," he admitted grudgingly.

"You are going to get married?"

Buck nodded abruptly. He didn't like to talk about it. "I'll marry the kid if that's what she really wants. I feel sorry for her. She got a bum deal on Pete's estate. Christ almighty, there wasn't anything left . . . the old bastard had spent the whole ball of wax."

Nora wanted to say that it served Connie right.

"At least she could've had those goddamn bonds if the padre . . ." Every time Buck referred to Foster these days his voice became that much more bitter. "If that asshole priest hadn't left them in crazy Oswald's car."

"Yes," Nora nodded. She'd heard it before. "And Oswald has set sail . . ."

"I hope the old fuck drowns," Buck said viciously. He stared at her malevolently for a second, then grinned. His attention span for revenge was no longer than for anything else. "You're looking more beautiful every day. I guess you're getting it regular these days . . ."

"Thanks so much, darling," Nora said sardonically.

She did look good, she knew it, in tailored black slacks, high heels and a black cashmere sweater with a single strand of pearls. Her black mink was stashed in the closet up front.

"Nora," he said reasonably, "we may as well have it off. We will eventually, you know. We travel together, stay in the same suite and everybody must think we're balling anyway like a couple of bears."

"Norm doesn't think so. He trusts me."

"Silly bastard. I wouldn't trust you as far as I could throw you."

Nora laughed. "You are nasty, *very* nasty and insulting."

"Well?" he taunted her. "What about Frazer. Has he asked you yet?"

She shook her head. "And he won't. He thinks I'm a pro."

"And you are," Buck said. He put his hand on her black-clad knee. "Tell me something . . . *when?*"

Nora smiled at him. "I'll tell you—if you can get yourself involved, somehow, I mean in an important way, on a Watson ticket . . ."

"You mean if I could get Defense . . ."

"Yes," she nodded, "if you do, then I'll let you."

"I get to throw you one? That's a promise."

"Sure."

"You say it so easily, you don't think I've got a chance."

"I think you do, if you work at it," she said throatily, touching his knuckles with her fingertips. She stared down at his hand. "If you got Defense, I'd let you *maybe* once a month as long as you're in the job—or until you got tired of me."

"Tired of you? No way, beautiful."

She leaned toward him, careless of the stewardess. "Yes, for that it'd be worth it, Buck. I could spread my legs . . . so wide . . ." she teased, watching his eyes dilate.

"Jesus . . ." He sighed heavily, his breath coming hard. "Beautiful, now listen . . . Goddamn it. I know you're making fun of me. Is that a nice thing to do, Nora? Does it make you happy?" She stared at him. "Nora, goddamn it, are you happy?"

"In what way?" she asked.